LINDA LAEL MILLER

Shotgun Bride

POCKET BOOKS

New York   London   Toronto   Sydney   New Delhi

Pocket Books
An Imprint of Simon & Schuster, Inc.
1230 Avenue of the Americas
New York, NY 10020

This book is a work of fiction. Any references to historical events, real people, or real places are used fictitiously. Other names, characters, places, and events are products of the author's imagination, and any resemblance to actual events or places or persons, living or dead, is entirely coincidental.

This Pocket Books paperback edition June 2021

POCKET and colophon are registered trademarks of Simon & Schuster, Inc.

For information about special discounts for bulk purchases, please contact Simon & Schuster Special Sales at 1-866-506-1949 or business@simonandschuster.com.

The Simon & Schuster Speakers Bureau can bring authors to your live event. For more information or to book an event, contact the Simon & Schuster Speakers Bureau at 1-866-248-3049 or visit our website at www.simonspeakers.com.

Interior design by Lexy Alemao

Manufactured in the United States of America

10 9 8 7 6 5 4 3 2 1

ISBN 978-1-9821-7150-6
ISBN 978-0-7434-2458-5 (ebook)

COURTING SUSANNAH

"Enjoyable . . . Linda Lael Miller provides her audience with a wonderful look at an Americana romance."

—*Midwest Book Review*

TWO BROTHERS

"A fun read, full of Ms. Miller's simmering sensuality and humor, plus two fabulous brothers who will steal your heart."

—*Romantic Times*

"Great western romance . . . *The Lawman* is a five-star tale. . . . *The Gunslinger* is an entertaining, fun-to-read story. . . . Both novels are excellent."

—*Affaire de Coeur*

ONE WISH

"[A] story rich in tenderness, romance, and love . . . An excellent book from an author destined to lead the romance genre into the next century."

—*Rendezvous*

"An author who genuinely cares about her characters, Miller also expresses the exuberance of Western life in her fresh, human, and empathetic prose and lively plot."

—*Booklist*

Also from Linda Lael Miller and Pocket Books

AUSTRALIAN SERIES
Moonfire
Angelfire

CORBINS SERIES
Banner O'Brien
Corbin's Fancy
Memory's Embrace
My Darling Melissa

LOOK BOOK SERIES
Don't Look Now
Never Look Back
One Last Look

THE MCKETTRICKS
High Country Bride
Shotgun Bride
Secondhand Bride

ORPHAN TRAIN SERIES
Lily and the Major
Emma and the Outlaw
Caroline and the Raider

SPRINGWATER SEASONS
Springwater
Rachel
Savannah
Miranda
Jessica
A Springwater Christmas
Springwater Wedding

QUAID SERIES
Yankee Wife
Taming Charlotte
Princess Annie

THE WOMEN OF PRIMROSE CREEK
Bridget
Christy
Skye
Megan

STAND ALONES
Courting Susannah
Daniel's Bride
Desire and Destiny
Fletcher's Woman
Knights
The Last Chance Café
Lauralee
The Legacy
My Lady Beloved (writing as Lael St. James)
My Lady Wayward (writing as Lael St. James)
My Outlaw
One Wish
Pirates
Two Brothers
The Vow
Wanton Angel
Willow

For my nephews:

Mike Lael
Jerome Lael
Chris Lael
Chandler Lael
Jesse Lang
Derek Readman
Andy Wiley
Bo Wiley

With love

Shotgun Bride

1

KADE MCKETTRICK RODE slowly into Indian Rock, that raw and ragged afternoon at the tail end of winter, hat pulled low over his eyes, the collar of his muddy black duster raised in a futile effort to warm his ears. He'd grown a beard in the weeks since he'd left the Triple M, at the old man's worried urging, in search of the recalcitrant brother riding beside him now. Far as he was concerned, the old man had nobody but himself to blame for all the problems. He'd been the one to pit his three sons against one another in the first place by issuing a decree that the first to marry and produce a child could get the ranch.

Now, Kade's hair was shaggy, his scalp itched, and he couldn't remember the last time he'd had a hot bath, a sound night's sleep, or a decent meal. After following a number of false trails, he'd finally tracked Jeb to Tombstone, where the little bastard had been having a high old time, and the whole experience had left Kade with a sour taste in his mouth. Right about then, he'd just as soon knock out a couple of Jeb's perfect teeth as look at him.

Jeb had come along willingly enough, probably because he'd been up to no good in Tombstone and gotten on the wrong side of some bad people, though if he'd wanted to stay, Kade would have had a fight on his hands. Jeb hadn't offered any insights into what he'd been doing, and Kade, being equally stubborn, hadn't asked for any, though he'd surmised on his own that women were involved. With Jeb, women were *always* involved.

The fact was, he was curious about his brother's exploits, but he was in no mood for Jeb's patented smirk and smart-ass rhetoric, so it was better all around to leave well enough alone, for the time being at least.

Main Street was uncommonly quiet, and the air had a certain weight, as though something were waiting out there, just beyond the edge of town, building up steam. Without exchanging so much as a glance, the brothers reined in at the livery stable, where Old Billy kept his blacksmith shop, saying as few words as possible to each other or the talkative proprietor while they made the arrangements and left their horses to be fed, groomed, and put up for the night. Kade wanted nothing so much as to get back to the Triple M, back to his books and his own bed and Concepcion's fine and consistent cooking, but night was coming on, and the animals were spent from several days of hard riding. The ranch was just two hours away, but it might as well have been twenty, in terms of the effort required to get there.

Leaving the livery, Kade and Jeb walked side by side down the broad wooden sidewalk, spurs jingling in discordant concert. The emptiness of the street made Kade edgy; he scanned the storefronts and roofs on either side—looking for what? Strangers? Riflemen? He didn't know, but something.

A skiff of a snowfall began, riding a stinging wind and putting a seal on his glum mood.

The Arizona Hotel was just ahead, spilling light from its windows, the new parts of it framed in with lumber but still skeletal, and Kade raised a hand to his beard as they approached, wishing he looked a mite more presentable. There was a good chance that Emmeline, their elder brother Rafe's wife, would be there, since she was part owner, along with her spirited and unconventional mother, and Kade had a tender place for his sister-in-law. Rafe he hoped to avoid, at least for a while. Ever since their father had laid down the law about the ranch, they'd been at odds.

Reaching the hotel's front door, Jeb put out one leather-gloved hand and wrenched it open in mocking deference. "After you," he told Kade. The look in his eyes was downright irascible.

Kade gave his brother a scathing once-over, squared his shoulders, and stepped over the threshold. The lobby was warm and cheerful, with curtains and carpets and china-globed lamps, offering a pleasant contrast to the hardship of the trail, and a blaze was crackling on the hearth of a newly added fieldstone fireplace. Steamy, savory smells wafted from the direction of the dining room, the only restaurant in town. It didn't compare to the ones in lively Tombstone, where there were any number of such establishments, including ice cream parlors, but if there had to be just one eatery in Indian Rock, Kade was grateful it was a good one.

A small nun with striking blue-green eyes stood behind the registration desk. His brain dulled by fatigue, Kade blinked once, certain he was seeing things, before he remembered meeting the young woman on a couple of other occasions, once at a party a few months back, on the ranch, and on a previous visit to the hotel. She'd come in on the stagecoach one day, by the account he'd heard, and Emmeline and her mother had seen she was down on her luck and offered her work at the hotel. Something about her worried at his memory like the teeth of a dog, but he put it down to being road weary and saddle sore.

Sister Mandy, she called herself, he recalled that much. He smiled a little and ambled toward her, with Jeb chinking along a few strides behind. Irreverently, he wondered what she'd look like in a party dress.

"Welcome to the Arizona Hotel," she said, watching him in a wary way, as though taking his measure. She looked about half-ready to bolt for the nearest exit. She probably figured him for an outlaw, with his seedy countenance, and that amused him as much as her disguise. Whatever Sister Mandy was, she was no more a nun than he was an outlaw; he would have bet his favorite saddle on that. Or traded it for a real good look at her.

"Would you gentlemen like a room?" she asked.

Kade remembered his manners—he hadn't had much call to use them of late, so he was somewhat out of practice—and removed his hat. "Two rooms," he said, without looking at Jeb. He'd been bunking on the opposite side of a campfire from that polecat for almost a week as it was, and he needed some elbow room, literally and figuratively. "Please."

Sister Mandy nodded and swiveled the registration book around for Kade to sign. He picked up the pen, dipped it into an open inkwell, and wrote his name with a flourish. Jeb penned his own signature underneath, barely legible, like always.

"I'll be wanting a bath," Jeb said. Seemed he hadn't forgotten how to talk after all, damn the luck.

"You need one," Kade observed, without looking at his brother. He was spoiling to tie into somebody, had been since they'd left Tombstone, but he'd bide his time. Becky had worked hard to make the Arizona Hotel a respectable place, and the last thing she needed—or would tolerate—was a brawl in her cheerful lobby. Besides, a lady was present. So to speak.

"Go to hell," Jeb responded blithely. Out of the corner of his eye, Kade saw his brother flex his left hand and knew he felt the same longing as he did to throw a punch and feel it connect.

"That's fifty cents extra," Mandy said, raising her voice a little, looking from one of them to another, clearly discomforted. The words they'd exchanged had been mild enough, but the testy undercurrent was unmistakable. Kade felt a moment's shame for alarming the girl, though he wouldn't credit Jeb with the decency to do the same. "With the room, that will be two dollars," she finished.

Jeb laid the money on the desk and gestured for a key with a beckoning motion of his fingers. Kade was reaching for his own wallet when Emmeline swept in from the dining room, looking flushed and plump and happy, and thereby distracting them all. She and Rafe had gotten off to an uneven start where matrimony was concerned, but if her expression was anything to go by, they'd resolved the worst of their difficulties and reached a comfortable accord of some sort.

"You're back!" she cried, pleased, approaching Jeb and Kade and rising on tiptoe to favor each of them with a sisterly kiss on the cheek. Kade found himself wishing, yet again, that he'd taken the time for a bath and barbering somewhere along the way. "We've been worried into a regular fret, every one of us. Where have you been all these weeks?"

Kade and Jeb glanced at each other in a desultory fashion, but when Kade turned back to his fair-haired, bright-eyed sister-in-law, he was wearing a stock smile. She was Rafe's and had been from the first, and he'd best be about accepting the truth of the matter, but facing it sounded a lonesome refrain inside him all the same. "That's too long a story to tell when I'm this hungry," he said. He cocked his head toward the lobby window overlooking the street. "Where is everybody? The place looks like a ghost town."

Emmeline reached back, fiddling with the ties of her apron. Some of the glow faded from her face and countenance. "Folks are—nervous. There's been some trouble—"

At the edge of his vision, Kade saw Sister Mandy put away his money and Jeb's, and set two brass keys on the desk. Her color seemed a little high. So there *was* a flesh-and-blood woman under that getup.

"What kind of trouble?" Jeb asked, reaching for one of the keys, before Kade could get the words out. Though he'd never said as much, Kade suspected that Jeb, too, had cherished a few sweet illusions where Emmeline was concerned. She'd blown into their family like a fresh breeze on a hot, dry day, arriving from Kansas City as a mail-order bride, and none of them had been the same since. Especially Rafe.

Emmeline bit her lower lip. "There's talk of some gunplay between the ranches." She inclined her head toward the hotel dining room. "Come along, and I'll get you both a plate of food—you probably haven't had anything that wasn't cooked over a campfire in days. I'll explain while you eat."

Jeb and Kade took a table by the window in the next room, and Emmeline brought them coffee first thing, bustling a little, then put in their orders for a pair of fried chicken dinners.

"Has there been any shooting?" Jeb demanded once Emmeline had served the food and joined them at the table. "Or just talk?" He looked even more amenable to the idea of a good fight than he had out there in the lobby, though now he seemed ready to take on half the territory, not just Kade. Typically, he didn't wait for an answer, but jumped to the first conclusion with a foothold. "It's got to do with Holt Cavanagh buying the Chandler place out from under Pa, hasn't it? He's gone and cut off the water to the Triple M." Cavanagh was more than just an irksome neighbor, he was a half brother to Rafe, Jeb, and Kade—Angus's son by his first wife, born in Texas and left behind as a babe when Ellie McKettrick had died and the old man had taken it into his head to go north. They hadn't known Holt existed until recently, when he'd hired on at the Triple M pretending to be a regular cowhand, and he was still a burr under their collective hide. Cavanagh's main reason for coming to Indian Rock, it seemed to Kade, was to rankle the McKettricks as much as possible, and while he had his agreeable moments, he was making a good job of it.

Emmeline hesitated, fidgeted a bit with her hair. A few people were venturing out onto the street by then, even though the snow was coming down faster, whipped into bitter little twisters by the rising wind. Kade was doubly glad to be in out of the weather, though he wished they'd had better news awaiting them. A bare-knuckle row in back of the barn with one or more of his brothers was one thing. A bunch of rowdy cowboys riding all over the countryside gunning for each other was another.

"It hasn't come down to bullets yet," she said. "Not so far, anyhow. But there's been some nasty talk between the Triple M and the Circle C, and a few other outfits have taken sides. Some fence lines were cut, some cattle rustled, that sort of thing."

Kade picked up a piece of chicken and bit into it. His stomach was so empty it seemed to be gnawing at his backbone, and he didn't figure he'd be able to think clearly until he'd seen to the matter. "What's Rafe got to say about all this?" he asked, taking advantage of a gap in his chewing and swallowing. Rafe was foreman of the Triple M for the time being, and their pa's mandate notwithstanding, that galled Kade. By his reckoning, Angus McKettrick had been flat wrong to give one of his sons authority over the others, but these days, his opinion didn't appear to account for much.

Emmeline sighed, fiddling with the checkered gingham curtains at the window. "He's worried," she admitted. "So far, it's just been mischief, mostly, but if there's violence of any kind, there could be a range war."

History had recorded many a bloody fight between competing ranchers all over the West, and Kade didn't want to see it happen on or around the Triple M. "Has he talked to Cavanagh?" he asked. Holt had a good-sized chunk of land, and the several springs that fed the creek running through the Triple M were squarely within his property. If he wanted to cause real grief for the McKettricks, all he had to do was change the course of the stream or build himself a dam.

"They've had words," Emmeline admitted. She tried to smile and fell a little short of the mark. "You know how hardheaded Rafe is, and Holt is as bad or worse. All they've done so far is lock horns and exchange accusations. A couple of times, I thought they might actually come to blows." Innocent Emmeline. She'd grown up in the city, in a household of women, even if it was a high-toned brothel, and she knew nothing of the ways of brothers raised to scuffle like bear cubs. Adjusting to life on the Triple M must have been a monumental effort for her, and Kade, for one, admired her grit and gumption.

"Where's our big brother now?" Jeb wanted to know. He'd evidently eaten as much as he cared to and pushed his plate away to sip the stout coffee. Kade, on the other hand, was seriously thinking about ordering another chicken dinner, since the first one hadn't hit bottom yet. Nothing much interfered with his appetite, including talk of a range war.

"He's out with a crew of men, mending fence and rounding up strays," she said. The wistful look that rose in her eyes was gone in a flicker. Kade wondered if, for all her apparent well-being, there might be a problem between her and Rafe after all.

"And you're staying in town?" Kade asked, summoning up a convivial smile. "What about that fine house Rafe built for the two of you over across the creek from us? Is it standing empty these days?"

Emmeline shook her head, and all of a sudden she looked tired. Kade felt a pang of concern; if Emmeline was in the family way, Rafe was certain to win control of the Triple M for good. Much as Kade would have liked to be an uncle, he wanted to be a father first. A father with a legacy to leave.

"Becky's been up in Flagstaff with John Lewis for a week," Emmeline said, "so I've been helping Clive and Sister Mandy look after the hotel." Becky Fairmont, also known as Becky Harding, depending on her state of mind and the phase of the moon, was Emmeline's mother, and John Lewis, the town marshal, was her beau. The two of them had churned Indian Rock's version of polite society into a regular dither, carrying on the way they did; the ladies down at the spanking-new church were bound to be spending more time on gossip than prayer and hymn singing. Good thing none of them knew the family secret, that Becky had been a madam back in Kansas City, before turning to innkeeping.

Jeb let out a long sigh and sat back, folding his arms. He looked as disreputable as Kade felt, being sorely in need of scouring, and he didn't smell much better than a sweat-lathered mule. "I'm heading for the Triple M tomorrow," he told Emmeline. "I'd be glad to borrow a buckboard from Old Billy and drive you out there." He was always trying to charm the women, Jeb was, and it didn't seem to matter much if they belonged to somebody else. Kade set his jaw briefly, biting down on a string of words better left unsaid.

"Like you did the first day I came here," Emmeline reminisced, with a little laugh that did a lot to raise Kade's flagging spirits. She shook her head, probably reflecting on the memory of arriving in the Arizona Territory, believing herself well and truly married to a man who'd just rolled through the doors of the Bloody Basin Saloon to land at her feet. Her introduction to Rafe had been an eye-opener, even by Western standards. "I remember wishing I'd signed on to marry you instead of your brother."

"That," Jeb said, with one of those crooked grins of his, "was your common sense talking."

Just then, a clamor arose in the street, horses' hooves clattering on the hard ground, saddle leather creaking, men calling to each other in raised voices.

"There he is now," Emmeline said, but even without her saying so, just by the way she leaped from her chair with her face all pink and shining, Kade would have known that Rafe had arrived. He felt a sore yen to have a woman light up that way for him and despaired of its ever happening.

Rafe strode right into the hotel, just as if he owned the place, bringing the frigid, snow-flecked wind and nine or ten rambunctious, spur-jangling range hands right along with him. When Rafe entered a room, it always felt as if the ceiling had dropped and the walls had sucked in like the sides of an empty bellows.

"Well," he said, towering in the doorway and jerking off his work gloves one finger at a time, "if it isn't my little brothers, home from the far country. Kill the fatted calf."

2

MANDY SPERRIN SNEAKED through the hotel kitchen, having avoided the dining room entirely, and took refuge in the alley beyond. Oblivious to the snow and the cold searing her flesh even through the heavy woolen habit she wore, she stood absolutely still, with her back pressed to the wall of the general store, one hand to her chest. Her heart thundered like a herd of runaway horses.

She was sure Kade McKettrick didn't remember her from that night five years ago down in Cave Creek, which both troubled and relieved her, but he'd given her a curious glance or two just the same. Doubtless, it was only because of the nun suit, she thought, grasping at straws. Next time she needed a disguise, she'd darn well pick a garment that didn't draw so much notice. Or itch like something off the floor of an abandoned teepee.

One moment, she was standing there, hiding out and battling the urge to scratch, and the next, she was pinned to the clapboard wall, nearly choking, with an icy rifle barrel pressed lengthwise across her throat. She scrambled onto her tiptoes and pushed with both hands to free herself, but it was no good.

Blinking with fear and breathlessness, she stared into Gig Curry's furious eyes. Curry would have been her stepfather, if he'd ever taken the trouble to marry her mother, though he never hesitated to claim the title if he saw any benefit in it. The old emotions rose up in her, bitter and violent but at the same time sustaining. Her blood burned like kerosene in her veins.

Slowly, degree by degree, Curry relaxed the pressure of the rifle, allowing Mandy to drop to her heels and draw a desperately needed breath. Curry was a thin man, not particularly tall, but full of rangy strength, and he'd been born pissed.

"Well, now," Gig crooned, his face so close to Mandy's that she felt a splash of spittle as he spoke, "so here's where she's been hiding, our own little Sister Mandy." He paused to shake his head. "Now, that's funny, you posing as a nun. That's downright *hilarious.*"

Mandy closed her eyes for a moment in a desperate bid for courage, then fixed Curry with a glare. He thrived on other folks' fright, and he could smell it, like the wild animal he was. She'd learned a long time ago not to show fear, whether he was around or not.

"What do you want?" she asked, chin raised and jutting a little. She thought of Cree, her half brother, and hoped he was far away, and safe.

Curry raised his free hand as if to backhand her, then apparently thought better of the idea and let it fall to his side. "I want to know where that little war-whoop brother of yours is right now. He's been bad-mouthing me, and messing in my business."

Mandy might have called out for help just then, if there had been more people on the street, but the nip in the air and the rising fear of trouble between the various ranches had driven most of them inside. "I haven't seen him," she said, and made sure she was snippy about it, though it might just earn her a beating. Or worse. "But if I had, I wouldn't tell you."

Gig looked as if he might be about to choke her again. "You double-crossing little—"

She tried to stare him down.

"Now you listen to me, Amanda Rose. If that savage gets the chance, he'll ambush me, and that means my life is on the line. There's one person in all the world he gives a good goddamn about, and that's you. So it does seem to me that you might need a little persuasion to get that memory of yours fired up."

As if she'd betray her brother for any reason. He was the only person in the world she'd ever completely trusted and, besides her mama, the only one she'd loved. "Cree's no savage," she said. "He makes ten of you."

Gig lifted his hand again, and this time, she knew he wouldn't hold back; he meant to hit her hard enough to loosen her teeth. The way he'd done with her mother so many times, and with Cree, too, before he'd got his fill of it, when he was just sixteen, and ridden out for good.

Door hinges creaked nearby, and Mandy's heart squeezed itself into her throat. In a glance, she saw Kade McKettrick standing on the back stoop, about to light a cheroot. He'd shed his trail-worn coat and left his hat inside, but a .45 rode low on his right hip, loose and ready in its holster. Mandy's attention went right to that gun and got stuck there for a long moment.

Kade put out the match he'd just struck, slipped the unlit cheroot into his shirt pocket. "There some difficulty here?" he asked easily, but some quality underlying his words reverberated through Mandy like the hiss of a rattler, invisible in the tall grass, primed to sink fangs into flesh.

Seeing Kade, Gig muttered a curse, and Mandy figured he must have been skulking around long enough to learn who was who around Indian Rock, starting with the McKettricks. His eyes blazed with a brief, ancient malevolence; he hated most folks, just on general principle, but especially the ones he perceived as privileged.

The display was quelled in an instant. Curry was part reptile himself; he could slither right out of his skin when it didn't serve his purposes and take on a whole new aspect, just that easy.

"No difficulty at all," he said, taking a step back. His smile was ingenuous, mild, and wholly false. Mandy reckoned the devil probably smiled like that while he was watching souls roast in the fires of hell.

She shuddered at the image. If stealing was indeed a mortal sin, she'd surely end up in Hades herself, turning on a spit.

Mandy forced herself to breathe slowly, by dint of will, and to calm down. Straightening her habit and adjusting her wimple, she struggled against an undignified inclination to dash over to the stoop and hide out behind McKettrick. Her fierce pride prevailed, though, even over the instinct to protect herself, and she stayed where she was.

"It's cold out here," her rescuer said moderately, addressing his words to Mandy, though his gaze remained fixed on Gig and slightly narrowed. "Maybe you'd like to come inside—Sister."

Mandy straightened her spine and let her shoulders down from her ears. She'd ponder over the cynicism she'd heard in the word *sister* later; right now, she just wanted to put as much space between her and Gig Curry as possible. "Yes," she said agreeably. "I think I would."

She felt Gig reach for her arm as she passed and just as quickly suppress the motion. She kept right on walking; ten more steps, seven, five . . . *keep going* . . . one foot in front of the other.

"You know of any ranchers lookin' to hire a good hand?" Gig called to McKettrick from behind her. "I'll be sticking around here for a while, I reckon."

A chill struck the length of Mandy's back like a wall of cold water.

"Nope," McKettrick replied. His gaze didn't shift from Gig, nor did he raise his hands from the railing on the stoop, but Mandy sensed a bone-deep vigilance in him as she drew nearer. He might not have been looking directly at her, but he was taking in every nuance of the situation, subtle or otherwise. He would be a hard man to deceive, should that become necessary. But, then, she'd known that since the episode in Cave Creek.

"I heard there was a fellow name of Cavanagh lookin' to take on some help," Gig said, friendly as could be, all smiles. Mandy thought she heard the sound of sinners sizzling on a griddle.

"That would be between you and him," McKettrick said flatly.

Mandy had gained the steps by then, and Kade stepped aside slightly to let her go by. When she considered lingering to see what would happen next, however, he passed her a look that made her think better of the idea.

"I'll be seeing you soon, Sister Mandy," Gig called in jovial warning, as she stepped over the threshold into the radiant warmth and temporary safety of the hotel kitchen.

Mandy's stomach pitched at the threat, but Emmeline was

there, solid and sweet and practical as an angel, just taking a fresh pot of coffee off the stove, and it wouldn't do to let the boss lady see how shaken she was. Kade McKettrick might have saved her bustle this time, but Gig would get to her sooner or later, or die trying.

Emmeline paused, taking her in with a concerned expression. "Are you all right?" she asked. Kade lingered outside on the porch, the door still open, and the faint scent of tobacco smoke curled into the room, oddly comforting.

Mandy forced a smile. "I'm just a little cold," she said to explain the visible shiver that went through her. She was generally brave when face-to-face with trouble, but afterward, when she let down her guard a little, well, that was when she was hard put not to fall apart. "Here—let me take that coffee."

Emmeline hesitated, then set the heavy kettle back on the stove and handed the pot holder to Mandy. "Thank you," she said, her gaze straying to the open back door, full of questions.

Mandy willed some starch into her knees, picked up the coffeepot, and headed for the dining room, which had filled, in the last few minutes, with cowboys and other customers. She poured coffee for Rafe McKettrick, Emmeline's husband, and for Jeb, his brother, along with the other men, all the while waiting for Kade to come back in, then moved on to the large corner table next to the window. A small group of young women had settled there, all of them impatient mail-order brides, gathered for one of their regular war councils.

Mandy wasn't without sympathy for the aspiring wives; all of them staying at Mrs. Sussex's boarding house to conserve funds, they'd come to Indian Rock from every direction but up, set on getting hitched to a McKettrick, and they'd all been sent for one way or the other. The problem was, only two marriageable brothers were left, not counting Holt Cavanagh, of course, and there were six brides.

So far, anyway. It seemed like every stage brought in another one.

Mandy smiled, momentarily amused, but the smile faded when she looked up and saw Gig Curry standing on the other side of the window opening onto the street, staring at her through the steam-fogged glass. The look in his eyes was colder than the heart of a high-country winter, and he needed no words to convey his message: if she didn't help him find Cree, he'd kill her for sure.

3

"WHAT DO YOU know about this Sister Mandy woman?" Kade asked Emmeline, after putting out his cheroot and stepping back into the kitchen, where his sister-in-law was busy cutting slices of peach pie and setting them neatly on plates. He felt a wispy recollection tugging at the edge of his mind again, but he couldn't quite catch hold of it. There was an element of fascination, too, which troubled him.

Emmeline looked back at him over one shoulder. A tendril of hair curled against her temple, and it was all he could do not to reach out and smooth it for her. Not to send her home to the ranch, or at least into the hotel's private parlor, to put her feet up and catch her breath for a while. He did none of those things because Emmeline was his brother's wife, not his own. *Keep that in mind, cowboy,* he thought.

"Not a great deal," she admitted. "She came in on the stage one day, and Becky gave her a job. We figure she's running from something, but she hasn't confided in us and we haven't pressed her much, what with all that's been happening."

"I thought being a nun *was* a job," Kade remarked, curiously irritated, pushing the door closed against the cold and folding his arms. He was in no hurry to go back to the dining room and deal with both his brothers at once—they were plague enough one at a time.

Emmeline shrugged. "Not being Catholic," she said, still busy, "I wouldn't know."

Kade was not religious himself, at least not in the conventional sense, but Concepcion, his father's longtime housekeeper, was devout. She knew all the saints on a first-name basis, said her rosary beads regularly, and paid visits to Father Herrera, at the Spanish mission on the other side of Indian Rock, to make confession. He meant to put the matter to her once he got back to the Triple M, though he'd have to wade through a flood of inquiry from her first. Concepcion would want to know everything that had transpired since he went looking for Jeb, and she wouldn't give an inch of ground until he'd described every tedious detail. "You shouldn't go trusting everybody who comes along and asks you for work, Emmeline," he said. He thought of the man he'd seen outside with Sister Mandy. "There are plenty of no-good drifters around."

She brushed at the escaped tendril, then took two pie plates into each hand and headed for the inner door, opening it deftly with her hip before pausing briefly to look back at him. Her mouth had a mischievous tilt to it.

"I assume you're still set on getting married," she said, as if in passing.

He'd forgotten that fact, blessedly, for all too brief a time, and the reminder brought a scowl to his face. "Yes," he said. His fondness for his sister-in-law was one matter, and his need for the Triple M was another. He intended to get a wife and make her pregnant as soon as possible; there was still a good chance that he could win out over Rafe and Jeb. "The sooner I do that, the better."

Emmeline smiled, and her eyes danced. "Well, then, here's your opportunity," she said airily. "There are six women out there in the dining room right now, all of them convinced they were meant to marry a McKettrick. Specifically, you."

Inwardly Kade groaned. *"What?"*

Emmeline chuckled at his expression. "It seems you put the word out that you wanted a wife. Well, they're here. Take your pick." With that, she whisked through the doorway and disappeared, leaving Kade reeling in her wake. It wouldn't do any good to call her back and point out that Rafe had sent for at least one of those women when he thought things were going to hell between him and Emmeline. Fact was, he *had* written a letter to the matrimonial people himself, and paid a fee, and he suspected that Jeb had, too, though the sneak probably wouldn't admit it. Jeb didn't appear to be worried about landing a wife, come to think of it, and he'd probably enjoy watching Kade roast like a pig at a picnic.

Kade's deepest instinct was to turn on one heel and bolt out the back.

"Hell," he muttered. He'd been on the road for weeks, looking for Jeb and then making the long journey home, so the old man wouldn't burst a blood vessel fretting about the little jackass, and he looked and felt about as appealing as an old bear just rousing himself from a long hibernation. He'd have given almost anything right then for some time to marshal his thoughts into some kind of order, but it didn't look as though he was going to have the luxury.

When he finally worked up the nerve to walk back into the

dining hall, the place was bristling with cowboy talk, the clinking sound of spoons in coffee mugs, and tittering women.

A moment went by before anyone took notice of his arrival, but a telling silence fell when they did, and he could have sworn every eye in the room was on him. He saw amusement in Rafe's gaze, along with a certain wry speculation, and Jeb was out-and-out grinning, his chair tipped back and his arms folded. Sister Mandy wouldn't look at him at all, but her cheeks glowed as if she'd been standing too close to the stove.

The gaggle of women at the corner table did enough looking for everybody, taking in his unkempt hair, his beard, his grubby clothes and battered, dirt-caked boots. He made himself look right back as a point of pride, but he couldn't have described a single one of the brides as an individual to save his life—they looked like a flock of fitful birds to him, colorful and beruffled and fixing to go on the peck directly.

One of the ladies rose from her chair, and then all the others got up, too, as if they were all rigged together somehow, like a team of mules hitched to the same harness.

Kade swallowed hard.

The boldest of the brides approached, a brittle smile fixed to her mouth, and Kade called upon all the restraint he possessed not to take a step backward. Try though he might, he couldn't work up any facial expression at all.

"Mr. McKettrick," the woman said, putting out a gloved hand, and the slight shrillness in her voice scraped at the underside of his spine, which brought on a shudder. He prayed Rafe and Jeb hadn't noticed the response, because they'd rib him until the day he died if they had. "My name is Sue Ellen Carruthers, and I am here to marry you."

Kade's tongue felt like a scared critter, trying to burrow into his throat. "H-howdy," he choked out.

Miss Carruthers, he decided, was a forthright type, and probably fertile, which meant she'd do for his purposes, but she was three days of hard riding from pretty. Since he reckoned he'd be spending upward of forty years looking at the woman he took as his wife, from across the table and his side of the bed, he was reluctant to propose.

Another woman elbowed Sue Ellen to the side and beamed at him. He caught a flash of bright yellow hair and cornflower blue eyes, but not much else. "Marvella Denhome," she told him, "and I was here before Sue Ellen by a good week."

Contentious, he thought. What was it the good book said about living with a contentious woman? Better to die in the desert?

"Abigail Bergen," said a third woman. She was nice to look at, and soft-spoken, too, but the mean glint in her eye gave Kade pause. She wanted either a husband or blood vengeance, and it seemed to him that one would do her as well as the other.

The next three candidates were a shifting blur of textures and colors, and by the time they got through prattling out their introductions, all Kade could think about was heading for the Bloody Basin Saloon and swilling down as much whiskey as the bartender could pour. He figured he would have swooned dead away, right there in front of his brothers and half the hands from the Triple M, if Becky Fairmont hadn't glided into the dining room just when she did, cutting a path between those women like the Lord parting the waters of the Red Sea so the Israelites might pass.

Emmeline's mother and the primary owner of the Arizona Hotel, Becky was a force to be reckoned with by anybody's account, and though the brides didn't look any too happy about it, they subsided all right, grumbling among themselves.

"Kade McKettrick," Becky said with brisk finality, putting her arm through his and steering him toward the lobby door, "just the man I wanted to see."

The brides erupted into chattering complaint behind him, and the cowboys were having a good laugh at his expense, but Kade would have followed the devil himself out of that room, if it meant escaping.

He didn't let out his breath until he and Becky were closeted away together in her office, behind the registration desk. Clad in smart traveling clothes and wearing a feathered bonnet, the former madam went straight to the liquor table and poured them each a double shot of whiskey.

Kade threw his back in one burning, restorative gulp, then collapsed into the chair Becky pushed into place behind him. He thought of the brides and considered shoving something heavy in front of the door.

"I've got a proposition for you," Becky announced, sipping her own whiskey and taking a seat at her desk. She was dark-haired, and still beautiful, but fragile, too. Like Kade's pa, Angus, she had a temperamental ticker, though it didn't seem to slow her down much.

"What?" he managed to ask, after a hopeless glance at the

whiskey decanter on the other side of the room. Those people at the Happy Home Matrimonial Service, back in Kansas City, were a mite too zealous about filling orders, as far as he was concerned. He might have asked for two wives, or even three, since he tended to be absentminded, but *six?*

"John Lewis and I want to get married and go on a proper honeymoon," she informed him, hands folded, all business. "Trouble is, this town is about to go off like a Chinese rocket over the trouble between the Triple M and the Circle C, among other things, and John says he can't leave it unattended. How'd you like to pin on his badge for a while and call yourself Marshal McKettrick?"

4

NEVER ONE TO decide weighty matters on the spur of the moment, Kade didn't give Becky an answer right away. They each had another whiskey, and he stewed over the offer through the evening and most of the night.

For all his deliberating, he was no closer to a decision the next morning. On the one hand, he belonged on the Triple M the way stones belong to a creek bed, and he knew it. On the other, he was fascinated with the law, having studied it for as long as he could remember, and the chance to exercise some of that knowledge had a certain appeal.

He took his breakfast with Becky and John in the hotel dining room, and promised to settle on a course soon.

The journey to the ranch was tedious, and when Kade and Jeb finally rode across the creek and up to the house, Angus was waiting on the front porch, as if he'd been expecting them. The old man looked like the scrapings from last week's batch of pinto beans, dry and gray and oddly concave, as if he were shrinking away from his own hide. He sat in a rocker with a robe draped over his legs, but a spark gleamed in his blue eyes as he watched his sons approach. It was pure cussedness, that spark, and not to be mistaken for fatherly affection, but seeing it reassured Kade a little, all the same. Angus McKettrick still had some fight in him, which meant the earth still revolved around the sun and summer still came after spring.

For most of the ride out from town, Kade had wrangled with the idea of taking the marshal's job, trying the case in his mind, arguing for and against, making no attempt to strike up a conversation with Jeb. Now, seeing his pa, he set the quandary aside.

"I ought to send the pair of you packing for worrying us the way you did," Angus growled with a cantankerous gesture of one hand. Being a contrary sort, he liked to bitch, even when he'd gotten what he wanted. "After a good old-fashioned horse-whipping, that is."

Concepcion slipped out the door to stand behind him, one competent brown hand resting lightly on his shoulder. She didn't offer a welcome, but Kade still cherished a fleeting and distracted hope that she wouldn't refuse to cook or wash for them, as she'd done in the past whenever they'd gotten on her bad side. She'd been keeping house on the Triple M since before their mother died, when they were boys, and in many ways she'd taken up where Georgia McKettrick had left off. Life would have been grim around the place without her around to soften things up a little.

Jeb swung down from the saddle first, leaving the reins to dangle, a go-to-hell grin on his face. Like Kade, he'd had a bath the night before at the hotel, but he still looked like a prospector gone to seed.

"I missed you, too, Pa," Jeb said.

Kade dismounted, more resigned than anything. He wasn't glib like Jeb, and he'd had a lot on his mind just since returning to Indian Rock, between the tin star he'd been offered, all those brides on his tail, and the grief brewing between the Triple M and Cavanagh's outfit. Making idle conversation was beyond him.

"I'm disinclined to claim either one of you," Angus fussed. "You call yourselves McKettricks? You look like a couple of road agents."

Jeb laughed, opening the front gate and leaving it to swing back against Kade's middle when he tried to follow. "And you look like a bony-kneed old lady, sitting there under that lap robe. Where's your knitting?"

Angus tried to keep his dudgeon up, but even he couldn't help grinning a little, for all his sour mien. Jeb could bullshit a hellfire-and-brimstone preacher into dancing a jig with the devil, if he put his mind to it. That was a gift Kade didn't possess, and when his guard was down, he envied it mightily.

As the two brothers mounted the wide porch steps, a ranch hand came to collect the horses, and Angus levered himself to his feet with a creaking sound that might have come from either the chair or his dry, old joints. Concepcion stayed close, Kade noticed, but didn't make the mistake of helping the old man rise.

"I hear there's a fight brewing," Kade said, because if he didn't speak up before Jeb started yammering in earnest, he wouldn't get a word in edgewise.

"You heard right," Angus said, reddening. His jugular vein stood out, and his right temple pulsed. "It's that half brother of yours that's behind it, too. I'd stake my life on it. Damn pigheaded cuss."

"Wonder where he gets that?" Kade asked lightly.

Concepcion gave him a reproachful look and spoke for the first time. "Same place you did, I would say."

Angus put out a hand, and Kade shook it. Old coot's grip was still stout as an ape's; could be he was putting on a good part of this peakedness, just to get himself some sympathy and attention.

Concepcion led the way into the house, prattling about scissors and razors. She was bent on dispensing shaves and haircuts, and once she got a notion like that into her head, the deed was as good as done.

Jeb and Kade paused to hang their coats, hats, and gun belts on the hall tree just inside the front door, and Angus tarried, keeping an eye on them. Maybe he thought they'd make a run for it if he didn't keep them corralled.

"Where the *hell* have you boys been?" he demanded in a raspy whisper. "I figured you both for dead, you were gone so long. And not a word to put my mind at ease. Either one of you ever heard of the telegraph?"

Kade shoved a hand through his hair. "We're both too mean to die, Pa," he said. "Just like you. And I figured if I sent a wire, you'd moan and holler about the extravagance."

Jeb offered no comment for once, but he was smirking a bit, always a bad sign, as he strolled past his father and brother and headed for the kitchen, where Concepcion was surely setting up her own barbershop.

When they were alone, Angus slapped Kade on the shoulder. "Thanks for finding Jeb," he said, low and confidential.

"I had to look under a lot of rocks to do it," Kade replied lightly. "I figured he'd turn up sooner or later, though, and sure enough, he did." In point of fact, he'd found his kid brother playing poker in the back room of a Tombstone whorehouse, drunker then hell, but he didn't see any benefit in elaborating. Not then, at least. The knowledge might come in handy later, though.

A blast of stove heat and the smells of good home-cooking struck Kade as he entered the kitchen a few moments later, and he began to think he might be able to round up his stray wits after all, make some sense of things, once he'd assuaged his empty stomach.

Concepcion already had Jeb plunked down in a chair in the middle of the room, with a checkered tablecloth wrapped around his shoulders, and the scissors snipped busily in her hand as she tried to make up her mind where to start. Kade ignored his brother and fetched the basin from the back porch, ladled in some hot water from the reservoir on the side of the stove, and sharpened a razor against a strop.

Locks of Jeb's dirt-blond hair lay on the floor by the time Kade had finished shaving, and the two of them switched places.

Jeb got through grooming first, making quick work of his own beard, and poured himself a cup of strong coffee, leaning against the sink as he watched Kade getting sheared. "I'm surprised you've been able to hold in the big news all this time, Brother," he said, with a glint of merry devilment in his eyes.

"What big news is this?" Concepcion wanted to know, but she didn't pause in her combing and whacking.

Kade darted a warning look in Jeb's direction, but he knew beforehand that it wouldn't do any good. Once Jeb opened his yap, the words just stampeded right out, and it was get out of the way or be trampled.

Jeb saluted him with the coffee mug. "My big brother is

about to be married. Soon as he figures out which of his many admirers to take up with, that is."

Concepcion stopped cutting, and Angus, who had stationed himself in his customary chair at the head of the table with coffee of his own, perked up like a mossy-antlered old buck catching something on the wind.

"That so?" he said. The idleness in his tone didn't fool Kade; Angus wanted his boys married, and he wanted them to be fathers, just barely in that order, probably. Rafe was out front in the race to win the ranch, since he had the wife, if not the child, but win or lose, it would take an act of Congress to get himself and Jeb off the hook. Yes, sir. The old man would see them settled down, right and proper, in their turns, or there would be hell to pay.

"There're six of them," Jeb marveled, with that mocking grin still plastered across his face. Kade would have liked to knock it off, but Concepcion had him pretty well hog-tied with two corners of the tablecloth tied behind his neck, and besides, she was armed with scissors. "And then there's the job offer."

"*Six of them?*" Angus asked, still snagged on the plentitude of brides, and he looked so thunderstruck that Kade couldn't tell whether he was pleased or aghast. "What the deuce would one man want with six women?"

Jeb's grin turned engaging. He'd saved himself many a trouncing with that grin—and brought on a lot more. "You *are* getting old, Pa."

Angus frowned at that, but then a look passed between the old man and Concepcion, like quicksilver, that made Kade sit up a little straighter in his chair. He would have bet Jeb hadn't noticed—he was too busy being a horse's ass, but Kade stuck the exchange away in the back of his mind, to be considered later on.

"What's this about a job offer?" Angus demanded, stone-faced. To his way of thinking, his sons belonged on the Triple M ranch, and nowhere else. Life might have been simpler for Kade if he hadn't agreed; he'd probably be practicing law in San Francisco or working for the Pinkerton Agency by now, if it weren't for his love of the land.

"I might fill in for John Lewis awhile," Kade said, glaring at Jeb, warning him with his eyes that there would be a reckoning, and sooner, rather than later.

"It seems to me, Jeb McKettrick," Concepcion said when a space opened in the conversation, so she could herd a few words through it, "that you ought to be doing some courting yourself, instead of tormenting your brother."

Jeb's grin broadened, and he shrugged. "It just may be," he said, smooth as cream rising on new milk, "that I've already got a wife." He held up his left hand and, sure as hell, there was a gold band on the appropriate finger. No doubt he'd used it to keep the brides at bay, back in town.

The room was so still that if it hadn't been for a piece of wood crumbling in the belly of the stove, Kade would have sworn he'd gone deaf as a post.

5

"I͟F͟ ͟Y͟O͟U͟'͟V͟E͟ ͟T͟A͟K͟E͟N͟ a wife," Angus challenged his youngest son, being the first to recover, "where is she?" After all, anybody could buy a ring, and Jeb was just crafty enough to do it.

"Yeah," Kade echoed. "Where is she?" He hadn't seen any sign of a bride since he'd hooked up with Jeb down in Tombstone, nor had he caught a glimmer of the wedding band, but that didn't mean the sidewinder wasn't hiding a woman away someplace and planning to spring her on them all at the worst possible moment; hell, she might already be breeding.

Jeb was ruminating on his answer, and enjoying the process a mite too much for Kade's taste, when the subject fell by the wayside all on its own. A wagon rolled up outside, raising a clamor, and Concepcion left off clipping to stand on tiptoe and peer out the window over the sink.

"It's Rafe and Emmeline," she announced, without turning around. "And they've got the little nun with them."

Kade closed his eyes, shook his head. He supposed he could tolerate Rafe, and he was out-and-out fond of Emmeline, like the rest of the family, but he had real misgivings about the nun. She wasn't what she appeared to be, which meant she was living a lie, and Kade had no patience with liars. Besides, she made him jittery.

There was some stomping on the porch, and then the back door swung open and Emmeline came in, followed by Sister Mandy and, finally, Rafe. He looked even bigger than usual, in contrast to two middling-sized women.

Emmeline was smiling, her cheeks pink with fresh air and cold, and she made a beeline for Angus, who, besotted, had risen to his feet in honor of her presence. She stretched to kiss his stubbly cheek.

"Are you happy now, Angus McKettrick?" she demanded with bright affection. "You've got all your rascal boys rounded up and roped in."

Angus chuckled and kissed her forehead, his big, gaunt hands resting lightly on her shoulders. "It's you I've missed most," he said shyly. Then he looked past her to Rafe, who'd enjoyed the status of firstborn son, until Holt Cavanagh had turned up, anyhow. He wasn't quite so sure of himself now, old Rafe, for all that he was first in line to run the ranch and, therefore, Kade's and Jeb's lives. "Took you long enough to fetch your wife home where she belongs," Angus told him, his gaze straying once to the gold glint on Jeb's ring finger. He wasn't happy if he wasn't grousing about something.

Rafe smiled, but when he linked gazes with first Kade, then Jeb, the expression didn't quite reach his eyes. "Emmeline's a hard woman to reason with, Pa," he said. "It takes a team of oxen to drag her away from that hotel."

Throughout all this, Sister Mandy stayed quiet, keeping to the fringes and looking as though she'd like to bolt for the timberline as soon as there was a gap in the throng.

Concepcion was having none of that. She took the girl's

hands into her own. "Amanda Rose," she said, catching Mandy's eye and holding it. "What a fine surprise. You will be paying us a long visit, *sí?*"

Rafe had gone to the stove to pour coffee for himself and Emmeline; when he offered some to Mandy, she demurred. "She's come to help out over at the house," he said with portent. "Emmeline's taking a rest from the hotel, letting Clive do the managing for a while, and Becky, when she's not off gallivanting with the marshal."

Emmeline colored up a little and Kade knew, with a sinking feeling in the pit of his stomach, that it wasn't because of Rafe's remark about Becky's romance with John Lewis. In his mind's eye, he saw his dream of running the Triple M retreat into the mists.

"Tell them," Rafe urged his wife gently, and when he looked at her, his chest seemed to expand, and pride glowed in his face.

She bit her lower lip and dropped her head, but when she raised it again, her eyes were shining with happy tears. "We just came from Doc's office. Rafe and I are expecting a child."

Angus let out a whoop of joy, and Concepcion, tears flowing, gathered Emmeline into her arms, hugging her fiercely. Soon after she and Rafe had moved to the new house, over beyond the creek, there'd been talk of a baby coming, but that had evidently ended in disappointment. This, Kade knew, was different.

Rafe stood still, watching his brothers. Waiting for their reaction.

Kade crossed the room, gave him a good-natured shove to the shoulder, then shook his hand. "Congratulations, Rafe," he said, the words scraping his throat as they passed.

"You mean that?" Rafe wanted to know.

"Hell, yes. But you still can't have the ranch."

Rafe laughed out loud at that.

Jeb came forward. "Damn right you can't," he said, as he and Rafe shook hands. "I'll be the one to run this place, not either of you sorry greenhorns."

"See what you have done, Angus McKettrick?" Concepcion piped up, but the reprimand was jolly. She dried her eyes hastily on the hem of her ever-present apron. "You have turned your own sons against each other."

"Well, it got them off their backsides, didn't it?" Angus asked. "Hallelujah, I'm finally going to have a grandchild! When is this blessed event supposed to occur, Emmeline?"

Flustered and beautiful, Emmeline beamed. "Sometime in November, according to Doc." She paused, exchanged a glance with Rafe, and went on, "Put away whatever you're cooking. You're all to come to dinner across the creek tonight, and I won't abide excuses. We're going to celebrate!"

No one could refuse Emmeline when she was smiling that way, Kade thought, and sure enough, nobody tried.

6

THE HORSEMAN SAT alone on the rise, looking down on the two glowing houses, one on either side of the moon-spangled creek, wondering why he gave a damn about any of the McKettricks, let alone the man who'd ridden off and left him with relatives before he was old enough to walk. Hands down, the best thing to do would be to rein his gelding around and ride straight back to Texas, where he reckoned he belonged, despite all that had happened there in recent years, but something nagged at him to stay.

He'd always been sure of his substance as a boy and as a man, and he'd elbowed out a place to stand wherever the trail led him, but that night, he felt more like a wraith than flesh and blood, as transparent and impermanent as smoke from a dwindling fire.

Holt Cavanagh cursed and spat. *Ride away,* whispered the still, small voice in the back of his mind, the one he'd learned to disregard only at his peril.

"The hell I will," he said aloud. Leaving now, however well advised, would feel too much like running from a fight. Trouble was, he couldn't seem to make himself wade in, either. The situation put him in mind of a mule up to its nostrils in mud.

There were horses grazing in front of Rafe's place, and a couple of wagons, too. The strains of a fiddle spun lively over the silvery grass, interspersed with an occasional burst of laughter. They grated on Holt, those sounds, pulling at him and driving him back, both at once. He wondered what they'd do, the high and mighty McKettricks, if he knocked on the front door, just like he was one of them, and joined in the celebration, whatever it was.

He sat awhile longer, resting one forearm on the pommel of his saddle, and then, no closer to making a choice than before, he turned his mount toward the log ranch house just five miles north of the Triple M, where there was no need for knocking at doors.

7

"Who are you?" Kade asked quietly when he caught Sister Mandy alone on Rafe and Emmeline's front porch, toward the end of the evening. She sat huddled in a wooden rocker, a plate of food in her lap, and she barely made up a shadow, swaddled in all that dark wool. She was going to be in misery when the hot weather came, he reflected, as sure as if she'd wrapped herself in an army blanket.

She started, evidently lost in thought, and barely caught Emmeline's piece of prized wedding china before it could slip off her knees to shatter on the floor. Light from the window spilled over her face, glinting in a wisp of golden brown hair escaping from the wimple.

"I'm Sister Amanda Rose," she said with a little thrust of her chin.

Kade leaned against the porch railing, a too dainty plate of his own in hand, and stabbed up a chunk of roast beef. "Like hell you are," he said easily.

She had backbone, he had to give her that. She wanted to run, he could tell by the way she stiffened, perched there on the edge of her seat, but she kept a tight hold on the reins. "Think what you like," she said with a sniff. "You will, anyhow."

He chuckled, helped himself to another mouthful of food, and enjoyed chewing and swallowing before offering a reply. "I reckon that's true enough. You on the run from somebody? The law, maybe?" He would have bet she was, wearing that imaginative but pitiful disguise. Her watchfulness gave her away, too; there was something tightly wound about her, as if she might lift her skirts and sprint up the road at any moment. Lord, he'd like to see her do that, if only to catch a glimpse of her ankles.

Her nervousness was palpable, but she didn't bend: "You planning to arrest me if I am?" Word that he was considering pinning on John Lewis's badge had apparently gotten around fast—no surprise in a town the size of Indian Rock. Around those parts, folks flapped their jaws over a lot less.

"Should I?" he countered.

She hesitated, as if she wanted to tell him something, but she didn't stumble. "I haven't broken any laws."

He considered the man he'd seen talking to her the day before, in the alleyway, the one she'd been so glad to get away from. "Might be I could help you, if you'd give me a chance," he ventured, feeling kindly disposed toward her, though against his better judgment. She was spunky, but she was also a woman, and the Arizona Territory was brimming with outlaws, renegade Indians, rattlesnakes, and sundry other perils.

"Might be you couldn't," she countered, determined to be contrary, and, after gazing at him steadily all that while, finally glanced away.

Inside the house, Denver Jack, a longtime fixture in the Triple M bunkhouse and an able cowpuncher, was giving his fiddle a workout. Feet shuffled on the bare wood floors, and Angus let out a roar of merriment, sounding almost like his old self. He was probably as happy about that new baby as Rafe and Emmeline were, in his own crusty way, and he'd make a fool of himself over the child, once it came. For Kade, the prospect was bittersweet.

He crossed to Sister Mandy, took her plate and silverware, set them on top of his own. "Who," he said, leaning down and lowering his voice, "was that fella I saw you with yesterday, out behind the hotel?"

Her eyes flashed as she looked up at him. "His name," she said in a burst, "is Gig Curry, and if you've got any sense at all, you'll stay clear of him." The instant the words left her mouth, she tightened her lips, as if she hadn't meant to let them get by. "Like as not, he's heading up a gang of cutthroats as bad as he is."

"What's he got to do with you?"

"Nothing."

"Lying is a sin, Sister. Or didn't you learn that at the convent?"

She stood, nearly clipping him under the chin with the top of her head, and he was forced to step back, their two plates rattling in his hands. He felt a peculiar quiver deep in his middle, being so close to her. "You might know a thing or two about sin yourself, from what I hear," she retorted, and slipped past him, hurrying into the house and letting the screened door slam smartly behind her.

Kade didn't move right away, and he was jolted to find himself grinning a little, for all his bafflement. The muscle under his belly was still jumping.

Presently, when he'd recovered a little, he went inside, carried the dishes through to the kitchen, and set them in the sink.

When he got back to the front room, Denver Jack was putting away his fiddle, and the cowboys who'd wandered over from the bunkhouse to sidestep Red's cooking and socialize a little were tipping their hats to Emmeline, offering shy congratulations and saying their farewells.

Kade caught Mandy's eye and smiled, and she responded with a glare.

The crowd had thinned appreciably with the cowboys gone, and Concepcion started looking about for her shawl. Jeb, who had been perched on the arm of an overstuffed chair for most of the evening, the ring no longer in evidence, made to rise, and Rafe yawned, though a smug light lingered in his eyes, as if he were the first man in the history of the world ever to get a woman pregnant. Angus, leaning against the framework of the broad doorway leading into the small parlor, straightened. Emmeline had begun casting glances toward the kitchen; no doubt her thoughts had turned to washing dishes. He'd never seen a woman who thrived on hard work the way she did, except for Concepcion.

Kade spoke up. "I believe," he said solemnly, "that an occasion like this calls for a prayer." He paused, waiting for the roof to fall in, but the beams held. "Sister Mandy, would you do the honors?"

Mandy reddened under the cheekbones and her aquamarine eyes took fire. Something tightened in Kade's groin.

"Sounds like a fine idea to me," Angus boomed. He was about as religious as the pump handle out by the horse trough, but his spirits were high that night, with three of his sons in one place and a baby coming, and he must have been feeling generous.

Emmeline looked amenable, and so did Rafe. Jeb was amused, as he was by just about everything; it was Concepcion who sliced a sharp glance in Kade's direction. He saw it out of the corner of his eye and steadfastly ignored it, though he reckoned he'd pay later.

Sister Mandy's eyes flashed again, fit to singe the fine hairs off Kade's flesh, but then she stepped resolutely into the center of the room and knotted her fists together in front of her chest. The knuckles, Kade noted with a satisfaction he knew was downright unbecoming, were white as a skull bleached in the desert sun.

A reverent silence fell. Concepcion and Emmeline folded their hands and bowed their heads. Rafe, Angus, Jeb, and Kade kept theirs up, and not a one of them shut their eyes.

Sister Mandy cleared her throat and shifted from one foot to the other before finally getting herself situated someplace in the middle.

"Good evening, God," she said. "This is Sister Amanda Rose talking. We—we've had a dandy time here tonight, and we're grateful. There was plenty of food and the music was tolerable. We'd appreciate it if You'd look out for all of us, but especially for Mrs. McKettrick and the babe she's carrying." Sister Mandy opened her eyes, caught Kade watching her, and squeezed them shut again. Her right temple throbbed. "Much obliged, Lord," she added as a seeming afterthought. "And amen."

"Amen," Emmeline and Concepcion chorused.

"Amen," echoed Jeb, Angus, Rafe, and Kade in gruff unison and a beat late.

"Now," said Mandy, with a that's-done motion of her shoulders, "I'd better get those dishes washed." At that, she turned on one heel and hustled off to the kitchen.

Kade tried to go after her, but Concepcion moved to block his path and elbowed him in the ribs for good measure.

Angus was already at the door, and Rafe stood by Emmeline's chair, holding her hand. Their fingers were interlaced. No doubt they would do some private celebrating once they were alone.

"Come along, woman," Angus said to Concepcion, who had driven him across the creek in a buckboard before supper. "It's late."

Kade cataloged the oddness of the remark with the other ragtag impressions he'd been storing up since his return from Tombstone, and promised himself that he'd unravel it all later. In the meantime, he got his coat and hat and followed Concepcion and Angus outside.

He offered Concepcion his arm when she went to climb up into the box of the wagon, and she shrugged it off and favored him with another scorching look. A moment later, she and Angus were rattling down the rocky bank toward the shallow place in the creek.

Jeb stood beside Kade, the reins of his horse in hand, watching as the pair made the crossing and trundled up the opposite side, wagon bed dripping, headed for the barn.

"That was a dirty trick, making Sister Mandy offer up a prayer in front of us all the way you did," Jeb drawled. He was holding a matchstick between his teeth, and he shifted it to the other side of his mouth. "Wish I'd thought of it first."

8

GIG CURRY SMILED to himself as he watched the homesteaders rushing hither and yon, trying to put out their blazing cowshed. Might as well stir things up a little, he'd thought, while he worked out his plans. He meant to conduct some business with the railroad, and with the McKettricks, too, now that the old gang had come together again, but he wouldn't have a peaceful mind until he knew where Cree Lathrop was.

Under a headstone someplace, he hoped. Should have killed that ornery little half-breed when he had the chance; now, if he didn't track him down and deal with him, he wouldn't be able to concentrate on the tasks at hand for looking over his shoulder all the time.

Curry shifted in his saddle and spat. He could feel the heat of the fire on his face, but he was hidden in a copse of oak trees, so he was in no hurry to ride on. He'd stay awhile and enjoy the spectacle while he ruminated on how to proceed. The stakes were big, and Dixie's boy was a wild card, a spoiler.

One thing would draw Lathrop out of the brush for sure, though, and that was Mandy. They were cozy, those two, and while Cree would cut a man's throat as soon as look at him, he'd go to hell and back for that lying, thieving little hoyden.

Sister Mandy. He chuckled and shook his head. He'd have to ask her where she'd gotten that getup, next time they crossed paths.

Meanwhile, the entertainment at hand was getting good. The homesteader's woman, a bony little snippet in calico and work boots, shrieked something at the man when the flames caught the dry grass and started racing toward the cabin. The sodbuster had his hands full, tending a couple of terrified plow horses and a razor-hipped milk cow, but his wife hoisted up her skirts and ran right alongside the fire. She had some spirit in her, he thought. Maybe he'd come back another time, if they stayed on, and pay her a social call. He turned melancholy on occasion, since Dixie had run him off, threatening to bring the law down on him if he came near her, though he didn't miss the aggravation.

The lady of the house sprang into the cabin just as the fire started climbing the eastern wall and came out quick with a bundle in her arms. Yes, sir, she had some gumption, all right. He did admire a frisky woman.

The shack went up just as fast as the shed had, and the nesters stood piteous but proud next to the trickle of a creek, with their flea-bitten livestock gathered around them, watching as fire took everything.

Still Gig remained, fascinated. It soothed something in him, watching ill fortune overtake somebody else besides him. He looked on until the flames died to embers, until the dirt farmer and his wife and the babe finally laid themselves down on the creek bank, spent by their efforts and their heartbreak.

When he was sure they weren't fixing to stir and catch sight of him, he pulled a cold branding iron from the scabbard where he usually carried a rifle, climbed down off his horse, and laid the business end of the rod in a patch of red coals to heat.

Light was gathering in the eastern sky by the time the iron was ready; he took it from the coals and pressed the Triple M brand hard into the charred trunk of an oak tree. The mark it left was clear, and he paused to admire his handiwork for a few moments.

He was humming under his breath as he mounted his horse, turned north, toward the Circle C, and rode off. A man needed his diversions, and if the boss man took pleasure in the news of the dirt farmers' calamity, once it reached him, Curry might just feel obliged to take the credit for a fine night's work.

9

They'd ridden to town on a spavined, swaybacked plow horse with singed hide, the sodbuster, his wife, and the child, and as they stood in John Lewis's office that cold morning, he despaired of going on a wedding trip with Becky anytime soon.

The family's clothing, probably little better than rags in the first place, was soot-stained and torn, but it was the look in their eyes that stabbed at something in the depths of the marshal's soul. They'd fought tooth and nail, these people, endured hardships of every sort, made all the sacrifices anybody could rightly expect of them, probably, but now they were beaten, even if they didn't seem to know it yet.

"It was the McKettricks," the man said before he'd even given his name. "They burned us out last night. Left their brand on a tree, like they was proud of what they done."

Tears welled in the woman's eyes—she was a plain thing, a mere scrap of a female, barely bigger, it seemed to John, than the child she clasped in both arms. "We weren't hurting anybody," she said. For reasons John would never understand, folks always thought nothing bad ought to happen to them if they weren't causing harm to others. It was a noble thought; too bad the world didn't work like that on its best day.

Belatedly, John recalled his raising in a good Christian home and thrust himself to his feet. He rounded the desk without a word, drew up a chair, and eased the woman into it. The baby, warmly wrapped and wiggly as a pup in a grain sack, made a small sound, part cough, part whimper.

"You folks hungry?" John asked. The man stood behind the woman, ignoring a second chair over by the wall, his hands resting protectively on her shoulders. His jaw was hard, his eyes too old for the rest of him, his body thin and slight. "I've got hot coffee here, and I can send over to the hotel for some food."

The woman swallowed, the man shook his head, quick and fierce. "We ain't got the money to pay," he said. "But thanks, just the same."

"Reckon we don't have to worry about that right away," John replied, throwing a chunk of wood onto the fire in the potbellied stove. The woman started at the sound and blinked. Sparks snapped in the chimney, and the good smell of seasoned mesquite filled the room. "You can always chop some firewood for the cook or something. Never enough help over at that place, especially since they started building on."

The man considered the matter, clearly weighing the semblance of charity against his wife's need, and his own. To his credit, he chose wisely. "If I can pay our way by workin'—"

John smiled to himself, went to the door, and gave a shrill whistle. That would bring one of the Sussex boys from down the street; they were a posse of snot-nosed rascals, freckled and knock-kneed and wholly wild, but fit to run errands when the need arose. John had a special weakness for the scruffy little buggers.

"What's your name?" he asked the farmer, when Harry Sussex had been dispatched to the hotel kitchen to bring back whatever vittles might be available. He set a mug of coffee on the desk for the woman, handed another to her husband. "I don't believe I've made your acquaintance before today."

"Sam Fee" was the response. Fee's work-chapped hands trembled as he closed them around the tin mug. "This is my wife, Sarah, and our little one, Ella Susannah."

Sarah Fee had relaxed a little; she peeled away some of the child's swaddling and held her against one shoulder while she reached for the coffee John had brought.

"If you'd like to let the baby lie down," John said, "there's a cot in the cell there. It's nothing fancy, but it's clean enough."

Sarah looked to Sam. He deliberated awhile, then gave his assent with one sharp nod of his head. Once Sarah had settled the child comfortably, she rejoined the men in the front office, but her gaze kept straying toward the little barred room where she'd left her baby.

"Tell me what happened last night," John said, refilling both their cups. "Start at the beginning."

The story was grim, and by the end of it, Becky had arrived with a picnic basket, and a plan. The Fees tried to eat slowly, but they were both famished, and they finished off the ham, biscuits, and fried grits with desperate good manners. John wondered when their provisions had begun to run low. No matter how well prepared the settlers thought they were in the fall of the year, the high-country winters generally starved them out long before spring.

"Much obliged," Sam said with a red tinge to his jawline. He fixed his sorrowful gaze on John's face. "We're grateful for the food, Marshal, but we need to know what you mean to do about the McKettricks."

Becky's eyes widened. "The McKettricks?" she echoed. They were her daughter's kin, and she tended to think well of them. So did John, for that matter, though he'd had enough go-rounds with those roughneck boys over the years to know they were wild as rutting stallions after the same mare. At one time or another, he'd had each of them right there in his jail, drunk, disorderly, or both.

"They burned our place," Sam told her. His tone was somber, with fury in it, but not a trace of self-pity. These were strong people, used to the hardships of life on the land. Like as not, they'd never known an easy day in their lives.

Becky paled a little at Sam's announcement, and it was all John could do not to go patting her hand and all like that. Fortunately, he knew better by experience; she hated fussing, this woman of his. Liked to stand on her own two feet and fight her battles personally, no matter what came at her. "That can't be," she said. "They wouldn't—"

Sarah spoke up. "The one they call Rafe," she said flatly, staring into space, "he came by to see us just last week. Told us we were on Triple M land and we ought to move on before there was trouble. Before there was trouble. That's just how he said it."

Becky closed her eyes, swayed. John's resolve not to coddle her wavered, but in the end it held.

"He said we was squatters," Sam put in. "We wasn't. Until that fire, we had documents to prove we bought our land fair and square. I showed him. McKettrick, I mean. He said we'd been cheated, that the papers was a fraud and we had no right to the place."

"Rafe McKettrick," Becky said, recovering, "would never—"

John caught her eye. Willed her to remember the Peltons, another family who'd settled on McKettrick land. The husband had shot himself through the head, and the wife had lost their child and ended up under Concepcion's care for a while, before taking the train back to Iowa or Ohio or some such place, where there were folks ready to take her in. Once they were both gone, Rafe had set fire to their cabin and barn and had even the rubble hauled off in wagons, and that wasn't the only time he'd burned something down, either. On another occasion, in a fit of sorrow and rage, he'd put a torch to the first house he'd built for Emmeline.

"I'll go out and talk to Rafe and the rest of them," John said, feeling gray and spent inside, and about a dozen years older than he was. "Get to the bottom of this."

Becky had rallied, but John couldn't help wondering when those seemingly endless inner resources of hers were finally going to play out, like a mine that's been scoured for its last flakes of ore. It made him hurt inside to think she might be using herself up before her time; a woman like her was a rarity, and there would not be another one along soon.

Her smile pushed back the shadows and rivaled the stove for warmth. "Well, now," she said, "we'd better get that baby out of jail and head on over to the hotel. Sam, there's plenty for a man to turn his hand to at the Arizona, and, Sarah, I wonder how you'd be at changing beds, watching over the registration book, and waiting tables in the dining room. I can't seem to keep regular help in that place to save my very life."

John strapped on his gun belt, checked the cylinder of his pistol to make sure it was loaded, and reached for his hat and coat. The weather was contrary; it could go one way or the other.

Pretty much like this situation with the McKettricks.

10

RAFE AND KADE were trying to pull a lame cow out of a mud bog when John Lewis rode up, toward the middle of the afternoon. He wore an earnest expression, the marshal did, and by Kade's reckoning, that didn't bode well. Clearly, the lawman wasn't just passing by—he'd come on badge business and gone to some trouble to make the journey.

"John," Rafe said with a nod, still hauling on his end of the rope Kade had fixed around the heifer's neck.

John nodded back, dismounted, and came toward them. "Give you a hand?" he asked, and without waiting for an answer, he waded right into the mud, where Kade had spent the better part of the last hour, fruitlessly pushing a cow's ass.

"Obliged," Rafe allowed, straining on the rope, "but I don't reckon you came all the way out here just to help us with the chores."

John gave the critter a good whack on the flank, and she bawled and sucked both her front legs out of the mire, slogging toward dry ground in a few awkward leaps. "I'm here about the Fees," he said, dusting his hands together as he made his way toward Rafe.

Kade took the rope off the heifer and sent her on her way

with a muted shout; she'd find the herd on her own. His attention was on Rafe and the marshal, and he had a real uneasy feeling in the center of his gut.

"Nesters," Rafe said.

"They say they had just claim to that land," John replied. "You burn their place, Rafe?"

Rafe's big shoulders shifted back a ways, and his spine straightened like a ramrod, the way it always did when he waxed indignant. "No," he said pointedly. "They saying I did?"

John took his hat off, shoved a hand through his stringy hair, and put the hat back on. "What they told me was, you warned them off a week or so back. The Triple M brand was burned into a tree about a hundred yards behind what used to be their barn." Kade must have looked as skeptical at that as Rafe did, because John went through the fidgety routine with his hat again before saying, "I stopped by there on the way out here and had a look. It's your brand, all right."

Kade cursed and drew John's attention.

"You know anything about this, Kade?"

"Hell, no," Kade replied. He tossed Rafe an irritated glance; there was no question in his mind that his brother was telling the truth, but folks would wonder just the same, between the McKettrick brand and Rafe's proclivity for setting things on fire. And their wondering might just tip the tenuous balance between peace and war. "It would be an easy matter to steal a branding iron, John. You know that."

"I do know that for a fact," John agreed, with a long sigh, before voicing Kade's private worry: "But it isn't my opinion that's vexing me. Feelings are running pretty high around Indian Rock these days as it is. A thing like this could set off all kinds of trouble."

Kade had heard enough. He whistled for his horse, and Raindance ambled over from a nearby stand of grass, bridle fittings jingling. "Best thing to do," he said, "is go to the source."

Rafe turned to him, frowning. "What—?"

"Where you headed?" John wanted to know.

Kade put a foot in the stirrup and swung up into the saddle. "Like I said. To the most likely source. Holt Cavanagh."

"I'll ride with you," Rafe said, and whistled for Chief, his own horse.

Kade looked down at his brother, adjusting his hat. "Thanks," he said, "but you're liable to make things worse with that temper of yours. Just stay here."

Rafe was formulating a protest, Kade could see it brewing in his face, but when he moved to mount and follow, John reached out and put a restraining hand on his arm.

"Kade's right," he said. "Could be you're in enough Dutch already, without beating the brush for more."

"Listen to the man," Kade told his brother, then he turned Raindance around, headed for the Circle C.

11

Mandy was reading down by the creek, the hateful habit pulled up around her knees, the wimple beside her on the grass, when Gig caught her by surprise for the second time in as many days. He crept up behind her, took hold of her hair, and jerked her head back hard.

She let out a gasp before she could stop herself.

"All I've got to do is scream," she said, when she caught her breath from the shrill pain, "and every hand on this place will be on you, that quick."

Gig just laughed, but he must have given the threat some credence, too, because he let go of her hair. Her scalp throbbed. "Looks like you're coming up in the world, Amanda Rose," he said. "You throwing in your lot with the McKettricks these days?"

She ignored the question. She wasn't "throwing in" her lot with anybody. She was the same outsider she'd always been, and that was one of the lesser reasons she hated Gig Curry. "Get out of here," she said, "and don't come back."

He settled himself beside her on the grass, just as if she'd greeted him cordially, as if they were fond companions, and not old enemies. "You don't want me to leave before I tell you all about your poor mama, do you, Amanda Rose?"

Everything inside Mandy tightened into a single aching knot, fair stopping her breath. She hadn't seen Dixie in two years, and the last time, down near Tucson, her mother had been real sick. "What about her?" she whispered.

Gig assumed a mournful expression, though the angry mirth lingered in his eyes. "It's a pity," he said, "how she's declined since they put her in that place to be doctored."

Mandy's throat ached fiercely. *He's lying,* her reason said. "What place?" she whispered, because this was bait she couldn't help taking, even though she knew a hook was hidden inside.

"It's a sort of home for people like her. Consumptives, they call them. Nothing fancy, but she's got a bed and a roof and enough vittles to keep body and soul together. That's more than you and I can say most of the time, isn't it, Mandy?"

"More than you ever provided for her, too," Mandy said.

For a moment, she thought Gig was going to grab her by the hair again, or even slap her, but he restrained himself with a visible effort. "Where's Cree?" he asked.

"I don't know." In this case, she was telling the truth, though she knew Gig wouldn't believe her. Even when the two of them were far apart, she and Cree generally found ways to stay in touch—letters, telegrams, messages carried by stage drivers, peddlers, drovers, and drifters. As it was, she hadn't heard a word from Cree in almost a year.

"Don't make me hurt you, Amanda Rose," Gig cajoled. "I'll do that, you can be sure that I will, if that's what it takes to smoke him out into the open."

She knew Gig wasn't bluffing. He'd kill her without a flicker of hesitation or remorse—but not if she was of some use to him.

"Suppose I did know where he was," she allowed. "I'd be crazy to tell you, wouldn't I? You'd cut his gizzard out just to eliminate the threat, soon as he showed himself."

"I reckon he'd come back if you were ailing or bad hurt," Gig mused, chewing pensively on a blade of grass and squinting as he watched the late-afternoon light frolic on the waters of the creek. "Or dead. He wouldn't miss your funeral."

Mandy felt a chill spill over her. She'd been a fool to stay around Indian Rock this long, pretending her life could be any different from what it had ever been, making believe she might find a way to fit in. If she'd moved on, found a Wild West show to join up with, the way she'd planned in the first place, maybe Gig wouldn't have caught up with her and she might not be in this fix.

"Cree's probably a thousand miles from here," she said. "If he heard I was dead, he'd be right sorry, but he's not stupid, Gig. He'd guess that you were laying a trap for him."

Gig took her chin in a bruising grip. "Get him here. Tell him you need him. I just want to talk to him, that's all. Come to some kind of terms. You do that, I'll ride out of here, and neither one of you will ever lay eyes on me again."

"You're a liar."

He drew back his hand to strike her.

The click of a rifle being cocked stopped him in midmotion. "I wouldn't do that," Emmeline said, calm as all get-out. Last Mandy had seen her, she'd been in the house, about to stretch out for a nap, but she looked wide-awake now, and her aim was dead-on.

Gig scrambled to his feet, hat in hand, smile anxious and affable. "Now, ma'am, don't you go shooting me. Sister Mandy and me, we're family, and we have our little tiffs, it's true, the way all kinfolks do, but I wouldn't do this sweet girl any sort of injury. Surely, ma'am, I wouldn't."

Emmeline didn't lower the rifle, and she still had Gig's head in the crosshairs. "Amanda," she said, "get away from that man right now."

Mandy got to her feet, groping for her book and wimple, and rushed to Emmeline's side.

"Now, ma'am," Gig rattled on, raising his hands at his sides, to show he wouldn't go for his gun, "you've misjudged me grievously—"

"Get out of here," Emmeline said with no wavering in her, anywhere. She might hail from the big city, but she was plenty tough, and she knew one end of that rifle from the other, for sure and certain. Rafe must have taught her. "This is McKettrick land. I'll thank you to get off it right now, and don't bother coming back."

Gig gave a sigh, as if he were being martyred, but he took his hat and went, disappearing into the trees down the creek a ways, where he'd surely left his mount. Emmeline lowered the rifle, but she and Mandy both stood still and utterly silent until they heard him riding away, his horse's hooves clattering on the rocky hillside.

"Tell me who that was," Emmeline said. "Right now."

Mandy lowered her head. "He was my mother's man," she confessed, ashamed even though it hadn't been her choice to bring Gig Curry into the household.

Emmeline looked puzzled. "Her husband?"

"Just her man." Mandy had lied to all sorts of people in her life, mostly out of necessity, and she supposed she'd go right on doing it, but right then, in that time and place, she found she couldn't wrap her tongue around another tall tale. Not with Emmeline, who'd been so kind to her.

"He came here to do you some harm."

Mandy avoided Emmeline's gaze. Shook her head. Dear God—Cree *would* come if something happened to her, set on revenge, and he'd surely get himself killed. One-on-one, her brother could handle Gig any day, but Gig never worked alone.

"Mandy," Emmeline insisted. "You're scared to death. Why?"

"Don't meddle in this, Emmeline," Mandy pleaded miserably. "Please." She might as well have been talking to a rock.

"I'm going to report him to John Lewis," Emmeline said decisively. "We'll go to town directly and have the rounder arrested."

"Please," Mandy repeated, with quiet fervor. "Leave this alone."

"That would be cowardly. Anyway, I have to tell Rafe."

"No," Mandy cried, surprising herself as much as Emmeline by grabbing her friend's free hand and clasping it. "No, Emmeline—you mustn't—Gig's fast with a gun, and he's mean, and he doesn't do his fighting out in the open like other folks do. Like as not, he'd bow and scrape to Rafe if he came up against him, then shoot him right out of the saddle one day just for crossing him!"

Emmeline paled. "That's all the more reason to go to the marshal. Besides, Rafe and I don't keep secrets from each other. We made a promise."

Mandy's knees nearly gave out; she fought to stay on her feet. It would have been better if Emmeline hadn't come along and saved her from Gig; that way, she'd have been the only one to suffer. If Emmeline brought any trouble down on Gig's head, a whole lot more people would be drawn into the resulting fray. "I'll leave, Emmeline," she said with mounting desperation. "If I do that, none of you will get hurt."

"I'm not afraid of that low-down scoundrel," Emmeline said with conviction, trying to help Mandy up and manage the cumbersome rifle at the same time. "And you're not going anywhere. Now, come on. He's getting away."

"Let him go," Mandy pressed. "I'm telling you, he's a kissing cousin to the devil himself."

Emmeline looked solemn, and her eyes seemed to search Mandy's very soul. "That's why we we're not going to let this pass."

12

THE CIRCLE C ranch house was square, made of fieldstone and mortar, and though considerably smaller than its counterpart on the Triple M, it made an imposing picture that afternoon as Kade approached. He felt a grinding sensation in the pit of his belly—maybe it was envy, but it sure as hell wasn't fear—just looking at the spread. Chandler, the cagey old buzzard who'd owned the place before, had always sworn that if he ever got itchy feet and decided to sell out, Angus would have first chance at it.

Instead, he'd sold to Cavanagh, and he'd gone behind the McKettricks' backs to do it. Taken his profits and moved on without a word of explanation.

Kade put aside his bitter musings as best he could and concentrated on the task at hand. Holt was on top of the barn with some other men, driving nails into new shingles, and Kade knew his half brother had seen him coming from a long way off. Cavanagh didn't acknowledge him with so much as a wave or a glance, and he took his Texas time climbing down the tall ladder set against the near wall, but when he walked toward Kade, his gaze was direct and his expression was just shy of affable. He was a big man, big as Rafe, with brown hair and shrewd hazel eyes. He wore work clothes that day, and his stride was even, though he'd broken a leg several months before when a pile of logs had broken loose from their chains and all but crushed him. Back then, he was still posing as an ordinary ranch hand, and helping to build Rafe and Emmeline's first house, the one Rafe had burned to the ground.

"I'd say it was a pleasure," Cavanagh drawled in that honeyed Southern voice of his, "but from the look on your face, I know better."

Kade dismounted and stood facing the interloper. He didn't put out his hand, and neither did Holt. "There are some things we need to discuss," Kade said. He'd been the one to come here, so it was up to him to get things started.

Cavanagh waited, arms folded. It would have been neighborly to offer a cup of coffee, or water for the horse, but Holt wasn't on neighborly terms with any of the McKettricks. While Angus had wanted to take his firstborn son right into the fold, back before the trouble started anyhow, Rafe, Kade, and Jeb weren't quite so ready to accept him. There was too much at stake.

Kade pulled off his riding gloves, stuffed them into the pockets of his duster. "Last night some squatters were burned out just west of our place. Somebody used a Triple M iron to mark a tree so they could put the blame on us."

Holt arched one eyebrow, shifted slightly on his feet, and didn't unfold his arms. "That so?"

Curiosity welled up inside Kade, strange and sudden, out of context and purely unbidden; he wondered about Holt, about his schooling and his growing up, the places he'd been and the people he'd known and the things he'd done in his life before he came to Indian Rock. He wasn't about to ask about any of that, though, so he resigned himself to knowing next to nothing about his father's son.

"I figure you or one of your men was behind it," Kade said. This conclusion didn't seem as sensible as it had during the ride from the Triple M, but he was here and that was the only reason he had for showing up.

A ghost of a grin quirked one side of Holt's mouth. "Do you, now? And why's that, since it was the Triple M brand they found, and not mine?"

"Whoever set that fire wanted everybody to think we were behind it." Just thinking about that made Kade fighting mad. The McKettricks had their share of enemies, always had. It was part of running the biggest ranch north of Tucson; folks got to feeling jealous sometimes, and that made them fractious and inclined to believe the worst. Incidents like the one on the Fee homestead could only exacerbate the problem.

"And you really think I did it?"

"You or somebody who works for you," Kade reiterated. "It's no secret that there's been some bad blood between us."

"Bad blood," Holt echoed in the tone of one reflecting upon great and grave matters. "Interesting term." He paused, pondering again, then skewered Kade with a narrow look. "Did our old pappy send you here to talk to me? I would have thought he had more backbone than to ask a boy to do a man's job."

Kade pressed his lips together briefly, then let out a breath. "I'm no boy," he said evenly, "and I don't run errands for Pa or anybody else. What I came here to say is that nobody needs a range war, but there's going to be one for sure if you don't back off."

A flush crept up Holt's neck to pulse under his jaw, and Kade took strong if unseemly satisfaction in the knowledge that the other man was rattled. Up till then, he'd acted as if butter wouldn't melt in his mouth. "Your men have been cutting my fence lines," Holt said, "and somebody's been slaughtering Circle C cattle and leaving them to rot on the range." He thrust a finger at Kade for emphasis, and it was a damn good thing he wasn't standing close enough to connect, because that would have meant a fight for sure. "Seems to me, *Brother,* that you and the rest of your outfit are the ones who'd best do the backing off."

Kade knew that one step forward would get him what he only then realized he'd wanted all along, a chance to take this Texan down a notch or two, but something held him back. It wasn't prudence that stopped him, that was all he could have said for sure. He'd never been afraid of any man in his life, and this one was no exception.

The front door of the house creaked open just then, and a woman stepped out onto the small stone porch. Kade recognized one of the brides he'd ordered up. Sue Ellen, she was called, if he recollected right. He didn't like her being there, even though he wouldn't have taken her out strolling, let alone married her, whether the Triple M was on the line or not.

"I thought I'd take a housekeeping job until you came to your senses," she sang out, and this time, it was Kade who reddened. "A girl has to make a living, you know."

"Sue Ellen's a fair cook," Holt remarked, apropos of nothing.

Kade tugged at the brim of his hat; thanks to Georgia McKettrick, and then Concepcion, the gesture was ingrained. "You do whatever you feel the need to do, ma'am," he said, as cordially as he could.

She pouted, and Kade observed to himself that while a pretty woman might have been able to carry off such an expression, Sue Ellen would have been wiser not to attempt it. "It's a sorry state of affairs," she said, "when a proper lady leaves the bosom of her home and family, expecting a man to honor his promise, and finds herself disappointed."

Holt smirked at that, and while Kade would have liked to hit him, he refrained and doffed his hat instead. "If you want to go back to wherever you came from, Miss Sue Ellen," he said smoothly, "you just say the word, and I'll put you on the next stagecoach."

Holt suppressed a snort of laughter.

Sue Ellen set her hands on her hips and glared. "I do believe that was an insult."

"I didn't mean it as one," Kade said, and he hadn't. He'd been trying to do right by the woman, since she had a legitimate grievance, that was all. Trust a female to twist whatever a man said around until it was as tangled and prickly as a coil of barbwire left out in the weather.

"Mr. Cavanagh," Sue Ellen said with shrill dignity and a huffy set to her countenance, "supper is ready."

Holt leaned toward Kade and spoke in an undertone, "I'd invite you to stay for a meal, but I really don't think you should eat anything Sue Ellen cooked. She might just poison you."

Sue Ellen turned on her heel at that—evidently her ears were good—stomped back into the house, and slammed the door smartly.

"Thanks anyway," Kade said, addressing both the retreating woman and Cavanagh himself. He hadn't accomplished anything by riding all the way up to the Circle C, except to make a damn fool of himself. He'd settled nothing with Cavanagh, and running into Sue Ellen had been just plain sorry luck. Some days, it didn't pay a man to roll out of his bunk and pull on a pair of boots.

"Wait," Holt said when Kade turned to mount up.

Kade turned back, wary. "What?"

"I didn't order that fire set. When I've got a bone to pick with you or anybody else in the McKettrick outfit, you'll hear it straight from me. Which is why I'm telling you right now, Kade— if I lose any more cattle to gunmen from the Triple M, if I find any more fence lines cut, I'm coming after whoever I have to come after to put an end to it. That includes the old man, as well as you and Rafe and Jeb."

Kade hadn't been in the habit of defending his pa of late, but he wanted to then. "You and Pa have your differences," he said with a moderation that was hard-won, "and that's to be expected, I suppose, given his walking out on you and all. But now I'm going to tell *you* something, Mr. Cavanagh. If any harm comes to him or to either of my brothers because of you, I'll find you, if I have to track you to the hind corner of hell to do it, and I'll kill you."

Something moved in Holt's eyes, maybe surprise, maybe amusement, maybe even respect. All Kade knew for certain was that it hadn't been fear. This Texan might call himself Cavanagh, but he'd been born a McKettrick, and he most likely didn't have the good sense to be scared of anything, even when it would have been the wisest course.

That recklessness, more than the ranch, more than the money and cattle and mines, was Angus's legacy, a mark of his bloodline. Damn the old fool, anyway. He'd get them all lynched one of these days, or shot full of holes.

"I'll keep it in mind," Holt said after some time. "Don't bother to ride all the way to hell, though. I'll be a lot closer at hand than that."

Something flickered at one of the windows, and Kade glimpsed Sue Ellen as she flung the curtain back into place and stepped out of sight.

There being nothing else to be said, by Kade's calculations, he gathered Raindance's reins, crossed them over the gelding's neck, and hoisted himself into the saddle. He wasn't even halfway comfortable until he'd ridden well out of rifle range.

13

John Lewis was at the supper table, along with Angus, Concepcion, and Jeb, when Kade walked into the house that night well after dark, frustrated, hungry, and saddle sore.

"Any of that fried chicken left?" he asked of everyone in general, and rather pointedly, since the platter looked empty, as he paused at the sink to roll up his sleeves and wash his hands with Concepcion's harsh yellow soap.

"In the warming oven," Concepcion said.

"John tells me you rode up to Holt's place," Angus put in. Kade couldn't tell from the old man's tone whether he was looking for an affirmation or a denial, but it didn't matter. All he had to offer was the plain truth.

"Yes," Kade said, heading for the stove. He remembered to get a pot holder before removing the plate Concepcion had kept back for him in the upper oven, hot and brimming with savory chicken, biscuits, peas from a jar, and gravy. Just the smell of it improved his mood a little.

"Well, damn it, what happened?" Angus demanded. He wasn't long on patience, and just then, Kade wasn't, either.

He carried his supper to the table, made a place for himself on the bench next to Jeb, and used both the salt and pepper shakers before answering. It wasn't like he had any news, unless you counted Sue Ellen's wanting to poison him for not marrying her. "I pretty much got nowhere," he said. "Cavanagh says he didn't have anything to do with what happened to that family of squatters."

"And you believed him?" John asked circumspectly.

Kade pondered that while he chewed the fleshy part of a chicken wing. Typical, he thought. If he hadn't been out chasing smoke, Jeb wouldn't have beaten him to all the best pieces of meat. Like as not, the little waster had scraped the gravy pan clean, too. He wasn't wearing the wedding band; he probably put it on only when it was convenient. "I got the feeling that if he had done something," he reflected aloud, in his own sweet time, "he'd have owned right up and taken pleasure in it. He's got it in his mind that we're behind the troubles he's been having, and I guess I might think that, too, if I were him."

Angus looked both unsettled and relieved. Whatever the problems between him and Holt, and they were considerable, he couldn't be blamed for not wanting to believe that his own son would set out to destroy everything he'd spent his considerable strength and resolve to build. "Downed fence lines and the like?" he asked.

"Worse," Kade said, chewing. "Somebody's been shooting his cattle, for the sport of it, evidently."

Angus muttered a low curse. Beef was his stock-in-trade, the lifeblood of his operation, and the wanton waste of such a resource went against everything he believed in.

"And he thinks we're doing that?" Jeb clarified, a note of disbelief in his voice. Kade couldn't tell for sure in the dim lamplight of that dark evening, but he thought his normally unflappable brother's color might have heightened a shade or two.

"Yep," Kade said.

"Well, it's a damn fool notion," Angus added. He liked to play the trump card, whether the stakes were high or not. Hell, there didn't even have to be a game afoot.

Concepcion spoke up, the cool head of reason, as she so often was. "Somebody else is doing these terrible things, trying to make trouble between Holt and the rest of you. Who—that is what we need to know—and why?"

"I reckon we'd better find out directly," Angus concluded, after some cogitation, "before somebody gets killed."

"Amen," said John Lewis, who never wasted a word if he could help it.

Concepcion swept all the McKettricks up in a single fierce glance. "If you know what's good for you, and for this place, you will saddle up your horses, all of you, first thing in the morning, ride up to the Circle C, and talk this out with Holt, once and for all."

Angus glowered; it wasn't his way to seek people out and come to terms with them. He liked them to come to him, preferably with hat in hand and abject apologies at the ready, whether they were at fault or not. "It isn't like he's going to welcome us," he said.

"You may be surprised," Concepcion replied.

Lewis smiled at that, pushed back his chair, and stood. "I thank you for the fine meal," he told Concepcion, "and for your gracious company." A quirk at the side of his mouth made it clear that the compliment was intended for Concepcion alone, even before he went on, "As for the rest of you, I'd be taking this good woman's advice to heart, and wasting no time doing it. Wouldn't hurt to pour some oil on the waters."

Angus got to his feet. "Now, John," he said, "it's late, and it's dark. There's been some tomfoolery going on out there. You ought to pass the night right here, and head for Indian Rock in the morning."

John sighed. "Yes, I ought to do just that. But Becky's been a little delicate lately, and I like to stay close by in case I'm needed." He headed for the row of pegs next to the back door, took down his gun belt first and strapped it on, then donned his coat and hat. On the threshold, he paused. "A lot of folks around here look up to the McKettricks. They'll watch what you do about this thing and decide on their own actions accordingly. Keep that in mind."

With that, Marshal John Lewis took his leave.

"One of you go after him," Angus said, a moment after the door closed. "Ride along as far as town. John isn't as young as he used to be, or as fast, and somebody's liable to jump him out of pure orneriness."

Kade had done all the riding he wanted to for one day, but he agreed with his pa. The times were uncertain, and tough as he was, the marshal wasn't invincible. Kade collected his own rigging, just as John had done, and went out the door.

Lewis and his mount were already splashing across the creek when Kade reached the barn, so he didn't call to the other man to wait. Raindance was enjoying a well-earned rest in his stall, and Kade spoke with gruff affection as he passed the animal by, choosing another horse for the trip into Indian Rock. The sorrel gelding was small, but eager to travel, and Kade saddled him quickly.

A mile up the road, Lewis was waiting, pistol drawn and cocked. "Who goes there?" he demanded.

"Kade McKettrick. Put that thing away."

In the thin moonlight, Kade saw the lawman release the hammer with his thumb and slip the gun back into its holster. Maybe the old fellow was still capable of taking care of himself after all.

"Angus decided I ought to have a nursemaid," Lewis surmised with a chuckle.

"Just some company," Kade replied, drawing up alongside.

"I reckon I wouldn't mind that."

They were within half an hour of Indian Rock, riding at a steady gallop, and in companionable silence, when all of a sudden John Lewis put a hand to his chest and pitched right off his horse, landing headfirst in the road.

14

"What the hell?" Doc Boylen demanded when Kade rousted him from his bed. Back there on the road, he'd gathered John up, thinking at first he'd been shot, though there'd been no report of a bullet and no blood, loaded him into the saddle he'd just pitched off of, belly-down this time, and brought him to town, traveling as fast as he dared. At the moment, Lewis was lying unconscious in the small surgery downstairs, where the doc kept his irregular office hours.

Kade prodded Boylen with the barrel of his rifle to get him rolling. "It's John Lewis. He bit the dirt a mile or so outside of town."

Doc finally got everything headed in the same direction and hoisted himself to his feet. He was dressed in a flannel nightshirt with garters on the sleeves, his wild hair was rumpled, and he fumbled for his spectacles. "Somebody take a potshot at him?"

Kade shook his head, impatient, gesturing toward the inside door with the rifle. "I think it might be heart trouble or something like that. No warning—he just went down."

Boylen sighed, taking his ancient sawbones's bag from the bureau top as he passed. "He's plum worn himself out, John has. Too old for that job. Too old for that fiery woman of his."

"I'd appreciate it," Kade said, falling into step behind the doc and doing his best to herd him along at a faster clip, "if you'd stop running off at the mouth and do something constructive."

Doc chuckled at that, feeling his way down the dark stairway by long practice. Kade had already lit a lamp in the surgery, after laying John out on the examining table and covering him hastily with the first thing that came to hand, which was his own muddy coat.

"Go on over and fetch Becky," Doc said, lifting one of John's eyelids and peering in as he opened his bag with his other hand and rummaged for the stethoscope. "She'll have all our hides if you don't."

Kade started to protest, saw the sense in Boylen's words, and banged out of the office, his strides long. The Arizona Hotel was just a block down the street, and the lights were out, except for a dim glow in the lobby.

Becky Fairmont appeared on the landing almost as soon as Kade stepped up to the base of the stairs and yelled for her. Her dark hair trailed down her back, and she clutched a lace-trimmed wrapper around her slender form. From that distance, she looked like a much younger woman than she was, and her eyes were round with alarm.

"Is Emmeline all right?" she asked, and even from that distance, he could tell that she was holding her breath as she awaited the answer.

"It's John," Kade said. "He took a spill from his horse on the way back to town from our place. He's over at Doc Boylen's."

Becky uttered a little cry and put a hand to her mouth as an afterthought, but she recovered quickly, whirling to vanish back into her room and reappearing only a few moments later, clad in a misbuttoned green dress and with her hair still down. She blew by Kade like a gust of wind, headed for the door.

"Heart attack," Doc Boylen said by way of a greeting when Kade and Becky burst into the surgery. John lay gray and motionless on the exam table, and for one terrible moment, Kade thought his friend was gone, and without Kade's ever telling him he was admired.

Becky rushed to John's side, clutched his hand. "John Lewis!" she cried. "You listen to me. Don't you go dying!"

It seemed that John's left eyelid flickered, but maybe it was a trick of the lamplight.

"What can we do?" Becky asked, fixing her gaze on the doc.

"Not much," Doc said, looking sad and old and very much the sort of doctor one would expect to find in a half-assed frontier town like Indian Rock. "He's alive, but just barely."

It reminded Kade of Emmeline, the way Becky straightened her spine, sucked in her breath, and gave the doc a level look. "Can we move him?"

"Maybe tomorrow," Doc said. "He oughtn't to be jostled around any more than necessary. He came to once, in a lot of pain, and I gave him a dose of morphine, much as I dared, anyway, and then he passed out again. No telling when he might run down, though, Becky, and that's the sad fact of it."

Tears shimmered in Becky's eyes and Kade would have bet they sprang from an inner well of determination, not just simple grief. She laid her forehead to John's and wrapped her arms around him.

"You hold on," she ordered. "You hear me, John Lewis? You *hold right on.*"

John made a sound, part gurgle, part murmur. Becky straightened as if struck by some sudden inspiration, went to the chair where the doc had tossed the lawman's coat after peeling it off him, and unfastened the nickel-plated badge from the lapel. Then, facing Kade, she pinned the thing to his shirt, and though she was looking up into his eyes, her words were directed to John, lying behind her on that hard table, fighting for his life. And losing, by the looks of things.

"You fix your brain on getting well, John," she said clearly, raising her voice a little, "and don't be bothering with anything else. Kade McKettrick's going to look after your town for you." She seemed to be staring into his very soul. "Aren't you, Kade?"

He raised one arm to give the badge a polishing swipe with his cuff. "Yes, ma'am," he said. He didn't have the first idea how to go about upholding the law, he realized, but he figured on learning, and learning fast.

15

Kade sat bolt upright on the jail-cell cot at the sound of his name, wrenched out of a deep and rummy sleep. When he peered through the bars, he saw Sister Mandy standing next to the desk, and the sight of her lifted his spirits a little, though he couldn't think why that ought to be so.

She was wearing the nun getup, as always, and her hands rested on her hips "You've got no business being marshal," she announced.

He shoved a hand through his hair, fixed his sights on the potbellied stove next to the far wall, and staggered over to throw on a piece of wood and see what he could do about getting some coffee started. "Well, thank you for putting your two cents in, Miss Mandy," he said amenably, and with a yawn, "but I can't see for the life of me where what I do is any of your concern."

Her cheeks turned a fetching shade of pink. "Don't be a fool. You've got no idea what you're going up against by pinning on that badge!"

The stove door creaked as Kade pulled it open and bent slightly to peer inside. The fire was stone cold, and he crouched to poke in some crumpled newspaper and kindling from the meager supply at hand. "I mean to find out," he said, without sparing her a glance. "What are you doing in town, anyhow? I thought you were set on taking care of Emmeline."

"I would, if she'd stay put," Mandy replied, still in a fine and un-nunly dither. "When we got word of what happened to Mr. Lewis, she made Rafe bring us straight to town."

Kade struck a match to the fire he'd laid, waited to see if it would catch, closing and latching the stove door when it did, then straightening. "Is there any word about John?" he asked quietly, reaching for the coffeepot.

"He's holding his own," Mandy said.

Kade's relief was swift and strong; he was glad he had the coffee dregs to toss into the street, the pot to rinse and fill, because that way he wasn't left standing with all his emotions right there on the surface for anybody to see. He looked up to John Lewis as an uncomplicated, forthright man and a square dealer, and seeing him down and out was a hard thing.

Outside, he dumped yesterday's brew, worked the pump beside the public horse trough, came back in, and set the works on top of the stove. A canister of coffee sat on a shelf nearby, and he measured in a generous portion.

"You have some business with me, Sister Mandy," he finally asked, "or did you just come here hoping to send me packing?"

She huffed out a sigh. "Why do you want to be marshal when you've got a perfectly good ranch to tend to?"

He hid a smile. "Why do you want to pass yourself off as a nun? You aren't even very good at it. 'Good evening, God.' What kind of prayer is that?"

"I reckon it's as good as any." She looked to be teetering on the brink of a first-class, down-home hissy fit, but in the end she brought herself under control with admirable dispatch. "Sometimes," she said, surprising him, "a body gets herself into something and flat-out doesn't know how to get back out again. Emmeline was bent on having a word with John, but now—"

He regarded her while he waited for the coffee to come to a boil. "I reckon Emmeline will be along presently, then," he said. "You could start by telling me what's on your mind." He considered her, wondered what it was about her that intrigued him so, and stirred things up inside him. "Wearing a regular dress wouldn't do any harm, either."

She sat down, if grudgingly. "You think it's that easy?"

"I don't think 'easy' has much to do with anything in this life. It's a tough row to hoe, any way you look at it."

Another sigh from Mandy. "Maybe so, but it sure would be nice if, once in a while, things didn't have to be such a bloody struggle."

Kade chuckled. The coffee was beginning to bubble a little, which meant there was hope for the day. "Best to keep your knuckles bare and ready."

She frowned. "Do you always look on the melancholy side of things?"

"Yep. I like to know what's there. Don't get taken by surprise so often that way." Kade pushed the brew to the back of the little stove to settle a bit, then rounded up a couple of battered tin mugs. "Have some coffee?"

She shook her head and stood. "I'd sooner drink watered-down creek mud." She let out an audible breath. "You aren't fixing to listen to reason and take that badge off while you still can, are you?"

"No. When John's ready to take it back, that's when I'll give it up. Might be a while before that happens."

She sighed again. "I reckon I've done all I can to warn you off, then." She sounded resigned. "I'd better get on over to the hotel and see if Emmeline needs anything."

"Wait a minute," he said crisply. "You still haven't told me why you came here in the first place."

"No use in it," she replied with brave dismay. "I can tell you won't listen any more than Emmeline did."

Kade was dealing with her going, and what it made him feel, when she opened the door, let out an exclamation, jumped back, and slammed it again.

"What?" he asked, pouring his lonely cup of coffee and venturing a tentative sip. The best he could have said about the stuff was that it wasn't swill, though the distinction was a fine one.

Mandy's whole manner had changed; she was grinning, and mischief cavorted in her eyes. "There's a committee headed straight for us," she said, wholly delighted by this development.

Kade frowned, confused. He didn't reckon he'd been on the job long enough to foul up and bring the town council down on his head, though he wouldn't be surprised to see a delegation of unhappy ranchers. "A committee?"

The door sprang open before Mandy could reply, and Kade counted five disgruntled brides clustered in the gap. They were wearing war paint, carrying parasols for spears, and they looked ready to use them, with little or no provocation.

Marvella, the voluptuous blonde, had evidently been elected spokeswoman. "Kade McKettrick," she said, pushing past Mandy, "we're tired of waiting. You're going to marry one of us, and that's that."

Kade's mouth dropped open, and he nearly spilled his coffee.

"Yes," agreed the one he remembered as Abigail, flushed with righteous indignation, as they all rushed inside, a human flash-flood of ruffles and ribbons and flowery scents. "We're not leaving until you make a decision and abide by it!"

For a moment, Kade seriously considered shutting himself up in the jail cell where he'd passed what had remained of the night before, once he'd seen to John, but he didn't figure that would save him.

"I do need a wife," he agreed thoughtfully. Rafe might be ahead in the race, with Emmeline wearing his wedding band and carrying their child, but he wasn't ready to quit on the idea of winning the Triple M, though he allowed as how that would have been the sensible thing to do. The place and the dream simply meant too much to him, and for all the things Angus had taught his sons, he'd left out the fine art of giving up.

Marvella took in the poor surroundings—John's beat-up old desk, the rough plank floors, the two narrow cells at the back, with their cots and bare mattresses, chipped basins, and slop buckets. "Of course we wouldn't be living *here*—would we?"

Kade hid another smile behind the rim of his coffee mug. "I reckon the mayor might spring for a room over at Mamie Sussex's boardinghouse," he said, knowing the brides were already housed in that unprepossessing establishment, and running up a bill that honor would require him to pay. "The ranch is too far from my work."

Abigail looked around, assessing. Then, spotting a broom, she commenced sweeping up. "A woman belongs at her husband's side," she announced with a churchy little sniff. "No matter where he happens to be."

Mandy put a hand over her mouth, maybe to stifle a burst of laughter, but wisely said nothing. The glance Kade sent her way was intended to wilt, but it didn't seem to take.

"It's going to be a hard matter, deciding between such fine ladies as yourselves," he said, taking the broom forcibly from Abigail, who was making him nervous with her fussing, and setting it back in the corner. "Maybe there ought to be some sort of— contest."

Mandy's eyes widened at that, and Kade knew, sure as Sunday came around once a week, that she'd have told him what he could do with his "contest," had she been in the running. Which, of course, she wasn't, what with her claiming to be a nun and all.

"Contest?" Marvella echoed.

"Any wife of mine," Kade said, riding a crest of foolish inspiration, "will have to be a good cook. I believe we ought to start with pies, since I particularly favor them."

"Pies," echoed a rather fetching little redhead with freckles. He didn't recollect her name. Penny would have suited her, with that coloring.

"Just put the foodstuffs you need on my account at the general store," Kade said with a generous wave of his hand. "I guess you could use the boardinghouse kitchen, or the one over at the Arizona Hotel."

The brides looked at each other in silent consultation, then made a herd decision and practically stampeded out the door, making for the mercantile across the street.

"Kade McKettrick," Mandy said, lingering on the threshold, framed in the light of a glowing spring morning, "you're either the bravest man alive, or the stupidest."

16

MANDY PAUSED ON the board sidewalk outside the mercantile, watching as the prospective brides placed their separate orders for flour and fresh butter and what fruits they could hope to attain in such a place as Indian Rock. A part of her was amused, watching their foolish scramble to please a lunkheaded man, but another part, one she couldn't readily acknowledge, wanted to outbake, outfuss, and outruffle every one of them.

She shifted her attention, by force of will, to the objects on display in the fly-specked window—tins of beans, stacked into a colorful pyramid, a basket brimming with wild hazelnuts, wormy for sure, and a pretty calico dress, ice blue with delicate white flowers and a modest trimming of lace on the collar and cuffs.

Mandy coveted that garment, with a sudden and startling wholeness of heart, in a way she had never coveted anything else in her life. She imagined shedding the cumbersome nun garb and slipping into that cool and lovely creation. Imagined brushing out her hair and looking like a woman, instead of one of those penguin birds from way down south, where the mountains were made of ice and the ground was always frozen. She leaned in a little, peering at the price.

One dollar and twenty-five cents. A fortune. She sighed, and deliberately averted her eyes, only to spot something she wanted even more than the dress. A brand-new double-barrel shotgun with a polished wooden stock and an inlay of ivory and of silver filigree. Lord in heaven, it was the prettiest sight she'd ever seen, that gun. She squinted at the little sign propped beside it.

WIN THIS FINE FIREARM.
CHANCES, FIVE CENTS EACH.

Mandy reached into the pocket of her habit and came up with four nickels. She'd earned wages working for Becky Fairmont at the hotel these past few months, but she'd sent most of that money off in the mail, some to Sister Mary Marguerite, to make up for stealing her clothes, some to a landlady, down near Tucson, who'd been good to Mandy and her mother when they had had a hard time making the rent. She'd spent the rest on dime novels.

She gave herself a little shake. She oughtn't to be dallying on the street, mooning over fancy shotguns and frilly dresses. She needed to see to Emmeline, and to keep an eye out for Gig, lest he take her unawares again. And if she bought anything, it would be a horse, so she could move on.

She'd been lucky so far, but time was wasting, and if life had taught Amanda Rose Sperrin anything in no uncertain terms, it was that luck could turn sour faster than a puddle of milk. If she stayed, she was putting a whole town at risk. On the other hand, if Gig ever got her truly alone, a likely event if she struck out on her own, she'd wish she were dead—better by half to be dragged off by a band of renegade Apaches and tattooed from head to foot.

Walk away, she told herself. *Walk away from this window and these foolish dreams. Forget about Kade and the strange, sweet things he makes you feel before you get him killed.*

"Like the dress?" Kade asked from beside her, scaring her half out of her scratchy woolen socks. So much for keeping her wits about her.

"It's all right," she allowed. She felt an ache take shape inside her and grow until she thought her skin would burst from the pressure. She wanted more than that bit of frippery, she realized with wounded clarity. She wanted to be the sort of woman who wore a getup like that, and that was a whole other bit of business. She wasn't Emmeline McKettrick, or one of those silly creatures looking to bake the best pie that ever came out of an oven, and bent on practicing till they got it right. She was the daughter of Dixie Sperrin, a fallen woman, and a long-gone outlaw husband, two or three men back from Gig, and she'd never be anything else, no matter what she put on when she got up in the morning. "I guess I'd rather have that shotgun than anything, though."

Kade grinned, and she noticed the little lines around his eyes. They came from a lifetime of laughter, those lines, and something about them made the throb in Mandy's spirit that much worse. Maybe it was the contrast between being a Sperrin, whatever that was, and being a McKettrick. The whole of the cosmos seemed to lie between those two things.

"What would you want with a shotgun?" he asked, hooking his thumbs under his gun belt. The silver star pinned to his shirt glinted, mocking Mandy, hurting her eyes as it caught the sunlight.

She bristled. "I can shoot."

He looked pleasantly skeptical. "That so?"

"And ride, too. Better than you, I reckon."

He laughed and shook his head as though he couldn't credit the possibility.

"You think I can't beat you?" she challenged, watching the brides cluster around the counter inside the store, anxious to settle accounts and get to baking. She's been riding *and* shooting since she was eight years old.

"I *know* you can't," he said without the slightest doubt.

She placed her hands on her hips and opened her mouth, and just like that her tongue ran away with her, wild as a yearling foal in a spring pasture. "You want to make a bet, Marshal McKettrick?"

"You'd need a horse."

Oh, she needed one of those, all right. "You've got plenty to spare on the Triple M. I could leave you in the dust riding any one of them."

He pretended to consider the proposition, but Mandy knew by the light in Kade's eyes that he was ready to race right then and there, just to show her up. He was cocky, like all men, sure of his supremacy. Good. He'll be eating crow soon enough. "What about stakes?"

Mandy leaned in a little. "Stakes?"

"Sure. You win, I'll buy you the dress *and* that shotgun and that will be that. You can do what you want with them."

Her heart started to thump. She knew an easy mark when she saw one; she'd been picking their pockets for as long as she could remember. She'd done the same to Kade once, though to her disappointment and her relief, he didn't seem to recall the occasion. "And if you win?" Not, of course, that there was any danger of that happening. Cree had taught her those skills early, and he had taught her well.

"If I win," he said, "you still get the dress."

She blinked. "I don't understand."

"And you have to wear it," Kade stipulated, in an undertone. "In public."

Mandy looked down at Sister Mary Marguerite's worn habit and considered the matter. "It's a deal," she declared after some time, and put out her hand to seal the bargain. What did she care about the terms? She'd be gone in no time, once she got that horse under her and showed Kade McKettrick up as the braggart he was.

"Not so fast, Sister Mandy," Kade said, ignoring the gesture. "Once you come out of hiding, you can't go back. *That's* the deal." He took her arm, probably noticing, as she had, that the brides were about to emerge from the mercantile and catch him out in the open, and shuffled her down the sidewalk toward the Arizona Hotel.

In front of the doors, which were propped open to the fresh air with rocks left over from the new fireplace, she wrenched free of his grasp. "Did it ever occur to you," she hissed, "that I might have a good reason to hide?"

"There is no good reason for not being who you are," he argued mildly. "Now, have we reached an agreement, Sister Mandy, or are you just too damn scared to come out from behind that act you're putting on?"

Inside the lobby, Emmeline and Becky were having a cup of tea next to a potted palm, talking quietly, their faces pinched and solemn. No doubt John Lewis was the topic of discussion, and Emmeline had forgotten all about the incident with Gig. Mandy wished she hadn't piqued Kade's interest by touching on the matter back there at the jailhouse; he was bound to follow up sometime.

Meanwhile, Clive puttered behind the registration desk, while a woman Mandy had never seen before polished a window from the inside, using a wad of newspaper.

"Why does it matter to you what I do or how I dress?" Mandy demanded, exasperated.

"Like I said before," Kade pressed, a grin hiding in his eyes and teasing the corners of his mouth, "I like to know the truth about things and people. And I am especially interested in the truth as it concerns you. I have a feeling it's an undiscovered country."

"Lordy, you are a contrary man!"

"Well, if you're scared of losing—"

Mandy flushed, felt herself topple right into the trap. "Get me a horse, Kade McKettrick," she snapped, *"any* horse."

17

LEWIS LOOKED LIKE death, stirred up and reheated over a dwindling campfire, but he was sitting up in bed, and he was conscious. By Kade's accounting, that was progress.

"Badge looks good on you," John said.

"So far it's been an easy job," Kade replied, setting his hat aside and drawing up a chair beside the bed in Becky's room. He hadn't wanted to approach Emmeline, frazzled as she was, and ask her what she'd been going to tell John, but he'd have to do it soon. Instinct warned that the lawman trade might turn a bit more complicated after that. "I think maybe you've been swindling the town out of your pay for a while now."

John's grin was as thin as the rest of him, but it was probably genuine. The marshal was parsimonious with such pleasantries, same as he was with words, but when he talked, it meant something. "I reckon it took me getting sick for the truth to come out," he joked.

"You feeling any better?"

"Not so you'd notice."

Kade waited a few moments, settling a booted foot on the opposite knee, dusting something off it with the tips of his fingers. "If you can tell me what I'm supposed to do, it would help."

"Keep the peace." The covers were drawn up to John's chest, and his hands lay folded over them, ghostlike fingers interlaced. "Some days, that means keeping those Sussex kids from stealing penny candy over at the mercantile or hanging around at the livery and making Old Billy's life a misery. Other days, it means stopping a gunfight or throwing some yahoo like your brother Rafe into the hoosegow for using his fists a little too freely."

Kade chuckled. "Rafe's tamed down some, now that he's married." He thought it was downright delicate of John not to mention that he'd spent a night or two behind those bars himself, back in the days of his callow youth.

John's expression turned serious all of a sudden. He cleared his throat, and his fingers twitched. Kade was past relieved when the old fellow didn't lapse into a fit, or up and die. He'd had enough of that sort of scare to last him.

"Cavanagh's got a herd coming in from Texas any day now," John said. "You know how things have been around here lately—real tense. You'd be in for your share of grief anyway, just 'cause you're a McKettrick, but your being the marshal, too, might just aggravate the situation."

Kade had had the same thought, of course, but he didn't see how he could turn away from the job now without seeing a yellow coward looking back at him every time he passed a mirror. "I've never turned away from a good fight," he confessed, "but I don't mind admitting that I'd like to see this one pass right on by."

"If it gets started, it won't be easy to stop," John said, his gaze steady and, at the same time, bone weary. "Holt, he might see reason. But he's got a few troublemakers on his payroll, and so does your pa, and that's the crux of it. Outsiders, most of them, the sort of men they'd be better off without. When this herd comes in, there'll be a couple of dozen hotheaded, trail-weary cowboys added to the mix, looking for excitement."

"If you've got any suggestions, I'd like to hear them."

"Concepcion had the right idea last night at supper." John settled back on his pillows, his strength close to spent. "You get your father and brothers and Holt together for a palaver, for a start. And it wouldn't do any harm to swear in a couple of deputies, either. Talk to Sam Fee. He's a good man in need of a place to take a stand, and he'll see reason if you tell him none of you burned his place."

Kade was skeptical, but he didn't see any harm in having a word with Fee. Seeing how Lewis was fading, he simply nodded and got to his feet, ready to leave him to take his rest. Becky swept in just as he was about to reach for the doorknob, his hat in his free hand.

"I'll arrange that meeting," Kade promised in parting. If he had to, he'd hog-tie Angus and Rafe, Holt and Jeb, and drag them onto common ground one by one, behind his horse.

"What on earth have you been up to?" Becky demanded of Kade in a whisper. She was carrying a tray with a covered plate, a cup, and a small china pot of fresh coffee. "My kitchen is full of women wanting to bake pies, throw them out, and start over, and Sister Mandy asked me if I had a pair of britches she could borrow—*britches,* mind you—for a horse race with you."

Given the serious turn of recent events, Kade supposed he shouldn't be bothering with things like pie-baking contests and horse races with would-be nuns, but a man needed some diversion. Besides, if the mail-order brides were busy in the kitchen, they'd be out of his hair for a while. He'd have a good time judging the pies, but it seemed best not to think too far beyond that point. "Is Rafe around?" he asked, letting Becky's questions pass unanswered.

She gave him a narrow look as she set the tray on John's bedside table. "He said he had some business at the bank," she said. "Then he planned to head back out to the ranch."

"Thanks," Kade said, and departed.

There was no sign of Mandy when he descended the stairs, or of Emmeline, either. He'd talk to her later. He put his hat back on as he crossed the lobby and made his way down to the corner and across to the Cattleman's Bank.

Rafe was just on the other side of that establishment's frosted-glass door when Kade opened it, and he did not look like a happy man.

Kade frowned. "Don't tell me. You meant to rob the place, and they're fresh out of cash."

Rafe didn't smile. "There was a big payment due for those cattle we sold the army last fall," he said, joining Kade out on the sidewalk and keeping his voice low, "and it hasn't arrived."

Kade felt a cold spot form in the pit of his belly. He'd been born and raised on a cattle ranch, and he knew that a clog in the cash flow could bring an operation down in short order, even a large and long-established one like the Triple M. "Maybe it's coming in on the stage."

Rafe gave Kade's badge a contemptuous glance. "We're talking about almost fifty thousand dollars in currency and federal gold, Marshal," he said, still talking quietlike and putting a fine edge on Kade's job title. "They promised us a cavalry escort."

"I never heard a word about this," Kade complained, jerking off his hat and then slapping it on again. "Why is that, since the last time I looked, I was still a member of this family?"

"Nobody knew it but Pa and me," Rafe replied, as if it were all right for the two of them to keep something that important to themselves. "Should have been here yesterday."

Kade muttered a curse. "Now what?"

"Now Jeb and I and some of the men go out looking for those cavalrymen. And our money."

"I'm going with you," Kade said.

Rafe poked him square in the center of his badge. "You've got a job to do right here. Try to keep a lid on this hellhole until we get back."

18

Confident that she would win the race against Kade, and thus win the shotgun, Mandy laid her money on the counter of the mercantile, lifted her chin, and looked Minnie, the proprietor and town gossip, straight in the eye. "I want to buy shells for that shotgun in the window." Now that the brides were busy with their pies over at the hotel, the store was quiet, and Mandy's words, intended to be private, echoed from one end of the place to the other.

Minnie's small, eager eyes widened a little. "Why, Sister," she said, leaning toward her, "what on earth would you want with ammunition?"

"Even a woman of God has to take care of herself," Mandy said, and then waited for the inevitable lightning bolt. It was a relief, and a bit of a surprise, when nothing happened.

"These are troubled times," Minnie agreed. "I wouldn't give you two hoots in Hades for that McKettrick bunch's chances, for instance."

Mandy stiffened, perturbed. "What do you mean by that?"

Minnie shrugged her skinny shoulders. She was a painfully plain woman, her flesh pockmarked, her hair wrenched back from her face, slick as an onion skin, but it wasn't those things that made her homely. It was, Mandy concluded, the way she relished seeing trouble come to other folks. "High and mighty, that's what they are. Well, now that Mr. Holt Cavanagh has come to live among us, and they've got some real competition, they might just take a fall. Long overdue, if you ask me."

But I didn't ask you, did I? Mandy thought sourly. "I reckon you'd be hurting without their business," she said out loud, holding the other woman's gaze. "Lots of folks around here would."

The store mistress had enough decency to color up a little, though it wasn't likely she'd see the error of her ways and change herself accordingly. In Mandy's experience, people either stayed the same or got worse.

Minnie took the twenty cents and doled out the shells, slapping them down with a small harrumph sound. "I still can't reckon up what a nun would need with shotgun shells."

Mandy smiled. "I suppose you'll keep on trying to work it out, just the same," she said sweetly, tucking her purchase into the pocket of her habit.

She got as far as the door.

"Sister?" Minnie called after her.

Mandy sighed before turning back and smiling a smile she hoped was a shining example of Christian forbearance. "Yes?"

"You tell John Lewis that folks are thinking about him."

Mandy felt herself soften a mite. "I will," she replied, and went out, but as she walked down the sidewalk toward the Arizona Hotel, with the shells in the pocket of her habit, she wasn't thinking about the stricken marshal, or even about Kade McKettrick, who occupied more space in her thoughts most times than she would willingly have accorded him. Gig Curry, her personal devil, was far from her mind, as were her misplaced and ailing mother and Cree.

On her way, she saw a poster—JIM DANDY AND HIS WILD WEST SHOW, she read. COMING SOON.

Her step quickened, and a warm thrill coursed through her.

19

THEY FOUND THE cavalrymen at midmorning the next day, a full dozen of them, all dead, and drenched in blood. Jeb's stomach did a slow, backward roll.

Some of the soldiers had been stripped of their trademark blue coats, as well as their shirts, others of their boots or trousers, and all of them had been relieved of their hair. The horses were gone, and so were the regulation carbines and the side arms issued to every soldier.

The hairs stood up on the back of Jeb's neck, and like Rafe and the others, he'd drawn his .45 as instinctively as a breath. "Sweet Jesus," he marveled, averting his eyes for a moment. "Indians?"

Rafe cursed, then spat. The stench from the dead men was all-encompassing, swamping the nostrils and throat, overpowering the other senses as well, and the flies, the flies were everywhere, crawling over every inch of bare flesh, droning in the otherwise echoing stillness. "Maybe they wanted us to think so," he said with a shake of his head, scanning the quiet countryside around them, in case of an ambush. He drew his bandanna up around his mouth and nose, as Jeb did, though it didn't help much.

A broken strongbox lay in the middle of the carnage, and for some reason it put Jeb in mind of the Triple M brand burned into the tree on the squatters' place a few days before. He'd have bet, though he was operating on pure instinct and not much else, that the two occurrences were connected.

"Charlie," Rafe said through his mask, beckoning to one of the men. "Ride back to that homestead we passed this morning and see if you can borrow a few shovels. Mitch, you head for town. Get a wire off to the fort first thing, and make sure Kade's told directly." He paused, scanned the blue sky grimly. "We're going to have to lay these men to rest right here. It might take the army a while to find us, and the bodies can't be left for the scavengers."

Jeb swung down from the saddle, resigned to the grim task at hand, and approached one of the fallen men. He and Rafe and the hands remaining after Mitch and Charlie had gone checked each soldier for any sign of life and found nothing.

By the time Charlie got back, the homesteader jostling alongside in a buckboard, they'd laid the corpses out in a neat row, doing their best to keep the flies away by swinging mesquite branches over them like fans. They'd gotten used to the smell, insofar as that was possible, and lowered their bandannas to hang around their necks. A small heap of personal mementos lay atop a large, flat rock—battered little booklike frames containing images of wives and children, mostly, held shut by ribbons, worn colorless by carrying, a clutch of thin pages torn out of a Bible, letters from home, a watch, somehow overlooked by the killers, engraved with the man's name.

"Brings back memories of the war," Zeke Bryant commented, his eyes fixed on a battalion of ghosts. He'd been a hand on the

Triple M for as long as Jeb could remember, and he was a tough old soldier, a veteran of the Confederacy, known for solitary ways and playing lonesome strains on a harmonica. "Wish I had me some whiskey."

"So do I," Rafe agreed, taking off his hat to shove a hand through his hair. Jeb noticed that Rafe's gaze kept straying to the strongbox. "There's work to be done," Rafe said finally, after another of the long, silent periods of reflection to which he was given. "Let's get to it."

They took four shovels from the homesteader's wagon, and spent the rest of the afternoon burying the dead. Not much was said during that time, but Jeb did plenty of thinking about the fragility of life, and he knew the others did, too.

"It's a hell of a thing to see folks come to an end like that," Jeb reflected, as they rode back toward the ranch, with the night bearing down hard and a dozen fresh graves behind them, many unmarked and painfully isolated. The photographs and other leavings were tucked away in Rafe's saddlebags for safekeeping and would be turned over to the army when the time came.

Rafe set his jaw. "Here's the worst of it," he replied. "That might not have been the end. I reckon it could well be a beginning, instead." He let Jeb ponder that awhile, Rafe did, and then he told Jeb what the loss of that money might mean for the Triple M.

20

BAKING THE PIES turned out to be a bigger project than antici-pated, fraught with early failures, for two full days had passed when they finally turned up, arranged in a tidy row on Kade's desk. He'd come back to the office after making the rounds to see that the town was settling down for a peaceful night, and there they were.

He hung up his hat, though he didn't take off his gun belt, and went straight for the coffeepot. Having set all day, the stuff was beyond even his ability to tolerate, and he started a fresh batch.

He was a mite hungry, so he wandered over to inspect the spread. Each woman had marked her own work in some way, one by stabbing her name into the crust with the tines of a fork. He smiled at that. *Jeanette.* He wondered if she was the redhead.

Using his pocketknife, he cut a wedge of Jeanette's pie— cherry, it turned out—and raised it to his mouth. No sense in dirtying a plate, especially since he'd be the one to wash it. He was finding his new job tedious, composed mostly of mundane tasks, and so far he'd had no luck catching up with Emmeline. He still wanted to ask her what it was she'd meant to report to John be-fore he fell sick, but since she didn't seem to consider the matter urgent, he didn't, either.

The pie was a trifle on the sweet side, and he nearly choked when the door crashed open with such force that it slammed into the inside wall.

One of the Sussex boys stood in the gap, and his eyes widened at the sight of all those pies. The kid gulped, and his Adam's apple bobbed. "Mitch Wiggins sent me over from the telegraph office," he blurted. "He made Ben open the place up so he could send a wire to the fort. I'm supposed to tell you that there was twelve soldiers found murdered over east of Horse Thief Canyon."

Jeanette's pie turned to ashes in Kade's mouth. He put the piece he'd been holding down on a wanted poster on the corner of the desk, and swore. The boy's gaze tracked the pie.

"Help yourself," Kade said.

"I got a lot of brothers," the kid replied, but he took one step toward the food, then another, more purposeful one. "One sister, too." The sister, evidently, was an afterthought.

"I've got a couple of brothers myself," Kade commiserated. "Take as many as you can carry."

"You mean it?"

"I mean it."

An enterprising lad, young Sussex proceeded to stack the pies one on top of the other. "Thanks, Marshal. We ain't had nothin' like this since Christmas, when the ladies from the church fixed up a basket for us."

Kade managed a smile. "You be sure and share with the other kids," he said as the boy hurried out, nimble as a circus juggler, the pies teetering in his grasp.

The coffee was ready, and Kade poured himself a cup, adding

a generous dollop of whiskey from John Lewis's desk-drawer stash. His first impulse had been to send to the livery stable for his horse and ride for the Triple M, but after a moment or two, reason prevailed. Right then, he couldn't do much but wait. Rushing around like a chicken with its head cut off would serve no purpose.

He was glad to see Jeb when he came in later, even smelling of death the way he did, and watched as his brother helped himself to coffee without a single word.

"Where's Rafe?" Kade asked when the silence stretched on too long for his liking. He wasn't used to so much peace and quiet, particularly when it came to Jeb, and it made him uncomfortable.

Jeb's shoulders sagged a little under his coat. "With Emmeline," he said, then raised the cup to his mouth and took a sip. He made a face. "Good God," he exclaimed, "I hope your marshaling is better than your coffee."

"Sit down."

For once in his life, Jeb did what he'd been told without quibbling. Things must have been pretty bad out there, Kade concluded. He felt a twinge of sympathy for his younger brother, for all his devious ways, and some guilt because he hadn't been on hand to take his share of the load.

Jeb set down his coffee, took off his hat and coat, and drew up a chair. "Son of a bitch," he said, tilting his head back and staring up at the ceiling. "You ever seen a dozen dead men, Kade?"

He hadn't, and Jeb knew it. He was just talking, and in view of the situation, Kade was inclined to let him run on awhile, get some of it out. He simply shook his head and waited while Jeb chose fresh words.

"I keep thinking that all of them had folks—mothers, or sweethearts, or wives and kids," Jeb said. "There were pictures in some of their pockets, and a few letters and things like that. We buried them side by side, and marked the places as best we could, but we didn't know most of their names."

Kade pulled open the bottom right desk drawer, pulled out John's whiskey, and leaned over to add some kick to his brother's coffee. "You did what you had to do," he said. The high country was wild, and it was brutal. There was no way they could have left those bodies unburied, so they could be collected and returned to their families, or even to the fort. Coyotes and wolves would have scattered the remains over five square miles of territory before the sun rose tomorrow morning.

"This could ruin us, Kade," Jeb said after another lengthy interval of grappling with his thoughts. "They were carrying nearly fifty thousand dollars in gold and banknotes, payment for the herd we sold the army last fall. According to Rafe, without that money, the ranch might go under for good."

There had been other close calls over the years. Angus McKettrick was a hardheaded old coot with a gift for turning a profit, and certainly no spendthrift, but the cattle business was full of risk, and sometimes bad luck seemed like the only kind there was. They'd lost hundreds of head to disease, to blizzards, to rustlers and squatters and hungry Indians, and they'd always managed to hold on, but this time might be different. If Rafe was worried enough to confide in Jeb, or in him, for that matter, they were up against it for sure.

Jeb lifted the cup in a weary toast. "It would be a hell of a thing if all this wife-getting and baby-making turned out to be for nothing, wouldn't it?" He laughed, but the sound was mirthless. "The mighty McKettricks. Maybe we've had our day. Maybe there isn't going to be any ranch to bicker over."

Kade emptied his coffee mug and then slammed it down on the desktop with enough force to make Jeb start in his chair. "You might be ready to tuck your tail between your legs and quit," he said, "but I'm not. First thing we're going to do is get that money back."

Jeb sat up a little straighter, and some spark leapt into his eyes. "Hell, Kade, this being the marshal is going to your head. By now, those bastards could be halfway to Mexico."

"They're not," Kade said, and he was sure of that, though he couldn't have said why it was so. It was an instinct, like being in a dark room and knowing someone else was there, watching and ready to pounce.

"You think Holt was involved?"

The question annoyed Kade, though he might have asked it himself, in Jeb's place. A rush of fury went through Kade. "He might do a lot of things, but I can't see him killing twelve men in cold blood."

Jeb considered. "I guess you're right." Under any other circumstances, Kade might have had those words carved in stone; he couldn't recall the last time he'd heard them, from Jeb at least. As the two youngest brothers, they'd done their share of scrapping over the years.

"I figure the army will have a detail here by morning," Kade said presently, thinking aloud.

"Yeah," Jeb agreed. "You'll be writing out reports and answering questions from now till God's angels descend and build a brothel across the street from the church."

Kade closed his eyes and wished John Lewis a swift recovery so he could take his damn job back. "Thanks," he said. Then he refilled his coffee mug, and Jeb's, and dosed them both with more whiskey. "According to Lewis, Cavanagh's got a herd headed this way, on top of everything else."

"That ought to liven things up," Jeb replied.

The words proved prophetic.

The army showed up while Kade and Jeb were having breakfast in the hotel dining room at around eight the following morning, and the herd arrived before their plates were cleared away.

21

MAIN STREET SWELLED with cattle, cowboys, and soldiers, and the dust rose in gritty clouds, as if a sudden storm had just swept in out of nowhere. The din of rowdy men and bawling beef added to the chaos, and Mandy took a step back from the window of the hotel room Rafe and Emmeline shared, shaking her head.

Emmeline, resting with her feet up and looking wan, laid aside the book she'd been pretending to read and favored Mandy with a strained smile. "Have we been invaded?" she asked, starting to get up.

"Looks that way," Mandy said, waving Emmeline back into repose. "You stay right where you are."

A small frown creased the space between Emmeline's eyes, but she rested against the pillows plumped behind her. "It's not as if I'm sick," she protested.

"No," Mandy agreed firmly, "but you might take a turn if you aren't careful. I promised Rafe and Becky I'd look after you, and I meant what I said." It was going to be hard, leaving Emmeline behind, but to Mandy's mind that was better than staying on and putting her and the rest of the town in the path of Gig Curry's wrath.

Emmeline smiled a little; she was strong, but maybe, Mandy

thought, she enjoyed being pampered now and then. "Did you tell Kade about that dreadful man bothering you down by the creek the other day?"

Mandy debated between truth and expediency, a quandary she often faced. "Yes," she said, averting her eyes. "He said he'd take care of it, and we oughtn't to worry." She poured a glass of water from the carafe and took it to Emmeline. "Drink this. You look peaky."

Emmeline took the glass, sipped. "You fuss too much, and so does Rafe." Her eyes twinkled, and she confirmed Mandy's suspicions: "But I like it."

As if conjured by the mention of his name, Rafe thrust open the door and stepped into the room. His expression, normally solemn, changed when his gaze fell upon Emmeline. He crossed to her, bent and kissed her smartly on the forehead.

Mandy felt a sweet sting of—something. She wasn't sure what it was—envy, perhaps, or simple loneliness. What would it be like, she wondered, to have a man look at *her* that way, with his heart in his eyes? Most likely, she would never know; such joys were meant for other women, not the spawn of outlaws.

Emmeline set the glass aside and laid a hand to her husband's cheek. "You look so worried," she said with a tenderness that struck Mandy to the heart. "Is there anything I can do to help?"

Rafe sighed and straightened. "Just stay well," he said gruffly. "I can handle most anything as long as I know you're all right."

Mandy felt a hot, dry sensation behind her nose, and her eyes burned. The moment was profoundly private, and there she was, an unwilling intruder. Kade's image filled her mind and she willfully pushed it away.

"I feel the same," Emmeline said softly, taking his big hand and giving it a squeeze with her own small one. "I realize you've got to find that money, Rafe, and I know it weighs heavy on you, that those soldiers died trying to bring it here, but I want your promise that you won't put yourself in the way of a bullet. I won't know a moment's peace unless you give me your word."

Mandy's heart came to a hammering stop in her chest. Only a moment before, she'd been caught up in a storm of poignant emotions, all of them secondhand. Now, she forgot everything but a single concern. "There was a robbery!" she gasped. "A killing?"

Both Emmeline and Rafe looked at her in surprise. Maybe they'd forgotten she was there or simply thought she'd known. Rafe explained that a detachment of privates and corporals had been murdered, and a great deal of money stolen.

Mandy gripped the edge of the bureau for support. "Gig and his gang," she murmured.

"Wasn't that the man—?" Emmeline began, frowning again.

Mandy didn't pause to reply. She was fixed on one thing, and that was finding Kade McKettrick in that confusion of men and cattle taking over the town. Urgency sent her blood speeding through her veins.

She tracked him to the Bloody Basin Saloon, after several false leads, and even though the place was jammed with mid-day revelers, a confounded silence fell when she pushed open the swinging doors and stepped boldly inside. Cowboys stared at her, mugs of beer and shots of whiskey poised halfway to their mouths. The balls on the billiard table froze where they were, and the roulette wheel ceased its familiar, rhythmic clatter.

The bartender trundled over, wiping meaty hands on a stained apron as he drew near. "Now, Sister," he began, breaking the ominous pause, "if you've come here to spread the word of the Lord—"

Mandy quelled him with a glance. "I'm looking for the marshal," she said clearly. Kade, seated at a table in a far corner of the room with Jeb, Angus, and a couple of men in blue uniforms, stood and ambled toward her, the shadow of a grin playing on his lips but just missing his eyes.

"Well, now," he said, coming to a stop a few feet away. The distance between them was at once too narrow and too wide. "What can I do for you, Sister?"

"I need to talk to you," she said, almost hissing the declaration. "Right now." She hiked up her chin, painfully conscious of the blush rising up her neck to pound in her cheeks. Her heart felt like a wild bronco trying to kick its way out of a chute. "Alone." Reluctantly, the customers went back to their carousing, but she was aware of curious glances coming at her from every direction.

Kade took her arm and hustled her out onto the street with less decorum than she would have preferred.

"What?" he demanded. "If this is about the horse race, I've been a little busy."

Mandy flushed again, and so deeply that it hurt. "It was Gig Curry," she blurted out, after glancing this way and that, lest she be overheard. The street was still jammed with cattle and men, but no one appeared to be listening. "He and his outfit were behind those murders, and the robbery, too. I know they were."

"Who?" Kade asked, frowning now. He had hold of her elbow again, and this time he squired her into the nearest alleyway. The noise and smell of the cattle subsided a little, which was a mercy.

"Gig Curry," Mandy went on, growing impatient. "He was probably the one to burn out those homesteaders, too. If there's trouble, you can bet Curry had a part in it!"

Kade's frown deepened. The lines around his eyes came into play, but this time it had nothing to do with laughter. His grip on her arm tightened, and his voice was a rasp. "What's he to you?"

Mandy jerked free. "He was my mother's man, till he deserted her, anyway. That was him, bothering me behind the hotel that day."

"And you think he was involved in the robbery?"

"I *know* he was."

"Where is he now?"

"Around someplace," Mandy said, wheeling her arms once in frustration. "I try my best to keep out of his way, so he and I don't socialize."

"You sure took your sweet time telling me about this!" He leaned in, and the look in his eyes stung her beyond reason. What was this man to her? Nothing, that's what. He lived in another world, one she could never enter or fully understand.

Mandy stood toe-to-toe, calling on bravado, her stock-in-trade. "I didn't know about the soldiers until this morning, when Emmeline mentioned it! Now, are you going to stand around here yelling at me, or are you going to find him before something else happens?"

"You're damn right I'm going to find him," Kade retorted, rapid-fire, "as soon as I'm through with you. You might not have heard about those men being killed, but you sure as *hell* knew what happened to Sam and Sarah Fee, and you knew the McKettricks were taking the blame on account of that brand! That makes me wonder—*Sister Mandy*—just whose side you're really on!"

Guilt washed over Mandy, and she subsided, if only slightly, unconsciously smoothing the hated habit. Drat, what she wouldn't give for a pair of pants, a cotton shirt, and boots. As for Kade's challenge, she let that pass; she was on her *own* side, and if Kade McKettrick couldn't work that out for himself, she wasn't going to lead him by the nose. "I guess I figured that thing about the brand would blow over," she admitted, still huffy.

"'Blow over'?" Kade rasped. "Range wars have started over a hell of a lot less than that! By God, if you weren't dressed up like a nun, I do believe I'd take you over my knee right here and now!"

"You want to draw back a bloody stump, Kade McKettrick, you just *try* laying a hand on me!"

Kade yanked his hat off, whacked the wall of the Cattleman's Bank with it, and slammed it back on his head. A ray of dusty sunlight caught on his badge. "One of these days, Mandy—"

"Don't you dare threaten me!"

It was right then, of all times, that he remembered their first meeting, five years back, in Cave Creek. She saw it happen, just what she'd been dreading all along, saw his eyes widen and then go narrow, saw his lips tighten. A muscle bunched in his cheek and he clamped his jaw down tight. "I'll be damned if you're not the little thief who took my wallet and sweet-talked your way out of a good paddling. I should have followed through when I had the chance!"

Mandy bit her lower lip. "But you didn't," she said quietly. She'd been just fifteen when she'd first encountered Kade, stealing to keep herself and Cree and her mama alive, and to keep Gig from beating the life out of them for coming back to camp empty-handed.

He relented, but not appreciably. "Amanda Rose," he said in a dangerous undertone, shaking a finger at her, "you and I are going to come to terms about a few things. I don't have time to hash this out right now, but you can bet your rosary beads it's going to happen, and it'll be soon!"

She sighed. "I reckon so," she said, resigned. Now that Kade knew her for what she was, she didn't have a chance with him. But, then, she'd never had one anyhow—had she? And since when had she even *wanted* one? It was all too confusing.

"If you know anything else about this Curry, if you have *any idea* where I might find him and the bastards he rides with, you'd better tell me right now!"

"I swear I don't," she said, squaring her shoulders and making herself meet Kade's furious gaze.

"Is this what Emmeline wanted to talk to me or John about?"

Pained, Mandy nodded. "He showed up on the Triple M the other day—Gig, I mean. He—he threatened me."

Kade spoke tersely. "What did he want?"

"He was asking about my brother, Cree. Listen, if you'll just lend me a horse, I'll hit the trail right away. Gig's sure to follow me, and—"

"That's a harebrained idea if I've ever heard one!"

That rankled. Mandy put her hands on her hips. "I told you, Kade. He's an *outlaw*. This town hasn't seen the beginning of the trouble he could cause, he and that gang he's probably running with!"

"And you figure getting yourself killed would save the rest of us? That's a damn fool notion, Sister Mandy, and I'll be horse-whipped before I'll let you follow through with it!"

"Have you got any better suggestions?"

He swore roundly, slapped his thigh with his hat. "No. But you're not going to be the sacrificial lamb. That much I'm sure of, at least."

"We need to smoke them out some way," Mandy mused.

Kade was simmering down to a steady boil. "How?" He snapped the word, and it cracked in the air like a whip.

"He wants to use me to get to my brother, Cree," she told him, barely able to get the words out. "If I'm the bait, he'll step square into whatever trap you set for him."

Kade stood silently for a moment, still visibly resisting the idea. "I believe we just decided against that course of action," he pointed out. "Too dangerous."

"Not as dangerous as having him running loose out there, with a bunch of killers to do his bidding," Mandy argued, gesturing with one hand. "I pinched your wallet, and you could have had me put in jail, so I figure I owe you. You want Gig Curry? Then let me help you get him."

"I don't like it," he said, after another interval of pondering the matter, and shook his head resolutely.

Mandy watched him, her arms folded. "The way I see it, Marshal, you're fresh out of choices. If Gig and his gang stole that fifty thousand dollars and killed those poor men, he'll lie low for a while, then strike again. Chances are, they're just biding their time until they can pull off something a lot bigger, and they might even be behind the squabble between the Triple M and the Circle C. They'd want to keep folks distracted while they got everything in place."

Kade took all that in and swore again. "You've got all that worked out in your head, and you were just going to hightail it out of here and hope he'd give chase? Did it ever occur to you that he might just ride straight back here, after he'd killed you, and carry on as before?"

"Hell—heck, no. I meant to shoot the scoundrel. He might get me, but he wouldn't walk away without a bullet or two to show for the effort."

"Your confidence is amazing. And that's purely the most idiotic theory I've ever run across!"

"Like I said before, if you've got a better idea, let's hear it."

Again, a curse from Kade, rounder and more colorful and vociferous than any that had preceded it.

"You've heard, I presume," Mandy observed triumphantly, "that using profane language is a sure sign of low intelligence."

He started to say something, closed his mouth, and turned to go back into the saloon.

"Kade," Mandy said.

He paused, stiff-spined. Waited.

"Let me help you."

He shook his head, shoved open the swinging doors, and vanished inside.

22

"Where's Curry?" the stranger asked, riding straight into the center of the camp. The lookouts were lying up yonder, with their throats cut from ear to ear.

The members of the gang sat around a low-burning fire; they'd been swilling whiskey and swapping yarns, from the looks of things, and not one of them went for his gun. They were too drunk for that, and it wouldn't have been a sound decision anyhow.

The stranger stared them down one by one, until an old soldier finally spoke up. "Took off in a temper," the soldier said, rubbing his hands along the thighs of his worn trousers. "You the law or somethin'?"

"Or somethin'," the stranger replied, swinging down from the saddle. He scanned the bleary, unshaven faces, all turned in his direction. "I've got more than twenty men looking on from the brush, so I wouldn't advise any foolishness on your part. Now, once again, where's Curry?"

"Gone, like I said," the old man told him. "Some other outfit horned in on a job we figured for ours. I reckon that would be your doin'."

The visitor smiled. Dismounted. "We'll be sure to find him."

One of the others held out a whiskey flask. It was as good as an olive branch, not that he'd be turning his back on any of these lowlifes anytime soon.

"Drink?" the outlaw offered.

"No, thanks," replied the rider, neighborly enough, letting his hand rest on the handle of his bowie knife, jammed bloody into its scabbard on his belt. "We can use some help, me and my men. Anybody who wants to join us will be welcome and get a share of the takings. Anybody stupid enough to flap his lips outside this camp will be dead before that campfire burns much lower. Have I made myself understood?"

One after another, the men stood, wavering on their feet, stinking of cheap liquor, long days on the trail, and cowardice.

Not a one of them elected to die.

As if Kade didn't have enough trouble, word of the horse race between him and Sister Mandy had gotten around, probably with a lot of help from her, and folks were hankering for it. On the off chance that the spectacle might draw Curry out of hiding—he wasn't likely to make an attempt on Mandy's life with so many witnesses around—Kade gave in and agreed.

Young Harry Sussex posted the notices all over town before the printer's ink had dried, pocketed the nickel Kade gave him, and waited hopefully for more pies.

Kade grinned and ruffled the kid's shock of dark red hair. "You might just make a deputy one day," he said, as they stood side by side in front of the mercantile, where the last poster had been hung.

Harry beamed, evidently distracted from the prospect of further pies, which was a good thing, because the brides were not inclined to bake another batch, if their attitude toward Kade was any indication. He'd told them the contest was a draw, and they'd been crossing the street to avoid him ever since, though he had no reason to think the respite would last. They each still wanted a husband, and he was the logical candidate.

Most likely, they were planning another assault.

"Would I get a badge like yours?" the boy asked. "If I was a deputy, I mean?"

"Absolutely," Kade answered, distracted. He'd seen another nickel-plated star in the desk at the marshal's office. Maybe John would be willing to part with the thing, if it didn't have some sentimental value.

Harry looked up at the poster with admiration. "Those folks over at the newspaper office did a good job with that."

"Yep." Kade read the notice, even though he knew it word for word. HORSE RACE. SISTER MANDY AND KADE MCKETTRICK. INDIAN ROCK. 2:00 PM MARCH 15TH.

Gig Curry was bound to get wind of it, if he didn't see the notice for himself somehow. Maybe, just maybe, he'd be fool enough to show his face.

A chill tripped down Kade's spine, but he shook it off. No one was going to hurt Mandy while he had a breath in his lungs. He reached into his pocket, brought out a five-dollar gold piece, and handed it to the boy. "Give that to your mama."

Harry stared at the coin in his palm, baffled. "What's this for?"

"Luck," Kade said, and walked away.

Rafe and Jeb were waiting for him in Becky's office, over at the hotel, with Angus and Captain Dixon P. Harvey, U.S. Cavalry. With all of them crowded into that small space that way, it was hard to breathe.

"Seems to me," Angus remarked dryly, as Kade stepped over the threshold, "that you've got better things to do than conducting horse races with nuns, Marshal McKettrick."

Kade felt his dander rise, but he held his tongue. The fewer people who knew he was trying to draw Curry out, the better the chances it would work.

Rafe regarded him impassively from his chair, while Jeb indulged in a faint grin, as if he were in on some big secret. The captain sat rigidly, tight-lipped and watchful, his uniform starched and spotless. He put Kade in mind of a lizard fixing to snap at a fly.

Kade took the time to close the door. "I appreciate your confidence, Pa," he said, now that he'd had time to rein in his temper, which wanted to break out and buck. "But it happens that I know what I'm doing."

Angus had the good grace not to let his skepticism show, but Kade reckoned it was there, just the same.

"You mind letting us in on your plan?" Jeb asked moderately, breaking the short, charged silence.

There were no chairs left, so Kade hung up his hat and leaned against the wall, arms folded. He was across from the window, where he could keep an eye on the street, a busy place since the arrival of Cavanagh's herd. The cattle had been moved onto the Circle C range, but the cowboys were back in town, with pay in their pockets and trail dust in their throats, and they'd already gotten into a few scuffles with Harvey's soldiers.

"That wouldn't be prudent," Kade answered, in his own good time. "You know I have one. That's good enough."

"Maybe it's good enough for a bunch of ranchers," Captain Harvey put in, his little mustache twitching over his mouth, "but we've got twelve good men dead and buried like a pack of dogs in the middle of nowhere. The United States army needs more than an assurance that you've 'got a plan,' Marshal."

Kade measured his words carefully. "I'm going to have to ask the United States army to show some patience. It won't have long to wait."

"You do realize," Captain Harvey said, flint-eyed, "that if you impede the capture of these criminals in any way, I can have you arrested, thrown into a military stockade—badge or no badge— and tried in a federal court?"

Rafe smiled slightly. Jeb shifted in his chair, as if he were in a bawdy house, waiting for the show to start.

Angus set his jaw, and his eyes glittered. "We want whoever did this thing as badly as you do, Captain," he said. "And not just because of the missing money, either. I'll tell you this much, though: you're not taking my son anywhere."

The captain lowered his head for a moment, then stood with a laborious sigh. His gaze sliced from Angus to Kade and back again, swift and sharp as the saber at his side. "This—*race* is set for tomorrow?" he asked tersely.

Kade nodded. At part of his mind was still snagged on what his pa had said. *You're not taking my son anywhere.* He was a man, not a boy, and responsible for his own safekeeping, but Angus's statement meant something to him, and he'd remember it.

"Well, Mr. McKettrick," Captain Harvey told Kade dryly, "if you know what's good for you, you'll win." With that, he left the room, in a blue swath of dignity.

23

MANDY STOOD BEFORE the mirror in the back of the mercantile, staring at her reflection, barely recognizing herself, now that she'd been transformed. The habit and wimple were gone, and in their place, praise be, she wore denim trousers, boots, and a man's blue work shirt. Her shoulder-length brown hair was brushed back from her face and fastened at her nape with a clasp.

The store mistress appeared beside her, peering intently at Mandy's image in the looking glass, and her mouth dropped open. "Land sakes!" she gasped. "I wouldn't have believed it if I hadn't seen you with my own eyes."

Mandy might have enjoyed shocking Minnie, and a few other people in the bargain, if it hadn't been that this race with Kade was meant to smoke Gig Curry out of whatever hole he'd crawled into. The certainty that he'd kill her for sure if the slightest thing went wrong, and maybe even if it all went right, took some of the shine off knowing she was about to beat Kade McKettrick at his own game, fair and square. She meant to teach that arrogant cowboy-marshal a thing or two before she left town forever, and if she had her way, he'd be smarting from the lesson for a good long while.

She turned away from the mirror without troubling to

answer the other woman, drew a deep breath, and lifted her chin. It was time to go outside, mount the horse Kade had provided, and win. Silently, she blessed Cree for teaching her to ride Indian-style, the way he did, as part of the horse.

Minnie followed her through the store and out the front door, wide-eyed with delighted scandal. Spectators lined the streets, cowboys and women in calico, soldiers and men in suits, but all Mandy's attention was for Kade, already in the saddle, his fancy gelding fidgety beneath him. He sat that horse as if he'd been born there and held the reins of a small pinto mare, equally eager to run.

Trying not to dwell too much on how good Kade looked, Mandy smiled, put a foot in the stirrup, grabbed hold of the saddle horn, and swung herself up onto the mare's back. She felt a quiver of anticipation go through the animal and leaned slightly to give it an encouraging pat on the neck. *We can do this,* she told the creature silently.

Prancing, the mare tossed her head and nickered, as if to agree. It was a female conspiracy, Mandy thought with satisfaction. *Find the horse's heart with your mind and tuck your own right inside it,* she heard Cree say. *Let them beat together, as one.*

Kade handed over the reins. They'd agreed earlier that the starting line would be the new schoolhouse at the start of Main Street, and the finish, a stand of juniper trees a little less than a mile the other side of town.

"You see Curry in this crowd?" he asked in a tone meant for her ears alone. "If he's here, I haven't spotted him."

Mandy smiled brilliantly for the benefit of the onlookers, but she was keeping a sharp eye out for Gig. She might have had a reckless streak, but she was no fool. "No," she said, as tension coiled in the pit of her stomach, "but he's surely here someplace, if only because he hopes I'll fall off this horse and break my neck."

"You're sure you want to do this?"

"Dead sure," she answered, and saw Kade wince at the words.

"I still don't like it."

"That's because you know you're going to lose in front of the whole town," Mandy replied airily. It was odd, how alive she felt, even though she knew Gig might be squirreled away in some nook or cranny at that very moment, drawing a bead on her with that rifle of his. He might shoot at her out of pure meanness, especially if he was a little drunk. Knowing Gig was a mediocre shot gave her a degree of consolation.

She and Kade rode together toward the schoolhouse, took their places at the line Harry Sussex had drawn in the road. The boy stood grinning next to the ditch, the pointed stick he'd used gripped in one hand.

"You're going to lose," Kade said lightly, though he was watchful, and she could feel the strain in him. "But don't worry about it. You'll look real pretty in that calico dress."

Mandy had noticed that the coveted garment had disappeared from the mercantile window, and she was pretty sure Kade had bought it. He might have been resigned, or just plain arrogant—her money was on the latter. He was a McKettrick, and the McKettricks weren't used to losing. In fact, she'd have bet that the possibility hadn't even entered his mind.

Time his horizons were broadened.

"Let's see what you can do, cowboy," she said.

Old Billy, from over at the livery stable, raised a pistol into the air, paused to relish the moment, and at a nod from Kade, fired.

Kade and the gelding shot into the lead. Mandy smiled as she leaned low over the pinto's neck. Her heart found the mare's and eased itself inside, snug and warm. Excitement surged through her; Gig or no Gig, she was in her element, and she wanted to shout for joy.

"Easy," she whispered, addressing herself as well as the horse. "Save it—save it—"

The distance between the two riders widened as they passed through town, streaking between the cheering crowds, and the mare gnawed at the bit, trying to take it between her teeth, begging in every sinew to be given her head.

Mandy knew just how that horse felt. Exultation raised her into another place, above her ordinary self, but still she waited, keeping a firm grip on the reins and on her own desire to fly away with the wind. "Not yet," she told the mare in an anxious whisper. "*Not yet.*"

The horse obeyed, a champion in a small body. Mandy bent lower still, and her palms sweated where she held the reins. They left the town behind; the juniper trees were visible in the distance, green clumps against an azure sky, and Kade and the gelding were two lengths ahead.

Mandy counted silently in her head, as Cree had taught her when they were kids, riding bareback on scrawny, green-broke nags and racing each other across fields and along rutted cattle trails.

"*Now!*" she cried jubilantly, at long last, and gave the mare all the slack she needed. The animal leapt forward in an ecstasy of speed and freedom. The wind buffeted Mandy's face, stealing her breath and filling her with fevered triumph. A hundred yards this side of the juniper trees, Mandy and the mare plunged into the lead.

Beside her, Kade rode full out, determined to win. He wasn't going to give up without a fight, she saw that in an instant, and she was glad. She didn't want anyone saying that he'd thrown the race; it was hers, had been from the first, and she would win it with no concessions on his part.

The shot rang out just as Mandy crossed the finish line, and for one terrible moment, she braced herself, waiting for the bullet to sear her flesh. In the next, she whirled in the saddle and saw Kade hurtling backward off the gelding's back, landing in a rolling tumble of arms and legs.

She screamed, forgetting the race, forgetting everything except that Kade had been struck down. In that instant, nothing else mattered, not Gig, not her own safety, nothing.

The mare was still running full out when Mandy hit the ground, staying on her feet, racing for Kade. Another bullet nicked the ground beside her; Kade raised himself onto one elbow, plainly winded, and fired the .45 into the trees.

Her gaze traveled over him, anxious and quick. There was no blood.

She stopped, staring, then dropped to her knees beside Kade. *No blood.*

Still resting on his elbow, his hat several feet away, he grinned at her. "I'm all right," he said cheerfully. "Nice to know you were worried, though."

If Mandy hadn't been so relieved, she'd have slapped him silly.

The surrounding terrain spun around her, and she swallowed a sob. She turned her head, saw Rafe and another man hauling a wounded Gig Curry over the slight rise at the side of the road.

"I won," Mandy heard herself say. *"I won."*

Kade laughed, getting to his feet, hauling Mandy right along with him. "I reckon you did," he agreed. He indicated Curry with a nod. "Thanks, Mandy."

Gig was bleeding from the right thigh, and the look he gave Mandy was straight out of her nightmares, but she met his gaze head-on and refused to blink. When he looked away first, it was a greater victory than winning the horse race against Kade. Mandy felt something shift, deep down inside her. Something unchangeable just up and changed anyway, right then and there, though she wasn't sure what it meant. She was different, that was all she knew, and the difference was likely to last.

Kade unhooked a pair of handcuffs from his belt, walked over to Curry, and yanked him around so that his back was to him. "I've got some questions for you, neighbor," he said, locking the prisoner's hands behind him with a decisive snap of metal against metal.

"I don't have nothing to say." Curry looked scared, and mad as a rooster doused with dishwater. "You gonna get me a doctor for this leg? You got something to answer for, Marshal, shooting me down that way. I wasn't doing nothing wrong. Just hunting for jackrabbits, that's all."

"Put him on the horse," Kade said, as if Gig hadn't spoken.

Rafe hoisted Curry onto the gelding's saddle, sideways and belly first. Curry howled.

"Shut up," Rafe told him. "It's nothing but a flesh wound."

"This ain't right!" Curry wailed from his ignoble position. "You're tormenting an innocent man here!" He might as well have been talking to himself, for all the attention any of the others paid him.

"We'll meet you back at the jailhouse," Rafe told his brother, dusting his hands together.

"I'll be right there," Kade replied. He was looking at Mandy; there might have been nobody else in the world except the two of them, the way he was watching her. It was as if he'd never really seen her before, and the intensity in his eyes was as if he'd just made some startling discovery and was baffled by it. "That was a hell of a race," he said.

She wasn't prepared for the lump that surged into her throat, nor did she know she was about to slam the heels of both hands into Kade's chest, nearly knocking him right back to the ground. "I thought you were hit!" she cried when she could get the words out. "You let me think you'd been shot!"

He didn't step back, didn't smile, didn't try to touch her. That same look lingered in his eyes, measuring. Surprised. Maybe a little alarmed. "I didn't really have a chance to make the situation clear," he reasoned. "Things happened pretty fast."

Tears filled her eyes, half blinding her; she dashed them away with the backs of her hands. "Damn you, Kade!"

He looked at her thoughtfully. "You could bake a pie."

Mandy gaped at him, certain that the fall had knocked something loose in his head, or that she hadn't heard him correctly. She tried to speak and stumbled over her tongue. A pie? He'd let her believe he'd taken a bullet, and he was talking about *pies?*

"Cherry's my favorite," he added. An impish grin rested

lightly on his mouth. He was sweating and covered with dirt and his hair was windblown, and to Mandy, he looked as handsome as a dandy in an eastern suit.

She laughed at his audacity, heard a note of hysteria in the sound, and rested her hands on her hips. "Why in blazes would I want to bake you a cherry pie?" she demanded, half-mad and stalling in hopes of giving her scattered wits a chance to wander back where they belonged.

He hoisted her onto the mare's back, just as if he had the right to do it, and grinned up at her as he handed her the reins. "To convince me that I ought to marry you, of course. You and I would make one hell of a team."

24

Gig Curry was already behind bars, lying on his cot and moaning in apparent agony, when a pleasantly befuddled Kade arrived at the jail. Rafe sat behind the desk with his feet up, flipping through a stack of wanted posters and ignoring the prisoner completely.

"Doc on the way?" Kade asked, hanging up his hat. He was trying to keep his mind on the business at hand, but it kept straying back to Mandy. The way she rode, like a Comanche on a raid and, Lord, the way she looked in those pants. Until that day, she'd been a pretty woman playing at being a nun, and nothing more. Now, she was an undiscovered territory, a universe ruled by a spirit the likes of which he'd never imagined, let alone encountered face-to-face.

"He needs to sober up a little first," Rafe said. "He'll be along presently."

Kade strolled over to the cell, rounding up these strange emotions the way he would a herd of cattle, driving them into the quiet canyons of his soul. "I guess we'd better have a look," he said, shrugging back into his skin. It didn't seem to fit the way it had before. "Make sure this polecat isn't going to up and die on us or something."

Rafe shrugged, hoisted himself to his feet, and wandered over. "You want to hold him down, or should I?"

"Doesn't matter to me." Kade's voice was still an echo, coming from somewhere beyond his own head. He renewed his efforts to get back to himself and succeeded, for the most part.

Curry stopped his carrying on and opened one eye, justifiably worried. "Why does anybody have to hold me down?"

Rafe took out his pocketknife, flipped open the blade, and inspected it closely. "There might be some pain involved if there's a bullet lodged in your leg," he said companionably. "Don't you fret, though. It'll feel real good when the hurting stops."

Curry sat bolt upright on the cot. "Nobody's taking a knife to my leg," he croaked. Sweat broke out on his forehead and along his upper lip.

"Then I reckon you ought to leave off complaining," Kade said easily as he walked away, aiming for the stove and the coffeepot.

The outlaw stood at the cell door, gripping the bars. "Am I charged with something? Because you can't keep me here if I ain't—I know the law!"

Kade took the lid off the coffeepot, peered in, and grimaced. Hell of a day. He'd been beaten by a nun in a horse race, and the whole town would hear about it, too. Now, he had a whiner on his hands. And, oh, yes, a riot was going on inside him.

"For the moment," he said coolly, and without so much as glancing back at the captive, "you're charged with being a no-good, snake-bellied son of a bitch. Then there's attempted murder. When I've got something more, I'll let you know."

"I done told you I was just hunting rabbits, and not out to

hurt anybody," Curry threw out. "It ain't like I don't have any friends, neither. You'll have them to deal with if you try to keep me here!"

"We're counting on that," Rafe said. He was back in the chair, with his boots on the desk again, cleaning his nails with the point of the pocketknife. "We'd surely like to make your friends' acquaintance, Mr. Curry."

"It's that Amanda Rose that's behind this here breach of justice. She's been lying about me. Well, let me tell you about her—"

Kade turned from his coffee making, everything inside him gone still as death. "Shut up," he said, "or I swear to God I'll dig a bullet out of you whether there's one in there or not."

Curry went pale, his throat working visibly as he swallowed. "That just wouldn't be right, your treating a human being like that"

"From what I gather," Rafe observed, "you aren't any such thing, so I wouldn't stew over the matter if I were you."

"This just ain't Christian," the outlaw replied.

About that time, Doc Boylen staggered in. His hair was in disarray, and his eyes seemed to be revolving in separate directions. He belched loudly. "I hear you've got yourself a wounded prisoner."

Out of the corner of his eye, Kade saw Curry shrink away from the bars.

"Fella's been caterwauling for fifteen minutes," Rafe said. "So it must be bad. Might need to cauterize the wound or something. Want me to put a poker in the fire?"

Doc swayed on his feet, fixed both eyeballs on Curry, which took some obvious doing, and sort of swung himself in the direction of the cell. He set his bag on the edge of the desk with a resounding thump, wrestled with the catch for a few moments, and finally got the thing open. "Fresh out of chloroform," he said.

"Stay away from me, you old quack," Curry warned.

Doc stiffened his spine, indignant. "Lay down on that cot and shut your trap," he said. "Rafe, come hold this feller to the bedsprings. He might be about to do some thrashing around. Besides, we don't want him getting away."

Grinning, Rafe got up to comply.

Curry let out a squawk when Rafe slammed him down onto the spindly cot, setting the whole thing to creaking mightily, and pinned him there by the shoulders.

Doc ripped the prisoner's pant leg and inspected the wound. "Bullet barely grazed you," he said, sounding patently disappointed. "Hell, I'm surprised it even tore your britches." He paused. "Still, we ought to pour in a little carbolic acid, just to make sure there's no infection. Kade, fetch me my kit."

Kade brought the bag, and Doc ferreted out a brown bottle, sealed with a cork.

"Is that the medicine you mean to dose me with?" Curry asked warily.

Doc popped the cork with his teeth and took a couple of noisy swigs. "Nope," he answered when he was through sputtering, "it's moonshine." He put the stopper back and brought out another jug, which apparently contained the carbolic acid. "I reckon this will hurt a mite, son," he said with a semblance of regret.

"Don't do it," Curry begged, flailing. "Don't you do it!"

"That leg could turn green and fall off if I don't. Stop carrying on, mister, and we'll get this over with."

Curry let out a shriek before the acid ever touched him.

"I do believe you're the biggest chunk of talking chickenshit I've ever come across," Rafe said. "Course, it takes a coward to shoot at a woman."

The pit of Kade's stomach dropped a notch; for a moment, he was back there on the road. He'd seen Curry come out of the brush in the space of a split second and draw a bead on Mandy with his pistol. With no time to draw his own gun, Kade had hurled himself backward off the gelding, hoping to distract the other man just enough to throw his aim off, and the trick, desperate as it was, had worked.

Thank God, it had worked.

"I told you it was an accident," Curry lamented. "When is this going to stop hurting?"

"Next week sometime, I figure." Doc was applying a bandage to the man's thigh. He gave the ends of the long strip of cloth a good yank before tying them off and turning away to walk out of the cell. Rafe released his hold on the outlaw and followed, closing the door with a clang and engaging the lock.

Doc focused on the coffeepot, now perking away on the stove. He belched again, resoundingly, and caught Kade's eye. "I hear you lost a horse race today. To a female."

Damned if the bastard wasn't right, and stone sober into the bargain. The drunken revelry had been an act.

25

Buying the dress had been easy enough, but it took some fast-talking on Kade's part to persuade Minnie to part with the shotgun. She'd promised it to somebody named Jim Dandy and would have to order another one all the way from Tucson if she let that one go. Kade offered her half again as much as she could expect to get, and a deal was struck.

He was on his way out of the mercantile with his purchase when two fine ladies of the community nearly ran him down, in their haste to get inside.

"She's no better than she should be, that woman," one blustered.

"Keeping a naked man in a hotel room," marveled the other. "It's just not proper, even if he *is* grievously ill."

Kade, in the act of tipping his hat, decided against it. "Ladies," he said, with a nod and a note of irony.

They ignored him. "You mark my words, Bertha," said the one with a single eyebrow and no chin to speak of. "Becky Fairmont has a *past*."

"Everything that is hidden," replied her friend, with stern certainty, "shall be brought into the bright light of day."

Kade shook his head, scratched under the back of his hat,

and stepped out onto the street. The pinto mare Mandy had ridden in the race the day before waited patiently at the hitching rail, reins dangling. He untied the lead rope, winding it into a loose coil and draping it over the saddle horn. The calico dress, wrapped in brown paper and tied with string, protruded from one of the saddlebags.

He led the mare down the street, doing his best to pay no mind to the good-natured taunts that came his way, all of them to do with his losing and Mandy's winning. Like as not, he'd be a long while living this down. And that was nothing compared to the struggle raging in his spirit.

In front of the hotel, he stopped and just stood there in the street, willing Mandy to appear. It scared him how much he wanted to see her, never mind touch her.

She must have been waiting for him, because she came outside right away. He'd thought he was prepared, but the sight of her fair took his breath away.

She'd forsworn the nun suit for a blue dress he'd seen Emmeline wear a time or two, and her hair was pinned up and soft around her face. She could have passed for a lady without half trying, though it wasn't the lady in Mandy that called out to Kade. It was something else entirely, something wild and ancient, never burdened with a name.

"I see you're a man who honors his debts," she said. She had the decency not to smile, but a glimmer of triumph shone in her blue-green eyes. She seemed unaware of the larger issue, her new power over him, and he was thankful for small favors.

"Absolutely," he said, sounding normal, and gave his hat brim a gentlemanly tug. He got the parcel from the saddlebags and handed it over, along with the shotgun. Maybe his hands trembled a little, though he liked to think he was mistaken about that part.

Mandy took them both, but she set the package aside on the bench just to the right of the hotel entrance to admire the rifle, holding it ably in both hands. After opening it to make sure it wasn't loaded, she put one finger through the trigger guard and gave the heavy piece a few showy spins before stopping it at her right hip with a precision Kade doubted he could have equaled himself.

His mouth dropped open.

Mandy smiled and propped the shotgun carefully against the side of the bench, facing him with her hands at her waist. "Thanks," she said.

"I guess you've given up pretending to be a nun," he said, and promptly felt stupid for stating the obvious.

She was looking at the horse. "You've got a good mare there."

He extended the reins. Inside, he was offering far more, though he didn't dare consider what.

Mandy stared at him in confusion, and her cheeks turned faintly pink.

"She's yours, if you want her," he said, like a kid offering a homemade present.

"Mine?" Mandy looked at once hopeful and wary and stubbornly proud. "That wasn't part of our deal, was it?"

Kade shrugged. Amazing, all that could stand behind such an ordinary gesture. When the hell was he going to come to his senses? "She needs riding, and a fair amount of attention. On the Triple M, mares aren't much use, except for breeding." He paused, reddened. He'd been living with his pa and brothers for too long, he decided. Concepcion's influence aside, he was about as polished as a porcupine at the far end of a three-day drunk.

"I don't imagine they are," Mandy observed, somewhat stiffly, and he knew she wasn't talking about horses. He could have kicked himself for opening his mouth a second time and stuffing his foot right in it.

She relented and stepped forward with a little smile, taking the reins from his unsteady hands, stroking the animal's muzzle with a gentle pass of her fingertips. "You sure are a pretty thing," she told the mare. "What's your name?"

There was a pause, as if they were both waiting for the horse to answer. Kade fought down a surge of envy, wanting her tender touch and sweet words for himself, though he didn't reckon he'd cotton to being called pretty.

"She doesn't have one," Kade said awkwardly. "There didn't seem to be any point."

"Every living creature needs a name," Mandy commented, still petting the horse, and Kade had to look away for a moment and tell himself to stop thinking and acting like an idiot. "I'm going to call you Sister," she told the animal. "Sissy for short."

Kade had no idea why he needed to take issue with the choice, but he did. "Now that's a damn fool thing to call a horse," he said. Only then did it occur to him that Mandy would probably skip town, now that she had the means to travel. In a fog of confused admiration, and profound relief that Curry hadn't killed her, he'd just given her everything she needed to do it.

And, damn, he didn't want her to go.

"If she's my horse," Mandy reasoned lightly, fixing him with a saucy look, "I can call her anything I like." She reached up to fondle the mare's ear, and in that moment, he'd have sworn she knew exactly what she was doing to him. "Isn't that right, Sissy?" She paused and, without looking at him, added, "Did you get anything out of Gig yet?"

Kade felt his shoulders sag a little. They'd gone to a lot of trouble to round Curry up, with Mandy almost getting herself shot in the process, but so far, that waste of hide and hair hadn't admitted to spitting on the sidewalk, let alone leading the gang that had robbed the U.S. army and left a dozen men dead. The circuit judge was a liberal-minded sort and might believe Curry's rabbit-hunting story. If he passed through before the outlaw started talking about his other crimes, like burning down the Fees' homestead, or they turned up some solid proof, Kade might have to let the son of a bitch go free.

"No," he admitted.

"Remember that he's not working alone," Mandy said in a conversational tone.

Kade hadn't forgotten. "You don't know any of these men?"

"I reckon we all know them," Mandy said, still fussing over the horse. It was one thing to be kind to animals, Kade thought grudgingly, but they oughtn't to matter more than a man. "Mama always said they were demons, wearing masks. It's their way to blend in, like a snake on a rock, and strike when it's least expected."

Kade resettled his hat. "He might be bluffing about how many there are—I never met anybody who could run off at the mouth like Curry does."

"He's too much of a coward to work alone, and he likes

having people jump to his tune," Mandy answered with quiet conviction, and a warning was in her eyes when their gazes met at last. Kade might as well have been standing in a mud puddle and pissing on a lightning bolt as looking into those eyes. The impact was the same. "They're as real as you and me. Ordinary cowhands, most likely. Drifters and the like. Some of them probably rode in with Mr. Cavanagh's herd."

"Curry claims they'll try to spring him."

Mandy shivered, though the breeze was warm. "They might, but not because they bear him any particular affection." Her eyes were so blue, they made something ache inside Kade. "Believe me, to know Gig Curry is to hate him. Those outlaws, they'll be afraid he'll turn on them, if you put the pressure on, and start babbling names."

She knew a hell of a lot about the workings of a gang, it seemed to Kade. One day soon, he'd better be finding out why.

26

STILL PENSIVE SOME five minutes after parting with Mandy, Kade felt a chill brush past his spirit when he went in to see John Lewis in his room at the hotel. Though he was sitting up in a chair by the window, the man's chest seemed to have collapsed, his lips were blue, and his cheekbones stood out beneath gray flesh. Nonetheless, he troubled himself to smile by way of a greeting.

"Hello, Kade," he said. "I hear you rounded yourself up an outlaw. Not sure I approve of the way you went about it, though. That girl could have been hurt."

Kade set his hat aside on the dresser, approached John, and took the other chair. "He's not talking. Except to complain about the food, of course."

Lewis gave a raspy chuckle, shook his gaunt head. His hair seemed thinner and grayer than before, like his skin. "The food's never been much," he allowed. "It's better here at the hotel, but Doc tells me the Sussexes would go under without the money Mamie gets from the town treasury for feeding prisoners, so I didn't give the business over to Becky."

The mention of the widow Sussex reminded Kade of the boy. "There's another badge over at the office," he said. "I'd like to pin it on young Harry. He's been a help."

"Good idea. Might give the lad something to be proud of. Those kids have been running wild ever since they came to Indian Rock, but I've got some regard for them, all the same." John paused, struggled visibly for his breath. "It'll be a good thing when that schoolhouse opens up. Give those little rascals someplace to go when their ma shoos them off, in the morning, at least."

Kade sighed. He didn't know much about the Sussexes, or their situation, mainly because he'd never paid them any mind. It seemed like an oversight of some significance, now that he was living in town. "What happened to her man?" he asked. "Mamie Sussex's, I mean."

John rearranged his covers, and even that much effort appeared to wear him out. Kade had made up his mind before he came upstairs not to stay more than a few minutes; now, even that seemed too long. "I'm not sure there ever was one in particular," the marshal said. "Mamie showed up one day, a couple of years back, with those screaming yahoos of hers loaded into the back of a broken-down wagon, and talked the banker into selling her that place on a hope and a promise."

"How do they live?" Kade asked, frowning. "Seems like most folks stay over at the hotel, if they need lodging." Except, of course, for the brides. He made a mental note to go over and square up the bill while he still had the money. The way things were going on the Triple M, he'd be lucky not to end up as a saddle bum; he sure wasn't getting rich in the lawman business.

John gave him a pointed look. "Mamie sells her favors," he said quietly.

Kade frowned. "Isn't that against the law?"

"There are times when a man might just as well look the other way."

Kade wasn't much for shutting his eyes to things, but he respected John Lewis more than any other man alive, except for his own pa, and if that was his policy, there must be some good in it. He got to his feet. "Is there anything I can do for you, John?" he asked, turning his hat in his hands.

The words seemed to echo in the room, bouncing off the walls, and the long, thoughtful silence from John only exaggerated the effect. "I've got a daughter, Kade," he said. "Last I heard, she was down in Tombstone, teaching school. I wonder if you'd send for her, as a favor to me."

Kade paused in mangling his hat. It was natural for a man to want to see his child, he supposed, but something in the way John had made the request made things grind inside him and raised the small hairs on the back of his neck. "Sure," he said hoarsely.

"I reckon I could have asked Becky to do it, but we haven't talked about Chloe much, and I'm not sure I have the strength to take up the subject with her at this late date. Not in earnest, anyhow."

Kade closed his eyes for a moment. "Just tell me where to reach her. I'll take care of the rest."

John took a scrap of paper he'd been using to mark his place in a book and picked up a pencil stub from the table beside his chair. He wrote out his daughter's name and address and extended the paper to Kade. His gaze was painfully direct. "Tell her she ought to hurry."

"John—"

"Send a telegram," John said gravely. "A letter will take too long." With that, he turned his head away and stared out the window, and Kade knew the conversation, and maybe a whole lot more besides, was over.

He met Becky on the stairway, carrying a tray of food for John, and she gave him a wobbly smile.

"It means a lot to him, your visiting," she said quietly. "Asking his advice about marshaling and the like."

Kade opened his mouth, closed it again. There was nothing to say, and he was his father's son; wasting words was like wasting cash money, or water, both of which were always at a premium in the high country.

"I know," Becky said, her eyes full of bravery and sorrow. "I know."

He managed a nod. "What will you do?" he asked, after a long time.

Tears glittered along her dark lashes. "The only thing I can do. Go on."

He considered that, nodded again, and went on down the stairs.

There was no sign of Mandy, or of Emmeline, when he passed through the lobby, and that was a disappointment, because just laying eyes on either one of them would have been a comfort just then.

He went straight from the hotel to the telegraph office, where he dispatched a wire to Miss Chloe Wakefield of Tombstone.

Come to Indian Rock as soon as you can.
John Lewis is ailing.
Kade McKettrick, Town Marshal

27

"A *DANCE*?" EMMELINE said, exchanging glances with Mandy before turning her attention back to her mother. "You can't be serious. John is—"

Becky Harding-Fairmont lifted her chin. She was a small woman, but in that moment, she seemed taller than the potted palm over by the main stairway. Her eyes glittered and pink fire glowed in her cheeks. "We need some music in this place," she said purposefully. "Anyway, it was John's idea. He says we're gloomy as undertakers, the whole bunch of us, and he's sick of our moping."

Mandy looked away, blinking rapidly until she was sure she wouldn't break right down and cry. She hadn't known John Lewis long, but he was a rare man, and his love for Becky was as deep and mysterious as an ocean.

Emmeline got up from her chair and crossed the room to lay a hand on Becky's shoulder. "Very well, then. If a dance is what's wanted, there will be one."

Becky's lower lip wobbled. "Thank you. I'm aiming for Saturday night. That gives us a few days to get ready."

Emmeline nodded. Then, on impulse, she took Becky into her arms and hugged her, hard. The sight made Mandy yearn for her own mama, wherever she was. Maybe, by now, Dixie had passed away. She'd been going downhill the last time Mandy had seen her, thin and coughing herself into exhaustion, a false flush of health shining beneath her transparent skin.

Becky was the first to break away. She sniffled and smoothed her skirts. "Amanda Rose, you take a plate of supper over to Kade. He shouldn't have to eat Mamie Sussex's cooking on top of his other trials and tribulations."

Mandy wouldn't have refused Becky's request for anything, especially under the circumstances, though she was in no rush to see Gig Curry again, even if he *was* safely behind bars. The prospect of a few minutes passed in Kade McKettrick's company had its appeal, too. Being around him fed something hungry inside her, even though he usually managed to make her mad.

"Yes, ma'am," she said, trying not to sound too eager. She reminded herself that she was planning to leave one day soon, now that she had Sissy and Gig was behind bars, but it didn't dampen her good cheer.

There was fried chicken downstairs in the kitchen, and a lot of it. The supper trade in the hotel dining room had been booming since the arrival of Holt Cavanagh's herd; the drovers were a hungry lot, and they had money to spend, having collected their pay at the end of the trail drive.

Mandy got a heavy china plate from the shelf, loaded it with vittles, ignoring accusatory looks from the Chinese cook, covered the whole mess with an upended pie plate, and set out resolutely for the jailhouse.

Lanterns were burning inside, and Kade was playing checkers with the grubby ruffian of a boy he'd befriended. The child, no more than ten years old, seemed enthralled by the game. A bruise marked his right cheek, Mandy noticed, experience having given her an eye for such things, and young Harry had been weeping, unless she missed her guess.

She'd almost forgotten about Gig, so busy were her thoughts, and when he spoke, she nearly dropped Kade's dinner right on the floor.

"Well, Mandy girl," Curry called, as if no hard words had ever passed between them, let alone hard blows, "thank heaven you're here. This stuff that boardinghouse whore brought over ain't fit to slop a pig."

Harry bolted to his feet, visibly scalded by the insult to his mother, his small, scabby fists clenched, and Kade put a hand to his shoulder, wordlessly pressing him back into his seat.

Mandy, who had frozen in her footsteps for a moment, thawed out and got herself moving again. She set the plate down on the corner of Kade's desk, still covered by the pie plate, and smiled at Harry.

"Don't pay Mr. Curry any mind," she said. "He's a coward and a thief, and his opinions matter about as much, in the scheme of things, as a pile of buffalo chips."

Harry was still flushed, but he seemed to simmer down a little.

Kade looked up at Mandy, smiled slightly, then turned his attention to the food she'd brought. "Smells like fried chicken," he said.

"The best pieces," Mandy confirmed.

Gig started rattling the bars, and Harry's gaze traveled to the meal Kade was just unveiling.

"I want some of that grub!" Gig bellowed, and nobody paid him any mind.

"I'll share with my deputy," Kade said to Mandy. "Looks like there's plenty."

Something tipped over somewhere in Mandy's heart and spilled, warm, down the walls. She was glad she hadn't stinted on filling that plate, even though the cook had fairly glared the hide right off her when she'd done it.

Gig hurled his own supper, a bowl of something, against the wall. "What am *I* supposed to do?"

Kade, having fetched another plate, was busy dividing the spoils. He handed the first one to Harry, who fairly dived to grab it. "Starve, I reckon," Kade answered, without sparing Gig so much as a glance.

"You think this is funny, Amanda Rose?" Curry demanded. "I see that snippy little smile on your face, don't you think I don't! You wait till I get out of here—you won't have much to smile about then."

"If you don't want me to lasso you and drag you two miles behind my horse," Kade warned idly, still not looking at Gig, "you'll shut your worthless mouth."

"You're gonna pay for the way you treat me, Marshal. Just like Amanda Rose is gonna pay."

"Where's my rope?" Kade asked, with his mouth full of fried chicken.

Gig took to rattling the bars again, setting up a fearsome clamor.

Kade jumped three of Harry's checker pieces between bites of food, and crowned his own man king.

"You want to know who I work for, Marshal Smart-ass?" Gig howled. "You been asking me over and over. Well, now I'm ready to tell you."

Mandy saw Kade's shoulders tense slightly under his cotton shirt, but she doubted that Gig knew he'd gotten a rise out of him.

"I'll tell you who hired me," Gig went on, fairly spitting, he was so mad. Mandy was briefly afraid he might actually wrench those iron bars right out of the wall and come after them like a bull bison with its backside ablaze. She'd seen his rages before and knew how strong he was when his temper was up. "Your brother, that's who!"

28

Kade's chair creaked ominously as he turned slowly around to face the prisoner. Harry's eyes were enormous, and Mandy felt rooted to the floor. She'd learned to read Gig well over the years, by necessity, and she knew when he was blowing hot air. This was not one of those times.

"Holt Cavanagh hired me, that's who," Gig sputtered. "He wants to put your pa and his whole outfit out of business, whatever way he can. He'll do it, too. Serve you all right, runnin' roughshod over everybody the way you do."

Kade rose slowly to his feet, overturning the checkerboard and sending the wooden pieces clicking to the plank floor. He didn't seem to notice.

Gig must not have liked what he saw in Kade's face, for he backed away from the bars, just out of reach. His eyes flashed with an ugly hatred, though, and he didn't seem to know that he ought to hold his tongue. "You get blamed for something you didn't do, nobody's gonna lose any sleep over it. Everyone knows how you McKettricks feel about squatters!"

"You burned the Fee homestead?" The words were toneless, but Mandy knew an ocean of hot blood was behind them, fixing to break through and boil the hide off everybody present.

"What if I did? You didn't want them there in the first place!"

"You stupid bastard. You could have killed those people!"

Gig was winding down by then, coming to his senses, looking sheepish in a recalcitrant sort of way. "Mind you, I wasn't precisely confessing to nothing—"

"Did Cavanagh tell you to burn them out?"

Gig's frustration took an upturn. "What's the use of my telling you if he did? He'll deny it, and leave me twisting in the wind. I was doing his dirty work, that's all."

Kade closed his eyes for a moment; Mandy and Harry both watched him, waiting, braced for some kind of eruption. Finally, he spoke, low and quiet and dangerously calm. "What about those dead soldiers, and the stolen gold?"

"I didn't have nothing to do with that!"

Kade turned, crossed the room, took his gun belt down from its peg, and fastened it on. The cold, murderous rage in his face frightened Mandy more than anything Gig could have said or done.

She hurried over to catch hold of his arm. "Don't be a fool, Kade. Gig wants you to leave him unguarded, that's what this is about. If he can get you chasing after Holt, those no-good friends of his might come and break him out of here. And if he can turn you against Holt Cavanagh, all the better."

Kade shook her off, and the brusqueness of the action made her feel as if she'd been slapped. "Harry," he said, his voice as flat and lifeless as a snake's eyes, "go home and stay there."

"I can't do that, Marshal!" Harry protested, going pale and casting a desperate glance at Mandy, as if seeking her help. "There's a man there with Ma. He's mean. I done already told you that, and you said I could stay."

Kade let out his breath, laid a hand on the boy's shoulder. "That's right," he said, with gruff gentleness. All the while he talked, he was looking holes into Gig's worthless hide. "I remember now. You go on over to the Bloody Basin and ask for Jeb McKettrick, then. Tell him I need a hand with something."

"What if he ain't there?" Harry wanted to know. He was already halfway to the door. Mandy reckoned the boy would have gone to hell if he'd been asked, anywhere but home. She'd felt the same way herself often enough as a child, so she could empathize.

"There'll be somebody from the Triple M," Kade said. "I'd prefer one of my brothers, but right now, I'm not too choosy. I need somebody to look after things here at the jailhouse for a while."

Harry nodded and raced out.

Gig laughed, a familiar sound that brought back fearsome memories for Mandy. "Well, now, Marshal," he said in the insolent drawl she had heard so many times before when he thought he'd gotten himself the upper hand. "I reckon I got your attention this time, didn't I?"

"I believe I told you to shut up," Kade answered, and at his tone, Gig wisely backed up another step. "Unless you've got something to say about the robbery and the murder of those soldiers, I don't want to hear another word out of you."

Mandy went over to the wall and took down John Lewis's rifle. She cocked it, slid a shell into the chamber, and stood ready for anything.

Kade was staring at her when she turned her attention his way. "What do you think you're doing?" he asked in a lethal undertone.

It took Mandy a moment to realize what he was thinking, that she'd take Gig's part against him, and when she did, she was mad enough to spit. How could he believe such a thing of her?

Gig apparently misunderstood, too. "Go ahead, Mandy girl," he said, wheedling. "Shoot him, and get your old stepdaddy out of this hole. We'll let bygones be bygones if you do, I promise you that."

Mandy aimed the rifle an inch to the left of Gig's head and fired, taking out a chunk of the log wall behind him. He leaped to one side with a yelp of fury and terror. "What the—?"

"I'd sooner let the devil out of hell as turn you loose," she vowed. Recollections came at her like birds startled from a hidden roost: Gig, slapping her mother until she sank to the floor, sobbing and bruised. Crcc, no older than eleven or twelve, going after him with a butcher knife, and taking a savage beating for his trouble. Herself, hiding on the floor of a wardrobe in some flea-ridden rooming house, making herself small, with both hands clasped over the top of her head. The remembered terror surged into her mouth, sour as vinegar.

"Put the rifle down, Mandy," Kade said reasonably. He sounded weary, as if he'd traveled a long, hard way to get to where he was. "You're liable to hurt yourself."

Her face felt as hot as a stove lid on a January morning, but slowly, she lowered the rifle.

"I'm sorry for misjudging you," Kade said.

She looked away from him and would not look back. She wanted to tell him so many things, but he'd never understand what it had been like for her, growing up the way he had as the son of a rich rancher, living in that fancy house, with folks to take his part and books to read, food he didn't have to steal and clothes that came from a real store instead of a charity box in some mission. And she didn't want his pity, wouldn't be able to endure it.

He crossed the room, took the rifle gently from her hands. "Mandy—"

The door crashed open, and Jeb and Rafe burst in, pistols drawn.

"What the devil happened here?" Rafe demanded, when he saw that everybody was still standing up and breathing. "We heard a shot!"

Kade grinned, but something hollow was in his eyes. "Mandy took a pop at the prisoner. Too bad she missed."

"I *didn't* miss," Mandy insisted, even as she cursed herself for being a stiff-necked fool for needing to clarify the point. Her chest swelled with the breath she drew. "I could split a gnat's wing at a hundred feet, Kade McKettrick, and don't you forget it."

Jeb slid his .45 back into its holster and laughed. "I'll be damned. The little nun isn't just a horse racer, she's a regular Annie Oakley. Will you marry me, Sister Mandy?"

Kade didn't look at his brothers; he was still watching Mandy as if she were a set of numbers that wouldn't add up. "Is Holt in town?" he asked, addressing Rafe and Jeb.

"He's over at the Bloody Basin," Rafe answered, clearly confused. "I just lost twenty dollars to him in a game of poker."

Kade set Mandy free of his probing gaze at last, crossed the room, and took his hat from the peg. "Stay here till I get back," he said to both Rafe and Jeb, with a nod in Gig's direction. "If that jackass tries anything, nail him."

"Now wait just one dad-blamed minute!" Rafe growled. He was used to giving orders, not taking them, and Kade's command clearly didn't set well with him. "You can't just go waltzing out of here looking for Cavanagh without one damn word of explanation!"

"Apparently," Jeb observed dryly, when the door slammed behind Kade a moment later, "he can."

Rafe turned his hot gaze on Mandy. "Explain!" he demanded, so sharply that she jumped.

The effrontery of it made her mad all over again, and she was still shaken to the core. "You watch how you talk to me, Rafe McKettrick," she warned. Much as she loved Emmeline, she wasn't taking any guff off anybody, from this day forward. She'd had her fill.

"Everybody," Jeb interceded, holding up both hands as if he were Moses about to read from the stone tablets, thus imparting the law to lesser folks. "Calm down."

Rafe dragged in deep, ragged breaths; his blue eyes bulged, and he looked for all the world like a bull, ready to charge. Gig had retreated to the back of his cell, where he was picking at the splintered wall as if he thought he could dig his way out with a fingernail. Jeb stood watching Mandy with affable interest, his hands resting on those narrow gunslinger's hips of his.

"I'm listening, Sister Mandy," Jeb prompted when she didn't volunteer any information.

It was Harry who answered, Harry, whom they'd all forgotten. He was crouched on the floor, gathering the wooden checker pieces as carefully as if they'd been jewels, spilled from a king's coffers.

"That feller in the cell," the boy said, the words coming out of his mouth so fast that they tumbled over each other like stones rolling downhill in a landslide, "he told Kade who he worked for and got him riled up good."

Mandy held her breath. *Please don't say any more,* she thought, though she knew it was a forlorn hope.

Jeb and Rafe waited, and the stillness was awful.

"Holt Cavanagh, that's who," Harry said, grimly triumphant.

The color drained from Rafe's face, while Jeb flushed furiously.

"Son of a *bitch!*" Jeb spat.

"I'll kill the bastard with my bare hands," Rafe added.

"Hold everything," Mandy put in hastily, fearing that the both of them would rush out and leave her and Harry alone with Gig. If his friends *were* close by, looking for a chance to break him out of jail, she'd be outgunned for sure, and they wouldn't let one scrawny little boy get in their way, either. "Curry started all this to make trouble. He's a bold-faced liar, and that's his *best* quality." She took a breath. "He wants the rest of you distracted, at each other's throats, so he can accomplish some purpose of his own!"

Rafe and Jeb looked at each other.

"You figure Kade's going to be all right?" Jeb asked Rafe. "There're a lot of men from the Circle C in that saloon. Somebody might jump him."

"One of us has to stay here," Rafe said regretfully, glowering at Gig. He'd done some fancy talking earlier, Gig had, but he didn't look so sure of himself now. He watched them all, over his shoulder, and went on messing with the hole in the wall, expressionless as a monkey in a cage.

"Only one fair way to decide." Jeb brought a silver dollar from his coat pocket, held it between two fingers for all to see. "Heads," he said, and gave the coin a practiced flip before catching it deftly in one palm. He looked at it, grinned, and went for the door. "I win," he called back.

"Damn the luck," Rafe muttered with a shake of his head.

Mandy started to follow Jeb, thinking she'd stop by the hotel and fetch her new shotgun before making for the Bloody Basin Saloon. Kade might be marshal, but he was only one man, and she wasn't going to stand by while he got his brains blown out.

Rafe took an inescapable hold on her arm as she made to slip past him. "Oh, no, you don't, Sister Mandy. If I have to stay here and cool my heels while my brothers kill each other, so do you."

Knowing as she did that Rafe's words could easily be prophetic, Mandy suddenly felt weak. She groped for a chair and sank into it. For a second, she thought she'd be sick.

Harry was putting the checkerboard away, his motions slow and methodical. Like Rafe and Mandy, he was probably trying to keep his mind off what might be going on over at the Bloody Basin.

"Your mama's sick and dying, Amanda Rose," Gig said mournfully. "She loves me dearly, you know. She'd want you to do me better than you have been of late, and that's a fact."

Mandy felt like crying; she knew Gig was telling a partial truth, the only kind he could manage. Her mother *was* sick and dying in some lonely place, or even already gone. And wherever she was, she *did* care for Gig Curry, God help her. She'd followed him all over the back acre of hell to prove it and dragged her children right along with her.

Rafe went to stand in front of the bars. "Come over here," he said to Gig, all friendly like, as if he might have changed his mind after all and decided to let him go, with Godspeed and no hard feelings. Gig, bumbling like a blind cellar rat, stepped right up to the door.

In the next instant, he crashed full force into the steel bars. Rafe, who'd grabbed the front of Gig's shirt in a motion that made lightning look slow by comparison, opened his hand and watched with satisfaction as Gig slid to the floor, out cold.

"That's enough out of him for a while," Rafe said, turning to smile at Mandy and the admiring Harry. "How'd you like to get whupped at checkers, boy?"

29

HOLT WAS SEATED alone at the far table, drawing on a cheroot and admiring his winnings, when Kade thrust open the swinging doors of the Bloody Basin Saloon and stalked toward him.

He must have taken note of the expression on Kade's face; from inside, it felt like a brand, etched deep and still smoldering. Whatever his perception, Holt didn't move, he just sat there, lounging, pleased with himself and all the world. He was the spawn of Angus McKettrick, all right, born convinced that he knew his way through life from beginning to end, and certain of every step along the path.

It was like looking in a mirror. The realization thundered through Kade, and in the wake of it, he sent everything flying— chips, bills, cards, and all—with a swift kick to the underside of the table. Only then did Holt get to his feet, easylike but watchful. He didn't go for his gun. "Now *that*, little brother," he said, exaggerating his down-South drawl, "was out-and-out rude."

"You're no brother of mine," Kade said, though he knew it wasn't the truth. He wondered at the heat of the rage burgeoning inside of him, knew it had its roots in something older and more elemental than Gig Curry's claim that he was on the Circle C payroll. It was a blood-and-marrow bond, one he didn't want to recognize and couldn't ignore.

"We've got the same father, God help us," Holt replied, still unruffled. Something glinted in his chameleon eyes, though, hard and cold as the barrel of a carbine. No doubt, he had his own reservations about an affinity he wouldn't have chosen. "In most folks' books, that makes us brothers. What's all this hoop-a-la about, anyway?"

A lot of other men were in that saloon, but it might have been empty of everything but mice and cooties, judging by the silence pounding in Kade's ears. "I've got a man named Curry over in my jail." The fingers of Kade's right hand closed and then opened again; it scared him how much he wanted to draw on Cavanagh right then and there, and devil take the consequences.

"Good place for him," Holt said. "But I confess I'm having some trouble reckoning up what that has to do with me."

Kade thought of the Fees' homestead, nothing but a pile of charred logs now, the broken and blackened skeleton of a poor man's dreams. He thought of the Triple M brand, burned into the trunk of a tree, and for no reason he could get a handle on, of his mother, falling sick after taking a harmless spill in the creek and dying the next day. Before he knew it, he'd landed a haymaker in the middle of Holt Cavanagh's face, a face too much like his own for ready acceptance, and sent him wheeling backward.

A murmur rose from the customers, but they were nothing but a droning blur to Kade. The whole world pulsed around him, like the heart of a monster buffeting the breath from his lungs.

"You hired him," he heard himself say as Holt got to his feet, bleeding from the mouth and feeling for loose teeth with one hand. *"That's* what it has to do with you."

Holt's hand came away smudged with blood. To Kade's furious amazement, the son of a bitch laughed. "You pack one hell of a punch, for a rich man's brat. Maybe I'll claim you after all."

"Why'd you do it?"

"Why'd I do what?" Holt snapped back, and it did look as though he was finally getting riled. About time, by Kade's assessment. "Hire Curry? I needed ranch hands."

"You paid him to help you bring down the Triple M. He set fire to the Fee place, on your say-so, and laid the blame on us."

Holt spat, but there was no sign of a tooth flying, more's the pity. "The hell, you say. I didn't tell him to set any fire. As for seeing the Triple M go under, well, it seems to me there'd be no effort required. All I have to do is sit back and let you boys and the old man run the place into the ground. You're making a fine job of it, as far as I can tell."

"Are you going to fight or not?"

"No," Holt said with maddening patience, "I'm not, and you'd better be glad of it, *little brother,* because getting your ass kicked from one end of this saloon to the other might just undermine your reputation as a big, tough lawman. We wouldn't want that, would we?"

"I *want* this settled," Kade said, feeling his ears heat up a little as a ripple of laughter moved through the Bloody Basin. "Here and now."

"And you figure my giving you a thrashing in front of God and everybody else would accomplish the purpose?"

"I *figure* you're a low-down, chickenshit bastard."

"And *I* figure you're a hothead with manure for brains," Holt answered mildly. "But that doesn't mean I'm going to wear out my knuckles trying to pound some sense into you. You're probably not worth the aggravation anyhow." The Texan locked gazes with Kade. "You going to help me pick up this money, or go right on making a fool of yourself?"

"It's your money. You pick it up."

"You and I are going to come to terms over this one day soon, little brother," Holt warned as he sifted through the sawdust, spit, and peanut shells for cards and coins and bills of currency. "Watch your back."

"What's wrong with right now?"

Holt grinned, fat lip and all. "I'd like to thrash you, but it's a private matter, between you and me. No need to make a spectacle of it."

Kade seethed. "Suppose I just tie into you?"

"I'll take the beating without raising a hand to you, and you'll look like the fool you undoubtedly are," Holt said, getting to his feet. "You're wanting a fight, and I'll give it to you for sure, but not here, and not now." He set handfuls of coins and currency on the green-felt surface beside him. "Meantime, you could use some help. You're up to your eyeballs in shit. How about swearing me in as a deputy?"

The question so surprised Kade that his bloodlust subsided a little. "What do you know about being a lawman?"

"I was a Texas Ranger for close to ten years. I daresay I learned a thing or two, riding for the Republic."

"Sounds like he's qualified, Kade," Jeb said from somewhere nearby. "I'd jump at the offer if I were you."

Kade turned his head and glared at his kid brother. "What are you doing here?" he demanded.

Jeb spread his hands and grinned ingenuously. "Free country."

Kade turned and stormed out, looking neither to the right nor to the left. Both Jeb and Holt were right on his heels, and he couldn't do a damn thing about it.

30

"WHY WOULD YOU want to help us?" Rafe asked Holt straight out half an hour later, when the four of them stood in front of the jailhouse, conferring. It was good and dark by then, and the Bloody Basin was doing a brisk business down the street. Harry was inside, sound asleep on one of the cots in the second cell, and Kade had personally walked Mandy back to the hotel. Or, more accurately, he'd strong-armed her, taking her by the elbow and marching her along the sidewalk. She'd called him names no nun had ever heard.

"Call it Christian duty," Holt said, standing with one foot braced on the edge of a horse trough. He was sporting a split lip, Kade noted with grudging satisfaction, though it still galled him plenty that Holt hadn't thrown a punch in return. "It's just too damn sad to watch you people fumbling around like a bunch of beetles in the bottom of a barrel."

Rafe took a step toward their half brother, and Jeb put out an arm to stop him. To Kade's surprise, Rafe subsided, though for a moment there, it was anybody's guess whether he'd land square in Jeb's middle. He wasn't the sort to suffer interference gladly.

"It's no secret that you've got a grudge against us," Jeb told Cavanagh reasonably, and if he'd feared reprisal from Rafe, he gave no sign of it. That was typical, given the way he lived, hell-bent for tomorrow, as if he didn't have a history of getting his butt whupped by his older brothers. "You expect us to believe that you've turned softhearted all of a sudden?"

Holt smiled idly and turned his gaze to Kade. A warning was in it. "At least one of you is prone to believe just about anything, it appears." Holt heaved a melodramatic sigh. "Listen," he went on after ruminating awhile, "we all know there's no love lost between the four of us, but it would kill the old man to part with that ranch, and that's a fact. We've got our differences, he and I, but he's still my father, damn his bristly hide, and I can't just stand by and watch him go under." He paused, thoughtful again. "Without me, you haven't got a chance in hell of getting back that money before the bills fall due. So let's put aside our grievances for the time being and get this thing done."

"What's in it for you?" Rafe asked suspiciously. The same question was in Kade's mind, and probably Jeb's, too.

Cavanagh shrugged. "I've hated Angus McKettrick for as long as I can remember. Now that I've actually clapped eyes on the old coot, well, that fire in my belly comes and goes. For the moment, I reckon I'm just tired of being at the mercy of that half-wild kid I used to be, the one who got left behind. In my own way, I'd be putting *paid* to a lot of things. Once that's done, maybe I'll sell out and move on."

Rafe, Jeb, and Kade were all silent for a few moments, as-similating what Cavanagh had said, weighing one thing against another. In a ring-tailed, back-assward McKettrick kind of way, it made sense.

Kade reckoned he should have gotten more pleasure out of the prospect than he did. Another matter to puzzle over, if he ever got the time. "We want that land," he said.

Holt grinned again, though his eyes were hollow. "I reckon you do. You're used to getting what you want, aren't you?" He paused, enjoying his advantage. "The way the old man's got things set up, two of you are going to be at loose ends one day soon, even if we manage to pull this thing out of the privy. I almost regret that I won't be around to watch you scramble."

A short silence ensued, during which Kade wondered how long he'd have to wait for that fight Cavanagh had promised him.

"You were really a Ranger?" Jeb asked out of the blue. There was still a lot of kid in him, even if he was nearly twenty eight years old. It made Kade think of Harry, and how proud he was of the tin star Kade had given him. Hell, maybe he should try to find one for Jeb, too, stuff it into the toe of a red flannel sock, and say it was from Saint Nick.

"Yup," Holt said. "I was a major."

"Why'd you give it up?" Rafe asked, skeptical. "Rangering is a hard life, but there must be some satisfaction in it."

Holt was quiet for a long time. "I had my reasons," he said, and Kade knew from the way he spoke—it was pure Angus McKettrick, that tone of voice—that they'd get no more out of him on the subject, no matter how long they deviled him about it. Still, Kade wondered about the smoky specters he'd glimpsed in his half brother's eyes.

"Tell me again why we ought to trust you any further than we can spit?" Kade asked.

The ghosts were still there when Holt met his gaze, though it was a direct look, and steady. "Because you don't have a choice."

Kade suppressed an unseemly urge to fling his hat down and grind it into the dirt with the heel of his boot.

31

ANGUS SAT IN the chair at his desk, and the set of his shoulders, so broad and strong only a season before, so dejected now, nearly broke Concepcion's spirit. She stepped in behind him, laid her hands on either side of his neck. She wouldn't have chosen to love this difficult man, but she'd lost her heart to him a long time before, watching him grieve for his lost Georgia. His sorrow had been a fierce and relentless thing, but through it all, he'd looked after his boys, in his rough way, and he'd held on to the ranch with a tenacity most mortals couldn't imagine, let alone match. One night, way back when, he'd come to her for solace, and she'd given it. They'd been together, in secret, ever since.

"A penny for your thoughts, Mr. McKettrick," she offered softly.

He gave a grim chuckle and reached up to lay a hoary palm to her wrist. "I reckon I could use one right about now, *Mrs.* McKettrick. A penny, I mean."

She didn't have to stoop to kiss the top of his head, even though he was sitting and she was standing. He was a big man, her Angus, and not just physically. He was an old lion, and the soul of honor. "You have faced hard times before," she reminded him gently, "and always you have come through them. This will be no different."

He sighed and pulled her gently around to sit on his lap. "It's not the ranch that's worrying me," he confided, when she'd settled in, laying her head on his shoulder. "Concepcion, you were right—I've turned my own sons one against the other. I wish I'd listened to you and left things as they were, given them each a fair share of the land."

She straightened his collar. "They are your boys," she said quietly, "with your good blood flowing in their veins. No matter what happens, they will find their way."

He didn't answer, which meant he wasn't convinced.

"You could call the whole thing off," she suggested, knowing even as she spoke what his reply would be. She knew the terrain of this man's mind and heart better than her own.

"A deal," Angus said, "is a deal. It wouldn't be fair to Rafe to go back on my word now."

She stroked his rough cheek. Even though he shaved every morning, at her insistence, he still had stubble by suppertime. He was a man in the fullest sense of the word, and the fire he'd kindled in Concepcion burned as hot as it ever had. It had been the subject of many a confession, the passion she bore him. "I wonder sometimes if we ought to tell them we are married," she confessed. The previous summer, during a party celebrating Rafe and Emmeline's union, the two of them had sneaked off and gotten hitched on a whim, swearing Father Herrera and their witnesses to silence. Concepcion had never regretted that night for a moment, though she wondered sometimes if Angus did. He'd cared deeply for both his other wives, Holt's mother, Ellie, and Georgia, and she knew he still suffered over the losses, though he tried not to let on.

"Far as I'm concerned," Angus said with a grim chuckle, turning his head to plant a husbandly kiss on her mouth, "you can have an announcement carved into the wall of Horse Thief Canyon or stand on the roof of the Cattleman's Bank and shout it to the whole territory."

Her heartbeat quickened slightly. "Really?"

"I love you, Concepcion," he said without hesitation, "and I'm proud that you're my wife. I'd have broken the news before now, but I figured you mightn't want folks to know a fine woman like you had taken up with an old warhorse like me."

She laughed, though tears were in her eyes, turning his grizzled face to a reflection shimmering on water. "'Old,' you say?" she teased. "Well, Senor McKettrick, suppose—just suppose—that Emmeline was not the only woman in this family with a baby growing under her heart?"

A log collapsed in the fireplace behind them; Concepcion heard sparks crackling in the chimney. Outside, a raw, blustery wind blew, rattling the windows of a house that was as sturdy as the man who had built it with his own two hands.

He held her a little away and studied her face. "Concepcion, if this is a joke—"

She giggled, feeling like a girl, instead of a woman of nearly forty, settled and thoroughly married. "I thought it was the change of life," she said shyly, "but I am sick in the mornings and I think my belly is beginning to swell."

A smile dawned in Angus's hard features, pushing back the shadows. "Glory be," he said, marveling. "I don't believe it!"

At his response, Concepcion was seized by joy. She hadn't expected this, had indeed feared that he might accuse her of being faithless, lying with another, younger man. "I am hoping for a girl," she said, and blushed. "We have enough men around here already."

Angus threw back his head and shouted with exuberant laughter. "A child!" he crowed, jubilant. His blue eyes, so worried of late, shone with pride. "Yours and mine!"

"*Sí*," she said softly.

He unbuttoned the bodice of her dress and slipped a hand inside to cup her breast. She gave a little moan as he caressed her. "I reckon we ought to take ourselves upstairs and do a little celebrating," he said, chafing her muslin-covered nipple to attention with the side of his thumb.

"It was our *celebrating* that got us into this," Concepcion said, gasping between the words. She was a girl again, in his arms, and the familiar passion besieged her senses.

He set her on her feet, rose from the chair.

Concepcion did not bother to close her bodice; to do so would be impractical, since he would only open it again the moment the bedroom door closed behind them.

He gave her bottom a proprietary swat. "Get moving, woman. I'm of a mind to have my way with you."

"Old bull," Concepcion said, but she headed for the stairs, her steps quick and light as those of an eager bride, and Angus was right behind her.

32

KADE KNOCKED RESOLUTELY at the door of Mamie Sussex's rooming house first thing the next morning, knowing full well that he was bound to run into a bride or two. Since he couldn't avoid them forever, much as he'd like to do just that, he might as well just tough it out, attend to his business, and get on with things.

Mamie herself answered, a blowsy woman with a conversely innocent face. She had a wealth of dark red hair, like her tribe of kids, and more freckles than there were stars in the desert sky. She was decently dressed, but the flush in her cheeks made Kade wonder if the man who'd smacked Harry in the face, leaving a bruise, was still somewhere around.

"Marshal McKettrick. What a surprise." And not a good one, by the hunted look in her eyes. She put Kade in mind of a field mouse cornered by a pack of cats.

The realization struck him that she thought he'd come to arrest her, and he hastened to reassure her. He took off his hat. "I understand my brides have been staying here. I came to bring the accounts up-to-date."

Mamie was a pretty woman when she smiled; he saw the

evidence of it now, though she was still tentative. "I don't understand," she said, stepping back to admit him. "I thought that gold piece you sent with Harry was for the ladies' expenses."

He tried not to look too closely at the poor surroundings. The place was clean enough, but the walls were thin, with old newspapers nailed up for insulation, and from the chill, the fire had been out for a while. The plank floor had no rugs, and the furniture was battered, probably scavenged from abandoned cabins and alongside the trail, where overloaded sojourners were wont to discard things. "It was a gift," he said. "The boy's been a lot of help."

A little girl wandered in, red-haired like the rest of the outfit, wearing shabby bloomers and a camisole that probably belonged to her mother. She hugged a grubby cloth doll and surveyed Kade with considerable reservation.

"Run along, Hortense," Mamie said hastily.

The child obeyed, but not graciously. According to Harry, the family had six kids; there was no telling what kind of mischief the rest of them were up to.

"I could brew up some coffee, if you'd like," Mamie said, trying to please and plainly uncertain how to go about it. He suspected she knew only one way to deal with a man and was at a loss when something else was called for.

Kade shook his head. "No, thanks." He sat when she gestured toward one of the mismatched chairs. He cast an anxious look toward the stairs. "The brides around?"

Mamie shook her head. "They're over at the church." She sat down on the edge of another chair. "There's a prayer meeting." She, too, looked worriedly in the direction of the stairway, but for a whole different reason, of course.

"I guess it must be hard, tending all these children on your own," he said, to let her know, once again, that he wasn't there to make trouble. Clearly, she'd had more than her share of that already. He reached into the inside pocket of his coat for his wallet. "If you'll just give me a figure for the brides' room and board . . ."

She named a modest sum, but when Kade tried to hand it to her, a clattering came from upstairs, and she pulled back as quickly as if she'd been burned. Her gaze flew to the ceiling.

"He'll take it away, if he gets wind that there's money in the house," she whispered.

Kade stood, folded the currency between her hands. "You come and tell me if he does," he said quietly, watching as she hid what must have seemed like a fortune to her under the cushion of her chair. "And Mrs. Sussex?"

She looked up at him, baffled, then recognized her own name. Waited tensely.

"Somebody gave Harry a shiner," Kade said. "He spent the night at the jailhouse, on one of the cots. I don't know for sure who it was that hit him— he wouldn't tell me—but I feel a need to make myself clear on this matter. If that happens again, I'll be back to deal with it directly."

Mamie put a hand to her throat, nodded. Pain and shame flickered in her eyes. "I try to keep them out from underfoot," she said in a meek whisper.

"I'd suggest you make a stronger effort." Kade didn't know what he'd do if the occasion actually arose since, to his consternation, it wasn't against the law to beat a child or a woman, any more than a dog or a mule. Kade found that situation wholly objectionable, and he made up his mind then and there to do whatever he had to, to change things.

Meanwhile, he glanced at the ceiling, tempted to take the stairs two at a time, drag whatever no-good rascal he might find up there out into the street and give him his just comeuppance. It would serve more than one purpose: the bastard had it coming, and he'd be able to let off some of the steam that had been building since he'd locked horns with Holt over at the Bloody Basin. "You ever need help," he added, "you come to me."

"Nobody ever said that to me before," she told him, and he believed her. He felt ashamed, partly because he knew he was a hypocrite—his right hand was still sore from punching Holt in the mouth and he still wanted a fight with everything in him— and partly because he'd never taken any notice of the suffering and everyday injustice that went on right there in Indian Rock, virtually under his nose. He'd been too caught up in his own concerns to see beyond them.

He nodded and headed for the door, and it didn't seem like an accident that he met Harry on the front steps.

"Is he gone?" the boy asked.

"I think he's still around," Kade answered. "You'd better come back to the jail with me. I might need a deputy."

Harry's thin chest swelled under his too-small shirt. They were walking along side by side when the boy spoke up again. Plainly, he'd been working up his nerve for a while. "Folks say you're wanting a wife," he blurted out. "My ma ain't spoken for."

Kade stopped, pushed his hat back, and faced the boy. He chose his words as carefully as any he'd ever uttered. "The truth is, I'm kind of taken with somebody else." He'd been wrestling with the fact for a while now and still hadn't made proper sense of it, but it was so and, if only for that reason, it wanted saying.

"Who?" Harry inquired. If Kade's response was a disappointment, Harry seemed to recover from it quickly enough. Maybe he'd just had a lot of practice in that area.

Kade sighed. "Mandy," he admitted to Harry, and to himself.

Harry's face lit up. "You mean the lady who brought us the fried chicken last night? The one who beat you in that horse race?"

Kade laughed. Harry had obviously taken this revelation better than Kade had; he was still trying to sort it out in his own mind. "That's the one."

"She's real pretty."

Kade nodded. "That she is." Then he hunkered down a little so he could look up into the kid's face. "You and me, we're always going to be partners. That all right with you?"

"I reckon it's fine," Harry allowed, swelling up again.

"Good," Kade said, rising. He ruffled the boy's hair with one hand. "That's good."

Old Billy had been keeping watch at the jail, and when Kade and Harry stepped through the door, he met them with an accounting of Gig Curry's many sins. Since these wholesale atrocities had taken place in less than half an hour, and with no visible damage to the property, Kade wasn't alarmed.

"I never been so insulted in all my days," Billy complained, jabbing a finger in the direction of the cell where Curry was making his home these days. "He called me old."

Kade struggled not to grin. "You don't say. Did you call him ugly?"

"I didn't think of that," Old Billy confessed.

"How about stupid?"

"Didn't think of that, either."

Kade laid a hand on the blacksmith's powerful shoulder. "Well, now, Billy, if you want to be in the jail-tending business, you'll have to be a mite meaner."

"I'd call him a coward," Harry piped up, "if I was calling him anything."

"I don't have to take this!" Gig protested.

"Yes," Kade replied, hanging up his hat, "you do."

33

KADE COULDN'T GET Mandy out of his mind, once he'd told Harry straight out, not to mention himself, that he had a soft spot for her. He'd kept the full extent of the damage private, though: fact was, the walls of the fort had fallen and he was occupied by enemy troops.

And *soft* wasn't precisely the right word for what he felt, he reflected miserably as he sat behind his desk ten minutes later with his feet up, Rafe-style. It was too damn quiet in the jail-house; he'd dispatched Harry on an errand, and Curry was taking himself a nap with snoring fit to rattle the bars of his cell.

Kade tried to herd his thoughts into some kind of sensible order. Why hadn't he known right away that Mandy was different from every other woman who'd ever drawn breath? He figured it must have been the nun suit that threw him in the beginning, though if he was honest with himself, he had to admit that he and Amanda Rose had been striking sparks from the first. Now that he'd seen her in a dress, not to mention a pair of tight trousers, everything was different, turned inside out and upside down. From there—maybe it was desperation—he commenced thinking about how long it had been since he'd had a woman. Too long, by his standards or any other man's, and he wondered if that was his whole problem. Maybe he just needed to ride over to Flagstaff and make a visit to a certain house on a certain street.

The trouble with that idea was, he didn't have the luxury of heading for a whorehouse every time he felt the need, now that he was marshal, with a shitload of grief on his hands. And he was plagued by another thing, too: it was Mandy he wanted, and none other, though he flat-out didn't trust her. She knew too much about the outlaw life for his taste—more than she was telling, by a long shot.

He picked up his enamel coffee cup, fortunately empty, and flung it across the room. It bounced off the stove with a clank.

At the sound, Curry came sputtering out of sweet repose, as rattled as if there'd been a shot fired; there was some satisfaction in that, at least. Since neither of them had much to say to each other, time dragged.

At noon, two of the men from the Triple M came by to relieve him, and he decided he'd have his midday meal at the Arizona Hotel. If he couldn't take Mandy to his bed—not that he actually *had* a bed, now that he was spending the majority of his time in town, and sleeping in the extra cell—well, he could at least look at her a little.

The dining room was bustling with cowboys, soldiers, and townspeople when he arrived, and Mandy was rushing about, helping Sarah Fee wait tables. The Fees' baby slept in a laundry basket set across the seats of two chairs. He peered at the kid briefly, then found himself a solitary seat.

"What'll it be?" Mandy asked as if he were just another cowpuncher, her pencil in hand, notepad at the ready.

He figured she'd douse him with hot coffee if he answered honestly. "What's the special?" he countered after groping for the words, and shifting uneasily in his chair.

"Liver and onions." She gave him a curious, searching look, as if he'd suddenly sprouted an extra pair of ears or something. "Are you all right?"

"Never better," he lied. "I'll have the liver."

She nodded and hustled away. He watched her backside as she went and entertained ideas he wouldn't have dared to think about a nun. He wasn't a particularly religious man, but he knew there were things the Almighty wouldn't tolerate from a saint, let alone a sinner like him. He glanced at the ceiling and almost jumped out of his skin when Becky paused beside his chair and laid a hand on his shoulder.

"We're giving a dance here Saturday night," she said, and the look in her eyes told him she'd guessed a lot more of what was going through his mind than he would willingly have revealed. What she said next confirmed it. "I don't think anybody's asked Mandy yet."

Kade felt a thickening in his throat. Mandy wasn't going to any dance without him, and she sure as hell wasn't going with another man. "I guess I'd better put in my bid, then."

Becky smiled. She was a strong woman, contending with trouble and heartache day to day and still planning dances. Little wonder Emmeline had turned out to be such a thoroughbred. "I guess you'd better," she agreed. "I saw Jeb watching her a little while ago, and I believe he's thinking along the same lines you are."

Jeb, of the on-again, off-again wedding ring. Kade pushed back his chair and stood. "That won't do," he said to no one in particular, and started for the kitchen.

Mandy was busy loading plates. Liver and onions sizzled in a pair of huge skillets on the stove, and the cook, a Chinese man whose name he couldn't recall, gave him a look fit to tan leather for invading his territory.

"Mandy."

She stopped, stared at Kade. "Is something wrong?"

He shook his head. He hadn't felt this shy, or this awkward, since he was fourteen and asking to walk Miss Alice Jean Gibbons home after a church social. He wondered fitfully whatever had happened to Alice.

"There's a dance here on Saturday night."

She looked puzzled. "Do we need a permit or something?"

He had to laugh then, at her and at himself. "I was hoping you'd let me escort you." He paused, feeling his ears heat up. "To the dance, I mean."

"Me?" she asked, as if she might have misheard. "Surely one of the brides—"

"I don't want one of the brides, Mandy. I want you."

She stared at him, evidently speechless.

"Well?" he prompted, unable to bear the suspense another second. If she refused, he'd just go off somewhere and shoot himself and be done with it.

She considered things further, probably unaware that she was putting him through the tortures of the damned, but possibly enjoying the moment, and finally smiled. "Sure," she said, and shoved one of the plates at him. "Here's your liver and onions. Now, get out of my way. I've got work to do."

He stood watching, plate in hand, as she swept past him, bumping the door to the dining room open with one hip. As innocent and ordinary as that gesture was, it left Kade without a doubt in his mind about one thing, anyway.

He was sitting on a wagonload of gunpowder, and it was about to explode.

34

Becky recognized the cowhand the moment he stepped into the hotel lobby, which had been cleared of furniture for that night's dance, and worse, she knew from his impudent grin that he remembered her as well.

He approached her boldly, spurs jingling. Maybe he'd ignored the discreet sign outside that said spurs weren't allowed inside the hotel, or maybe he flat couldn't read. "It's a small world," he said, taking off his hat and pressing it to his chest in a parody of good manners, "just like folks say."

She kept her gaze level with his. "Much as we might like it to be otherwise," she said sweetly, "it surely is."

He was a good-looking boy, if a little rough around the edges, but a mean light glittered in his eyes. She remembered that he'd raised a hand to one of her girls that night in Kansas City, and she'd promptly had him thrown out of her establishment for good. Plainly, he was still smarting from the perceived injustice of it all.

"Jesse Graves," he said, as if his name mattered spit to her. When she didn't answer, he evidently felt called upon to dig himself in deeper. "I hear you're the marshal's woman now."

The lobby was still mostly empty, since the evening was

new, but a few eager guests were within earshot. Becky fervently hoped the cacophony of the cowboy band, tuning up their fiddles, washboard, and guitars, would drown out the exchange. "Kade McKettrick's the marshal," she said. "He's a mite young for me."

Graves smiled, confident as a pup. "From what I've seen, you aren't all that particular about a man's age, long as he's got money in his pocket."

Rage surged through Becky, but she held it in check. She'd known, after all, that her nemesis would ride in one day, and she'd tried to ready herself for the inevitable revelations. Now, face-to-face with her past, she realized some things simply couldn't be prepared for ahead of time. "I run a respectable business here," she said, "and I'll have you tossed into the street, same as I did in Kansas City, if you don't mind your manners."

He shook his head and made a tsk-tsk sound. "And I was about to offer you a deal."

"I'm not interested in any 'deal' you might have in mind, cowboy," she said, relieved to see Rafe and Emmeline coming down the stairs. They were laughing quietly, dressed in their fancy finest, ready for a lively evening. "You can stay and enjoy the festivities, as long as you conduct yourself like a gentleman, or you can go. The choice is yours."

The cowboy glanced at Rafe and something tightened in his face. Maybe he was having an attack of common sense, though Becky didn't hold out much hope for that. "You're acquainted with my son-in-law?" she asked lightly, though the pit of her stomach was clenched like a fist.

"He's a McKettrick. That's about all I need to know."

The brides came in as a group, spiffed up and anxious. Not

for the first time, Becky considered taking them aside and explaining that wolves hunted in packs, but smart women did their tracking alone. She wondered how long it would be before they figured out that Kade's heart was already taken—probably about the time he did.

"You have a bone to pick with the McKettricks?" Becky asked.

"Maybe I do," Graves allowed. "Some folks just plain have too much of everything." He'd spotted the brides, and his cocky smile was back. "Those some of your girls?"

Becky's spine stiffened. "This isn't a brothel, Mr. Graves. It's a hotel, and one of the best in the territory. And those ladies are just that—ladies. You will treat them accordingly, or answer to me."

He smiled, wolflike, as he admired the colorful clutch of young women. "I reckon it depends on your definition of what's according."

"Step out of line under this roof," Becky retorted sweetly, "and you'll be worried about another definition entirely. Find yourself a dictionary, if you can read, and look up the word *incarcerated*."

Rafe and Emmeline were coming toward them now, which was both a relief and a concern to Becky, though she didn't let any of that show in her face or bearing.

Jesse Graves registered their approach, as surely as she did, and made for the brides with some haste.

"Who was that?" Emmeline asked, a little frown furrowing her brow. Rafe had stopped to speak with Denver Jack, the leader of the band, probably about ranch business.

"Trouble," Becky said.

Emmeline stiffened. "Should I get Rafe?"

Becky sighed. "It wouldn't do any good, sweetheart." She summoned up a smile. Her store of them was dwindling, now that John was ailing, but she always seemed to have just one more at the ready when she had need of it. "Don't you look a picture in that new dress."

"I feel fat."

Becky laughed. "A small price to pay for bringing a brand-new life into the world." She felt better for remembering that she'd be a grandmother by the time the snow flew. It was something to hold on to. She straightened her shoulders, turned her gaze to the stairs. "I'd best go and see if John is well enough to come out on the landing. He told me he wants to watch the rest of you cut a rug, even if he can't join in." Doc had gotten an invalid's chair from someplace, and he was with John now, examining him and no doubt warning him not to overdo.

Emmeline caught Becky's hands in her own when she would have walked away. "Just you remember," she said, in a low voice, seeking Graves out with her eyes and frowning again, "that whatever happens, you're my mother, and Rafe and I will stand by you."

Tears filled Becky's eyes. Once, they'd been rare for her, but now, with John's health failing so rapidly, she wept almost daily, though usually privately. She blinked the wetness away and kissed Emmeline's cheek. "That's all I need to know," she said, and hurried up the stairs to the one and only man she'd ever truly loved.

He was waiting for her. He cherished her, even though he knew all her secrets. His soul was twin to hers.

And he was dying.

35

THE BRIDES HAD Kade cornered in the lobby of the Arizona Hotel before he even took off his new hat, bought special for the occasion, and they were loaded for bear. Sue Ellen, arriving with Holt, but a little apart, joined up with them right away.

Kade tried to look past them, scanning the crowded, noisy room for Mandy, but there was no sign of her. By his reckoning, that was both a problem and a mercy.

At his side, Jeb gave him an elbow. "Speak up, Brother."

Kade swallowed, darted a look at his sibling, and did as he'd been bidden. "This is my brother Jeb," he said to the brides, seeing them as a flock, just like always. "He's in the market for a wife himself."

Jeb's grin was ready and wicked. Kade sidestepped a second and more forceful jab to the ribs. "I declare you ladies are lovely enough to make a man forget the sacred vows of matrimony," Jeb said smoothly, showing that damn disappearing ring of his. "I'm sure my patient wife wouldn't object to a little dancing, though."

The brides looked every bit as confused as Kade felt, though the redhead accepted Jeb's hand when he extended it and allowed him to lead her into the swirl of dancers in the middle of the floor. The rest of them backed off a little after that, and seemed amenable when Captain Harvey's soldiers and a few fancied-up cowboys ventured forward to request a dance.

"If you've got a wife," Kade demanded, when he and Jeb were momentarily alone, fifteen minutes later, with the brides temporarily off their trail, "where is she?"

Jeb looked smug, fiddling with the ring. "That would be my business, wouldn't it?"

Kade decided it would be unseemly to smack him right there in Becky's crowded lobby. "I think you're lying; ring or no ring."

"Think whatever you like." With that, Jeb walked away to find himself a dance partner.

If Mandy hadn't chosen just that moment to come down the stairs, looking grand in the calico dress he'd bought her at the general store as part of the stakes for their horse race, he might have gone after his brother and choked a straight answer out of him, party manners be damned. As it was, he made his way through the crowd like a sleepwalker, all his thoughts centered squarely on Mandy.

"You look—" he began, and it came out sounding so raspy that he had to start over. "You look real nice."

She smiled. "Thanks," she said, preening a little under the compliment. "Who's watching the jail? Not poor little Harry, I hope."

"Old Billy's there," Kade said with a tilted smile that felt unsteady on his mouth, as if it might not hold. "He's got a rifle, and I'll be stopping by regularly to check on the situation."

Mandy sighed and assessed the gathering almost wistfully, as though she couldn't believe she was really there, and a part of it all. When she looked at Kade again, fretfulness was in her eyes.

"You must know that Old Billy won't be able to handle that gang, if they decide to come for Gig."

"I almost wish they would," Kade said. "That way, even if they got away, we'd have somebody to track. Someplace to start."

"One thing I know about trouble. You don't have to go out beating the brush for it. It'll come right to you, sure as sunrise."

"I'm pretty much counting on that," he said, relaxing a little. The music was playing, and he wanted to take her into his arms and let the whole town of Indian Rock know that she was there with him and nobody else. "May I have this dance, Amanda Rose?"

She went pink in the face. "I don't really know much about dancing," she confided, "since I've never had much call for it."

He smiled and set his hat aside on a table, with a dozen others. He was wearing his best waistcoat and a string tie, and he'd even had his good shirt washed and pressed over at the Chinese laundry. "Just follow my lead," he said, and pulled her out among the other dancers. It felt powerfully good to hold her.

Mandy was awkward at first, but she soon learned the steps, and the way she smiled up at Kade as they moved to the music made him feel like a much better man than he really was. He decided to enjoy the illusion while it lasted.

When they were both winded after several sets, she excused herself, saying she wanted a word with Emmeline, and Kade, though unwilling, accepted the parting with as much grace as he could summon. Spotting John Lewis up at the top of the stairs, seated in a wheeled chair with a blanket over his legs, he went to pay his respects.

"Did you send that wire?" John asked urgently.

"Yes," Kade said. "I reckon she's got it by now."

"But there's been no answer?" The ex-marshal looked downcast, and fragile, as if the light of a dim lantern would shine right through him.

"Maybe she's on her way," Kade suggested, hoping for his friend's sake that that was the case. "Could be, she just lit out for here as soon as she got the news, and didn't take the time to send a telegram."

"She'd best hurry." John met Kade's gaze, swallowed hard. His eyes blazed, the way a fire will just before it goes out.

"Sounds as if you've plumb given up on yourself," Kade remarked, putting on that he was affronted. In reality, he felt lost and more than a little helpless, and he hated that. He was accustomed to taking action, *doing something* about things, though lately he'd been forced to mark time, more than anything.

"A man knows," John answered quietly, "when things are shutting down inside him. It's like I'm stepping back from myself somehow."

Kade was surprised, but he tried not to show it.

"What's done is done. Maybe this is what I deserve. I was in jail once, a long time ago. Pulled a robbery. Did I ever tell you that?"

Just then there was a stir downstairs, and Kade peered through the rails of the balustrade to see his father and Concepcion walk in, arm in arm and spit-shined. Again, he had the odd sense that he was missing something he ought to have noticed.

John must have been reading his mind, because he chuckled and inclined his head toward the newcomers. "You young people," he said with a telling sigh. "Think you invented passion, like it's some brand-new thing, all your own."

Passion? Kade had never connected the word with Concepcion, let alone his pa. Still, the two of them glowed as if they'd each swallowed a pint jarful of lightning bugs.

"You'd better get back to Mandy," John counseled with a faded remnant of his old smile. "Seems to me she's drawing a lot of notice from those young soldiers, and not a few of the cowboys, too."

Kade sought Mandy with his eyes, found her by the punch bowl, talking with a corporal. He was clear downstairs before he realized he hadn't told John good-bye, or even that he'd never hold an old mistake against him.

36

"Becky Fairmont is nothing but a whore, Bertha," said the woman with one eyebrow, a cup of punch raised to her taut lips, having whispered the pertinent word. "I heard it from a reliable source, just five minutes ago." She paused, obviously enjoying the confirmation of her suspicions. "What do you think of that?"

"I'm not at all surprised," Bertha replied with lofty distain. "I told you that woman was no better than she should be."

"Why, you old bats!" Mandy erupted, clean out of patience, and she couldn't tell who was more shocked, the pair of gossips or the corporal who'd been hinting for a dance.

Bertha leveled a quelling look at her, but Mandy was not quelled. Not by a long shot. "You are as shameless as *she* is," Bertha said. "I declare. Posing as a nun, of all things, then entering a horse race in pants and fawning over Kade McKettrick for all the world to see!"

Mandy had heard enough. She went for them, heedless of her calico dress and carefully rehearsed manners, set on clawing out their eyeballs. She would have done it, too, if Kade hadn't caught her around the waist from behind and lifted her clean off her feet. "Excuse us, ladies," he said cordially, and hauled Mandy away, through the open doors of the hotel, and onto the sidewalk.

Mandy was fit to be tied. "Put me down!" she cried, kicking. The punch cup was still in her hand, though she'd spilled most of the contents, and she was sorely tempted to bonk Kade over the head with it.

He set her on her feet with a great sigh. "All right," he said a moment after the fact, "but if you start acting up again, I'll have to douse you in the horse trough."

This remark made her almost as mad as the comments that had passed between Bertha and her friend. Angry tears sprang to her eyes, and Kade being the one standing with his back to the water, it was all she could do not to turn the tables on him and give him a good push. "Those terrible women!" she cried. "They called Becky a—a—" She couldn't say the word; it stuck in her throat like a ball of dry thistles.

Kade laid his hands on her shoulders, and the gentleness of his touch was nearly her undoing. "Is this truly about Becky?" he asked quietly.

She let out a wail of fury and sorrow.

He led her over to the bench next to the doors and sat her down. Then he took the place beside her, holding her hand, interlacing his fingers with hers. "Well?" he prompted.

"*No.*" She sniffled, taking the handkerchief he handed her and wiping angrily at her face.

"I didn't think so. Whatever Becky was or is, she can look after herself, and everybody with half a brain knows it." He paused, squeezed her hand lightly. "What put a match to your fuse, Mandy?"

She could have told him it was what they'd said after that, about her, but that wouldn't have been the truth, either. She didn't much care what anybody thought of her—except Kade McKettrick. "My mother," she said miserably. "She was—she sold herself. She had to, or Cree and I would have gone hungry more often than we did."

"I reckon lots of women would do that if they had to. As if to illustrate his point, Mamie Sussex came out of the hotel just then, on Doc Boylen's arm.

The two went right on by, talking quietly, without noticing Mandy and Kade.

"I bet *your* mother wouldn't have," Mandy said. "She was a fine lady, I imagine."

"She was never put in that situation," Kade said reasonably. A smile warmed his voice, though Mandy couldn't quite bring herself to look at him. "She was spirited, though. One time, when Rafe was about ten or so, he took it in his head to play matador. Stole a red-and-white checkered tablecloth off the clothesline and headed for the bull pen. Ma took the fence in one leap, skirts and all, and faced off with that critter, all the while telling Rafe to git. The bull came at her, and she grabbed him right by the horns. The way I remember it, she wrestled him to the ground, but that part's probably my imagination."

Mandy sniffled again, picturing the scene and certain to the core of her being that her mama would have done the same thing, in the same circumstances. She'd just had one weakness, Dixie had, and that was men like Gig Curry, making pretty promises that were never kept. "Did she whup him afterwards?" she asked.

Kade chuckled. "The bull, or Rafe?" he teased. Then he sighed and stretched his legs out in front of him. They were long and strong, those legs, fit to take him places. "Ma didn't believe in violence, and that included tanning our hides, much to Pa's irritation. She made Rafe memorize the Book of Malachi and recite it back to her, word for word. He stayed clear of the bull after that."

Mandy laughed in spite of herself. "I wish I'd known her."

"Me, too," Kade agreed easily. Then, prompted by some inner shift, he sat up straight and tall again. "Mandy, I've got something on my mind."

She turned to him, curious. Everything had pulled tight inside her, all of a sudden, churning up a strange, sweet tension that made her feel vaguely scandalous.

"I was wondering if you'd marry me."

She stared at him. Blinked. "What did you say?"

"I think you heard me the first time."

"Why?" she blurted. "Why would you want to marry me, of all people, when you could have any one of those mail-order brides with a crook of your finger?"

"They aren't you," he said simply.

"I don't understand."

"I don't understand, either," Kade admitted with a long expulsion of breath. "And it isn't like my prospects are all that good. I might inherit the Triple M, if we don't lose it first, but it seems pretty unlikely, given that Emmeline is in the family way."

All Mandy could latch onto was his proposal. She might have accepted, if it had been another man asking, just to have a home and regular kin for a little while, but she couldn't bring herself to deceive Kade. Maybe it was because he seemed to understand about her mama, because he hadn't judged Dixie harshly and dismissed her as no-account, the way so many other people had.

"Kade, there's a Wild West show coming to town. When it pulls out, I plan on going with it."

"You're not Annie Oakley, Mandy," he said, as if it were going to come as a revelation to her.

"I could be," she replied, feeling prideful. "I can shoot as well as she can, and I can ride even better."

"Well, if that doesn't beat all," Kade said, and he sounded fractious.

She wanted him to understand, wanted that in the most desolate and hopeless way. "It's my chance to be somebody, Kade."

"You're somebody now."

"Somebody special," she clarified. She'd been to just one year of school, during a brief and peaceful stay with her aunt Dora, down in Waco, and gotten the foundations of reading, writing, and ciphering that way, building on her knowledge by happenstance after that, poring over whatever book she could beg, borrow, or steal. She had a lot of making up to do when it came to learning, and to living. She flat-out wasn't smart enough for a man like Kade, either, and if he didn't know that, she did.

"You're that, too. Special, I mean. Give this a chance, Mandy. Marry me, and if you're not happy, then you can just go your way."

She digested that. The idea was more attractive than she would have liked. She felt as if she were standing on the edge of a precipice, with a penchant to jump. "What if there's a baby?" she asked when she'd worked up the courage.

"I'd expect you to leave him with me, if you joined the circus."

"Not the circus," Mandy said, exasperated and not a little indignant. "Jim Dandy's Wild West Show."

"Same thing," Kade told her flatly. "Either way, it's no place for a child to grow up."

Mandy's thoughts were racing ahead of her, dragging her behind them over rough ground. A child, hers and Kade's. Tarnation, it would half kill her to give birth to a baby and then go off and leave the little thing behind. Maybe Kade knew that, was counting on it. "Why should I agree to a crazy idea like this?" she asked.

He turned her face, bent his head, and kissed her, lightly at first, and then with such thoroughness that she expected her stockings to roll down to her ankles.

"That's why," he said hoarsely, an eternity later, when he drew back.

She came up out of that kiss like a swimmer, plunged too deep, knowing neither up nor down, desperate to breathe. When she broke the surface, she gasped for air.

"No," she heard herself say. "No." But everything within her, every hope and instinct, every image of heaven, shouted *yes*.

37

"Fine," Kade said without apparent rancor. "If you won't marry me, then I guess I'd better get myself hitched to one of those brides as soon we can round up a preacher."

Mandy's mouth dropped open. She didn't know what she'd expected Kade's reaction to her refusal to be, but it certainly wasn't this instant and apparently easy shift of plans. "You're not serious," she said.

He got to his feet, his expression implacable in the relative darkness of the street. "Oh, yes," he said, sighing the words. "I reckon I'm about as serious as anybody has ever been about anything. I want that ranch."

"But Rafe and Emmeline are already expecting a baby. Emmeline told me about the contest."

"Until there actually *is* a baby," Kade said, "this game isn't over. I'm not taking any chances. I should have married one of those women first thing, but I thought—"

Mandy felt as though a mule had just bunched its haunches and kicked her square in the belly with both hind legs. She stood. "You thought what?" she asked, in a stricken whisper.

His voice was flat, void of all emotion. Mandy would have preferred fire, or even ice, to this bland resignation. "I thought you and I might be able to build something together. Something nobody's ever had before." He paused, the moonlight framing his broad shoulders and his hair, putting Mandy in mind of Saint George, the dragon slayer. Inwardly, she flinched. "Guess I was wrong."

With that, he walked back into the hotel, leaving Mandy to watch him go, feeling broken and furious, fighting an unbecoming urge to rush after him, say she'd changed her mind, anything to stop him from leaving her.

It was the memory of her mother, doing the same thing with Gig, begging, willing to pay any price for peace, that stopped her.

Inside the hotel, Kade stopped, wanting to go back. Ask for Mandy's hand again, this time using pretty words. Damnation, he was a fool. Jeb would have known better than to state his case so bluntly; he would have quoted poetry, gazed into Mandy's eyes, told her he loved her, whether it was true or not. Hell, even Rafe, with all his brawling and blundering ways, could have shown him up in the romance department.

He might have turned on his heel and tried another proposal out on Mandy if it hadn't been for Marvella. She materialized out of the crowd, looking all warm and curvy and willing, and slipped an arm through his.

"You look lonely," she said.

She had that right. Just then, Kade felt as though the whole universe had dissolved, leaving him with nowhere to stand. "I'd be obliged if you'd dance with me." The words came out gravelly, making him wish he'd cleared his throat before speaking. Something curdled in the pit of his stomach.

Marvella batted her thick eyelashes and smiled. "Best offer

I've had all evening," she said, and pulled him into the flow of dancers.

It wasn't so bad, squiring Marvella around the floor, and it got better when he caught sight of Mandy out of the corner of his eye, standing just inside the doors and watching him as though she'd never seen him before.

After Marvella, he danced with Abigail, and after that, he lost track, but he was always conscious of Mandy, as if the two of them were linked by an invisible cord. He noticed when she danced with Jeb and seethed with private rage when one soldier after another offered her his arm, but he never once glanced in her direction.

He finally decided on the redhead, Jeanette. He liked her hair, and she made a decent pie.

"Will you marry me?" he asked at the end of a waltz.

She stared at him, flustered at first, then visibly pleased. "Well," she said. "Yes."

He squeezed her hand and smiled, wondering why he didn't just go out behind the hotel and cut his throat. It would have been more direct, and less painful. "Good," he said. "Let's get it over with."

Jeanette blinked. "Now?"

"Why not? I need a wife and a baby, in that order."

She paled. "What about a courtship?"

"I don't have time for a courtship." He could feel Mandy watching him; a flush crept up his neck. He took a firmer grip on Jeanette's hand and half dragged her toward the stairway.

She resisted, but only a little. "Mr. McKettrick—"

He looked back at her. "What?" he snapped.

"Where are we going?"

He realized then that she thought he was hauling her straight to bed, and softened slightly. "I'm going to make the announcement."

"Oh," she said, and followed more willingly.

It seemed like everybody in the room took note of their progress; Rafe stopped right in the middle of a dance with Emmeline, his eyes watchful, and Angus, Concepcion glowing beside him, wore a curious, faintly amused expression. Kade came to a halt in the middle of the stairs, Jeanette breathless and blushing beside him.

The music stumbled to a tinny halt.

"Jeanette and I are getting married," Kade said bluntly. "Soon as we can round up the padre."

The silence was ominous.

Angus frowned and sought Mandy with a piercing gaze. Rafe glowered and raised his eyebrows, and Holt shook his head, looking bewildered. Jeb stood with his arms folded and his face set in stone.

Kade didn't dare look at any of the other brides. He just hoped none of them were armed.

Somebody clapped, tentatively, and stopped when no one else joined in.

Mandy made her way through the party to stand at the base of the stairs, staring up at Kade.

"All right." Her voice was quiet, but it seemed to ring from the walls. "You win."

Jeanette began to fidget. "I don't think—"

Kade was watching Mandy, unable to look away. He let go of Jeanette's small, sweaty hand, and she made a dash for it.

As far as Kade was concerned, there was no one else in the world besides him and Mandy. The whole party receded into a dizzying blur of featureless faces and dim colors. "You mean it?" he asked. "You'll marry me?"

"Fifty horses and whatever you've got in your bank account," Mandy said, looking neither to left nor right, her chin at an obstinate angle. "That's the deal."

"What about the baby?"

Her chin rose another notch, her eyes flashed. "That's something separate." It didn't sound as if she meant to give any ground. "If I go, any children we have go with me."

Kade swallowed. He'd met his match in this woman; life with her would be an up-and-down proposition. Anything could happen. "All right," he conceded. Somehow, someway, he'd win out over the Wild West shows of the world and make her want to stay. He'd worry about the how part of it later. "All right." He put out his hand.

Mandy hesitated, then mounted the steps and put her hand in his. Side by side, they faced their baffled audience. Angus's face came into focus first, and it was at once rigid and hopeful. Plainly, the old man was torn between offering his congratulations and taking a horse whip to his middle son, then and there.

Concepcion, her eyes shining, gave Angus a little push in their direction, but Becky was the first to reach them, hugging Mandy and then Kade. "You got it right after all," she told Kade. "For a minute there, I was worried."

Kade waited for his tongue to climb back up out of his throat, then glanced down at Mandy, standing stiffly, her hand hot in his. She indicated Jeanette, cloistered in the center of the little band of brides, with a nod of her head.

"Apologize to that woman," she said in an undertone, "or I'll skin you alive."

"Now?" Kade asked, taken aback. In point of fact, he'd intended to do just that, but it stung that Mandy thought she had to goad him into it.

"Now," Mandy said.

Kade squared his shoulders, let go of Mandy's hand, and excused himself as he edged past Becky to do as he was bidden.

The brides, all of them flushed and flashing, planted their feet and wouldn't have parted to let him through if Jeanette hadn't pushed her way to the fore.

"I'm sorry," Kade said. The words were inadequate, but they were all he had to offer at the moment.

To his chagrin, Jeanette smiled. "That's all right."

"It *isn't* 'all right,'" Mandy put in from somewhere near Kade's right elbow. "He used you. He deserves to be put in his place!"

Jeanette's smile was steady, and Kade wished the floorboards would part so he could drop through. "Looks like you can manage that just fine," Jeanette said. "Anyway, I want a man who wants me. It's obvious that Mr. McKettrick prefers you."

The brides turned away as one, in a sniffing huff. Jeanette lingered a moment, saying nothing, her gracious manner filling Kade with shame, then Holt asked her for a dance, and she let him lead her away into a busy, determined resurrection of music.

"You're a skunk," Mandy said, and marched off to dance with a soldier.

A brisk tap on Kade's shoulder brought him back from the haze.

"May I have a word with you?" Jeb asked amiably. "Outside?"

"Sure," Kade said, confused.

Jeb made for the doors, and Kade followed. On the sidewalk, in a wash of light from inside, the two brothers faced each other.

"What?" Kade asked, feeling peevish and, at the same time, grateful for a timely rescue.

"This." And then Jeb landed a haymaker in the middle of Kade's face, dropping him to his knees.

Kade shook his head, one hand to his bleeding mouth, confused. "What was that for?" he asked, as Jeb helped him to his feet.

"For being an asshole, that's what," Jeb hissed back. Then he just stood there, waiting for the fight to begin. "You had no call to shame that woman in front of a whole town."

"I reckon I had it coming then." Kade had been wanting a row, and here was his chance, but he couldn't seem to work up the steam. In Jeb's place, he would have done the same thing.

Just then, Rafe joined them, coatless and pushing up his sleeves. He stopped when he saw Kade was already bleeding.

"Well, hell," he said, shifting his narrowed gaze to Jeb for a moment. "You beat me to it."

"Damned if I didn't," Jeb said with grim satisfaction, rubbing his scraped knuckles.

Rafe was never one to leave well enough alone. He jabbed an index finger into the middle of Kade's chest. "You know better than to treat a lady like that," he growled. This from a man who had made his wife's acquaintance while lying on his back in front of a saloon.

"I said I was sorry," Kade retorted, feeling indignant. It was one thing to take a punch, and another to stand still for a tirade.

"Not sorry enough," Rafe replied. And then, with no more warning than Jeb had given, he set the heels of both palms against Kade's chest and shoved him backward into the horse trough.

He came up sputtering, wet to the skin, covered with scum, and mad as a newly castrated bull. Shaking the water from his face, he gripped the sides of the trough and started to thrust himself out, only to be knocked smartly down again, this time by the sole of somebody's boot making contact with his chest.

He expected to see Rafe when he surfaced again, but the frame looming at the foot of the trough was Holt's.

"If I were you," came the familiar Texas drawl, "I'd just stay right there awhile and consider the error of my ways."

Speechless, Kade looked from Holt to Rafe to Jeb. They all stared back at him, their arms folded, their expressions hard.

"Shit," he said.

One by one, his brothers turned their backs on him and went into the hotel to rejoin the festivities.

Kade rose slowly out of the water, dripping and cursing under his breath. The bottom of the trough was slippery with algae, and his boots were full. Pride demanded that he follow the three of them inside and have an accounting, but reason protested that he'd already made enough of a fool of himself for one night.

He went to the jailhouse instead, where he had another set of clothes.

Harry and Old Billy stared at him, opened their mouths to ask what had happened. He glared them both into silence.

Gig Curry was not so easily intimidated. Gripping the bars and grinning, he looked Kade up and down. "Looks like you got your comeuppance from somebody," he said, pleased. "Wish I'd been there to see it."

Kade peeled off his ruined coat and threw it on the floor with a splat. "Shut the hell up."

Harry fetched him a dry shirt and trousers from the trunk in the second cell.

"You and Billy can go now," he told the boy.

Harry's eyes were wide. "You sure?"

"Just go."

Reluctantly, they obeyed.

"All these doings have something to do with Mandy?" Gig speculated, when Kade had exchanged wet clothes for dry and commenced to building up the fire in the stove.

Kade ignored him. Slammed the door on the blaze he'd just fed.

"She's trouble, that little gal," Curry warned gleefully.

"You'll get no argument from me, not on that score, at least."

Wisely, perhaps reading a warning in Kade's bearing, Curry subsided, but he sat humming in his cell, pleased.

38

Kade was beginning to wonder if Mandy had changed her mind about marrying him when, later that evening, after his prisoner had settled down to snoring, the door of the jailhouse creaked open to admit a female figure.

The sudden leap in his chest dwindled to a flutter when he recognized Emmeline.

"Are you all right?" she asked, crossing the room to peer at his sore and swollen lip.

He did not want to be fussed over or mollycoddled; in truth, he did not even want to be noticed, but there was no escaping Emmeline's concerned examination. "I'm *fine*," he grumbled.

She frowned, her gaze still fixed on the place where Jeb's punch had landed with the impact of a boxcar rolling downhill. "You don't *look* fine. Maybe I ought to fetch Doc."

Kade thrust himself up out of his chair, rising on a swell of impatience. "*No*, Emmeline. Just let me be."

She smiled, undaunted by his temper. As a McKettrick wife, she'd learned to mark off a piece of ground and plant her heels on it. "Not a few people would say you got what you deserved." Her expression turned serious and her hands came to rest on her hips. "That was a disgraceful thing you did, dragging poor Jeanette up in front of the whole town and saying you were going to marry her, when all the time you really wanted Mandy."

Kade flushed. "Maybe it was."

"Maybe, nothing. You're lucky Mandy had the courage to step in. You might have ruined her life and Jeanette's, not to mention your own."

He shoved a hand through his hair. "What the devil do you people want from me? I apologized to the woman, and my brothers took it out of my hide."

Emmeline raised an eyebrow, surveying him pensively. "Do you think saying you're sorry is enough? Talk is cheap, Kade. Unless you do things differently from now on, your apology isn't worth a puddle of horse pee."

A chuckle escaped him, rueful and raw. "Is that any way for a lady to talk?"

Emmeline was still framing her answer when the first shot splintered the door of the jailhouse.

Without thinking, Kade grabbed her by the arm and thrust her hard to the floor behind his desk, crouching beside her as another bullet fragmented the window.

"Stay down!" he ordered, jerking open the bottom drawer of John's desk and grabbing the .38 he kept there for emergencies. His own gun was way over by the door, holstered and hanging from a peg.

"What's happening?" Emmeline whispered, pale, one hand resting on her abdomen.

Outside, horses whinnied and stomped, and a man's voice shouted, "Send Curry out!"

After another glance at Emmeline, Kade made his way across

the floor, scrambling like a monkey, the pistol heavy in his hand. "The hell I will!" he yelled back. He took a chance, stole a glance out the broken window, and nearly got his right ear shot off for his trouble.

Probably a dozen men were in the street, mounted, their faces in shadow. He hadn't recognized any of them in that instant of looking.

"I told you they'd come!" Curry shouted exultantly from his cell. "You're a dead man, Marshal!"

"Stay down and shut up," Kade responded, still hunkered down under the window.

"Kade," Emmeline said, and her voice sounded weak.

Dread struck Kade, real as a bullet, and shattered something inside him. "Are you hit?" he asked, making his way back as more shots thunked against the walls and clanked off the stove.

She grasped his hand when he reached her, shook her head. "I don't think so," she whispered, and he realized that he'd been holding his breath. "I'm scared, Kade."

"Don't be. If they get to you, it'll be over my dead body."

There in his cage, Curry laughed like a demon. "A man can always hope," he said.

"It's Rafe I'm worried about," Emmeline confided, in a desperate whisper. "Rafe and the others. They'll come to help. They'll be out in the open."

He squeezed her hand. "They're not idiots, Emmeline. Rafe will come, but he won't make a target out of himself, and Jeb is the fastest gun I've ever seen." That last part wasn't something he would normally have admitted, except under pressure.

Behind them, another shot sounded, and Curry let out a yelp.

"Christ," he gasped, "somebody just tried to shoot me through the window! They're looking to *kill* me!"

Kade swore under his breath, pushed Emmeline as far into the well of the desk as he could, and sighted in on the tiny, barred opening in the cell wall. Sure enough, the shape of a man loomed there, probably on the back of a horse. Kade took aim and fired, there was a cry, and the shadow gave way to a flow of moonlight.

Outside, there was more shooting, and more shouting. Then the thunder of hooves. The door crashed open, and Kade heard a blessed sound.

Rafe's voice: "Kade!"

An hour before, he'd been ready to come up out of that horse trough and tear his brother apart, limb by limb. Now, he was hard put not to kiss his boots. "I'm here," Kade responded.

The shooting receded farther and farther into the distance. Kade got to his feet.

"Are you all right?" Rafe demanded, furious with concern.

Kade set the .38 on the desktop and took in the damage to the place. Curry was unhit, having crawled clean under his cot, but the stove was dented, the front window was a memory, and everything was pockmarked. He nodded in answer to Rafe's question, catching his breath, and leaned down to offer Emmeline a hand up.

Rafe's eyes bulged at the sight of her. He gasped her name.

She took a stumbling step toward her husband, faltered, and fell.

Rafe rushed to her, knelt, gathered her into his arms. The look on his face was terrible to see; he crushed her against his chest, felt frantically for wounds.

Her lashes fluttered; she reached up to touch Rafe's cheek. "The baby. Oh, Rafe—the baby."

That was when Kade saw the blood staining the skirts of her party gown.

"Sweet Jesus," he gasped.

Rafe's gaze hooked into his and held. "This is your fault."

"Rafe," Emmeline interjected. "No—"

"You wanted this to happen!" Rafe spat. He got to his feet, a big man, awkward in his grace, Emmeline resting broken in his embrace. He glared at Kade for another infinite moment, then turned and rushed out.

Kade stood stricken in the center of his ruined office.

This is your fault.

You wanted this to happen.

Rafe was wrong on the second count, he thought, as something inside him shuddered mightily and then crumbled, but the first was another matter. If he hadn't earned himself a punch in the mouth from Jeb and a dousing in the horse trough from Rafe, Emmeline would not have been there when the shooting started.

39

FOUR MEN WERE lying sprawled dead in the street, but Mandy didn't stop to see if she knew any of them from the old days. Angus had held her back when the shooting had started and had let her go only when Jeb and Holt and most of the other men at Becky's party had chased the outlaws out of town. Only one person was on her mind from the beginning to the end, and she sought him with her eyes, with her heart, as she burst through the doorway at the jailhouse.

Kade stood in the middle of the floor, his head bowed, his hands limp at his sides.

She went to him. Hesitated, then put her arms around him.

He let his forehead rest on her crown, drew in a deep breath, and embraced her, tentatively at first, then with a ferocious need. She felt wetness seep through the strands of her hair to rest, warm, on her scalp.

"Emmeline," he ground out. "She was here—"

"Shhh," Mandy said.

"I threw her down—didn't want her to get hit—she's bleeding."

She held him.

"I didn't mean—Rafe thinks—"

"Shhh," she said again. She pulled back, took his hand. "Come on. We're going home."

"I can't," he protested. "The prisoner—"

"Damn the prisoner," Mandy replied, and led her man out of the wreckage.

Kade was in a stupor. Jeb, Holt, and the others had returned, most of their horses wandering loose in the street, and he knew without being told that they'd lost the outlaws in the darkness. Jeb, squatting beside one of the bodies, caught Kade's eye, stood, and walked toward him.

"That one," he said, inclining his head toward the corpse he'd just left, "is Jesse Graves. He gave Becky some grief at the dance tonight." His gaze narrowed; the keenness of it cut like a fresh-stropped blade. "Kade?" he prompted.

Kade tried to shake off his mental fog, but it wasn't going anywhere. He thrust a hand through his hair, while Mandy's grasp tightened on the other one. "Emmeline," he said miserably.

Jeb laid a hand on his shoulder, the same one he'd used to fatten Kade's lip earlier in the evening. "What about her?"

"She shouldn't have been there," Kade muttered. "I pushed her down, out of the line of fire, and—I think she's losing the baby."

Jeb ducked his head for a moment, and his hold on Kade's shoulder tightened briefly. He looked at Mandy, saw something in her face, and turned his gaze back to Kade. "I suppose Rafe blames you?" His voice was quiet.

Kade nodded. "Yeah."

"He's probably out of his head, Kade. In time, he'll see reason."

Kade wished he could be so certain. "There's another man behind the jailhouse. I shot him through the cell window."

"We'll see to him," Jeb said. His gaze shifted to Mandy, and something unspoken passed between them.

"Anybody recognize any of the riders before they got away?" Kade asked.

"One of them was Davy Kincaid," Harry put in from somewhere nearby. "He comes to our place sometimes, to see Ma."

Kade's blood froze at the realization that Harry had been close by when the bullets were flying. He didn't dare turn toward the kid; if he did, he might shake him out of sheer relief. Instead, he focused his thoughts on Kincaid. He'd never really known Davy, who had a reputation for drinking a mite too much, but he'd seen him around a time or two, and he'd met his slow-witted brother, Avery, once, a couple of years back, when Kade was riding fence lines. Caught out by a freak snowstorm, he'd holed up in one of the line shacks to wait for better weather, and Avery had sought shelter there, too, coatless and wild-eyed, saying nary a word and hunkering down in the corner all night, like a dog expecting to be whipped. In the morning, Kade had awakened to find Avery gone, along with half his own rations and some tobacco. He'd shaken his head and put the incident aside, not being one to dwell overmuch on the curious workings of other men's minds. The convolutions of his own kept him busy enough, most times.

Now, it seemed to Kade, it was time to get to know the Kincaids a little better. He'd start by paying a call on them, first thing in the morning. In the meantime, he needed to lick his wounds.

"What you require is a posse," said Sam Fee, stepping out of the crowd. He wasn't a big man, but he looked able, and agile, too. "I'd be willing to sign on."

Considering that his place had been burned to the ground, and the McKettrick brand left behind, putting a signature to a clear statement, Kade was taken aback by the offer. "I didn't figure you were on our side," Kade said.

"I been talking to John Lewis," Fee replied grimly. "He said it was probably that outlaw in there that burned our place, not the McKettricks. His word is good enough for me."

"Obliged," Kade said, conscious of Mandy beside him, holding his hand. He wondered what she'd think if she knew she was holding him upright.

After Sam stepped forward, a dozen other people volunteered, cowboys mostly, some from the Triple M, and some from the Circle C, but one or two townsmen threw in with them, too, including Ben Hopper, the manager of the telegraph office, and Wiley Kline, who printed the newspaper. They made plans to meet in front of the marshal's office at sunrise, ready to ride, and the crowd finally dispersed.

Kade looked around, found Jeb standing close by. "I'll keep watch here at the jail," Jeb said. "You go on back to the hotel with Mandy."

Mandy tugged at Kade's hand. "There's nothing more you can do tonight," she urged. "Let's go."

He went.

40

BECKY SAT STIFFLY by John's bedside, holding his hand and wait-ing. Her eyes ached with tears that would not be shed, no matter how vast the need, and she was past coherent thought, wandering in a reverie of sorrow.

Lamplight bathed her beloved's gaunt face, and he opened his eyes. "I heard shots," he said weakly. "What happened?"

"Some thugs tried to break Gig Curry out of jail to kill him, evidently," Becky said.

"Anybody hurt?"

She swallowed, looked away, shook her head. It was a lie, and he probably knew it: Emmeline was down at Doc's office right at that moment, probably losing her baby, and Becky felt as though her own soul were being torn asunder, but she could not leave John, not now. It was Rafe's place to be with Emmeline, but knowing that didn't ease her grief.

"You just concentrate on pulling through," she said thickly, tightening her grip on his hand, as if she might somehow hold him back from the beyond, keep him with her for a little while longer.

He raised their clasped hands to his mouth, kissed her knuckles lightly. She felt an echo of the sweet shivers his touch had so easily stirred in her before the framework of creation itself had buckled at its core and come crashing down around her, pillar by pillar. "Somehow," he labored to say, "I'm going to find a way to stick by you, Becky, and I won't let the grave stop me. Once I know for sure that you're going to be all right, I might move on to whatever's next, but until that day, I'll be waiting, just on the other side of your next heartbeat."

Her throat closed with the intensity of all she felt. "I love you," she said. She'd uttered those words too seldom in her life, and heard them too rarely, until she'd met John. Now, they were infinitely precious, all that was important or true.

"I know," he said quietly. "And I love you. But I don't want you wasting your tears over me, Becky, now or when I'm gone, and I won't have you wearing black and pining for me, either. You've got to promise that you'll live as long and as well as you can. Emmeline needs you, and so do a lot of other folks."

She put her free hand over her face and let out the small, desolate sob that had been strangling her. "Can't you stay?" she asked, moments later. "Can't you hold on, and get well—for me?"

He shook his head. "The decision wasn't mine to make, but it's been made all the same. I've had my turn."

She wept openly then, from the depths of her shattered soul. She'd begun to hope again when she met John, to believe and trust in fate. Now, he was slipping away. "It isn't fair," she protested. "We didn't have enough time."

He smiled. "I don't think eternity itself would be enough time." He was weakening, and yet something was gathering in him, visible in his eyes, something he wanted to say before it was too late. "We need to talk about Chloe. I asked Kade to send for her, but I don't think she's going to get here soon enough, if she comes at all."

Becky smoothed his forehead, trying to erase the worries that furrowed his fine brow. "Your daughter."

John let out a deep sigh. "I'm sorry now that I never told you more about her." Every word was costing him, and Becky wanted to tell him to save his strength, but she knew it would be wrong. He had a right to die in his own way, and to empty himself of words first, if that was what he needed to do. "We were never married, Chloe's mother and I. Rachel found herself a respectable husband while I was in prison, though, and they raised Chloe together, in Sacramento. I've visited her a few times—Chloe, I mean—but she thought I was an uncle."

"I wouldn't have minded knowing about Rachel, John. It isn't like I thought you'd lived your life as a monk."

John chuckled hoarsely. "Rachel hasn't mattered to me in a long time. I'm not sure why I couldn't bring myself to talk more about my little girl, though. Maybe because it hurt too damn much, and I was a coward."

"You might be a lot of things, John Lewis," Becky scolded, watching him through a glaze of tears, "but you're no coward. Some things are just too private to share with anybody, that's all."

"Chloe'll be a handful, if she shows up at all," John went on, with a mixture of amusement and fond lamentation. "I've had half a dozen letters from my daughter over the years—like I said, she thinks I'm a brother to her late pa—and she is not one to hold back on her opinions. She'll have a lot of questions once the truth comes out, and she'll make some judgments, too. Maybe harsh ones."

Becky dashed away her tears and smiled. "You're saying she's headstrong."

He rolled his eyes. "Now there's an understatement for you. Chloe is a pain in the hind end, is what she is. She's full of fire, but she's mine and I love her."

"Then I'll love her, too, if she'll let me," Becky promised. "One more willful woman oughtn't to make much difference around here."

John gave a raspy, rattling chuckle. "Oh, she'll make a difference, all right. Brace yourself, Becky. And warn everybody who'll listen."

She was astonished that some laughter was still left in her, for all that her heart was breaking. "You make her sound more like a hurricane than a young woman." Humor twinkled in John's pain-weary eyes, and she knew she would cherish the memory of it, along with so many other things about him, most of them profoundly ordinary.

"That's a fitting description of her nature," John said with certainty, and then they were quiet for a long time. "Once she hits this town, things will never be the same."

"Maybe that's good," Becky allowed gently. "Indian Rock could use some shaking up."

They fell into an easy if poignant silence after that.

When John closed his eyes for the last time an hour later, Becky didn't move, or let go of his hand, nor did she call for anyone to come and hear the news. She just sat, still as a snowy morning, listening to the steady ticking of the mantel clock, the sound bearing her, against her formidable will, into a world where there was no John Lewis.

41

MANDY LOOKED NEITHER to right nor left as she brought Kade through the now empty and darkened lobby of the Arizona Hotel, up the stairs, and into the small room at the end of the hall.

There, once again, she took him into her arms.

"Mandy," he whispered, and it seemed to her that one word became a small universe in itself, that it held all his misgivings, all his hopes, all his sorrows.

"Just now. That's all we're going to think about, Kade. Now." She splayed her fingers and buried them in his hair.

He kissed her, and everything inside her, everything real, rose to meet him in some strange and singular space, heretofore undreamed of, let alone explored, rarefied and apart from commonplace things like floors and walls and windows.

The kiss deepened, and when it was over, Kade cupped her face in both his hands and held her firmly. "Mandy, you have to be sure."

She merely nodded. She'd never been more certain of anything in her life; there could be no going back.

He lifted her into his arms, carried her to the narrow bed where she had dreamed alone, so many nights, since coming to Indian Rock. She knew that when she rose from it again, she would be a different person, for better or worse, and she was glad.

The light of the moon gilded his hair, rimmed his head and shoulders. For what seemed like a long time, he simply gazed down at her. When she extended her arms, he lay down beside her, and touched her as gently as any man had ever touched a woman.

They were a long time shedding their clothes—a button here, a sleeve there—the process was a ritual of ancient magic, full of mystery. Presently, they were both naked, and the spell deepened even as their caresses became more urgent.

"Mandy," he said again, braced on his elbows as he lay between her legs. It was a question, it was a statement, it was a plea.

"Yes," she said simply.

He entered her then in one powerful thrust, and the pain was blinding, but joyous as well.

"Dear God, Mandy," Kade rasped. "You've never been with a man."

Fire seized her in the wake of the sweet injury he'd done her; she ceased being one woman and became all women. She laughed softly, and hers was the mirth of a goddess set loose from her bonds, free to soar. "That," she answered breathlessly, "might have been true a moment ago."

She felt a charge of passion surge through him, answered in her own body, and she was more than flesh, she was essence.

"Sweet God," he muttered, "I thought—"

"Never mind what you *thought*, Kade McKettrick," Mandy gasped, straining to take everything that was this man, seen and unseen, inside her. "Stop talking and make love to me!"

He laughed at that, a ragged sound, purely masculine, and began to move upon her, slowly and with a consummate control that soon drove her straight into madness.

Mandy lost herself in that madness, willingly, in celebration of everything holy.

There would be time enough for penance in the morning.

Kade was gone when Mandy opened her eyes to the first pinkish gray threads of dawn. She lay still a few moments, letting her melted limbs turn solid again, fighting off an army of regrets and expectations, clinging to the sweet peace of her soul.

She heard horses and men in the street below, quiet voices in the hallway outside.

Last night, she'd been to heaven; today, she might see the far horizons of hell. She got out of bed, washed, and dressed, putting on trousers, a shirt, and boots.

She met Becky in the hallway, a brave and befuddled wraith, holding herself together by God knew what means.

"Emmeline lost the baby," Becky said.

Tears sprang to Mandy's eyes, and words failed her.

"John—" Becky paused, reached out to set one hand against the wall, as if to keep her balance. She drew a deep, tremulous breath, met Mandy's blurred gaze. "He's gone, Mandy. What will I do without him?"

A sob caught in Mandy's throat; she went to Becky and took her into her arms, held her hard. She wasn't sure whether she was giving comfort or taking it—both, perhaps.

They clung to each other, two women, one broken, one newly made.

"I won't say it'll be all right," Mandy said.

"Don't you dare." Becky stepped back, clasping Mandy's hands, and took in her riding clothes. "You're going . . . ?"

"With Kade. If he'll let me."

Becky shook her head. "Mandy—"

"He's headed out after those outlaws. I have to be there, even if I can't do anything."

Becky started to protest, stopped herself, and nodded. "I think you're a damn fool, Amanda Rose, but I understand. I'd have done the same thing for John, I suppose." She squeezed Mandy's hand. "God help us both."

"Amen to that," Mandy said ruefully. Then she hugged Becky once more and left her, descending the stairs in a hurry.

42

THE POSSE GATHERED in front of the jailhouse at dawn, as agreed the night before. Captain Harvey and his troops presented themselves, grim faced and ready to ride, as did Jeb and Holt and a good many of the townsmen and ranch hands from every spread within a hundred miles. Kade, fresh from Mandy's bed, where he'd known impossible delights, had been met with two kinds of bad news when he reached the street: Emmeline had miscarried in the night, and John Lewis was dead. He felt disjointed, torn between the pleasure he'd known with Mandy and pure sorrow.

Then he spotted her, his attention veering toward her like scattered metal shavings scrambling for a magnet. She kept to the back of the crowd, mounted astride Sister, the pinto mare, and carrying the spanking-new shotgun he'd bought himself at the mercantile.

He strode between horses and men to stand looking up into Mandy's stubborn face. Her eyes were red-rimmed, probably from weeping over John and Emmeline, her hair was tucked up into an old hat, and her chin stuck out.

"Get off that horse and go back to the hotel, where you belong," Kade said evenly, taking hold of the bridle. He'd had no choice but to set his own grief aside, to be reckoned with later. John would want those outlaws caught, first and foremost, and Emmeline would recover, if there was a God in heaven. In the meantime, Kade was determined to fix his mind on the job at hand—finding the gang that had shot up the jailhouse—and he meant to see the task through, no matter what it took.

"I'm not accountable to you, Kade McKettrick, not yet, anyway," Mandy said, with a toss of her head. "I can ride and I can shoot, and the plain fact is, you need my help, whether that sets well with you or not."

Kade closed his eyes, counted mentally, accompanied by a murmur of laughter from the rest of the posse, the members of which had obviously been listening shamelessly, then looked at her again. "What I need," he said, in what he hoped was a reasonable tone of voice, "is to know that you're safe. If you really want to help me, Mandy, you'll stay here and look after Becky and Emmeline."

She probably didn't give a damn whether he was worried about her or not, but he could tell that he'd gotten to her, and he didn't hesitate to press his advantage.

"How are they holding up?" he asked.

Mandy raked her lower lip with her teeth, sniffled once. "Becky's staring at the wall of her room like she can see right through it, and she won't talk to anybody. I haven't seen Emmeline."

Then Rafe appeared, leading his horse and looking like a man who'd just spent the night wrestling with the devil.

Kade left off arguing with Mandy, for the moment, and approached his brother. "What are you doing here?" he asked quietly. There was an incendiary element to Rafe's countenance, as if he'd explode at a single spark.

Rafe wouldn't meet Kade's eyes, and maybe that was for the best. "Same thing you are," he said. "We've all got a stake in this."

Kade wanted to lay a hand on Rafe's shoulder, the only way he knew to offer comfort, but he didn't dare; everything about Rafe warned him to stay clear. So he held back, not for his own sake, but for his brother's. "I'm sorry about the baby."

"Better if we don't talk about that just yet." Then Rafe turned his back on Kade and swung up into the saddle.

Kade stood for a moment, absorbing yet more grief, then turned back to Mandy.

Her chin remained at that familiar, obstinate angle. "Rafe was right," she said. "I've got a stake in this, just like everybody else."

"Are we set to ride, Marshal?" one of the men called from the safety of anonymity. "Or are you going to stand out here jawing with the little woman all day?" This query was followed by a few others, all of them calculated to get right under Kade's hide, which they surely did.

He simply watched Mandy, willing her to give him a break. "Think about Emmeline," he said. "If you were in her place, and she were in yours, what would you want her to do?"

Mandy's cheeks went bright pink and her eyes snapped with rebellion. "Damn you, Kade, that isn't fair."

He raised an eyebrow, waited.

"Oh, all right," she said in the end. Then she reined the pinto around and rode off toward the hotel, her head high and her back straight. On the one hand, he was relieved, considering that he would have been forced to lock her up someplace if she hadn't seen reason. On the other, he felt knee-high to a bedbug, seeing the slack in her shoulders as she rode away.

43

With Old Billy guarding the prisoner and Mandy headed for the hotel, Kade mounted up and divided the posse into smaller groups, sending each one in a different direction, some looking for tracks, some fanning out over the countryside. Captain Harvey and his men went their own way, while Kade and Holt and two men from the Circle C set off for the timberline, and the Kincaid place.

It took nearly two hours of hard riding to reach the shack of a cabin, which was wedged up against a cliff of red rock, affording the residents a clear view of anyone approaching, and plenty of time to prepare.

Their greeting came in the form of a rifle shot, missing Holt's head by two inches and splitting the trunk of a mesquite tree behind him. The oldest man Kade had ever seen came hobbling and wobbling out of the cabin, clad in faded red long johns and mincing along on bare feet. He carried an old carbine, its barrel still smoking from the howdy, and he was already reloading.

"Hold your fire, you old coot," Holt called out to him. "We're not here to make trouble and we sure as hell don't want any from you."

Kade wouldn't necessarily have put it that way; if Davy Kincaid was around, there would be trouble for sure. The place had an empty look about it, but that didn't mean much of anything. Avery was not the sociable sort, and Davy might take a shot at them at any moment, from any point on the compass. Only difference was, he wasn't likely to miss, the way his pappy had.

Kade rode straight up to the scrawny little figure in the union suit, touched the brim of his hat by way of saying hello. "We're looking for your boy Davy," he said, straight out. Obviously, Pappy Kincaid wasn't the patient sort.

"Ain't here," Pappy said, and spat. "Polecat. He took my three dollars and half the ammunition I had. How's a man supposed to defend hisself and his property, I ask you, without no bullets?"

"Don't rightly know," Kade allowed. "That is a problem." He shifted in the saddle. "You have any idea where Davy might be now? Maybe I could get your money and shells back for you, if I could find him."

Pappy looked a little more interested, now that his grievances had been addressed. His toothless mouth worked furiously, gumming at something, and his eyes went squinty and narrow. "You one of them McKettricks?" he asked. "You put me in mind of a fella I knew once. Angus was his name. Big Scotsman from down Texas way. Mean sum-bitch."

Kade suppressed a smile, though he felt tension coiled in the pit of his stomach, like a snake. "I'm a McKettrick, all right." He leaned in the saddle to put out a hand. "Name's Kade." He wouldn't have predicted it, but the man he'd privately dubbed Pappy responded with a handshake. "Angus would be my pa."

Pappy drew back his hand, wiped it unconsciously on the stained bottoms of his skivvies. A look passed between Kade and

Holt, tinged with amusement and shared curiosity. "He's a sum-bitch," the old man repeated.

Holt leaned on the pommel of his saddle, pushed his hat to the back of his head. His tone was conversational, with a conspiratorial note to it. Kade felt his neck redden, even though he knew well enough what Cavanagh was up to. "I've got my own score to settle with Angus McKettrick," he said easily. "What's yours?"

"Took my cattle, that's what he did. Had me two good heifers and a bull, and he just *took* 'em. Said I'd stolt 'em from his herd. Lyin' sum-bitch. His wife gave me them critters herself. I tolt him that a couple of days after her funeral, and he still wouldn't give 'em back. Drunk as a fish, he was. Had me thrown clean off his place."

Kade had gone still inside. He recalled the incident clearly, now that he'd been reminded. Back then, Angus had been wild with grief, and he wouldn't have been inclined to listen to anybody, least of all a crazy old man trying to lay claim to three head of cattle. The truth was, Georgia McKettrick had cut the heifers from the herd herself, and turned them over to Kincaid personally, telling him to come back for one of the bulls. Kade had witnessed the whole exchange, but he'd forgotten in the storm of sorrow that had swept over the Triple M after his mother's passing.

"You'll have your cattle," Kade said. At the corner of his eye, he saw Avery slinking toward them on foot, out of the scrub pine trees at the timberline. He didn't appear to be armed.

Pappy stared up at Kade, squinting. "You mean it, mister? You really gonna make this thing right, after all this time?"

"Yes, sir, I am," he said. "Avery's not fixing to do anything stupid, is he?"

"You just never know with Avery," Pappy replied sagely.

Avery hid behind the chicken coop. Kade turned his horse and rode slowly toward him. "I'm looking for your brother."

Avery was thin, and as bald as his father, though he couldn't have been more than twenty. His eyes were bulbous, giving him a buglike air. "You got any more tobacco?"

Kade smiled. Seemed like Avery wasn't so crazy as folks thought; he obviously remembered the snowy night at the line shack well enough, for all the time that had passed since then, and the pilfering he'd done while Kade had slept. "I might have. And I might not. Depends on whether or not you can tell me where Davy is right now."

Avery looked all around, as if to make sure nobody had crept up close enough to listen in. "I reckon he could be with that red-headed woman in town, the one with all the kids."

Kade shook his head. "He's not there. Your brother's in some trouble. Where does Davy hide out when he feels a need to lie low, Avery?" Kade took a half dozen cheroots from the inside of his coat pocket—all he had—and showed them to the other man.

Kincaid swallowed visibly. "I ain't supposed to tell nobody nothin'. That's what Davy said. Said he'd break my toes one by one if I did."

Kade made sure he looked properly reluctant and moved to put the cheroots back in his pocket.

"Wait," Avery said. "He warned me agin' talkin', but he never said nothing about showing somebody the way."

Kade tossed down one of the cheroots, along with a wooden match, and Avery made a handy catch.

"Don't you go running your mouth, boy!" Pappy ordered, gimping in their direction, elbows akimbo. "Davy'll skin you alive for sure."

Avery struck the match on the side of the chicken coop, lit the cheroot, and drew deeply on the smoke, patently ignoring Pappy. "You'll give me the rest of them little cigars if I take you to Davy's hideout?"

"I'll see that you get enough of them to last a year," Kade said.

"Avery!" Pappy squalled in hopeless protest.

Again, Avery paid his father no mind, but turned and started purposefully across the clearing, headed back toward the trees. Kade, Holt, and the two other riders followed at a discreet distance, and Pappy tried to keep up for a while, flapping and squawking like a hen come up one short on the last egg count. Finally, winded by the chase, the old man gave up and went turkey-trotting back toward the cabin.

Kade drew his pistol, checked to make sure it was loaded, and followed a crazy man into what might well be an ambush.

44

EVERYBODY TURNED TO look when Becky stepped into the town's only church that Sunday morning, with her eyes burning and her soul turned to dust. There was no preacher to lead the congregation, since the enterprise was fairly new, but a homesteader stood in front of the rustic altar, the good book open in his calloused hands. She saw pity in a few faces, and stone-cold condemnation in others. Word of John's passing in the night had surely gotten around the small community by now, along with news of Emmeline and Rafe's lost baby.

She raised her eyes to the plain wooden cross on the wall behind the pulpit and, drawn to it, started up the aisle between the benches serving as pews. She was midway to her goal when a tall, thin woman stood up and moved to block her way.

"Sit down, Mavis," said the man she'd been sitting beside. His bald pate gleamed in the sunlight pouring in through the windows.

A murmur arose like faraway thunder, a mere hum in Becky's ears. She stepped around the woman and marched on, knowing all the while that the cross was nothing but two pieces of scrap wood nailed together, but she needed to feel the texture of the thing just the same.

She was aware of folks getting to their feet behind her, but she didn't stop, didn't turn to look back. This effort was for John, and for the baby, as much as for herself, though she couldn't have said what she hoped to gain by it.

"Trollop!" a female voice shouted.

"Leave her be," said another.

"Defiler!"

The words bruised Becky like stones, the kind ones as well as the cruel, but she reached her destination and put out one trembling hand to the rough wood. Waited for lightning to strike—and sure enough, it did. Something seared her from the inside, white-hot, nearly dropping her to her knees. Stricken, she straightened her spine and turned to face the gathering, eyes blazing.

"Sinner!" cried the recalcitrant Mavis, sitting flushed and flustered beside her husband, next to the aisle.

Becky pushed her shoulders back and raised her chin. "That's right," she said clearly. "In all your days, you'll never meet a bigger sinner than I am." She paused, swept them all up in the imperious gaze she'd perfected long ago. "I heard this was the place for people like me, but it seems I was mistaken."

An uncomfortable silence descended, but Becky waited it out.

After an eternity had passed, a small woman near the back stood, adjusted her bonnet strings, and drew a breath so deep that it might have risen from the floorboards under her feet. She seemed to grow visibly taller, and when her husband tried to pull her back down onto the pew, she brushed his hand away.

"I say she has a right to be here," the woman said.

Another silence rolled in, heavy as the air before a storm, throbbing with tension. Then a second woman stood. "Essie's right," she said. "If Mrs. Fairmont has to leave, then I'm going, too. And if I leave, Mavis Potter, I won't be coming back. Not ever."

A third woman rose and echoed her opinion, then a man, then another person and another. In the end, only Mavis and two other women remained seated. The lay preacher was still standing next to the altar, openmouthed, the Bible drooping over his hand.

"I'm obliged," Becky said to one and all. Then she marched over to the front pew, sat herself down, and folded her hands.

After some shuffling and muttering, the service resumed, and Becky listened intently, her soul as dry as a desert gulch.

45

DAVY KINCAID'S HIDEOUT was a cave, it turned out, all but hidden from view by a cluster of scrub brush. Kade swung down from his saddle, his .45 springing into his grasp seemingly of its own accord. Avery watched from behind an oak tree, his eyes darting this way and that, as if they'd leap right out of his head at the slightest provocation.

No horse was in sight, but there were plenty of fresh tracks, and Kade found a cold fire inside the cave, along with some scattered gear, half a dozen rumpled bedrolls, and a few empty tins of beans.

"They won't be back," Holt said from the entrance.

The words angered Kade, probably because he knew they were true. Like any wild animal, Davy would know that his den had been disturbed, and he'd stay clear. There was, of course, no sign of the Triple M's lost money, but a military button lay on the hard-packed dirt, imprinted with a cavalry insignia. On closer inspection, after he'd pushed past Holt into the daylight, Kade saw the flecks of blood dulling the brass and shut the thing up tight in his fingers.

"At least we know who to go after," Holt said quietly.

Avery crept forward with his hand outstretched, and Kade gave him the remaining cheroots, as promised, along with a five-dollar gold piece. "Let's see where these tracks lead," he said to his brother.

Holt grinned wanly and slapped him on the back. "Whatever you say—Marshal."

Avery scurried into the underbrush, nimble as a jackrabbit, and Kade dropped the button into his pocket, slipped the .45 back into its holster, and headed for his horse. A hard ride lay ahead and most likely a hell of a fight at the end of it; best get on with things.

"He might go after the old man and that poor idiot," Holt remarked as they mounted their horses. "We'd better send these men back to fetch them over to the Circle C for safekeeping."

Kade merely nodded, and Holt gave the order. The two cowhands riding with them set their faces toward the Kincaid place, one of them snatching a smoking, squirming, yelping Avery right up off the ground and onto his horse as they passed.

"I counted six bedrolls in there," Holt reflected when they'd been riding awhile, and each had done some private pondering. "That doesn't mean there aren't more of them, and they could meet up someplace and decide they ought to do something about us."

Kade spared him another nod. "If you're scared," he said dryly, "go on home, take your boots off, and sit by your fire. I'll understand."

Holt's laugh was quick in coming. "Shhhhhhhit," he said,

drawing the word out Texas-style. Then he said it again, this time shouting to the skies, and gave a rebel yell as he slapped his horse's flank with the reins. The animal bolted forward, and Kade had to spur Raindance to keep up.

That it was an effort galled him not a little.

46

Mandy stood at the lobby windows of the Arizona Hotel, staring out at the street and willing Kade to ride in safe and sound, bad-tempered and hungry, bossing her around in that offhand way he had, as if it were a surety that he'd be obeyed. Emmeline appeared at her elbow looking pale and tired; she had to be one of the bravest, most cussed women Mandy had ever run across. Despite attempts to keep her in her bed, she was up and around, determined to go on in spite of everything. Too, she was surely as worried about Rafe as Mandy was about Kade.

"You should be resting," Mandy scolded, but gently.

"I can't. I need to move around as much as I can."

Mandy squeezed her friend's hand. "How's your mother?" Becky had gone to church that morning, of all places, and come back in a deeper daze than when she'd left.

Emmeline sighed. "I gave her a dose of the sleeping powder Doc left. I don't know if it will take, though. You're watching for Kade, aren't you?"

Mandy wondered if Emmeline knew she'd taken Kade to her bed the night before, and decided it didn't matter. She tried to smile. "Yes. That man vexes me something fierce."

"That's because he's a McKettrick."

Mandy put an arm around her friend's waist and squired her to the nearest chair. "Is that supposed to make me feel better?" she teased gently, taking a seat facing Emmeline. "How is Rafe?"

Tears sprang to Emmeline's eyes, and she shook her head. "He's hurting, but he's too strong and too stubborn to fall apart."

She paused, searched Mandy's face with worried eyes. "Why did you agree to marry Kade?"

Before Mandy could think of a sensible answer, Becky appeared in the dining room doorway, looking for all the world like a sleepwalker. "Emmeline, you should be in bed."

Emmeline just looked at her mother.

Becky's eyes were blank. "I must see John," she said, wringing her hands.

Emmeline rose to embrace her. "We've got to let them go."

Mandy was ashamed of what she felt in those moments, watching Emmeline and Becky together: it was sheer envy. Even in circumstances as tragic as these, she would have given anything to have her own mother close, or just to know she was still among the living. Her thoughts turned to Gig, and right then, she could cheerfully have shot him for keeping Dixie's whereabouts from her.

"You tell me how to do that, Emmeline," Becky fretted. "You tell me how to turn loose and I will."

Emmeline dashed at a tear with the heel of one palm. She looked done-in again, broken and gray. It was too much to ask of one woman, losing a baby and a friend in the same day.

Mandy got hastily to her feet. "I'll settle Emmeline in her room," she said, taking charge. "Then you and I will go over to

Doc's. In return, I want your word that you'll lie down when we get back."

Becky nodded tremulously. "Thank you."

Emmeline didn't resist, but let herself be led back up the stairs and tucked beneath a quilt on her and Rafe's bed.

"You stay put," Mandy ordered.

Emmeline smiled, closed her eyes, and slept.

Mandy and Becky found Doc in his small office, pen in hand, paper before him, writing. When he looked up and saw Becky, his homely old face contorted with a thousand secret sorrows. "Becky," he said, rising. His tone held a gentle rebuke. "You're wearing yourself to a raveling. Do I need to remind you that your heart won't stand much of this?"

"My heart," she said, "is broken beyond repair. When I find all the pieces, we'll see about putting them back together."

Doc crossed to her, took her hands in his. He looked sober, which Mandy counted as a blessing. With Doc, it could go one way or the other. She wondered what devils he was trying to drown in all that whiskey. "John wouldn't want you grieving like this," he reasoned gently. "And you'll be no good to Emmeline and Rafe if you fall apart."

Becky hiked her chin up a notch. "I won't let Emmeline down. Right now, though, I need to see John. I need to touch him, get it straight in my mind that he's really gone."

"All right," Doc said with a heavy sigh. He inclined his head toward the examining room. "He's in there."

Becky moved toward the inside door with all the wounded dignity of a bereaved queen, and Mandy went with her, even though she didn't particularly cotton to the idea of looking at a dead man so close up. Since it was Mr. Lewis lying on a table, and he'd been decent to her in his quiet way, she forced herself to set her misgivings aside.

John didn't look like himself, stretched out there, all still and colorless. His eyes were closed and weighted with pennies, and he'd been stripped of his shirt, vest, trousers, and boots, then covered to his shoulders with an Indian blanket.

Becky moved to stand at his side, taking one of his hands in both her own. "So cold," she whispered, then sought Doc out with her eyes. "Is there another blanket?"

To his credit, Doc didn't raise the obvious argument; he simply fetched the blanket from a cabinet against the wall and handed it, still folded, to Becky. She shook it out and spread it tenderly over John's body.

"There," she said, her voice soft as a lullaby.

A sob escaped Mandy's throat, and Doc led her away, settling her in a chair in the outer office. "She'll be all right," he said, quietly, as Mandy gave in to tears. "So will Emmeline." He paused, studying Mandy intently. "You're not going to go to pieces on us, are you?"

Mandy nodded then, in the grip of paradox, shook her head. Doc handed her a handkerchief and waited while she worked things through.

She was crying because the body laid out on that hard table could so easily be Kade's. The reckless fool—did he think a bullet couldn't penetrate that tough McKettrick hide of his? She was crying for her mother, poor, bewildered Dixie, she of the gentle and winsome soul, and for all the lost children, born and unborn. Some of her tears were for Cree, too, and for herself.

"I keep trying to make sense of things," Mandy finally replied when she could trust herself to speak, wiping furiously at her swollen eyes.

Doc smiled sadly. "Now *there's* a fool's errand. There are a lot more questions than answers in this world, it seems to me. But we've got to go right on living all the same, Miss Mandy, whether it suits us or not."

Mandy was beginning to compose herself when Harry appeared, his face so white that his multitude of freckles seemed to stand out. Her heart stopped at the sight of him; she knew he'd come with bad news about Kade. She just knew it.

"What's the matter, boy?" Doc asked, rising yet again from his desk chair.

In her mind, Mandy saw him and Mrs. Sussex strolling past her and Kade the night before, and she wondered about that.

"We've got sickness over at our place," Harry blurted. "Ma said it might be the diphtheria, and you need to come quick!"

"Oh, Lord," Doc murmured, casting about for his bag, finding it, closing a hand over the grip. His eyes were weary as he caught Mandy's gaze. "Take Becky home," he said. "And look after Emmeline as best you can." Then he was gone, following Harry out of the door and leaving it gaping open behind him.

Mandy dried her cheeks, took a deep, restorative breath, and stood. "Becky," she said firmly, when she stood in the inner doorway. "It's time to go back to the hotel now. You promised, remember?"

Becky nodded. "I remember." Then, with heartbreaking purpose, she leaned down, kissed John's forehead one last time, and murmured a final good-bye.

47

THE SUN DIPPED in the western sky, blazing with pink, purple, and orange light, and though the tracks of the outlaws' horses had vanished long before, there was plenty of sign to follow. Holt finally insisted that they stop and make camp for the night; given his choice, Kade would have ridden through till dawn.

While Holt built a fire, Kade shot a couple of rabbits for supper, skinning them next to a footwide creek. Now that the day was ending, and he had the time, he had to think about John Lewis being gone for good, whether he chose to or not. He felt diminished by the loss, as though his friend had carried a part of him away when he went. And then there was Rafe and Emmeline's baby, never living to see the light. The last time he'd glimpsed that kind of rendering sorrow in his elder brother had been when their mother died.

And there was another thorny matter. Kade blamed himself for Georgia McKettrick's passing, at least in part, though he'd never confided that to a living soul. She'd been riding after strays when she was thrown into the creek and caught the chill that bore her away within twenty-four hours. Rounding up those wandering cattle had been his chore, but he'd been late getting home from town, where he'd talked himself into a poker game, and his mother had stepped in to keep him from catching hell from Angus.

Now, beside the narrow creek, Kade washed the rabbit carcasses and then his hands before heading back to camp. Too bad he couldn't wash away his regrets as easily.

Holt had a good, hot fire going by the time Kade returned, and he'd rigged up a spit for roasting the rabbits. Kade longed hopelessly for hot, fresh coffee and eyed the hard ground where he'd be spreading out his bedroll. He was grimly amused to find himself hankering mightily for the cot back at the jailhouse, with its thin, lumpy, and none-too-clean mattress. Mandy's bed would have been better, of course, but after the scene in front of the jailhouse that morning, he didn't reckon he'd be welcome there.

He put the rabbits on the spit and stood beside the fire awhile, warming his hands against the high-country chill. Holt sat nearby, one leg bent at the knee, the other stretched out straight. He stared into the blaze, thinking his own thoughts.

As a general rule, Kade was no conversationalist, but that night, sadder and wiser, with the ranch in danger and one of his best friends dead, he felt the need to talk. "You remember your mother?" he heard himself ask.

It was a mighty personal question, and Holt couldn't be blamed if he chose not to reply, but after a long while spent watching the fire, he shook his head. "She died when I was a baby. Pa rode out soon after that, so I don't have any recollections of him, either."

"Who raised you?" Kade shivered as a cold wind blew down off the distant, snowcapped peaks. His bones felt brittle, and he yearned for Mandy's singular warmth.

"Some kin of my mother's," Holt answered flatly.

"The Cavanaghs?"

Holt sighed and threw Kade an irritated glance, but he finally shook his head in response. "No. I took that name from the first rancher I worked for—started as a stable hand. He was a good man. It was because of him that I joined up with the Rangers."

Kade was quiet, absorbing this revelation. He was powerfully curious about this half brother of his, and he hoped he wouldn't be forced to admit as much. He didn't know how to frame the words without sounding like he gave a damn. "You never called yourself McKettrick?"

"No reason to," Holt said, watching the campfire again. Kade wondered what he saw in there—something, for sure, if the solemn expression on his face was anything to go by.

"You came up tough, I guess."

Holt pondered that, then nodded. "I reckon I did."

"What was it like, riding with the Rangers?"

"You planning on starting up your own newspaper or something?"

Kade allowed himself a weary grin. "A man lives his whole life never knowing he's got a third brother out there someplace, and then meets the fella face-to-face. It makes for curiosity."

Holt kept his eyes on the flames, and their reflections flickered across the rugged lines of his face. Being fairly certain that he wouldn't be flattered to hear how much he resembled Angus, Kade didn't remark on the fact, though it struck him square in the gut. "I knew about you and Rafe and Jeb," Holt said, "and I still had plenty of questions."

Kade crouched, raising his collar against the wind and

hoping it wouldn't snow during the night. He waited, knowing his brother had more words in him, and somewhere in the near distance, a wolf howled plaintively, perhaps calling back the vanished moon.

"Angus wrote me, once I was old enough to read," Holt said. "By that time, I'd been adopted by my ma's sister and her husband, Dill, but I guess the old man thought I'd want to know all about his new family, so he turned newsy every other year, around my birthday. Christ, I used to hate getting those letters."

Kade sighed. "It would be a hard thing, growing up that way. Pa should have brought you home to the Triple M."

"He'd have had to hog-tie me."

"But you're here now."

Holt engaged in a bitter smile. "I never planned to stay."

"Then why'd you buy the Chandler place and bring in that herd of cattle?"

Their gazes met across the dancing fire, and locked. "I knew Angus wanted that land. Seemed like a good way to piss him off."

Kade laughed, but the sound was raw in his throat, and no joy was in it. "You did that, all right. You still trying to get under his skin, or are you serious about ranching?"

"A little of both, I figure."

The rabbit meat began to sizzle and the smell made Kade's empty stomach growl. He went to unsaddle and hobble his horse, and took care of Holt's mount as well, while he was at it. When he returned to the fire, supper was ready.

Kade had used up his store of words for the day, so he laid out his bedroll, took his share of the food from the spit, as did Holt, and ate in silence.

"I'll take the first watch," Holt said. They both knew that Davy and the men he rode with might double back at any time, and it wouldn't serve to be taken unawares.

Kade didn't expect to sleep, weary as he was, given the hardness of the ground and the thoughts churning in his head, but the next thing he knew, Holt was shaking him awake to stand lookout, and his blanket was covered by a light dusting of the snow he'd dreaded earlier.

The rest of the night was long, dull, and cold, and Kade was relieved when dawn finally broke. Breakfast was jerky from their saddlebags, and he and Holt were soon mounted and on their way.

The snow had covered the trail they'd been following, and they were about to turn around and head back when they saw the blood.

48

THE MURDERED MAN lay belly-up in the red snow, with half his chest blown away and his scalp neatly separated from his skull. The carcass was gruesome, awash in crimson gore, a fresh kill as savage as the leavings of any wild animal.

"Sweet Jesus," Holt said, scanning the surrounding area quickly, gun in hand, as Kade did the same. No one was in sight. The stillness of that high and lonesome place resounded through Kade, an echo of nothing.

Bile surged into the back of his throat, and he spat before getting down from the horse and approaching the body. If people kept dying at the rate they had been lately, he reckoned Indian Rock would be a ghost town in no time at all.

Kade recognized the corpse right away, though he and Kincaid hadn't been acquainted.

"That him?" Holt asked, standing in his stirrups to peer at the dead man. "Pappy's boy?"

Kade glanced back at him over one snow-dusted shoulder, nodded. "Reckon so."

Holt dismounted, too, glanced once at what was left of Kincaid, and crouched to examine one of several sets of hoofprints in the snow.

Kade got to his feet, doing his best to keep down the jerky he'd eaten on the trail. He straightened his hat and made a wide circle, searching for anything that would indicate where the killers had gone from there.

"What now?" he muttered, talking more to himself than Holt.

"We take the poor bastard home to his father and brother."

"We have to keep going."

"The tracks lead nowhere, Kade. Whoever these people are, they've had a lot of experience at eluding posses. They killed Kincaid to make sure he wouldn't talk and deliberately left him here for us to find, which means they know we're after them. By now, they're miles from here."

Kade cursed. "You're probably right," he said, grudgingly.

Holt was unfastening his bedroll from behind his saddle. "I sure as hell am," he replied flatly. "Let's get young Davy home to his kinfolks, such as they are. If they've gone on to the Circle C with Charlie and Pete, we'll head there."

They wrapped Kincaid's remains in the blanket, rigged up a litter with tree branches and rope, and dragged him back down to Pappy's cabin. When they arrived, there was no sign of the two men Holt had sent back to protect the old man and Avery.

Once again, Pappy came out to meet them, but this time, he wasn't shooting. It was a small consolation but, at the moment, Kade was willing to take what he could get. "That Davy in there?" the old man asked cautiously, peering around Kade's horse at the travois, and the bloody bundle it carried.

"Yes," Kade said.

"I warned him this would happen, he kept runnin' with bad

companions." Pappy drew nigh the body, his movements tentative, as though he thought his son might spring up and take him by the throat. He made no move to touch Davy, but instead peered up at Kade. If he felt any grief at all, it wasn't evident. "You get my three dollars and my bullets back?"

Kade ran the back of a gloved hand across his mouth and linked gazes with Holt. "No," he said, after some hesitation.

"What about my cattle? You promised me them cattle."

"You'll have them," Kade replied. There would be no mourning Davy Kincaid, it appeared, and even though the son of a bitch probably hadn't been worth a pitcher of warm spit, it was still a pitiful thing to know. He got down off the horse, moved past Pappy to unhitch the travois.

"Where are my men?" Holt asked, looking around. His jawline had gone hard; plainly, he expected his orders to be obeyed. Just like Angus, Kade thought, and under any other circumstances, he would have been inclined to smile.

"Took Avery and left," Pappy said. "I tolt 'em I wasn't going nowheres."

"We'll need a couple of shovels," Kade said, exhausted in a way that a month of sound sleep couldn't cure. "Where do you want him buried?"

"Don't give a damn, long as you don't put him too close to the well." With that, Pappy trotted off toward the cabin, leaving birdlike footprints in the melting snow.

"Angus McKettrick," Holt observed, dismounting and coming to help Kade with Davy's body, "is beginning to seem downright sweet-tempered."

49

KADE PARTED WAYS with Holt at the turnoff to the Circle C and rode wearily on to the Triple M, arriving there around three o'clock, just as Concepcion was laying out an early supper. Jeb and Angus were at the table, sleeves rolled up, preparing to dish up. Everybody was glum, and with good reason. Emmeline's miscarriage had come as a blow to them all, and then there was John.

"Any luck picking up the trail?" Jeb asked as Kade hung up his coat and hat by the kitchen door.

"Davy Kincaid was part of the gang," Kade said, with a shake of his head, unstrapping his gun belt and setting that aside, too. "They killed him."

Angus winced. "Lordy," he said, studying Kade closely, perhaps looking for signs of wear. "Was it bad?"

"Bad enough not to talk about while folks are fixing to eat." Kade went to the sink and began washing his hands in the hot water Concepcion had ladled into a basin, making good use of the strong yellow soap she brewed in batches every fall after the butchering was done. "How about you?" he asked Jeb. "You turn up anything in your travels?"

"Nothing to speak of," Jeb said. "Captain Harvey's got his tail in a twist. He's threatening to bring the whole cavalry in and go over every inch of ground between here and Utah."

"That's all right with me," Kade replied, drying his hands. He looked at Angus, then at Concepcion. They were carrying on, but they both looked peaked. "You two holding up all right?"

Concepcion averted her gaze, sniffling, and Angus grumbled and shuffled around in his chair a bit. "It's a damn shame about John, and Emmeline, too. You seen Rafe?"

Jeb and Kade exchanged glances. Evidently, Jeb hadn't been holding forth on their elder brother's state of mind.

"He's taking it hard," Kade said. He braced himself for a hide-stripping; since Rafe blamed him for what had happened, it might be that they did, too.

"Hope he doesn't burn anything down," Angus fretted.

Jeb grinned at that, though not with his usual spirit. "He'll work it through in time."

Kade paused to lean down and kiss Concepcion's cheek on the way to his chair, and she offered him a fleeting smile. Thin as it was, that smile took some of the chill of the trail, and Davy Kincaid's grisly murder, from his bones.

"If we'd gotten the chance," Angus said out of the blue, "Concepcion and me would have made an announcement of our own at the dance the other night."

Kade waited, bracing himself, with no idea what to expect.

"What?" Jeb wanted to know.

"We've been married awhile," Angus imparted.

The silence was thunderous.

"I'll be damned," Jeb said, finally. It was something of a relief to have the conversational logjam broken, even if it did gall Kade that his younger brother had been the one to do it.

Kade let out his breath, tossed a mischievous glance in Concepcion's direction. "What I can't fathom," he said, taking his customary place next to Jeb and reaching for the platter of roast beef, carrots, and potatoes, "is what a fine woman like you would see in an old reprobate like my pa." Concepcion was probably the only woman in the territory who could abide the old man, to Kade's way of thinking, though in truth he felt a renewed affection for Angus, having noted the contrasts between him and Pappy Kincaid.

Angus laughed at that, a note of jovial relief in the sound. It touched Kade in a surprising way to realize how much Angus wanted his sons' blessing on the marriage. Had he expected recriminations? Maybe so, given the way they'd reacted to the news of an extra son.

Jeb offered no further comment, for once; he just waited impatiently for the platter and then speared two good-sized slabs of beef and scraped half the spuds onto his plate for good measure.

"I promised Pappy Kincaid three head of cattle," Kade announced presently, figuring that was as good a time to break the news as any. "Two heifers and a bull. I've already sent a couple of the hands up to his place with them."

A heavy silence settled over the room. Jeb looked as if he were poised to duck under the table, and Concepcion wore a mighty serious expression as she tried to catch her husband's eye.

"Why in blazes would you do that?" Angus demanded, his considerable ire trained on Kade alone. So much for matrimonial bliss.

"To pay a debt," Kade said, meeting his father's gaze and holding his ground. "Seems to me some of the things folks say about our dealings have a bit too much truth to them for my liking."

Angus flushed, disgruntled. "He's crazy as a wood tick, that old man. You go giving cattle to everybody who thinks they've got some claim against the McKettricks, we won't have a herd left."

"It's done, Pa," Kade said. Concepcion had gotten up to pour him a cup of her blessed coffee, and he took a mouthful, relishing the taste of the stuff. "Best leave it alone."

It looked like Angus was bent on an argument, but a second glance from Concepcion subdued him, and after that small hitch, the talk turned to finding the money that would save the Triple M. That the task seemed more impossible with every passing day did nothing to diminish Kade's private determination to do it.

"Will you stay the night?" Concepcion inquired half an hour later, while she and Kade stood side by side, washing and drying the supper dishes. Angus had retreated to his study and Jeb was off to the bunkhouse for a game of poker with some of the ranch hands.

The thought was inviting—Kade had missed his room, his bed, and his books—but he shook his head. He was still the town marshal, and that meant he was needed in Indian Rock. Besides, Mandy was there, and they had some things to square away between them.

"I have to get back," he said, making no attempt to hide his regret. His eagerness to be near Mandy, in her bed or not, was too personal to share.

Concepcion nodded her understanding. "Angus and I will be heading that direction in the morning. We want to be there for John's funeral and see what we can do for Rafe and Emmeline."

Kade's throat tightened. He dreaded the disappointment in Emmeline's eyes, the furious grief in Rafe's, and even more, he dreaded seeing John Lewis's coffin lowered into the ground, but there was no question that he'd attend the service. "It won't be an easy day," he said with some difficulty.

Concepcion laid a hand on his arm and spoke frankly. "I know you feel a duty to see this job through, but you need to remember that this ranch is your home. It is in your blood, this place, and staying away is like denying yourself food and breath and water. It will shrivel your soul." Her eyes gleamed with love and tears as she looked at him. "You belong right here, Kade."

He'd come to realize that himself, over recent days, but he couldn't take off the badge in good conscience until those killers had been rounded up and brought in and a new marshal had been found. And then there was the money. He nodded, set the last dish aside to be put away, and hung up the dish towel. He thought of Rafe and Emmeline's sturdy house, across the creek, and wished he had a place like that to bring Mandy home to. In his mind, he was already making plans to build one, and he would do it with his own hands. He wanted his children and grandchildren to grow up there.

He gave Concepcion a nod as a belated answer, and peered out the window. It was still early, but town was a couple of hours away, and he didn't much relish riding in the dark. "I'd better go," he said with resignation.

50

SOME FOLKS MIGHT be good at minding their own affairs, but Mandy had never been one of them. She'd gone straight to the Sussex house after seeing Becky safely back to the hotel, where Sarah Fee was looking after Emmeline, and she'd been there with Doc, doing what she could to help, ever since.

Mamie Sussex, the mother of the brood, was in no state to be effective, and the brides, with the exception of the one called Abigail, had fled the place, bag and baggage, afraid of taking sick. Since they hadn't been at the hotel when Mandy was there earlier, she could only assume that they'd been taken into various homes around the town or had gone to the mercantile to sit on their trunks and valises, waiting for the next stage out of town.

Mandy was too busy to care what they did, as long as Kade wasn't a factor in their doing. Like Doc, she'd been awake all night and all that day, and she was running on pure obstinacy. Every nerve in her body seemed to be fluttering on the outside of her skin, bared to the elements.

There were six Sussex children, all with their mother's rich auburn hair, but otherwise so dissimilar of face and feature that no two could possibly claim the same father. Five of them had been prostrate with fever when Mandy got there, their little bodies soaked and shuddering, their eyes rolled back in their heads.

"There's been enough death around here lately," Mandy had said to God, right out loud, at one desperate point somewhere in the wee hours, "the least You could do is let these children live!"

Doc, kneeling next to another child, in another bed, bathing him with cool water to bring down his temperature, had smiled at that. "You tell Him," he'd said.

Abigail, busy at the same task, with yet another child, had pursed her lips at first, but then relented. "Amen," she'd said.

The hours stretched on while the Almighty made up His mind. Darkness dissolved into daylight, then twilight was gathering again. Diphtheria was a swift and savage killer, and Mandy had seen whole families wiped out by it between morning and evening. She didn't have much hope, truth be told, but they hung on, those little devils, and they hung on tight. They were accustomed to scrapping, like Mandy herself, and would not give up easily.

Long after sunset, she was sitting on the front step with Harry, keeping him company and trying to catch her breath, when Kade rode up and swung down from the saddle. Mandy was so glad to see him that she had to stay herself from jumping up, running to him in the street like a hussy, and throwing her arms around his neck. Harry rushed to his side, and Mandy felt her heart turn over behind her breastbone, watching as Kade squeezed the boy's shoulder.

"They're all down with the diphtheria," Harry said in a burst of words, "all of them but me."

"So I heard," Kade replied gently. His gaze found Mandy. "Any news?"

She shook her head, all but overwhelmed by the things she felt. Oh, there was grief for John Lewis, and of course for Emmeline and Rafe, but there was ever so much more, too, and all of it seemed to have its beginnings in this irresistible, hardheaded man. She'd given herself to him without reservation night before last, and she supposed she ought to regret that, but she didn't. Just because something was impulsive didn't mean it was wrong.

He came to sit beside her on the step, clad in his trail clothes, his long gunslinger's coat, and his weariness. Again, she knew a woman's desire to comfort in a woman's way, and it made her blush, remembering how it felt to have his hands, his lips, on her bare flesh.

He smiled, just as if he'd read her mind, and maybe he had. They were crafty, those McKettricks; Mandy had been around them enough to know that for sure. "The padre is in town for John's funeral," he said. "I was thinking we could get him to marry us tonight." His gaze touched her in places he'd already explored in much more intimate ways. "Wouldn't want any scandals to arise."

Mandy swallowed, and heat rushed through her. She wondered if she wasn't too old, after all, to come down with the plague that was ravaging Mamie's children. She certainly seemed to be running a fever. "Tonight?"

"I didn't reckon you'd want our wedding anniversary to fall on the day we buried John," he said reasonably, letting nothing of his hopes, whatever they might be, show in that unfairly handsome face of his. "I've already spoken to Father Herrera, and he's agreeable if you are."

All manner of joy rose up in Mandy at his words, in spite

of everything. *Fool,* taunted a too familiar little voice inside her, *get on a horse and ride out of here, like you planned.* "Yes," she said, as much to spite the voice as anything. "Yes." She could no more have stopped the smile that came to her mouth than she could have kept the moon from rising. "But I still want those fifty horses and the money. And you'd better not stop me from riding with you next time the posse goes out."

"You drive a hard bargain, Miss Mandy," he said with another grin. "But a deal's a deal, and you'll have what I promised you."

Her mind was racing. "I don't have a proper dress," she fretted. "Or a ring to put on your finger."

"There are dresses aplenty at the mercantile," Kade said with a small smile, "and we can worry about the rings later."

"Can I go to the wedding?" Harry asked with such eagerness that Mandy nearly wept for him. "If Ma will let me, I mean?"

"Sure," Kade said. "I couldn't get married without my best deputy there to make sure everything went all right."

"Will there be cake?" the boy asked.

Kade smiled again. "I reckon. The cook was building one when I left the hotel, on orders from Becky." He turned back to Mandy. "I stopped there on the way, looking for you."

She let herself lean against him for a moment, taking an improper pleasure in his nearness and his strength. "I'll have to come straight back here afterward," she said. "Doc and Abigail have their hands full with these kids." Harry was already banging his way into the house, no doubt to ask his poor, distracted mother if he could go to the wedding, where there would be cake. "These little ones are in a bad way, Kade," she added when the boy was out of earshot.

He took her hand and squeezed it, and they sat like that, in companionable silence, for several moments. When Harry came back outside, Doc was with him, looking three years older than dirt.

"My mother told me to take up the law instead of medicine," he said. "I should have listened."

"We'd be in a hell of a snarl if you had," Kade observed, getting to his feet. "I need to speak with Mamie. Is she in a fit state for a visit?"

"She's sitting in the kitchen," Doc said. "As for the state she's in, well, I couldn't rightly say that she'd notice if a cannon went off in the next room."

Kade nodded grimly at that, stepped past Doc, and walked into the house. Mandy burned with an unholy curiosity, but she did not allow herself to follow.

In a few hours, she would be somebody's wife. Tarnation.

51

THE WEDDING PARTY was necessarily small. Just Kade and Mandy, Becky, Father Herrera, and Harry were there, clustered at the front of the raw-wood church. Sarah Fee had lit the candles, and she and Becky had scared up a dress somewhere, hastily basted to fit Mandy. Harry kept peering this way and that, probably hoping to catch a glimpse of the cake.

Kade reckoned his pa and Concepcion would be considerably put out when they learned that they'd missed the ceremony, but he wasn't inclined to wait. Once the idea of making Mandy his wife had lodged in his head, it had gained depth and breadth until it possessed the whole of his being. Besides, now that he'd bedded her, it was the only honorable thing to do.

He didn't know if he loved her; he had no frame of reference for such sentiments, since he'd never felt this way before. Besides, life was an uncertain proposition; the proof of that was all around him.

Mandy, standing beside him in front of the padre, pretty as an angel in her borrowed dress, was visibly nervous, and more than once, Kade had half expected her to call the whole thing off and bolt right out of there.

The marriage license had been signed, and Father Herrera

opened his wedding book. "Shall we begin?" asked the Jesuit in his precise English.

Kade gave a solemn nod.

The words were said, the promises exchanged. Kade felt himself growing taller with every vow he made, and by the time he got to "I do," he figured he was about to knock out a few ceiling beams with the top of his head.

"I now pronounce you man and wife," Father Herrera said, and closed the book on all the days and all the nights gone by. "You may kiss the bride."

Kade would have done that even without the padre's permission. He took Mandy in his arms, tilted her chin up with one finger, and lowered his head to place his mouth firmly on hers. There was something different in this kiss, though the preceding ones had been powerful, and it left Kade shaken and Mandy flushed to her ears.

"Where's the cake?" Harry piped up.

Mandy laughed and leaned down to kiss the boy on the forehead. "Back at the hotel. Let's go have some."

Kade and Mandy left the church arm in arm, and a small and unlikely crowd, made up of half-drunk cowboys and prim ladies in stays and bonnets, had collected outside to throw rice. Except for the remaining brides, that is—they seemed more inclined to throw rocks.

Kade wanted to start the honeymoon straight off, carrying Mandy upstairs like the spoils of a hard-won victory, but it wasn't to be. The Sussex kids were still under the weather, and damn the luck, he was still the marshal of Indian Rock.

While Mandy went to change out of her finery and back into

practical calico, Kade lingered downstairs, watching Harry devour his fourth piece of cake. Kade thought of Mamie Sussex, and how she'd wept when he'd told her Davy Kincaid was dead, and marveled that such a man could arouse so much sorrow in the heart of any woman. Only when she'd raised her face from her hands, after those first few minutes had passed, had he known it was relief making her cry like that, not bereavement.

Mandy descended the stairs in a hurry and caught Kade's hand in hers as she blew past. "Come on, Marshal. We've got work to do."

52

Doc was outside again, smoking his pipe this time, when Mandy got back to the Sussex house, and he reacted elaborately to the sight of her, pretending to be stunned, though a glint of tired amusement was in his eyes. "What are you doing here?" he demanded. "Land sakes, it's your wedding night! And where's your bridegroom?"

Mandy drew a resolute breath. "He stopped by the jailhouse, and you know damn well why I'm here."

He laughed at her audacity; she was a little pleased by it herself, truth be known. "Well, you just get yourself on out of here," Doc said. "The kids are still mighty sick, but they've turned the corner. I think they'll be all right in time."

Mandy was unprepared for the rush of emotion that brought tears to her eyes and weakened her knees. "Thank God for that," she whispered.

"I reckon God owed us one," Doc allowed. "He's been a mite heavy-handed of late, to my way of thinking."

Abigail came to the door, put her head out, and looked Mandy over, maybe to see if she'd changed in any visible way, now that she was married to the man she'd expected to have for herself. Doc tapped his pipe against the rail of the stoop, turned, and went back inside, easing past Abigail.

"It's done, then," Abigail said.

Mandy nodded. She wished she had a ring to show, but only briefly. Horses and shotguns and calico dresses mattered to her, but jewelry didn't mean much, in the scheme of things. "There are plenty of other men around here wanting wives," she said quietly, because she wasn't without sympathy for Abigail, or any of the other brides. They'd come a long way, all of them, just to be disappointed at the end of their journey, and that was a hard thing to reckon with.

Abigail smoothed her hair with one graceful hand and gazed off into the distance. "Not ones named McKettrick," she said.

Mandy couldn't refute that. "What will you do now?" she asked gently. "Go back home?"

"I don't have a home to go to," Abigail replied with an utter lack of self-pity. "Guess I'll make the best of things right here. Mamie could use some help getting this boardinghouse to pay."

Mandy was silent for as long as she could manage. "You know," she began cautiously, and in a low voice, "that Mrs. Sussex sees men for money?"

"I've been living under this roof for a while," Abigail said sensibly. "I couldn't help knowing that." She looked solemn for a while, then she smiled, and it transformed her face. "With a little work on my part, she could turn this into a respectable place." She inclined her head toward the street. "Here's your husband, Mandy. If I were you, I'd go to him."

Mandy turned her head, and sure enough, Kade was walking toward her. Her heart skipped right out to meet him and tarried there.

Reaching Mandy's side, Kade nodded slightly to Abigail.

"She must make good pies," Abigail said.

There was a beat of silence, then Kade laughed. "I don't know if she can cook a lick, but the way she rides and shoots," he allowed, "she might make a pretty fair deputy."

"I still think you're three kinds of a scoundrel, Kade McKettrick," Abigail responded, leaning against the rail in much the same way Doc had done earlier, "but I wish you well. Both of you."

Mandy felt Kade's hand close around hers. Tighten. "Thanks," he said.

Abigail nodded, a mite stiffly, and went back into the house.

Kade looked down at Mandy, a question in his eyes.

"Doc says the kids are better," she said. "He as much as told me to go straight back to you."

"Funny," Kade said with a quirk of a smile at the corner of his mouth, "Jeb said something similar when I went by the jailhouse. He and three soldiers are standing guard over Curry, and they've got a poker game going."

Mandy ducked her head, and they started back toward Becky's place, and the little room at the end of the upstairs hallway.

Kade didn't once let go of her hand.

Reaching the hotel, they walked into the light spilling through the open front doors. Clive was at the desk, but the place seemed deserted otherwise, and Mandy was grateful. This thing she and Kade had found together, whatever name it bore, was precious and private.

They climbed the stairs, Kade remembering to take his hat off as they went, and once they were inside their secret place, Kade closed the door, turned the key in the lock.

"My shotgun bride," he said huskily, taking her in with a sweep of his gaze. "You are so beautiful."

She didn't know what to say to that. *Thank you* didn't seem precisely right, and protesting the compliment probably wouldn't do, either.

He took a seat in the one chair the room boasted. "Come here." He was in shadow now, and she couldn't read his expression, but his voice was low and a little hoarse.

She hesitated, then went to him, unable to do otherwise, and he drew her down onto his lap, ran one hand along the length of her arm. Goose bumps rose, even with the sleeve of her dress making a barrier between her flesh and his.

He touched his mouth to hers.

"Wait a second," Mandy interjected, placing her palms against his chest.

He sighed. "What?"

"The other night, when we made love the first time, you said something."

"Women," he marveled.

"You were surprised that I was a virgin." There, it was out, but Mandy was as anxious as she was relieved, awaiting his response.

He traced the side of her cheek with an index finger, pondered her awhile. "I guess I couldn't credit my good luck," he said at long last. "A woman like you . . ." He paused, no doubt seeing the storm gathering in her, and started again. "You're like a wild-flower, Mandy. You're lovely to look at, and you smell like heaven, but your roots are shallow. You haven't led the most sheltered life, from what little you've said about your past. If some sweet-talking man had noticed you before I did, well, he might have put everything he had into persuading you." He searched her eyes, and she wondered if he saw the passion there, with all the other things she felt, desperate and beautiful, every one of them. "I don't mind saying I'm glad to be the first, and I sure as hell mean to be the last."

In the short time she'd known Kade McKettrick, she'd never heard him say so many words at once; they flung a thousand doors open inside her, and light poured through them all.

She put her arms around his neck. "Hold me," she said. "Hold me tight."

They sat like that for a long time, with their arms around each other, and then the kissing started again, and that led to the inevitable.

Presently, their lovemaking ebbed, and Mandy drifted off to sleep, vaguely aware that Kade got out of bed somewhere in the depths of the night and pulled on his clothes.

She dreamed, yearning for him, but too sated and spent to go in search of him. Then he was back; she heard him moving across the room.

"Amanda Rose."

Not Kade. *Who then?* Her heart seized in her chest.

She sat bolt upright, clawing the covers up to her chin, too startled to make the smallest sound, never mind scream.

"You married yourself a McKettrick," the intruder said. "You did good."

Her breath caught in her throat, and she leaned forward slightly, blinking, waiting for her eyes to adjust to the darkness. Her voice was a ragged whisper, sawing at her throat.

"Cree?"

53

"How's my little sister?" Cree asked.

Mandy was about to fling off the covers and run to her brother when she realized she wasn't wearing a stitch of clothing. She watched, barely trusting her eyes, as he crossed the room and sat down in the chair where she and Kade had made love so very long ago. "What are you doing here?" she asked, having regained some presence of mind. "How's Mama?"

"One question at a time," Cree scolded, and his grin flashed white as a translucent moon against a dark sky. The lantern had either burned itself out or Kade had extinguished it before leaving the room. "I'm here because you are, mainly. And Ma is—well, she's puny, but she's holding on."

Mandy cast a furtive glance at the door. She was sure Kade would have locked it on his way out. She was also sure her new husband wouldn't be pleased if he came back and found an uninvited guest in their room, even if that guest *was* her half brother. "How did you get in here?" she asked.

Cree sighed good-naturedly. "Another question." He waggled the deft fingers of one gloved hand. "Picked the lock."

Mandy was glad to see Cree, more than glad, but she was

somewhat uneasy, too. She told herself it was because of Gig, who'd kill him if he got the chance and never turn a hair over it.

"Are you insane?" she whispered. "Gig's right down the street, in the jailhouse, and if he finds out you're here, he'll tear the bars out with his bare hands and come after you for sure!"

Cree's handsome face hardened. He wore his gleaming black hair long, and his cheekbones were high and sharp in the poor light straying in from the street. "I'm not worried about Curry. You oughtn't to be, either."

"He means to kill you!"

Cree shrugged. "He's in jail. Not that that isn't a piss-poor setup over there. I could get out in five minutes."

"You might get *in* in less time than that, if you're not careful." Keeping herself covered with the blankets, Mandy bent over the side of the bed and groped until she'd snagged her dress, bloomers, and camisole. Still beneath the covers, she wriggled into them. "I can't believe you'd come here, bold as can be, if you knew Gig and his gang were around."

"I knew, all right," Cree said, and Mandy was certain he was wearing a smug expression even before she made her way to the bureau, struck a match, and lit the lantern, so she could see his face clearly.

She faced him, her hands on her hips. "No more stalling. I want to know more about Mama."

Cree hoisted himself to his feet and strolled over to the window, spurs jangling, to hold the curtain aside and look out. It wouldn't tell him much, Mandy reflected distractedly, since the main street was on the other side of the building. "She's in a bad way," he said, without turning around.

"*Where* is she?" Mandy demanded. A part of her was listening for Kade's footsteps in the hall, hoping he'd come back, while another was willing him to stay away. "Gig said she was in a hospital, but I don't believe him. He couldn't spend the money."

"She's in a place outside of Phoenix," Cree said, turning from the window at last. "A rancher and his wife took her in. After I gave them a pouch full of Mexican silver, that is."

Mandy closed her eyes. "Tell me they're good people," she pleaded.

"Good as any," Cree said with another shrug. "I told them I'd be back to look in on her regular-like, and that I expected to find her comfortable and in good spirits."

It came then, the sound she'd both awaited and dreaded; Kade was walking along the corridor, putting his key in the lock.

Quick as only he could be, Cree reached the window and slipped through the opening as if he were boneless, with no more substance than smoke. Standing there, staring at empty space, Mandy could almost believe that she'd never seen him at all, that she'd dreamed the whole encounter.

Kade stepped into the room and shook his head, smiling a little, when he saw that she was up and dressed. Sunrise was still several hours away.

He took off his hat, tossed it into the chair where Cree had been lounging only moments before, and looked around. For the space of a heartbeat, it seemed as if he'd picked up the other man's scent, the way a wild creature guarding its territory might do.

"Where have you been?" Mandy asked, because for reasons she didn't fully understand, she didn't want to tell Kade about Cree's visit. Not yet, anyway.

He raised one eyebrow. "Over at the jailhouse. I figured I ought to spell Jeb and the soldiers for a while." He took in her clothing again, and Mandy, looking down, realized she'd misbuttoned the dress. "Were you planning to go someplace?"

It was a hell of a time to realize that she couldn't lie to Kade, and an even worse one to admit she'd just had a visit from her brother. "No," she said, and didn't explain further.

He sighed, kicked off his boots one by one, and started to unfasten his shirt. "I need some sleep. Lord knows, it'll be light out soon enough."

Mandy watched, transfixed, as her husband stripped to the skin and got into bed. He lay propped on the pillows, his hands clasped behind his head, frowning at Mandy as though she were a puzzle to him.

"What's the matter?" he asked when she didn't volunteer anything.

She shook her head, raised slightly unsteady hands to the buttons of her dress. "I was just fretting about my mama." Dixie was sick, and Cree had left her in the keeping of strangers and paid for her care with money he'd likely stolen. Suppose the law was on his trail?

"Tell me about her," Kade said, watching as she came to the side of the bed, shed her dress, and crawled in beside him, still wearing her bloomers and camisole.

She settled in as best she could, dismayed to discover that she was near tears. She was tempted to tell him about Cree instead, but again some instinct stopped her. "Her name's Dixie. She's pretty, and she's got a gentle spirit," she said, slowly and softly, feeling calmer now that Kade was near. "She used to sing all the time, except when things were bad between her and Gig. She's sickly now."

Kade slid an arm beneath Mandy's shoulders and drew her closer. "I reckon you must want to see her pretty bad."

She nodded, blinking back tears.

"When this is over, I'll take you to her."

Mandy raised herself on one elbow. "I could go on my own."

"No," Kade said flatly. "It wouldn't be safe."

"Are you going to be a bossy husband, Kade McKettrick?" she asked, relaxing into his shoulder. Just then, it seemed the only safe place in the world.

He laughed. "Afraid so." And then he turned onto his side and kissed Mandy, all the while working the buttons of her camisole, and soon there was no room in her head for thoughts of anyone or anything but him.

54

It seemed fitting to Kade that the day of John Lewis's funeral dawned bitterly cold. A harsh, sharp-edged wind blew out of the north, and the trees, just beginning to sprout spring foliage, bent in the face of it.

The service was held at two o'clock that afternoon, and half the town crowded into the little church to hear Father Herrera preach over John's casket. Becky sat, composed and oddly serene, in the front row, with a fragile but blooming Emmeline at her side, listening intently, as though she were absorbing the words through her skin, storing every one away in the innermost chambers of her heart.

Mandy held Kade's hand tightly, squeezing it every once in a while, and he was thankful for her presence. Angus sat next to him, and he was grateful for that, too.

Kade, Rafe, and Jeb were all pallbearers, as were Holt and Angus and Doc Boylen. When all there was to say had been said, the six of them carried the pine box slowly down the aisle and out onto the street, and the wind stole Kade's hat right off his head, sent it rolling like a wagon wheel for Harry to chase down and bring back.

The cemetery was at the edge of town, a fair distance away,

but the coffin felt light, as though it were empty. Underneath the branches of a stately oak tree, a grave had been dug, yawning dark in the earth.

Kade bit his lower lip, remembering another funeral, as he was sure his brothers were doing. When their mother had died, they'd still been more boys than men, stunned and bereft. Angus, broken by the loss, had been little or no use, but Kade, for his part, had never blamed him. If anything, he'd been moved by the paradox of a man strong enough to let himself fall apart. A circuit preacher named Henry Woods had offered the prayer that day— it was cold, like this one—and they'd laid Georgia McKettrick to rest high on a ridge overlooking the Triple M.

Angus still went there often, though he didn't say much about it. Kade, on the other hand, had been back only once, the day after she was buried, when he'd gone alone to say he was sorry. Sorry for not being there to round up those strays; she'd have been safe in her parlor if he had and never fallen into the creek, taken sick, and left them all before they were ready to let her go.

Sorry he hadn't been a better son.

Now, helping to lower John Lewis's casket into the ground on a loose net of ropes, his throat constricted to such a point that he could barely breathe. Stealing a glance at his brothers, he saw grim composure in their faces and supposed they were grappling with similar memories, all their own. He knew Jeb and Rafe about as well as one man could know another, but the three of them had never talked much about losing Georgia. Secretly, Kade had always believed that they blamed him, at least in part, just as he blamed himself.

The coffin settled neatly into the deep pit, and the ropes were withdrawn, wound into coils, handed off to other mourners. Becky stepped forward to stand at the foot of John's final resting place and toss in a handful of blue crocuses, salvaged from between dirty patches of hardened snow. She wore a starched black gown and a veiled hat, and her shoulders were fiercely straight.

"I know you said you'd stay close by," she said clearly, as if she and John were the only ones there, and he able to mark her words, "but it would be selfish to keep you, so I won't. You go on now. One day, I'll catch up with you, but in the meantime, I'll be all right, so don't you fret about me, you hear?"

Emmeline, standing next to Rafe, gave a small sob, and Rafe slipped an arm around her waist, drew her against his side. She turned, clinging to him, and wept against his shoulder.

Becky lifted her gaze from the grave, raised her veil, and surveyed the other mourners with calm affection.

"Thank you," she said. "Thank you all for coming. There'll be refreshments served over at the hotel, and you're all welcome to join us." She touched her lips to the palm of her elegantly gloved hand, tossed the kiss to John. Her mouth moved, making no sound, and then she turned and walked away, a lonely, stalwart figure.

Emmeline wept all the harder, and Rafe led her back toward the hotel.

"Damn sad thing," Angus said, watching them go. "I declare, some things in this life are just about beyond bearing."

Jeb laid a hand to their father's back as he passed, but said nothing. Mandy looked up into Kade's face, her eyes full of concern.

"Are you all right?" she asked softly.

It was nearly his undoing, the tenderness in her voice. He almost put his arms around her, buried his face in her soft, fragrant hair, but the place was too public for that, and his feelings were too complex and too raw. He managed a nod. "You go on ahead to the hotel," he said gruffly. "I'll be there in a little while."

"I don't like leaving you."

He started to raise a hand, again wanting to touch her hair, pinned up in a ladylike arrangement the way it was, and coming loose, tendril by tendril, in the wind. "I have to say good-bye," he told her.

She hesitated, then nodded her understanding and went off alone, a little behind the others. He watched her until his vision blurred, then turned back to the grave.

Old Billy and a couple of unemployed cowhands were shoveling raw dirt into the hole, and the sound of it striking the top of John's casket was as bleak as any Kade had ever heard.

He had no words; with all that he'd read in his life, he'd have thought some would come to the surface now, but his head was empty. His heart, by contrast, was so full and so heavy that he feared his knees might buckle under the weight. He held his hat and remembered, because that was all he could do. He remembered a man who had done his job simply and without complaint, never expecting anything more than his pay in return, a man who'd thrown him in the hoosegow more than once for carousing and, when he was younger, given him lectures through the bars. Told him to take hold, stake out a piece of ground for himself, and make something worthwhile happen.

The recollection of those discourses, John leaning against the edge of his beat-up old desk, arms folded, face earnest, himself sitting on the same cot where he'd slept so often of late, some-times rebellious, sometimes ashamed, brought a faint smile to hover just back of his mouth, not quite ready to come through.

"Good-bye, John," he said finally, his hat in his hands. "And thanks."

55

CREE FELL INTO step beside Mandy as she passed Doc's office on her way back to the hotel following the funeral, and she started, as she always did when he sneaked up on her like that. He was half-Apache, Cree was, the son of a long-dead renegade who'd taken the white name of Lathrop, and he prided himself on making no sound, leaving no footprints, when he walked.

"So, it wasn't a dream," she said, and kept right on walking. Maybe her stride was even a little quicker than before.

"You've changed, Amanda Rose," Cree observed, taking no apparent notice of her peevish tone and stiff-backed manner. "For one thing, you don't look like a tomboy anymore."

She was aching inside because John was gone forever, because Dixie was dying among folks she did not know, and because Kade was hurting and she couldn't help him. Much as she'd missed Cree all these months and fretted over what devilment his wildness might have led him into, she wasn't in the mood for one of their sparring matches. "What are you doing here?" she asked as she had in the night. She hadn't gotten a straight answer then, but she was bound and determined to have one now.

His grin was cocky, and his dark eyes flashed with secrets. She knew he was going to sidestep the truth before he even opened his mouth. "I told you, Amanda Rose. I wanted to see my baby sister."

"Either you've turned stupid, or you're lying. Gig is here. His friends are probably around someplace, too. You wouldn't have stuck your head into a noose like this just to pay me a visit."

He feigned a wounded expression, keeping pace with her as she hurried along the sidewalk toward the Arizona Hotel. When she didn't respond, but simply tightened her mouth, he decided to play one of his trump cards. He always had a sleeveful of those. "I'm working for Jim Dandy's Wild West Show."

That made her stop, right on the sidewalk, and look up at him, hugging herself against the persistent wind. She felt a chill, deep inside, as she gazed into those dark and often unreadable eyes, and knew it had nothing to do with the crisp spring weather. "Doing what?" she demanded. "Riding? Shooting? Throwing that knife of yours? What?"

"Some of everything." Cree stepped back a half stride, though Mandy doubted he was aware of doing so. "Mainly, I just travel ahead of the show to stir up a little excitement, do some fancy riding and shooting, post some bills, sell a few tickets."

Mandy wanted to kick him, though she wasn't sure precisely why. Might have gone ahead and done it, too, if Kade hadn't caught up just then.

He looked Cree over without a whit of reticence. "I don't believe I've had the pleasure." No trace of friendliness was in Kade's voice or his manner, but that was understandable, she supposed, given the nature of the day.

"Kade, this is my brother, Cree Lathrop. Cree, my husband, Kade McKettrick."

Cree put out his hand first, and Kade hesitated, almost imperceptibly, before taking it. He didn't smile.

"Congratulations," Cree said. "My little sister is a prize worth the winning."

Kade slanted a look at Mandy, questioning, but tender, too. "Yes. She's that, all right." He indicated the hotel with his hat, which he carried in one hand, so that the wind ruffled his hair. "There's a gathering up ahead to honor a departed friend," he added quietly. "Maybe you'd like to join us."

"I surely would," Cree answered, edging the words with polite regret, "but I've got some things to do. Maybe we can talk later."

A look passed between the two men, and it made Mandy feel pushed aside, and frightened, too.

"I'll be over at the jailhouse after a while," Kade said.

Cree inclined his head affably, but the look in his eyes was watchful and wary. "I might see you there."

"What's his business here, Mandy?"

"He's working with a Wild West show."

Apparently satisfied, Kade put an arm around Mandy and steered her toward the hotel. It was warm inside, crowded with John's many friends, and Sarah Fee and Clive were handing out cups of steaming spiced cider. Mandy accepted one and let it warm her icy fingers, avoiding Kade's gaze when she felt him studying her.

She might have dwelt on her uneasiness over Cree's arrival if it hadn't been for Becky. She was a vision, even in her mourning garb, weaving between the little clusters of people, speaking to this one, touching that one lightly on the arm, even smiling now and then. Watching her, Mandy felt profound admiration, for she'd glimpsed the depths of this woman's suffering, and she knew what it must be costing her to seek others out and offer them comfort.

In time, she came to Mandy. "Joy in the midst of sorrow," she said, and taking Mandy's hand, she kissed her on the cheek. "You made a lovely bride, Amanda Rose. If I neglected to offer my congratulations last night, I apologize."

"You came to the wedding," Mandy said softly. "You can't know what that meant to me, especially . . ." Her words fell away, and she flushed with misery. "I mean—"

"I know what you were trying to say," Becky said gently.

"How can you be so strong?" Mandy couldn't stop herself from asking. "You loved John so much, and yet here you are, trying to make other people feel better."

Becky raised one eyebrow, smiled a little. She was still pale, and an ache pulsed in her eyes, but she was coming back from wherever she'd gone in those first cruel hours after the tragedies, and so was Emmeline. "It's *because* I loved John so much that I'm determined to go on as best I can," she said softly. Her grip on Mandy's hand tightened momentarily before she released it. "You and Kade, Rafe and Emmeline—all of you are so lucky to have found each other so early in your lives. Make the most of it, Amanda Rose. Love that man with everything you are and everything you have and, more important still, let him love you back."

Mandy swallowed, lonely for Kade even though he was only a dozen feet away, talking quietly with his father and Jeb. Was it love, what she felt for him? She didn't have the experience to know. "I keep thinking it all happened too quickly," she confessed. "That it can't last."

"Just be glad it happened at all," Becky said. "And *make* it last. The choice is yours to make, my girl." She gave Mandy a little push in Kade's direction and moved on to accept a kiss and a word of consolation from Doc.

Angus smiled down at Mandy when she reached Kade's side. "Doc said you were quite a hand with those Sussex kids," her father-in-law said. "Makes me proud to call you daughter."

Tears burned behind Mandy's eyes, and she blinked them back. She didn't know what to say, didn't, in fact, trust herself to speak. No one had ever told her they were proud of her before, not like they meant it, anyway. Coupled with the things Becky had said, and coming from the head of the McKettrick clan, it was nearly enough to overwhelm her.

"Have you seen Emmeline?" Concepcion asked, appearing at Angus's side with fresh mugs of cider for herself and her husband. "I am worried about her. She was so upset at the funeral."

Mandy was ashamed that she'd forgotten her friend even for a moment. "I'll find out how she is," she said, and after exchanging a glance with Kade, she headed for the stairs.

She knocked lightly at the door of the room Rafe and Emmeline shared when they were in town, and entered at Rafe's gruff "Come in."

Emmeline lay still on the bed, her eyes closed, and Rafe had drawn up a chair to stay close and hold her hand. The expression in his eyes was bleak when he looked up at Mandy, but that McKettrick strength was there, too.

"I'll sit with Emmeline awhile," Mandy told him. Then, taking a chance: "Why don't you go downstairs and talk to Kade?"

56

RAFE STOPPED AT the base of the stairs and swept the lobby with his gaze, and it came to rest, with no great willingness, on Kade, who was standing alone by the front window, staring out. He seemed oblivious of the other people in the room, but then, that was Kade. He was bookish, more interested in the dead and dusty philosophies of the Greeks and the Romans, most times, than living folks. It wouldn't have surprised Rafe to find out Kade was going over some ancient battle in his mind, drawing parallels between that and the outlaw situation and trying to extract a strategy.

With a sigh of resignation, Rafe started moving again. He crossed the room, stood next to Kade. The street looked empty to him, but there was no telling what Kade saw there.

The silence was awkward, but Rafe knew it fell to him to break it. He'd presented himself, and he figured he had to do the talking.

"I hear you and Mandy tied the knot."

Kade lifted a glass of punch to his mouth, took a sip, but didn't turn to face Rafe or even glance in his direction. "That's right," he said in his own good time. "How's Emmeline?"

Rafe bit back a terse response. "I reckon she'll mend in time."

Kade took more punch. With him, the mills ground slowly. "What about you?"

"I've been better." Rafe folded his arms, wondering what it was about that lonesome track that fascinated his brother, and forced himself to go on, get it over with. "I was wrong the other night. When I said it was your fault that Emmeline lost the baby, I mean. You probably saved her life."

At last, Kade turned toward him, a look of sorrowful amusement in his eyes, and batted at his ear with the palm of one hand. "Funny thing," he drawled. "I thought I just heard Rafe McKettrick apologize."

Rafe scowled. "Don't make too much of it."

Kade laughed and shook his head, but then his expression turned solemn again. "I want to win the ranch," he said with the forthrightness that was their common inheritance, "and I mean to have it if I can. But I wouldn't have wished that kind of sorrow on you for anything."

Rafe was tempted to lay a hand to Kade's shoulder, but something, maybe pride, stopped him. "You won't get the Triple M if I have anything to say about it," he said, and he meant it.

"Fair enough." With that, Kade turned back to surveying his moldy Romans and prissy Greeks, making their invisible parade down the street, and Rafe went in search of something to eat.

When Rafe came back to watch over Emmeline, after being gone an hour or so, Mandy made her way downstairs. The lobby was empty, and so was the dining room, except for Jeb. He was sitting at one of the tables, with several untouched pieces of pie in front of him, and he stood until she took the chair opposite his.

"Everybody ran off and left me," he said cheerfully, apparently explaining the excess of pie. He'd finished off at least two pieces himself, judging by the debris. "Pa and Concepcion went to pay some social calls, and Holt's gone back to the Circle C. Kade's down at the jailhouse, if you're wondering, making some repairs."

Mandy sighed. "I knew he meant to go there." She was glad to have Jeb to sit with, because it would be dark soon and she didn't want to go back to her and Kade's room alone. Cree was her brother and her closest friend, but he'd scared her the night before, and she still felt skittery.

Jeb took a pack of cards from the pocket of his suit coat, which was draped over the back of his chair, and shuffled. "Poker?"

Mandy smiled in spite of herself. "Sure."

He dealt, watched as she pretended to puzzle over her hand, rearranging cards and frowning.

"This is some honeymoon," he observed at considerable length.

Mandy pulled a piece of pie in her direction, then pushed it away again without picking up a fork. "Yes," she conceded.

His eyes danced. "I'm not sure this is a fit game for a lady."

"Kade thought the same thing about horse racing."

Jeb laughed. "He sure enough did." He picked up his cards then and studied them, and his grin lost a little of its luster.

"Not a betting man?" Mandy teased. She had a straight, ace high.

Jeb's pride was his undoing, the way it was with most men. Without a word, he fished a coin out of his trouser pocket and tossed it into the center of the table, then raised his eyebrows, waiting for her to bet.

"Will you take a promissory note?" she asked sweetly.

"Since you're my sister-in-law, I reckon that would be all right."

"Good."

By the time Kade returned two hours later, looking as though he'd been dragged backward through a knothole, she was up three heifers, a buckboard, and a fancy Mexican saddle.

57

CREE LATHROP WAS kin, now that he and Mandy were married, Kade reflected as he opened the door of Curry's cell the next morning, a plate of Mamie Sussex's questionable cooking in his free hand, but that didn't mean he had to like the man.

Curry lay on his cot, staring up at the ceiling. He was sweating, and he looked like a husk with everything inside rotted away. He'd been that way since the shootout the other night, hardly moving or speaking.

Kade, watchful, set the plate down on the floor beside him and took a step back. "Looks like that gang of yours turned on you. Got themselves a new leader or something."

"Leave me alone," Curry moaned. "I'm sick. Real sick. Maybe my wound is fixing to take an infection."

Kade shook his head, stepped out of the cell, shut the door, and locked it.

Cree Lathrop was standing just over the threshold when he turned around, and it gave Kade a start, though he was pretty sure his reaction didn't show.

"Mornin', Marshal," Cree said with a slow grin that said he knew he'd caught Kade off guard, and he'd intended to do just that. "Or should I call you brother, now that you and my sister are man and wife?"

"My given name will do," Kade said, willing the hairs on the back of his neck to lie down flat.

Lathrop was a lithe man, clad in fitted gear, probably bought in Mexico. He pulled off his black gloves with graceful, methodical motions and tucked them into his gun belt. His weapon was a .44, unless Kade missed his guess, and the holster looked worn. He carried a bowie knife, too.

Cree heaved a grand sigh. "Looks like we're not destined to be friends, you and I," he said with insincere regret. "I was afraid of that."

Kade wanted coffee, but instinct warned him not to turn his back on Cree, even long enough to pour brew into a mug. He gestured toward a chair. "Have a seat." They'd talked the night before, but only briefly, and not in much depth, since Old Billy had been hanging around, along with a few of Captain Harvey's soldiers.

Cree moved with the grace of a mountain lion, sitting down easy, stretching his legs out in front of him. His spurs were hammered silver, and he'd taken the trouble to polish them at some point. "You have any sisters, Kade?"

"Just brothers." Kade regarded Emmeline as a sister, now that he'd moved on from his initial fascination with her, but he didn't care to mention her, not to Lathrop, anyhow.

Another philosophical sigh. "Well, it's a special thing, having a sister. Hard to explain. On the one hand, it's a burden." He made the accompanying gesture. "On the other, it's a sacred trust."

Kade didn't comment, he merely listened. He did take note, as he had the night before, that Cree was well-spoken; like Mandy, he'd had some education somewhere along the line.

Cree's voice was soft, even, with an odd sort of rhythmic underbeat, like the ticking of a metronome in a distant room. "Amanda Rose is wild as a range filly in spring," he went on. "She's never lived in one place long, and she doesn't know what it is to have fine things." He indicated Curry's cell with a slight inclination of his head. "Thanks to that devil's saint in there, she and I both learned to look out for ourselves, early on."

"I reckon you intend to make a point somewhere along the line. You mind getting to it?"

Cree smiled slowly, and the answer was a while in coming, too. "I came here as a favor to you," he said, lounging. "You look to be a good man, and it only seemed right to warn you that she'll just up and leave one of these fine days." Another gesture, this time with both hands. "Best you know ahead of time, so it doesn't come as a shock."

The thought of Mandy taking to her heels wasn't new to Kade, not by any means, but it still made his gut grind, hearing someone else say it out loud. Especially someone who surely knew Mandy better than he did. "I plan on convincing her to stay," he said evenly.

Cree pulled a mournful face, but the light in his nearly black eyes and the easy confidence in his manner gave the lie to his expression. "She tell you that I'm with the Wild West show?" he asked mildly, and this time, Kade knew damn well that the other man had read him clearly, because he gave a little smile. "Mandy's always wanted to join up with one of those outfits, see the country, ride fine horses, have a little money of her own to put by for the future. Jim and the rest of the company will be here in a week or so. The show will run another week after that. And when we pull out, Mandy will go with us."

Kade felt as though he'd been punched in the belly, but he kept his composure. "Her choice," he said with a detachment he didn't feel. "If she wants to leave, I won't try to stop her." Like hell he wouldn't.

"Fair enough." Cree got to his feet. "Mind if I have a word with the prisoner? I've got no use for him myself, but he means something to my ma."

Kade glanced pointedly at the .44. "Not if you take off that iron first, I don't," he said, expecting an argument. Hell, part of him craved one, complete with fists, bruises, and blood. "The knife, too."

Cree merely shrugged, though, unbuckled his gun belt, and set it aside on Kade's desk, along with the gloves. They were made of thin, supple leather, those gloves, designed for shooting, not honest work. He pulled the knife from its scabbard and laid it down, too. "I won't be long."

Kade watched as Mandy's brother strolled back to the cell and stood looking in, gripping the bars. Since a good ten feet stretched between Cree and the bowie and the .44, he figured it was safe to pour himself a cup of coffee, and he did.

Lathrop spoke in the same low, even tone he'd used with Kade, the words pitched just a shade too low to catch hold of, and if Curry offered a response, Kade didn't hear it.

Presently, Cree came back, nodded cordially to Kade, strapped on his gun belt, reclaimed his knife, and left.

Kade waited until he was gone, then approached the cell himself.

"What was that little powwow about?" he asked without a hope in all creation of getting an answer.

Curry was still staring at the ceiling, his meal untouched on the floor beside the cot. His clothes were soaked with sweat, and his throat moved visibly when he swallowed.

"Said he'd cut my throat first chance he got," Curry said, and squeezed his eyes shut like somebody trying to get over a bad dream.

58

MANDY WATCHED, ARMS folded, as her brother nailed a poster to the clapboard facade of the mercantile. SHOOTING EXPOSITION, it read. FRIDAY AFTERNOON AT FOUR O'CLOCK. FREE TO PUBLIC, COURTESY OF JIM DANDY'S WILD WEST SHOW.

Cree turned his head to smile at her. "What do you think? Better than the one I sent ahead of time, right?" he asked. His smile was ingenuous; this was the mischievous Cree she remembered. She'd been silly, she decided, to be so uneasy. Probably it had been all the dying and sickness that had gotten to her, and nothing to do with her brother at all. Sure, his arrival had been unexpected, but then, Cree had always been a pilgrim of the wind.

"I think you're a show-off," she said.

He laughed, approached her, touched her hair with one gloved hand. "You're just jealous. The truth is, Mrs. McKettrick, that you wouldn't mind doing a little showing off yourself." He shook a finger under her nose. "I heard about that horse race. Didn't anybody ever tell you women are supposed to sit with their hands folded, batting their lashes, and never, *ever* put on pants, jump onto a horse, and leave their own husbands in the dust?"

"Not this woman. And he wasn't my husband then." The fact was, she'd changed since she'd married Kade—she didn't mind wearing dresses, putting her hair up, or even batting her lashes all that much. She especially didn't mind the things she and Kade did when they were alone together, though of course she had no intention of mentioning anything so private.

Cree gazed thoughtfully toward the jailhouse. "I always heard the McKettricks were ranchers. Not lawmen."

"They are," Mandy answered, wishing, for the thousandth time in her life, that she could see inside her brother's head and reason out what was going on there. "Why?"

"Trust you to take up with a town marshal," Cree said in that same distracted way, as if he hadn't heard her question. More likely, he'd just decided to brush it off.

Mandy felt a sting of annoyance. "What's that supposed to mean?" she snapped. "I might expect a remark like that from Gig, but coming from you—" She caught her breath. "You're not in trouble with the law, are you, Cree?"

He chucked her under the chin, a gesture she had always secretly loved, since affection of any kind had been a rare thing for her, but now, it only unsettled her. "Of course not. I was teasing, Amanda Rose. What's become of your sense of humor?"

She felt herself softening toward Cree; it had been that way as long as she could remember. He could pull her hair or leave her behind when he went off on some grand adventure, then get around all her objections with a simple grin.

She gave him a little push. "I've got things to do. I can't be standing around watching you put up signs."

"What things?" He spoke lightly, but she sensed a quietness

in him, a deep, listening silence. Vast places lay within Cree, dark and secret landscapes that no one else ever glimpsed, but then, she supposed that was true of everybody.

"Errands," she said, shaking off the shadows, pleased to have the upper hand for once. She walked a little way past him, then turned to look back over one shoulder. "Join us for supper? Six o'clock, in the hotel dining room?"

He hesitated. "I'm not sure that's such a good idea."

She stood absolutely still for a moment, seized by some nameless dread. "Why do you say that?"

"I don't know if you've noticed it or not, Amanda Rose, but your fine new husband doesn't have a lot of use for me." Having tossed off that disturbing statement, Cree turned and walked away.

Mandy watched him for a few moments, hurting inside. Then, resolved to make use of the day, she headed for the mercantile, her original destination. There she bought books and a newspaper for Emmeline, along with a rainbow of embroidery thread, and all the while she was making her selections, Minnie chattered—wasn't it something how Becky Fairmont had turned the church on its collective ear by turning up at Sunday service, expecting to worship right along with good Christian folks? Hadn't John Lewis's funeral been the best one ever, even with a Catholic overseeing the service? Wasn't it something that Mamie Sussex, who was no better than she should be, hadn't lost a one of those thieving brats of hers to the diphtheria? Didn't it make you wonder what the good Lord knew that they didn't, when somebody like Emmeline suffered a miscarriage? And what about that fine-looking half-breed, traipsing all over town putting up posters?

By the time she'd signed the account book and gathered up her parcels, Mandy's ears were burning and her resolution to hold her peace had deserted her. "That 'fine-looking half-breed,'" she said tautly, "is my brother, Cree Lathrop. Becky is probably one of the best people who ever set foot in any church, anyplace, for any reason, and John's funeral was indeed memorable. If the good Lord takes a shine to anybody, it ought to be Emmeline. As for Mamie Sussex and her children, they're just trying to get by, and it might be a little easier if folks like you spared them a kind word once in a while."

Minnie's mouth was open, and she was red to her hairline. "You, Mandy whatever-your-name-is, are impertinent."

"McKettrick," Mandy said crisply. "My name is McKettrick." She leaned forward over the counter and dropped her voice to a stage whisper. "And, yes, I'm almost certainly no better than I should be."

Minnie was still sputtering when Mandy left the store.

She took the thread and books back to Emmeline, stayed with her for a little while, then raided the hotel kitchen, putting together a substantial midday meal for her husband, and making sure there was extra, in case Harry was around.

Kade was alone when she reached the jail, except for Gig, of course, who was brooding in his cell. Mandy caught the briefest glimpse of him, sitting on the edge of his cot with his head clasped between his hands.

"I brought you something to eat," she told Kade, smiling. He was seated at his desk, going over some official-looking papers, and when he looked up at her, she saw a kind of reserve in his eyes, as though he were drawing back from her.

He spared her a responding smile, but it was short-lived, and a little forced, in her opinion. "That was downright wifely of you," he said, and though she knew he was trying for a light note, the effort missed the mark by a considerable margin. "And I admit to being hungry."

She busied herself taking the food from the covered basket, setting things out on the surface of the desk. "Where's Harry?"

"Helping out at home."

She was glad she'd brought him several servings of the pork roast the cook intended to offer as the evening special over at the dining room, because he seemed pleased. There were biscuits, too, along with mashed potatoes, gravy, and green beans boiled up with bacon and onions.

Her heart squeezed painfully as she watched him eat. "You must be missing John a whole lot," she surmised, pulling up a chair and sitting as close as she thought proper, in the broad light of day.

Kade nodded. "I've got a few other concerns, too," he allowed without looking at her. For him, that was a soul-baring revelation, akin to the speech he'd made before, about her being a wildflower and having shallow roots. It chafed, that part about the roots.

"Is there anything I can do to help?" she asked.

Kade pushed the plate away, half-finished, and met her gaze directly. "Yes," he said, seriously. Then his smile came, blinding and impudent. He leaned toward her and added, in a brazen whisper, "You can give the sun a good push in a westward direction, so it will get dark sooner and I can take my wife to bed. That seems to be the only place I'm comfortable these days."

Mandy blushed, though the prospect of their lovemaking

caused her nipples to harden under her everyday dress. "Kade McKettrick!"

He laughed and reached over to pass his hand lightly over her breast. "What?"

"You're too bold," she hissed.

"You're not exactly hidebound yourself," he replied, McKettrick-smug.

She blushed again, casting about for a change of subject. "Who's going to look after this place?"

"Won't be anything to look after." His expression betrayed misgivings, as well as relief.

Mandy stared at him, gestured toward the cell. "What about Gig?"

"Army wants him." He laid a hand on the documents he'd been reading when she came in. "That's what these papers are about. Captain Harvey and his pony soldiers are taking Curry to the stockade at the fort sometime this afternoon."

Mandy had no objection to Gig's leaving, but at least she'd known right where he was at all times, since he'd taken up residence in the Indian Rock jail. He was a slippery son of a gun, though, and even Captain Harvey and his soldiers might not be able to hold on to him. Soldiers, like cowboys, tended to be honorable sorts, working in the open, and outlaws liked to take advantage of that kind of complacency.

"What do you think?" she asked carefully.

He drew his plate back and stabbed another forkful of pork roast. "Two words. *Good* and *riddance*."

"Aren't you worried about recovering the Triple M's money?"

"Now that I won't have to play nursemaid to Curry for the better part of every day, I'll have time to find it."

Mandy sat back in her chair, thinking before she spoke, then venturing carefully onto uncertain ground. Kade knew a little about her outlaw childhood, but she didn't want him dwelling on it, lest it color his current and mostly favorable opinion of her. "They might ambush Captain Harvey and his men. The other members of the gang, I mean."

"I do believe the Captain and his men are hoping that's what will happen," Kade's appetite had obviously returned, but Mandy wasn't sure she'd be able to swallow so much as a bite, unless and until she knew for sure that Gig Curry was either locked up in prison for all time, or under six feet of hard dirt. "One thing for sure: the army ought to be ready this time. If they capture that gang, I figure one of them's bound to talk, if only in the hope of saving his own skin."

"What if the thieves have already spent the money?"

Kade pondered that, then shook his head. "They haven't had the chance. They've been holed up around here someplace, within striking distance anyway, and if there'd been any significant amount of cash changing hands, somebody around town would have noticed. And commented."

The theory made sense, but Mandy was still troubled. She tried to put a brighter face on things; maybe she was wrong to feel jittery. "I invited Cree to have supper with us tonight," she said, testing the waters. "Over at the dining room."

Kade lowered his fork slowly back to his plate, and something altered in his face, a change so subtle that she almost missed it. He spoke evenly. "Did you, now?"

Mandy stiffened; old affronts, with their beginnings in other people and places, came back to haunt her. "You don't like him."

"I didn't say that," Kade replied moderately.

"You didn't have to," Mandy accused. "Is it because he's part Apache?" She knew, almost as well as Cree did, how folks felt about mixed bloods. Breeds, they called them. She'd grown up with the insults, the sly looks, the shutting out, not just by the whites, but by the Indians, too. Hadn't she just encountered that kind of prejudice over at the general store?

Kade stared at her, angry and astounded. "Is that what you think? That I'm the kind to judge a man by the color of his hide?"

Mandy bolted to her feet, sat down again. Fought back tears of frustration and disappointment. She could fool herself all she wanted, call herself Mrs. McKettrick and parade around in fine dresses, but the truth was that nothing really changed. She and Cree would always be outsiders wherever they went.

"Mandy?" Kade prompted gruffly when she didn't speak.

"Yes," she answered in a burst. "That's what I think! You hate my brother because he's an Indian."

"I don't hate your brother." Kade's voice was low, seething with suspicion.

"Maybe you don't," Mandy accused bitterly, "but you'd just as soon he moved on, wouldn't you?"

"Yes."

"Why?" It was a demand.

Kade didn't answer for a long time, and when he did, Mandy wished he hadn't. "Because I think he's an outlaw."

"You're wrong!"

He studied her. "Am I, Mandy?"

"Yes! Yes, you're wrong, you—you *McKettrick!*" With that, she turned and headed for the door, half hoping that Kade would call her back.

He didn't.

59

GIG CURRY, KADE soon concluded, had recovered from his melancholy spell. He gave a hoarse burst of laughter as Mandy slammed out the front door. "Well, Marshal, seems to me the honeymoon is over."

"Shut up," Kade said without turning around, "or you won't have to wait for Cree Lathrop to cut your worthless throat, because I'll do it myself."

At the mention of Lathrop, Curry subsided, though grudgingly.

"You're afraid of Lathrop," Kade said, turning in his chair to study the prisoner.

"Ain't scared of nobody," Curry replied, but the look of him belied his words.

Kade shrugged, though he was still troubled. He knew he wasn't going to get any more out of Curry, however, so he turned back to the paperwork on his desk. It was an effort to concentrate, with Mandy on the peck.

An hour later, Captain Harvey rode up with a lot of brass-jingling and military flourish, and Kade went out to meet him. The aging soldier and his troops made an impressive picture, filling the street the way they did, with their blue uniforms and their polished buttons.

"Captain," Kade said by way of a greeting, tugging at his hat brim.

Harvey nodded. "We're here to collect Curry," he said with the kind of authority that comes from being obeyed unquestioningly and on a long-standing basis.

"I trust you'll let us know if you manage to get anything worthwhile out of him," Kade said.

"You have my word on that," Harvey answered, his grim expression holding firm. "The United States army wants to recover that money as much as you do."

Kade rather doubted that, since the United States army didn't stand to forfeit a ranch they'd bled and sweated to build. "Whatever you say, Captain," he replied with a semblance of a salute.

The big vein in the soldier's neck stood out. He raised a hand, and two of his men dismounted at the signal, one carrying handcuffs, the other, shackles. Gig Curry's ride to the fort was not going to be commodious—now *there* was a pity.

Kade turned, led the way into the office, and unlocked Curry's cell. The pair of corporals dragged him up off the cot and fixed him handily for transport with a lot of clanking.

Curry, far from balking, looked flat-out relieved to be putting Indian Rock behind him, no matter what might lie ahead at the fort.

"So long, Marshal," he said. "If I ever see you again man to man, I'll give you good cause to regret the shameful way I've been dealt with here."

"I'm sorry," Kade said insincerely, "if you found our hospitality lacking."

Before Curry could dredge up a reply, the soldiers took him

by the arms and dragged him through the doorway. To their credit, they showed a complete lack of consideration for the prisoner's dignity and comfort.

Kade ambled outside and watched, along with most of the town, as Curry was hoisted into a saddle, shackles, cuffs, and all. He did feel a moment of poignant sympathy—for the unlucky horse appointed to carry him.

He almost missed seeing Cree Lathrop standing across the street, his arms folded, his gaze fixed on Curry. A flash of movement drew Kade's attention, a gloved hand going for the .44 in that well-used holster.

Kade's own weapon was in his hand in the same instant; he didn't recall drawing, or even making the decision to do so. For better or worse, Angus McKettrick had taught all his sons to shoot as soon as they could hold an iron steady.

Lathrop saw him, made a show of spreading his arms at his sides, and smiled benignly.

Kade put the .45 away, but he kept an eye on the other man until Captain Dixon Harvey and his troops had ridden out with Curry in their midst, leaving dust and horse manure in their wake.

Lathrop stepped down off the sidewalk and walked across the street toward Kade, still sporting that smile, strangely empty now; his attitude said he was bent on placating the overanxious lawman.

"You're pretty fast with that .45," Cree remarked, facing him.

Kade shrugged. He wanted to find Mandy, try to make things right with her, since they'd parted on unfriendly terms. "You were going to shoot him," he said. "Curry, I mean."

"I confess that I was tempted," Cree admitted lightly, as though gunning a man down, even one like Curry, who barely qualified as human, meant nothing at all. "I wouldn't have done it, though."

Kade disliked double-talk and wanted to throw Lathrop against a wall, but he restrained himself. After all, this man was Mandy's brother, which most likely meant they'd be having dealings with each other right along, whether either of them liked it or not. "Since I had no way of knowing what you intended," Kade said, after willing his jaw to relax so he could get the words out, "I most likely would have dropped you where you stood."

Cree sighed. He was wasted with the Wild West show; he should have been traveling with a theater troupe instead, starring in melodramas. "That would have been a shame. Amanda Rose would never have forgiven you, I reckon."

Kade looked the man up and down. "She says she invited you to supper. Seems like you might be busy doing something else, now that you think about it."

Cree's face hardened. "We got off to a bad start, you and me," he said, feigning chagrin.

"I reckon we did at that."

"Give Amanda Rose my sincerest regrets," Cree said with another shrug, as Kade turned toward the open door of the jailhouse.

Kade didn't look back. "I will," he said. Then he went inside, banked the fire in the potbellied stove, took the master set of keys from the desk drawer, and locked the place behind him.

He was still wearing the badge as he walked away, but as far as he was concerned, his brief career as a peace officer was as good as finished. All he needed to do was find a replacement, and he'd be back on the Triple M, where he belonged, tending to ranch business.

He'd start by recovering the stolen money. Damned if he'd see the land go, to be broken up into a lot of small spreads, run by Johnny-come-latelies. In point of fact, he'd die first.

Deliberately, he turned his mind to his second objective, selecting a site and building a house for Mandy. He wasn't at all sure she would stay—Cree's warning carried weight, and he remembered only too well how her eyes had gleamed when she'd told him she wanted to be another Annie Oakley—but he meant to do everything he could to convince her that her place was on the Triple M, with him.

He was sorting through these thoughts, and others, as he walked down the street, crossed over, and approached the hotel.

He found Mandy bustling around the dining room, serving meals to a crowd of cowboys, and taking their good-natured, if rowdy, joshing in her stride. When she caught sight of Kade, she stiffened and nearly dropped the roast-pig dinners she was carrying in both hands.

"I want to talk to you," Kade said.

"I'm busy," she replied, all bristly-like.

He leaned in close and spoke softly, but in all earnestness. "I will carry you out of here over my shoulder, if need be, but you *are* going with me, Mrs. McKettrick. Right now."

She flushed with obvious indignation, turned and banged the plates down in front of a couple of startled cowpunchers, then ripped off her apron, sought out Sarah Fee, and made her hushed excuses.

A few of the cowhands called out manly encouragement as Kade ushered his furious wife up the stairs, and when they reached the second-floor corridor, she wrenched free of his grasp on her elbow and spat, "I have never been so mortified in all my life!"

He shouldn't have laughed, but he couldn't help it. She was a sure-enough sight to behold when her temper got the best of her.

Plainly incensed by his amusement, she drew back her hand to slap him, hesitated, then decided to go through with the original plan. Kade caught her wrist just shy of his face.

"Tell me about your brother, Mandy."

She glared at him. "You wouldn't listen anyway!"

He let go of her wrist, spread his hands. "I'm listening."

She sighed, settled down a little. Kade had taken a seat on the edge of the bed, and he beckoned her to sit beside him. Cautiously, she did. "He might have been in some trouble," she allowed, "when he was younger, I mean. But he *isn't* an outlaw."

"Gig Curry is scared shitless of him," Kade pressed, watching her face. "Why is that, Mandy?"

She considered her words carefully. It would be so easy for Kade, or anyone else, to misunderstand. "When we were kids, Curry taught us to steal. He *made* us steal. Whenever Cree talked back to him, Gig beat him senseless. He hated Gig—we both did—and he swore a blood oath that he'd kill him one day, for all he'd done to all of us."

Kade's expression revealed none of what he was thinking. "Go on."

"Cree ran away when he was sixteen. Once in a while, he'd

come to see me, always in secret, asking about Mama, bringing money. Each time he visited, he was a little stronger and little faster with a gun. He wanted me to go away with him, but I was afraid to leave Mama alone with Gig, so I always said no."

"But you did leave her, at some point," Kade prompted. She could still read nothing of his thoughts by searching his face.

She nodded. This was the hard part. "Gig wanted—he started—"

Kade's jawline clenched. "Touching you?"

Mandy blinked back tears, nodded. "I had to go then, so I lit out on my own. I ended up at St. Jude's Mission, north of here."

"I know the place." Kade had taken her hand, interlaced her fingers with his own. "A priest and couple of nuns, running an Indian school."

"I fell sick with a fever right after I got there, and the sisters took care of me." She felt a hot flush surge beneath the flesh of her face. "I repaid them by stealing a habit and a mule and taking to the trail. The mule died along the way, and a passing stagecoach picked me up the next day. The first stop was Indian Rock, and I didn't have the money to travel any further, so I got off. Becky and Emmeline took me in."

"Why the nun suit?" The question was blunt, but the faintest note of a chuckle was couched inside it.

"It was what I had. The sisters burned my clothes while I was sick."

"You could have told Becky the truth."

"No," Mandy argued quietly. "I knew Gig was out there someplace, and if he found me . . ." She shook off the horrors of that possibility, reliving the moment when her worst fears had come upon her that day in the alley behind the Arizona Hotel. "I didn't reckon he'd be looking for a nun."

Kade was thoughtful, but he put his arm around her and held her against his side. "From now on," he said presently, "you don't have to be anybody but yourself."

The idea was balm to Mandy's gypsy soul, but she couldn't help asking herself the obvious question.

Who, exactly, was she? Dixie's daughter? Cree's little sister? Kade McKettrick's wife? That was when the realization struck her. She'd better find out, before it was too late.

60

CREE LATHROP HAD vanished, and that troubled Kade far more than the man's unwelcome presence ever had.

The day of the much anticipated "shooting exhibition," heralded by bills posted all over town, came and went, and a sense of uneasiness settled over Indian Rock, causing Kade to pin on his badge again. He sent wires to other places, inquiring about Jim Dandy's Wild West Show, and the various town marshals and prominent citizens he contacted replied, to a man, that they'd never heard of the outfit.

Though Mandy had seemed forthcoming about her past, though they both caught fire in bed every time they lay down together, which was often, a certain distance still stretched between them, because there were still secrets Kade didn't know how to breach the gap, either with his mind or his body, and when he tried to talk to Mandy, she withdrew.

A week of this had gone by when two things happened that changed everything. The first was a telegram from the U.S. army, sent by Captain Dixon Harvey:

GIG CURRY ESCAPED STOCKADE LAST
NIGHT. TWO GUARDS KILLED BY ACCOMPLICE
OR ACCOMPLICES. ADVISE CAUTION.

Kade was still absorbing the implications of that when Concepcion burst into his office at the jailhouse, pale and dusty from a hard ride.

"Something's happened to Angus!" she blurted.

Kade crumpled the telegram into a wad and tossed it onto his desk. "What?"

Fresh tears followed the tracks of others, already shed, leaving streaks on Concepcion's face. "He saddled up yesterday and rode out," she managed, as Kade eased her into a chair. "He said he was tired of being holed up in the house and wanted to feel like a man again. I begged him not to go, but he wouldn't listen."

Dread curdled in the pit of Kade's stomach. "I take it he didn't come back."

She shook her head. "I sent some of the men from the bunkhouse out to search for him right after sunrise."

Kade took three or four slow, deep breaths. "No word from them?"

Again, Concepcion shook her head. "I waited as long as I could bear to. I could think of nothing to do but to come and find you. I don't know where Rafe and Jeb are—like I said, I came straight to you—but now you must all go and look for him."

Kade was already strapping on his gun belt. "Rafe is with Emmeline at the hotel," he said, cataloging facts for his own sake as well as his stepmother's, "and Jeb is probably at the Bloody Basin, fleecing some cowboy out of his wages over a game of poker."

"I am going with you."

"No," Kade replied flatly. "You'll only slow us down. I'll get somebody to take you back to the ranch. Pa's probably already there, wondering where you've gone." If only he truly believed that. Unfortunately, his gut was telling him something different.

"You know that is not so," Concepcion accused, dark eyes snapping with frustration and fear.

"Right now, I don't know much of anything," Kade said, putting on his hat. "Go home, Concepcion. If Pa is in trouble, he'll need you to be there waiting when we bring him back."

With that, Kade went out.

Harry was idling at the horse trough out front, with his feet swinging in the scummy water. Kade sent him to the livery stable, to tell Old Billy to get a buckboard ready, then made for the Bloody Basin.

He pushed open the swinging doors, scanned the dark and smoky interior, and saw Jeb at a table in the back, with cards in his hands and a big pile of chips in front of him. Kade beckoned, and Jeb laid down his hand, excused himself to the other players, and came toward him. Two cowboys, both riding for the Triple M brand, pushed away from the bar and joined them.

"Jake, Tom," Kade said tersely, to get the greeting out of the way, while Jeb stood close by, "Concepcion's at the jailhouse. I want you to pick up a wagon over at the livery and take her back to the ranch right away."

The cowhands nodded and vanished, their drinks unfinished on the bar.

"What the hell is going on?" Jeb demanded. "I had a royal flush—"

"Pa's gone," Kade interrupted.

"What?"

"Concepcion says he saddled up yesterday and left. She hasn't seen him since."

Jeb swore. Behind him, the game had resumed with some grumbling, but he didn't so much as look back. "Where's Rafe?" he demanded, resettling his hat and unconsciously laying a hand to the handle of his .45.

"Hotel," Kade answered, turning. "Let's get him and ride."

After collecting Rafe, they set out, and they hadn't traveled more than a few miles when three shots, fired in quick succession, drew them off the trail and onto the range, traveling west. They rode hard, which made it that much more of a marvel when Mandy caught up to them, mounted on the little pinto Kade had given her, fleet as an Indian.

Three more shots came, twenty minutes later, and Denver Jack was fixing to fire another three when they came upon him and another ranch hand, Zeke Winters.

Angus McKettrick lay sprawled facedown in the sweet grass with a bullet hole in his back, and Kade was off his horse and running well before the animal came to a stop. Rafe and Jeb were right behind him.

"He ain't dead," Denver Jack said, scanning their faces and slipping his pistol back into its holster.

"God's own wonder, too," Zeke put in.

Kade crouched next to his father, with Jeb, while Rafe took the other side.

"Pa?" Kade rasped as he and Rafe turned the old man over onto his back.

Angus's face was filthy, gray with pain, but he laughed, a raucous sound. "I thought you'd never get here."

"You're going to be fine, Pa." Jeb sounded as if he was trying to convince himself, more than Angus.

"Hell, yes," the old coot said. "Takes more than a few gun-slingers to put me in the ground."

"Just lie still till we figure out what to do," Rafe urged, yanking the bandanna from around his neck, presumably to use as a bandage.

"Do I have to tell you boys everything?" Angus demanded, crotchety as ever. "Zeke, Jack—you ride back to the ranch and get a buckboard. A bottle of whiskey might be a good thing, too. In the meantime, I'll do my best not to bleed to death."

Plainly relieved to have a course of action laid out for them, the two mounted up and rode out, headed for the ranch house, which was a good ten miles away.

"Who did this?" Kade wanted to know. He and Rafe helped Angus to sit up, and Rafe applied the bandanna to the wound. Jeb went back to his horse for a canteen, unscrewed the stopper, and held it to Angus's cracked lips.

Angus drank, sputtered, then spat. "Claimed they were from the Circle C," he said finally, "but I didn't believe 'em."

Rafe, Jeb, and Kade looked at each other, and a charge passed among them, elemental as lightning.

"They were outlaws, plain and simple, drunked up and yam-mering on about some train robbery they meant to pull off up around Flagstaff." Angus couldn't be blamed for not wanting to accept that Holt Cavanagh might order his murder, but his re-maining sons weren't so sure. At least, Kade wasn't.

Angus blinked and tried to shield his eyes from the early-afternoon sun with one gnarled hand. "Mandy?" he asked, squinting and plainly surprised. "Is that you?"

She stood at his feet. "Yes, sir." Kade took in her trousers and shirt. She was wearing boots, and carrying the shotgun loosely in one hand, and she didn't spare Kade so much as a glance. "It's me, all right."

"Dag-nab it," Angus complained, "it's been a long night, and I'm cold to the center of my bones. Hungry, too. Any of you got vittles in your saddlebags?"

Mandy smiled gently and shook her head. "No food," she lamented, "but I've got a bedroll tied on behind my saddle. I'll get it."

Jeb fished a couple of lint-covered hard-boiled eggs out of his coat pocket; no doubt, he'd purloined those from the usual saloon spread at the Bloody Basin during the poker game. He offered them to Angus, who ate them in two bites, muttering a grudging thanks, letting it be known that he'd have preferred something more substantial. A steak, maybe. Hell, all they'd have to do was shoot a cow, skin it, and roast chunks of it on a spit.

Kade watched Mandy, bemused, as she turned and walked away to fetch the blanket. A bedroll? She'd have had no reason to carry one of those, unless she'd been planning to make a long ride, and she surely hadn't mentioned anything like that to him.

Damn it, she'd been going to light out without a word of farewell, just as he'd feared she'd do all along. He'd been the one to say her roots were shallow.

She'd been at the livery, collecting Sister, most likely, when she'd heard that Angus was missing and decided to follow Kade and his brothers when they'd gone looking for him.

The sting of the betrayal rushed through Kade's veins like snake venom. He slowly got to his feet.

Paying him no mind, she brought the blanket back, unfurled it, and tucked it around Angus as tenderly as if he were a lost child found after much searching. It galled Kade beyond all reason that she wouldn't meet his eyes.

"These men you tangled with," she asked mildly, but with an edge of worry in her voice, "did they mean to rob you?"

Angus shook his head, washed down the pickled eggs with another swig from Jeb's canteen. "Nope. My horse turned up lame, and they closed in, four of them, out of nowhere it seemed like, when I got off to see if old Zeus had picked up a rock. I figured they were just having some fun, but then one of them said us McKettricks needed a lesson. I went to draw then, and one of them shot me from behind. Damn cowards."

"You didn't recognize them?" Mandy pressed, but cautiously.

"One of them was an Indian," Angus recalled. "Never seen him before."

Kade couldn't stand it any longer; he took Mandy by one elbow and dragged her away from Angus and the others.

She wrenched free of his grasp.

"Your brother did this," he growled. He kept his hands off her, but if she made a move to walk away, she wouldn't get far.

"That's not fair," Mandy hissed, turning pink. "Cree isn't the only Indian around here!"

"You were leaving, weren't you?" Kade insisted, just as furiously. "Where were you going, Mandy? To join up with your brother and his gang? Or maybe it was Curry you were going to meet. Did you know about his escape from the fort? Maybe you even helped plan it."

She drew back her hand and slapped him, and the report of it rang out like a rifle shot. He didn't move, but simply glared down at her, letting his accusations reverberate between them.

Jeb sauntered over, pushed his hat to the back of his head, spoke affably. "Take it easy, both of you. This is neither the time nor the place for a spat."

Kade kept his wrath focused squarely on Mandy, and it rolled out of him in waves of heat. "Damn you, you little Judas," he spat.

She flinched, just as if he'd struck her, but she glared right back. "I wanted some time to think, that's all."

"This is Mandy you're talking to, Kade," Jeb said quietly, moving between them. "This is *your wife*."

Kade reached out with one stiff arm and thrust his younger brother aside. His eyes were narrowed, his lips taut, as he stared Mandy down. "You were leaving for good."

Now, Rafe had joined the party. If Kade had taken the trouble to look, he figured he'd probably see Angus trying to crab-walk over there, too. The trouble with this family was, nobody minded their own business. "Kade," Rafe warned, in a gruff undertone. "Get hold of yourself. We've got to think about Pa right now. He's putting on a show, but *he's been shot,* and he's been out here all night, and this kind of carrying on will only get him riled up."

Kade ignored his brother's counsel and advanced on Mandy, his fists clenched at his sides. "Where were you going to meet your brother?"

The pain was incomprehensible. Mandy staggered under the weight and shock of it, and Jeb put an arm around her waist from behind, holding her up. "I wasn't leaving because of Cree!" she cried. "I wanted to get away from you, Kade McKettrick, you and your suspicions and your silences and your long stares. But I would have come back!"

"You aren't going anywhere until I get to the bottom of this!" Kade yelled.

At that, the hurt got to be too much, and Mandy made to launch herself at Kade, claws bared. Jeb restrained her, hoisting her clean off her feet and swinging her away from his brother.

"Get her out of my sight!" Kade spat, and turned his back on her.

"Jesus, Kade," Rafe growled, "what's the matter with you?"

Kade was immovable. "Take her to Indian Rock," he ordered. "Take her anywhere! But don't let her sneak off—maybe Curry and Lathrop got away, but she won't!" He turned and stormed back to his father, who was still sitting on the ground, huddled in Mandy's blanket. Rafe stalked after him, fists clenched, and all three of them came to a steady boil, like pots with their lids rattling.

Mandy might have collapsed if Jeb hadn't been supporting her. A few moments before, she'd been blind with rage; now, in the face of Kade's cold fury, she felt drained, ripped apart, discarded. *That's what you get,* the voice in her head taunted, *for ever thinking you could be one of them.*

Jeb was still holding her firmly, and his sigh ruffled her hair. "He didn't mean it, Mandy," he said gently. "He's scared for Pa, that's all."

She shook him off, shook off his kindness and his pity. She didn't want anything, *especially* pity, from any of the McKettricks, ever again. Kade's orders meant nothing to her; she raced over, snagged up Sister's dangling reins, swung into the saddle, and rode off with no direction in mind except *away.*

She heard Kade shout something, but it was Jeb who came after her, rode alongside, keeping pace, but making no effort to stop her flight. She kept Sister at a full-out run until the little mare began to tire, stumbling, her coat lathered and her sides heaving.

Coming to her senses, at least where the animal was concerned, Mandy reined her in, patted her neck in silent apology, and headed for the creek she'd spotted in the near distance. Jeb and his gelding stayed right with them.

"Go back to your pa and Kade and Rafe," she said, avoiding her brother-in-law's gaze. "I can get where I'm going without help from a McKettrick."

"Mandy," Jeb said reasonably, "you *are* a McKettrick. And I'm not going anywhere, so you might as well get past that."

Reaching the stream, she slid down off Sister's back and let the mare drink. "You're all stubborn as jackasses, you McKettricks!" she cried. "Every last one of you!"

Jeb dismounted, chuckling. "That must be why you fit in so well with the outfit." Then his face turned tender, which was the one thing Mandy knew she couldn't bear. "Mandy, listen to me. This thing's got Kade going three ways from Sunday. He doesn't really believe any of the things he said, and you know it. Give him some time to cool off and get his thoughts in order, and he'll come around."

Mandy used the backs of both hands to dash away an embarrassing abundance of tears. "He'd be wasting his time if he said he .was sorry!" She kicked furiously at a number of stones until some of her rage was spent. "He as much as called me an outlaw! I'd sooner spend the rest of my life cozied up with a mangy coyote than married to him!"

Jeb caught her by the chin and made her look at him. "How you going to tell the difference?" he asked with a twinkle.

She gave a sniffly laugh, shook her head. "I don't rightly know."

Jeb chuckled at that, but when he looked at Mandy again, his eyes were gentle. "Mandy, Mandy. My brother can be a bastard, no getting around it, but he's a good man. Maybe the best of all of us. Don't give up on him."

She spat her reply. "It's too late. Don't you see that, Jeb? You heard what he said. You know what he thinks of me. You're a poker player—you've got to know that there are times when the only thing a person can do is cut their losses and run!"

He stood with his hands resting on his hips, his head tilted to one side as he studied her. "I didn't figure you for a quitter," he said lightly, with a shrug in his voice, "or a coward, either. Guess I was wrong on both counts."

Mandy wanted to jump back on Sister and ride, just ride, as fast and as far away as possible, but she couldn't, because the horse was spent and wholly dependent on her good judgment. Where the mare was concerned, she hadn't shown much of that, and she was mortally ashamed.

She began to pace, striding in one direction, then whirling to stride just as purposefully in the other. "I am *not*," she yelled, swinging her arms for emphasis, "a coward—*or* a quitter!"

Jeb simply watched her. "Prove it."

"I don't have to prove anything!"

He shook his head. Sighed. "Mandy, we all have things to prove. Show Kade he was wrong about you. If you light out now, you'll never know what the two of you could have had together.

A whole family of ornery, stubborn little kids will never be born. Is that what you really want?"

She began to cry again. "No," she admitted, because he'd forced it out of her, left her with no choice. Just like a McKettrick. "But I've got some pride, damn it, and I'm in over my head here. That's why I wanted to go away for a while, to clear my head. I can't be what I'm not. Now I know I just plain don't fit in, and I never will, and that's the plain truth."

Jeb raised one eyebrow, folded his arms. "Is it?"

"Do you people ever give an *inch* of ground?" Mandy ranted.

He grinned. "Not if we can help it." He nodded toward his horse, grazing peacefully nearby. "Come on. You can ride with me, and we'll lead the mare."

"Not until you tell me we're not going to Indian Rock," Mandy said, digging in, folding her own arms.

"Okay," Jeb said easily. "We're not going to Indian Rock."

"Where, then?"

"You drive a hard bargain, Mandy McKettrick." She should have objected to his calling her by that name, but a part of her still liked the sound of it. He sighed. "We're going to the Triple M, and that's the end of it. And don't give me any more trouble, or I'll have to hog-tie you."

"I'd like to see you try it!"

He shook his head again, scuffed idly at the ground with the toe of one boot. "Oh, no, you wouldn't."

He was probably bluffing. She fumed, not quite daring to test her theory. "You're not holding all the cards here, Jeb McKettrick," she informed him, but when he took hold of Sister's reins and then mounted his own horse, she got on behind him. "If I'm going back with you, I want something in return."

He looked back at her over one shoulder, grinning a little. "What?"

Mandy was willing to grasp any distraction. "You've been claiming that you've got a wife someplace. Is that true?"

He frowned. "Sort of." He urged the horse into an easy stride.

"What do you mean, 'sort of'? You're either married or you're not." She was talking to the back of his neck now, but she kept on, mostly because silence would have driven her crazy just then. She felt the sigh move through him.

"Just between you and me, Sister Mandy," he said, keeping his face forward, "I made a mistake."

"What kind of mistake?"

The answer was a long time coming, and when it arrived, she knew it was all she or anybody else was going to get out of him, without the use of a hot poker. "I married a woman, and then I found out she really belonged to somebody else," he said. "So when Kade came to Tombstone to fetch me, I figured it for a sign to move on."

They met the buckboard, driven by Denver Jack, with Zeke riding shotgun, less than an hour later. They'd made good time getting to and from the ranch.

"Angus still holding on?" Denver Jack asked worriedly.

"He'll outlive us all," Jeb said.

The sun was setting when they reached the McKettrick place.

61

RAFE AND KADE lifted Angus into the back of the buckboard as carefully as they could, while Denver Jack held the team steady and Zeke went to catch Zeus, the old man's horse. Then, when the two brothers were halfway to their own mounts, Rafe moved to block Kade's way. "If it weren't for the shape Pa's in right now, little brother, I'd kick your ass all the way back to the barn!"

Kade stepped around him, deliberately slamming his shoulder against Rafe's as he passed, throwing him off-balance. "Soon as we get him settled at home, I'll be happy to oblige you with any kind of fight you might be looking for."

Rafe swore roundly. "You damn fool," he hissed. "Doesn't it bother you at all that you went and insulted the best woman you're ever likely to come across?"

Kade's jaw ached; he consciously relaxed it. "Leave it alone, Rafe. She's protecting somebody, and it's either Curry or that half brother of hers."

"What half brother?"

"Cree Lathrop," Kade said, grabbing his horse's reins and mounting up. "He's the grandstander who put up all those Wild West show flyers."

"The one that never turned up," Rafe mused, standing beside

his horse. The buckboard was rolling back toward the main house, more than an hour away.

Kade shifted in the saddle. "I don't like him."

Rafe wheeled his arms. "Well, *hell*," he exclaimed. "You *don't like* him. That settles it for sure—let's lynch the bastard!"

Kade shook his head, irritated beyond all logic and reason. "Damn it, it's more than that."

"What?" Rafe challenged.

Kade felt his shoulders, held rigid for much of the day, give way a little. Like every other part of his body, especially his heart, they were sore. "You wouldn't understand."

"You're right, little brother. Right now, I really don't understand." Rafe mounted up. "From where I sit, it looks like you're doing your damnedest to ruin a good thing."

"You'd be an expert on that," Kade said dryly. "It's God's own wonder that you didn't drive Emmeline right back to Kansas City before you came to your senses."

"When are you planning on coming to yours?" Rafe countered.

62

CONCEPCION REACHED THE ranch house only moments after Mandy and Jeb did, riding stiffly in a buckboard driven by one of the ranch hands. Doc was with them, and another cowboy rode alongside. Jeb dismounted, leaving Mandy to get down on her own, and went to meet them.

Mandy saw Concepcion relax at his words, which didn't carry, then bury her face in her hands to weep, most likely with relief. He and Doc helped her out of the buckboard, and Concepcion flung her arms around Jeb, who held her tightly until she'd gotten her strength back.

There was a lot to do in the next little while; Mandy and Concepcion rigged out a bed downstairs in a back parlor, and made supper, Mandy having relayed the news that Angus had been complaining of hunger when she'd last seen him.

Concepcion had plied Mandy all the while with anxious questions, and Mandy had answered them as thoroughly as she could. Inwardly, she worked hard at keeping thoughts of Kade and his terrible accusations at bay, but for all her busyness, it was a fight.

In time, Kade and Rafe arrived with Angus, and that was when Mandy made herself scarce. She locked herself in the room she knew was Kade's and listened to all the commotion down-stairs.

Hours went by, and the house grew quiet.

Mandy lay sleepless in the big bed far into the night, until the lamp on the bureau guttered. She should have asked to sleep in the spare room, she reflected miserably, or even the barn. Though she'd never set foot in Kade's room before, reminders were every-where she turned. Her estranged husband's unique smoke-leather-snowy-morning scent permeated the sheets and blankets and certainly the pillows. His clothes hung in the wardrobe, his good hat awaited claiming on a peg next to the door. There were enough books to start a library, most of them, she'd noted earlier, while snooping, the kind of lofty-minded stuff that would put ordinary folks into a coma. Emerson. Thomas Aquinas. Shake-speare. Somebody named Plato. He must have been foreigner.

Tarnation. Mandy was a reader herself, but her experience was mostly limited to thirdhand dime novels about cowboys and schoolmarms, or knights and lovely ladies who coughed deli-cately at intervals and then turned up their toes at the end of the book, just when you were starting to like them. She would have given one of her front teeth for something like that to lose herself in right then, but no luck.

Things went from bad to worse when she realized she re-quired a chamber pot, and there wasn't one handy. Evidently the high-and-mighty Marshal Kade McKettrick didn't find the need to relieve himself in the middle of the night, like ordinary mor-tals.

With a little huff of disdain, she tossed back the covers, and that raised his damnably appealing scent again, so easily recognizable that he might have been right there in the room with her, taking up all the space. She'd have given him a piece of her mind if he had been, that much was sure.

She got up, pulled on her trousers and boots, then donned one of Kade's shirts over her camisole, leaving it unbuttoned. Some women might have been afraid to venture out into the night in search of an outhouse, but Mandy wasn't the sort to fuss over minor inconveniences. For much of her life, she would have regarded even the smelliest privy as pure luxury.

Leaving the lamp behind, since it was nigh on useless anyhow, she crept along the corridor to the back stairs, then descended to the kitchen. A faint glow of light warned her that someone had gotten there ahead of her, but she expected Jeb or Doc or perhaps Concepcion, and she was quite unprepared to stumble across Kade instead.

He sat at the table, with his back to her, bent over an open book, and when he turned around, she saw that he was wearing spectacles with wire rims. There was no accounting for her reaction, a sort of aching tenderness that plucked at her heart, just as if there were strings humming in there. She drew in a deep breath, because when Kade McKettrick was in a room, he used up most of the air.

His face was void of expression as he took the spectacles off, set them aside, and looked her over. She pulled the shirt closed and fumbled to button it.

"I figured you'd be asleep in the bunkhouse or something," she said, because the silence was intolerable and Kade plainly wasn't going to be the one to break it. Oh, no. He was far too stubborn to make a concession like that.

"And I figured you'd be crawling out a window and heading for the hills," he retorted, his voice revealing no more than his face had.

She straightened her spine, painfully aware that she had to get to the outhouse and, at the same time, damned if she'd let him think for a moment that she was intimidated. Even though she was, and mightily so.

"Guess we both figured wrong," she said.

He let his gaze run over her again, slow and discerning and without a trace of friendliness. "If you're of a mind to run off now, forget it."

She felt herself flush, and her chin jutted right out. "I'd never go anyplace without my shotgun."

He smiled at that, but it was a grim offering. "My mistake."

She eased toward the back door. If Kade wanted to argue, he'd just have to wait a spell; she had personal business to attend to, and nature would not be denied. "I reckon you've made lots of those," she told him, taking care to sound haughty. "Mistakes, I mean."

"More than my share." He stood up. "Where do you think you're going?" He meant to press the matter, the jackass.

She squeezed her thighs together. "That needn't concern you."

He chuckled, finally taking note of her discomfort. "The outhouse."

Mandy bolted and, to her chagrin, soon realized that Kade was right behind her. "You just stay put," she called back, hurrying toward a privy-shaped shadow about a hundred yards from the house.

"Not a chance. I mean to keep an eye on you." Damn, but he was cussed. "Emmeline came out here once," he added, gaining on her, "and ran into a rattler. Broad daylight, too. No telling what you might come across."

She reached the outhouse door, wrenched it open, and dashed inside, taking precious time to lower the latch. "I'm not some city girl," she told him, dancing a little as she struggled with the buttons on her trousers. "Rattlers don't scare me. Anyway, they don't come out at night—it's too cold." By that point, she wasn't just keeping up the conversation; she didn't want him to hear her making water, and it was a long way from the hole she was sitting on to the pit beneath. "Not that I'd speak a word against Emmeline," she prattled on. "It's not her fault she's a McKettrick. She's been real nice to me, unlike some people I could name."

He laughed, damn him. She could just see him standing out there on the path, with his arms folded. King of the mountain, nothing he didn't know all about, backward and forward. Hellfire and spit, he was the most irritating man she'd ever had the misfortune to come across.

"I thought she was a handful, till I made your acquaintance." Just her luck that he was on one of his rare talking jags. "Next to you, my sister-in-law is a candidate for sainthood."

Figuring if any situation ever called for bravado, this was it, Mandy unlatched the door and flung it open with such force that it banged against the outside wall.

"I reckon if you thought so highly of Emmeline, you should have married *her*."

"I would have liked to," Kade replied, standing just as she'd imagined him, square in the middle of the path, "but when she got here, we all thought she was already hitched to Rafe."

Mandy's curiosity was aroused, in spite of her high dudgeon, which had not abated. Kade McKettrick had as good as called her a murdering outlaw that very day, and she wasn't about to forget that. Not immediately, anyhow, and not without a lot of persuasion—which probably wasn't forthcoming. "You *thought* she was married to Rafe?"

"So did she. Turned out there was some kind of mix-up at the mail-order-bride outfit, back in Kansas City, and the two of them had been living in sin. It was quite a scandal."

Mandy knew any number of people who had lived in sin, including her own mother, but they usually did it deliberately, not by accident. "I've got better things to do," she said loftily, trying without success to get around him, "than stand around yammering with you about other people's business."

"Mandy," he said, catching hold of her arm when she would have dodged off the path to pass. "You know something about those outlaws, even if you think you don't."

"If that was supposed to be an apology, it was a piss-poor one!"

"It wasn't an apology—not exactly, anyway."

Mandy folded her arms, partly because she was furious, and partly because it was cold in the high country at night. Poor Angus must have suffered, lying there on the ground in the dark, wounded and alone. "Then what—exactly—was it supposed to be?"

"The start of a reasonable conversation."

"There was nothing 'reasonable' about calling me an outlaw!"

"I didn't call you an outlaw," he said, taking pains with each word. A muscle bunched in his cheek. "And you're doing your level best not to hear what I'm saying here."

She waited, shivering a little, and too stubborn by half to say anything at all. That very afternoon she'd made up her mind never to speak to this man again as long as she lived, should she ever be unfortunate enough to encounter him, and now here she was, face-to-face with the rascal, and smack in the middle of a jawing fest.

"You're cold," he said, and putting an arm around her waist, he steered her toward the house.

She blinked back tears; when he yelled at her, she could hold her own, she'd had so much practice with Gig, but simple kindness invariably threw her for a loop. She let herself be led, though, because she knew if she balked, he'd just pick her up and carry her inside, and the very idea of that made her pride smart.

Once they were back in the kitchen, he indicated the table with a nod of his head. "Sit down."

She considered her options, which were anything but spectacular, then sat.

He went to the stove, picked up the coffeepot. "Want some?"

She shook her head. She'd never seen anybody drink coffee the way he did, at all hours of the day and night. It was a miracle that he ever slept at all. "Too much of that stuff can make your gun hand shaky," she felt obliged to point out.

"Never been a problem." He brought his cup back to the table and took a seat.

"I'm still leaving," she said, careful not to look at him. "First chance I get. It was a damn fool idea to marry you in the first place."

He seemed to be smiling behind the rim of his coffee mug, though his eyes, usually expressive, were flat as mirrors, and just as opaque. "Maybe it was, but you're not going anyplace until I round up those outlaws and get my pa's money back. Unless it's to lead me to their camp."

Mandy threw up her hands.

After that, it was a stare-down, not a conversation, and Mandy tried her best not to look away first, but in the end, Kade prevailed. She felt a crushing shame, thinking back on all the things she'd done in those early years, lying as a matter of course, stealing whatever she could, whenever she could. She'd hated that life, that was the God's truth, but Kade would never truly believe her. He'd already said as much.

Presently, Kade pushed back his chair, stood. "Get your rest, Amanda Rose. We're going after some outlaws in the morning."

The way he used her full name wounded her in some strange way, and when she looked up, his face was like stone.

She shook her head, despondent. Her throat ached; a powerful instinct to reach out to him came over her, and she was nearly swamped by it. In the end, though, her fierce pride saved her, if what she was feeling could be termed *salvation*.

"You're staying in my room?"

She nodded.

"Then I'll sleep in the bunkhouse. Good night, Amanda Rose."

There it was again, her given name. Why did it do her so much injury to hear him say it? She bit down hard on her lower lip and nodded again, and he took his infernal coffee and left the house by way of the back door.

Mandy sat still at the McKettrick table for a long time. Then, weary of soul, she took the lantern from the middle of the table and used it to light her way up the stairs.

THEY LEFT THE Triple M just after sunrise, Kade riding Raindance, Mandy mounted on a bay gelding named Dickie. Sister nickered and whinnied at being left behind in the barn, but she'd put in a long, hard trek and needed resting up.

Kade didn't bother to tell Mandy where they were headed; after bending her ear the night before on the path to the outhouse, now he wasn't talking at all. His hat brim was pulled down low, casting a shadow over his features, and his shoulders were as straight and stiff as a railroad tie. Mandy burned with curiosity, not to mention indignation, but she would have died before she'd put even the simplest question to that man. Let him simmer in his silence, like a chicken carcass in a kettle.

After nearly two hours, they came upon a cabin, backed up against a wall of red rock like a living creature, scared and looking for someplace to hide. Smoke twisted from the crooked tin chimney, and an old man in disreputable red underwear trotted out to greet them, sporting a toothless grin.

"Pappy," Kade said with the tone of a howdy, though he didn't return the smile.

"You sent them cattle up, just like you said you would,"

Pappy exulted. "I never credited as how you'd do that." He turned to Mandy, regarding her speculatively. "Who's this here?"

"Amanda Rose," Kade said, and Mandy all but winced.

"She your woman?"

"She's my wife." He said it lightly; most likely the fact carried no great weight in his mind.

Pappy looked patently disappointed. "That's too bad. I could use a female around this place for cooking and the like."

Mandy suppressed a shudder, and when Kade dismounted, she stayed put. For all she knew, her devoted husband meant to leave her here to be Pappy's woman; not much would have surprised her at that point.

"I've got some questions about Davy," Kade told Pappy, "and don't bother lying to me, because I'm not in the mood for it. Who was he riding with?"

Pappy looked cornered, but a crafty light showed in his little pigeon eyes, too. "Didn't catch their names. Fifteen or twenty of 'em, maybe more, riding real good horses. That's about all I know."

Kade took a gold piece from his coat pocket and tossed it to Pappy, who caught it handily, bit it, and tucked it away in a place Mandy didn't want to think about.

"I do recall that there was one fella, real good with a knife," he said, straightening. "Reckon he was the one that peeled back Davy's hair for him. I tolt that boy he oughtn't to run with thieves and killers, but he wouldn't listen, no, sir. Knew better than his old man. And just look where it got him."

Mandy's stomach had come to an acid boil at the mention of the knife, and she couldn't help recalling that Angus had said one of his attackers was an Indian. *Coincidence,* she told herself. *Plenty of those around, and lots of folks can handle a blade, besides Cree.*

"Now how'd you know that, Pappy?" Kade asked easily. "You never saw the body, remember? My brother Holt and I buried Davy without ever taking him out of the bedroll, and we didn't figure it would be delicate to tell you the particulars."

Pappy hawked and spat, and once again, Mandy's stomach threatened revolt. "Don't recollect. Must have heard it from Avery."

"Avery wasn't there," Kade said, quiet and relentless. "Holt's men took him back to the Circle C, and far as I know, he's been there ever since. Who told you about the scalping, Pappy?"

Pappy hopped from one foot to the other, as though the ground had suddenly turned to a sizzling griddle, burning him right through the worn soles of his boots. "The Injun," he said, after trying to wait Kade out and failing. "Said his name was Jim Dandy."

Mandy grasped the saddle horn with both hands, sure she'd topple to the ground if she didn't hold on for all she was worth. Out of the corner of her eye, she saw Kade slant a glance at her sharp enough to break the skin. The hotcakes he'd served up for breakfast back at the Triple M surged, scalding, into the back of her throat.

"This Jim Dandy," Kade said carefully, "he actually told you that he scalped Davy?"

Pappy looked at the ground, swallowed visibly, and nodded his balding head. "Davy and some other folks, too. Said he'd do the same to me, if I tolt anybody, even if I didn't have no hair to start with."

Leather creaked as Kade got back in the saddle. He took a tighter grip on the reins, though Mandy had observed that he usually let them rest easy in his hands. "When was this?"

"Day after you and your brother laid Davy in the ground."

"You seen him since?"

Pappy ruminated awhile. "God's truth, I ain't," he answered finally. "And I hope I never do, neither."

Kade adjusted his hat, which meant he was getting restless, ready to ride. "If you're scared to stay here, you can bunk in at the Triple M for as long as you like. Avery, too, if he comes back."

Pappy made a loud snuffling sound, as if he were clearing his sinuses, only backward. "I figure he'll stay on at the Circle C. He favors steady wages and don't mind muckin' out stalls and the like. As for me, I cain't leave this place. My woman's buried down there, by that stand of scrub oaks, and I give her my word a long time back I'd not go off and leave her alone." He paused, reflected. "Reckon if that fella Jim Dandy turns up again, I'll just shoot him out of the saddle, on sight."

"No," Mandy heard herself say.

Kade's gaze came right to her, and it felt like the broad side of an ax when it landed. He tipped his hat to Pappy, reined his horse around, and leaned to take her gelding by the bridle, pointing her and the horse back toward the trail they'd just traveled.

"I'm going to find your brother, Amanda Rose," he said, "and I'm going to bring him in."

64

THEY HADN'T TRAVELED more than a few miles when the truth struck Mandy with the force of a thunderbolt. Kade had been right all along—she *did* know where Cree was.

Kade's gaze swung to her as surely and swiftly as if she'd spoken aloud. "What is it?"

She swallowed hard. "That mission where I got the nun clothes," she said in a small voice. "Back when I was running from Gig, I—well—I knew where to find the place because Cree told me about it. He stayed there two whole years one time—Gig was in jail, and Mama and I lived in a rooming house in Tucson. The lady who ran it was real nice, but she wouldn't let Cree in because he was an Apache."

Kade stopped his horse, listening with his whole body, it seemed, and not just his ears. "And?"

"Cree loved it there. He didn't want to leave when Gig got out and went to fetch him back," she said miserably, unwillingly, barely breathing the words. "There was a canyon nearby, he said, where he used to fish and camp whenever he didn't have lessons or chores."

Kade waited, his gaze intent, his whole body still.

"That's where he is. That canyon."

Something eased inside Kade; she felt the shift as surely as if it had happened in her own being, instead of his. "Did he say exactly where it was?"

"South of the mission," she said, feeling sick. "There's a spring there, and some white oaks. It was a magical place to him. He said he could be an Apache there."

Kade nodded grimly. "I'll see you back to the ranch before I head out."

Mandy's response chafed her throat. "You can't go by yourself." Bloody images of what could happen when these two men collided all but overwhelmed Mandy; she saw Kade lying dead, and then Cree, and her heart split right down the middle. "What if he's not alone?"

"Then he's not alone." And that, apparently, was that.

Rafe and Jeb were nowhere around when they reached the main house; according to Concepcion, who came out to meet them, they'd gone to pay a call on Holt up at the Circle C. Mandy knew from the other woman's worried expression that they meant to confront their half brother about what had happened to Angus, and about his attackers' claims that they were riding with his outfit.

Mandy closed her eyes. God only knew what would happen.

"I'll send somebody after them," Kade said. "They're on the wrong trail." With that, he rode toward the barn, dismounted, and led his horse inside.

"He means to track those outlaws on his own," Mandy confided to Concepcion while they were alone, deliberately neglecting to mention Cree. "When Rafe and Jeb get back here, tell them to come quick and bring all the help they can round up."

Concepcion paled. "What about you?"

"I mean to follow Kade. I'll pretend to stay here, but once he's got a start, I'll be right behind him."

"Mandy, you cannot do such a foolish thing—I will not allow it!"

"I have no choice," Mandy said wistfully, watching as Kade led a fresh horse out of the barn. He carried his saddle and other tack over one shoulder, and he didn't even glance in her direction as he got ready to ride again. "I'm probably the only person who can keep Kade from getting himself killed. Please, Concepcion, if you care about him, and I know you do, then help me."

Tears stood in Concepcion's eyes. "Kade and Rafe and Jeb, they are like sons to me, all of them. I could not bear for anything to happen to them."

"Then help me," Mandy pleaded softly. She described the canyon, gave its location as best she could, so Rafe and the others could catch up.

Concepcion hesitated, then nodded.

Mandy got down from Dickie's back, led the horse toward the barn, giving Kade a wide berth. He finished saddling the horse, got on, and rode off.

Half an hour later, that being as long as Mandy could restrain herself, she picked up his trail.

65

KADE WAS SO caught up in his thoughts that he was well on his way before he realized, to his chagrin, that he was being followed. It didn't take a Supreme Court justice to work out who was behind him, though. He drew up behind a pile of red boulders and waited, and sure enough, Mandy came by shortly thereafter.

She had the shotgun out of the scabbard and aimed square at his belly in the space between one heartbeat and the next.

"Jehoshaphat!" she cried, lowering the weapon, slipping it back into its scabbard. "You scared the hell out of me—I thought you were Gig."

Kade rode toward her, purely confused as to whether he was glad to see her or mad as hell that she'd disobeyed his orders. He decided on both. "You don't take instruction too well," he observed.

"That's right, I don't." Mandy looked as if she could spit red-hot cobbler's nails at any further provocation. "If you want me to stay behind, you'll have to tie me to a tree, and I don't see you doing that."

"The suggestion has a certain appeal." Kade leaned a little in the saddle, with an accompanying creak of leather.

Her horse was fidgety, anxious to get on with things, which

only went to prove the animal had no more sense than its rider. She subdued the critter with a few quick words and some deft rein-work, then fixed her determined gaze on Kade. He felt it like a slap across the face. "I want your word that you won't kill my brother."

"I can't give it," he replied without hesitation. "If he draws on me, I'll take him down."

"What if you're not fast enough?"

"I'm fast enough."

She went pale. "I don't want you to get shot," she said, real soft. "Or him, either."

"Then we're in agreement on one thing, at least. There'll be as little bloodshed as possible, Mandy. That's all I can promise."

She absorbed that, and he suppressed an untimely urge to take her into his arms and hold her close. With the sun headed steadily west, though, and Cree Lathrop's roost still a fair distance away, he didn't have the option.

"All right," she said. Then she reined the gelding back onto what passed for a road. "You coming?" she asked, turning to look at Kade over one shoulder.

For no good reason he could think of, he laughed.

They traveled swiftly after that, and in silence, leaving the trail after a couple of miles and riding overland, in case lookouts were posted along the way. The gang was big, at least twenty strong if Pappy Kincaid could be believed, and they had the manpower to cover a lot of ground.

Twilight was gathering when they reached the rim of the canyon, leaving their horses behind to crawl onto the edge of one wall and look down on the campsite.

Kade counted twenty-three men, in various states of drunkenness, and concluded that several more had to keep watch, but since no alarm had been raised, he and Mandy most likely hadn't been spotted. Cree was clearly visible, his dark hair gleaming in the light of a sizable bonfire, his upper body bare and bloody. Nearby was the body of Gig Curry, tied to a spindly tree, his throat slit from one ear to the other.

Kade reached over to press a hand to Mandy's mouth before she could cry out. "Take it easy, Mandy," he whispered. "If we draw their attention right now, we're as good as dead."

She nodded, her shoulders trembling, and he withdrew his hand. Except for a glance or two at Mandy, he'd kept his gaze fixed on Cree Lathrop the whole while, and now he saw the other man pause, turn slowly, and stare in their direction. He couldn't possibly have seen them, or heard anything, but uncannily, he seemed to know they were there, just the same.

"Shit," Kade rasped.

"I think I can reason with him, Kade," Mandy said. "I've got to go down there."

"The hell you do!"

Cree took a tentative step in their direction, seeming to sniff the wind like a wolf scenting prey.

Mandy scrambled to her feet before Kade could drag her down, and caught him square in the side of his head with one bootheel in the next moment, no doubt because that was the only way she could keep him from stopping her, and from following.

He swore under his breath even as darkness pooled around him and swallowed his brain whole. When he came around seconds later, Mandy was headed downhill on foot, slipping and skidding. Kade struggled to focus his eyes and gather his wits, and when he did, he realized that she'd left her shotgun behind.

I'd never go anyplace without my shotgun, he heard her say.

Damn it. God*damn* it. She was taking on that whole band of outlaws unarmed, and worst of all, she was doing it to save his sorry hide. She probably had some fool notion that he needed the gun to protect himself.

He watched, helpless, as Cree came forward to meet her, at home on his sacred ground; she flung her arms around his neck and clung to him, blood and all. Every instinct Kade possessed urged him to go after her, but he didn't move. He had no alternative, at the moment, but to trust Mandy with his life and her own. Her plan was woefully inadequate, but he didn't have a better one at the moment.

The Apache held her at a little distance, looking her over. Kade couldn't read the other man's expression from that distance, but he knew by the way Lathrop held himself that he was suspicious.

Mandy talked fast, and Kade would have given a strip of tender skin to know what she was saying, but all he could make out was the prattling lilt of her voice, the words just beyond the bounds of his hearing.

Careful not to move too quickly and risk drawing someone's notice, Kade wiped the blood from the side of his head, trying to think. There'd been no call for Mandy to kick him quite so hard, he was sure of that, if not much else.

He watched, like a man trapped in a nightmare, as Mandy allowed herself to be escorted into a pit of snakes. She didn't so much as glance in the direction of Gig Curry's body, hanging there, bled out like a pig at rendering time, nor did she give any indication that she'd brought company. Kade reached for the shotgun, sighted in on Lathrop's head just to make himself feel better, then laid the gun aside and waited. The thing was no good at that range, anyhow, and if he fired it, the rest would be on him in seconds—after they'd shot Mandy.

One of the outlaws, clad in a stolen cavalry coat like many of the others, rose shakily to his feet, approached Mandy, spoke to her. Lathrop's pistol sprang into his hand as if it had flown there, and he shot the poor bastard in the belly, watched with what was probably satisfaction as he fell, and looked around to see if any of the others had a word to say to his sister.

Not surprisingly, none did.

Mandy didn't move a muscle, though she was too smart not to be terrified. God, she was a marvel—and when Kade got his hands on her, he meant to wring her neck. Right after that, he'd tell her that he loved her and ask her to forgive him for all the stupid things he'd said and done. Hell, he'd beg if he had to, and gladly, because if they got to that point, it would mean they were both alive.

"Easy," Kade whispered, with his heart pushing its way into his throat as he eased one hand back for his .45. "Take it easy, Mandy."

That was when he heard a gun being cocked behind him; before he could draw his pistol, roll over, and fire, he felt the barrel pressed, cold as spring breakup, into the nape of his neck.

"Looks like the fun's not over yet," said the outlaw. "We got us a McKettrick."

66

CREE SHOOK HIS head slowly from side to side as he watched the lookout prodding Kade down the hillside, a rifle shoved into the middle of his back. "Amanda Rose, Amanda Rose," he scolded ruefully. "To think I trusted you."

Mandy looked on in horror as Kade stumbled ahead of the guard. "You're hurt," she said, and took a step toward him, only to be wrenched back to Cree's side. The smell of Gig's blood and his fear came out of the darkness like a monster, fairly choking her. She'd hated Curry and would never mourn his passing, but she couldn't condone that kind of slaughter, either.

Kade actually smiled, the wretched fool, and touched his head. Didn't he know they might both be dead by sunrise, and wishing for it long before then? "That oughtn't to surprise you, Mrs. McKettrick," he said, "since it was your doing."

Cree took a step toward Kade, his knife drawn. Mandy felt a chill that had nothing to do with the temperature, which was steadily dropping. "In all the world," Cree said, "there was one person—*one person*—I could count on. And you turned her against me." He drew a deep breath, his thumb flicking the soiled blade, drawing his own blood. Mandy had seen him do that on hunting trips, before he skinned out a deer carcass. "You're going to die for that, McKettrick."

Kade grinned so broadly that Mandy began to wonder if she'd knocked his brain loose when she'd kicked him. Did he think this was a game? Cree was in deadly earnest. "Is this your Wild West show?" Kade asked. "Looks like a sorry outfit to me."

Cree's face contorted. "Shut up."

"Did you burn out the Fees' place, Cree?" Mandy demanded. She wanted to know, but she was trying to stall, too.

"Gig set the fire on his own, for fun," Cree said without looking at her. "I took over his gang while he was in jail."

"What about those army men, and the gold?"

He smiled. "I did that. Partly for my people, partly for the money."

"And Angus McKettrick? Cree, why would you want to shoot an innocent man?"

Cree spat, his gaze on Kade, and unwavering. "Innocent? Look around you, Mandy. The McKettricks, and men like them, have taken everything, so there's nothing left for people like us. I tried to get them fighting against each other—all the big, greedy ranchers. It would have been sweet justice if they'd killed each other."

Kade still wanted a fight, the damn fool. He'd taken in all Cree had said, and he craved vengeance. "Let's get to it," he said, beckoning. "You and me, Lathrop, man to man."

A murmur rose among the outlaws, pistols were drawn and cocked, and Mandy's breath got stuck in her throat, sharp as a double-edged sword.

Cree whirled on them, the knife he'd used to butcher Gig

gleaming in his fist, and swept them all up in a single fevered glance. "One of you moves a muscle—just one—and I'll cut his liver out and roast it over the fire."

The men were utterly still.

"Guns on the ground," Cree hissed, his gaze moving, molten with an ancient hatred, from one man to the next, and the pistols were dropped.

Cree turned back to face Kade. "Fool," he spat. "Why did you come here? And why the *hell* did you bring Amanda Rose?"

Kade was rolling up his sleeves, his motions as casual as if he'd been about to engage in a friendly brawl with his brothers back of the barn, or out behind the Bloody Basin Saloon, instead of in a battle that would surely end in either his death or Cree's, if not both. "I came for all the reasons you just named, and because I want that money back." He swung a glance in Mandy's direction. "As for bringing the lady, well, that wasn't my choice to make. She pretty much goes where she pleases, in case you've never noticed."

Cree actually laughed at that, but it was a frightening sound, one Mandy had never heard from him before. When—*when*—had he turned into a madman, and why hadn't she noticed when it happened?

She stepped forward, caught her brother by the arm. "Stop this while you still can, Cree," she pleaded. "There's a posse on its way. Hasn't there been enough killing?"

With a chilling shriek of rage, he backhanded her hard across the mouth, and she went stumbling, arms flailing, then fell. Kade bellowed like an enraged bull, his whole being bent on murder, and lunged for Cree.

"Kade, no!" Mandy screamed.

Cree swiped at Kade's middle with the knife, tore his shirt open, if not his belly. Kade was breathing hard, his eyes blazing with contempt as he tracked Cree. Probably because of the blow to his temple, for which he had Mandy herself to thank, his reflexes seemed slower than they might have been.

"You're nothing but a thieving, murdering coward, little warrior," Kade taunted. "Why, without that blade in your hand, you'd be just another man. And not much of one at that."

Mandy scrambled to her feet, edged around to where she could see both men clearly. "For God's sake, Cree, Kade—stop—don't do this."

Cree paid her no mind, but glared at Kade, his eyes glinting with the demons she would have recognized in him long ago if she'd allowed herself to see him for what he was. All the suffering, all the pain, all the hatred, had taken root in his soul somewhere along the line, and rotted it away.

"Please, Cree," she begged. "For me. For Mama. Put down the knife and let this be over."

"You're a traitor, Amanda Rose," he snarled, without sparing Mandy a glance. "Shut up before I kill you myself."

Mandy knew it was not an idle threat—the brother she'd known and loved was long gone—but she wasn't afraid for herself, not yet anyway. "I love you, Kade McKettrick," she blurted. "Do you hear me? I love you!"

Kade didn't look at her. He was watching Cree, but the words he said found their way into the center of her soul: "I feel the same way about you, and I'm sorry as hell for getting you into this."

Cree laid his free hand to his heart and made as if he would swoon. "Such tender sentiments," he raved. Then he dropped the knife and hurled himself into Kade, like a sea storm striking land, tearing up everything in its path.

The struggle was ferocious; Kade and Cree both fell with the impact and rolled on the ground, Cree fueled by rage, Kade by sheer desperation and the will to survive. The sound of men and horses echoed into the hidden canyon, and the outlaws scattered, running for their own mounts, but the battle between Kade and Cree only intensified, growing fiercer with every blow, every grunt of pain, every gasped curse.

There were shouts in the gathering darkness, and gunshots, but Mandy didn't so much as turn her head. She might as well have been in the center of the struggle between her brother and her husband, fighting right along with them.

They rolled close to the fire, back again, and then, suddenly, Cree was on top of Kade, getting him by the hair, slamming the back of his head hard onto a rock. He went still, and Cree groped for the discarded knife and raised it high in his right hand, where it caught the crimson light of the campfire.

Mandy took a step, stumbled over something, grabbed it up.

It was her own shotgun, brought to camp by the man who'd captured Kade. She felt her palm go moist as she gripped it, drew a bead on Cree, and shot him square in the chest.

67

KADE OPENED HIS eyes, blinking, and watched, baffled, awash in his own blood and that of his enemy, as Cree flew to one side, his chest a sickening pulp, and landed on his back, his arms spread wide as if to embrace the night sky and gather it into his broken body, like a final communion.

"Mandy?" Kade sat upright, his head pounding, and looked wildly around in search of her. If she was dead—oh, *Christ*, if she was dead . . .

But she wasn't. She was on her knees, a few feet away, the shotgun clasped in both hands, the barrel still smoking.

Kade went to her, half crawling, threw the gun aside, and wrenched her into his arms, crushing her against his chest, wanting to take her inside himself and shield her with his own flesh. "Mandy," he said again.

She shuddered, and he felt it in his own body. "I killed him," she whispered. "I *killed* Cree—"

"Shhh," Kade said, kissing her temple. The posse, led by Rafe, Jeb, and Holt, poured into camp. Kade saw his brothers out of the corner of his eye, but he didn't turn his head, and he didn't let go of Mandy. He wasn't sure he'd ever be able to unlock his arms.

She began to sob, clutching at his shirt, and he pressed her head into his shoulder, murmuring to her, his chin propped on the top of her head.

Rafe sprang down off his horse and walked slowly toward them. "Are either of you hurt?" The concern in his voice found a place deep inside Kade and took a firm hold.

He stood, raising Mandy up with him, supporting her, still with both arms, as he finally met his brother's gaze. "Not where it would show," he said. "Took your sweet time getting here, didn't you?"

Rafe shook his head, swept off his hat, scanned the camp. "We got the bastards. Twenty-four of them. Bunch of one-legged roosters, they hardly put up a fight." His gaze fell on Cree's body lying shattered in the firelight, half-naked and gruesome with blood. "Jesus," he breathed.

"I shot him," Mandy said, straightening against Kade and wiping at her eyes with the back of one hand.

Kade stroked her hair, held her tighter, if that was possible, kissed the top of her head. "I need to get Mandy home," he said to Rafe.

Rafe nodded. Several of the posse members were cutting Curry's corpse free of its bonds, and Jeb and Holt came out of the cave about then, lugging a strongbox between them. The Wells Fargo name was painted on the side in gold letters that reflected the firelight. "We'll ride with you," Rafe said, laying a welcome hand to Kade's shoulder.

Sam Fee stepped out of the darkness. "A bunch of us figured on taking the prisoners to the fort, where they can accommodate 'em," he said to Kade. "That all right with you?"

"Yup," Kade said. "I reckon the army's beef with them is even bigger than ours, given those twelve soldiers they killed."

Jeb and Holt set the strongbox down by the fire and opened it to examine the contents. "Looks like most of the money's here," Jeb said. There would be some celebrating tomorrow, Kade figured, but right now, there was too much blood for that.

"What about Cree?" Mandy asked, her voice small as she looked up into Kade's face. "We can't leave him behind."

"We won't," Kade promised. He addressed Ben Hopper. "Get him back to town, will you? Take him to Doc's office, for the time being."

Ben nodded grimly, and he and another man, Wiley Kline from the newspaper office, found a blanket and rolled the body up inside it. Mandy watched bleakly as they laid her dead brother facedown across a saddle and secured him there with ropes.

Kade cupped her face in his hands and made her look at him. "What you did was a hard thing," he said gruffly, "but you did it, and that's that. You saved my life, and more importantly you saved your own. You've got to put this behind you, Mandy, and go on from here."

She nodded, but she looked uncertain. "It's a heavy load, Kade. Maybe too heavy."

He kissed her forehead. "I'll carry as much of it as you'll allow me to," he promised. "Now, let's get you back to the Triple M, where you belong."

She fell a little short of a smile, but it was the effort that counted. Someone had rounded up her horse, and Kade's, and led them into camp, and he hoisted her into the saddle before climbing up behind her, reaching around her to take the reins. One of the ranch hands took charge of the other gelding.

She was asleep when they reached the Triple M several hours later, and Kade woke her gently. "We're home," he said.

She was limp as he handed her down to Holt, who held her until Kade had dismounted and taken her back again.

Angus, bandaged but ambulatory, waited in the kitchen, along with Concepcion, probably awakened by the arriving riders, and when Concepcion got a look at Mandy, then Kade, she put a hand to her mouth and cried out.

"What the devil?" Angus demanded, looking as if his ticker was about to give out on him then and there.

Jeb, coming in behind Kade and Mandy, closely followed by Rafe and Holt, who'd decided to join the posse when a ranch hand had come looking for his brothers, did the answering. "They tangled with those outlaws." Jeb was lugging the strongbox, and he set it in the middle of the table. "Here's your money, Pa. I think I can speak for all of us when I say we'd appreciate it if you'd manage things a little better from here on out."

Angus stared at the box. "You got it back?" he marveled, sounding almost as if he were afraid to hope such a thing could be true.

"Kade did," Jeb said. "And Mandy."

"I'll be hornswoggled," said Angus, beaming.

Concepcion, ever practical, but clucking like a hen, was already busy at the stove, building up the fire, putting on coffee, sending Rafe and Holt for water to fill the reservoir for the washing up that would need to be done.

Kade was intent on just one thing: carrying Mandy up the

stairs to their room, getting her undressed, looking her over for injuries. She was in shock, and she might have been hurt without realizing it.

She was shivering in one of his shirts, cold no matter how many blankets he added to the bed, when Concepcion knocked at the slightly open door and then admitted herself without waiting for an invitation. She carried a basin of steaming water, soap, and some clean cloth. "Go on downstairs, Kade," she said quietly, but in a manner that brooked no objections. "You are covered in blood, in case you've forgotten, and your father will not rest until he sees how much of it is your own. I will attend to Mandy."

Kade turned to his wife, his eyes questioning, and she nodded. "Don't be long," she said. "I reckon I'm going to need considerable holding in the next little while."

He leaned down and kissed her lightly on the mouth. "I love you, Mandy McKettrick. When you start to sort all this through, take that into account."

She smiled, and the effort it must have taken lodged in his heart like a splinter of steel. "I like the sound of that," she said, stroking his cheek.

"Which part? The 'I love you,' or 'Mandy McKettrick'?"

"One's as good as the other," she replied, and closed her eyes.

68

KADE WAS PROFOUNDLY relieved when Mandy chose the town cemetery for Lathrop's and Curry's final resting places. He couldn't have buried them on the Triple M; that kind of evil would taint the earth, and every inch of the ranch was holy to him. Still, he stood beside her next to Cree's grave, and he held his hat in his hand. She settled against him, empty of tears, for she'd cried plenty in the three days and nights since they'd ridden out of that canyon together.

"How could I have missed seeing what was happening to him?" she whispered, looking up at Kade, her eyes full of memories he couldn't share. "It must have been a long time in the making."

"We see what we look at, Mandy," he said quietly, tightening his arm around her waist. "Anyhow, everybody's got a lot of different sides to them. The part of Cree you saw was real enough—it just wasn't the whole man."

She smiled tremulously, and he leaned to kiss her forehead. "How'd you get so smart?" she asked.

He chuckled grimly at that, shook his head slightly. "Maybe I'm not so sharp as folks give me credit for. I've lived around here all my life, but there was a lot I didn't see, just the same. I didn't take note of Harry, for example, and how he and those other kids were doing without, even though he was right under my nose the whole time. I never thought much about people like the Fees, trying to put food in their mouths and make it through from one day to the next. I thought, and acted, like a McKettrick, as if that was all anybody had the right to ask of me."

"What else could you be, besides a McKettrick?" she asked reasonably, and laid her head against his shoulder, though they weren't alone. Half the town had come to see Lathrop and Curry laid to rest, not out of grief, but to see the thing ended, and as a way of accepting Mandy into the fold. The appreciation he felt for that kindness had settled in deep, made itself a part of him forever, like the love he bore his wife.

He gave a rueful half smile. "I don't rightly know," he said. "Guess you'll just have to take me as I am."

She stood on tiptoe to kiss his cheek. "Nonsense," she teased. "You need some work, but once I get you trained, you'll be close to perfect."

He laughed at that, though the cemetery surely wasn't the proper place for it. "That might take a while."

She smiled, and this time it was full strength. "We've got a lifetime. Especially now that you've turned in that nickel-silver star you were wearing."

He slanted a glance at Sam Fee, sworn in that very morning by the head of the town council. Sam stood proudly beside his wife, with his shoulders back and his head high. He'd be a good marshal; he had the grit for it. Rafe was having a little clapboard house built for the Fees, just down the street from the jailhouse, and the town was pooling its modest resources to furnish the place from top to bottom.

"I don't figure I'll miss that badge much," Kade allowed. "I was born to be a rancher, and that's the trail I'll follow from now on. What about you, Mandy?"

She looked puzzled. "What *about* me?"

"I seem to recall that you wanted to be Annie Oakley and see the world."

She gave another smile, muted, but still bright as light on creek water. "That job's taken, and this is enough world for me right here." Then she added saucily, "I still want my fifty horses and the money you promised me, though."

If they hadn't just seen two men buried, he'd have laughed out loud, picked her up, and spun her around, just for the sheer joy of doing it.

Doc approached, clearing his throat. Mamie and the little ones stood at a little distance in a red-haired cluster, looking on. The old man nodded to Mandy, put his hand out to Kade. "You did a fine job of cleaning out that nest of murdering rats," he said forthrightly. "Both of you. Which is not to say it wasn't out-and-out stupid to go about it the way you did."

Kade grinned, shook the doctor's hand. "I'll take that for a compliment." Then nodding to indicate the Sussex tribe, he said, "You thinking of settling down and staying sober, Doc?"

Doc flushed, but a twinkle was in his wise, pouchy, old eyes. "Maybe I am."

"Good," Kade said, and he meant it.

The physician turned his attention to Mandy. "You keep an eye on this rounder," he warned. "He's got a wild streak in him, just like those brothers of his. Some of us thought Kade'd never get through sowing his oats, but loving you, that's changed him for the better, just like marrying Emmeline changed Rafe." Doc looked around, found Jeb in the crowd. "Two down, one to go," he finished. Then he turned and went back to Mamie, who waited with a sweet smile and shining eyes.

In the distance, Kade heard the clamor of an approaching stagecoach. "Well, Mrs. McKettrick," he said, "if we're going to catch the four o'clock to Flagstaff and make our train to Phoenix, we'd best be heading for the mercantile."

She squeezed his hand. "Thank you for doing this, Kade. Seeing Mama will give me some peace."

He nodded. They'd left their bags on the sidewalk outside the general store before the funerals. Kade doubted if anyone had missed the irony of those two coffins, Curry's and Cree's, sitting side by side in the front of the church, but he was ready to put the events leading up to that strange state of affairs behind him for good.

Concepcion, turning plumper by the day, smiled at them and left Angus's side to walk alongside them for a ways. Not to be outdone, the old man soon caught up, though he was using a cane and still looked a little puny.

The stage pulled into Indian Rock and came to a noisy, dust-raising stop in front of the store, right on schedule.

Angus faced Kade, slapped him hard on the shoulder. Fortunately, Kade had some experience with his pa's exuberance, and he'd braced himself for the blow. "When you get back," Angus said, "Concepcion and I will have moved into your old room. You'll take ours, you and Mandy. It's anybody's guess which of you boys will wind up running the ranch, but one of you ought to head up the household, and you'll do as well as anybody."

Kade was startled, and he didn't try to hide it. "Pa, that isn't necessary. That room, that house is yours—I'll build a place for Mandy and me."

Angus shook his head; plainly he'd made up his mind. "Rafe is set, across the creek there with Emmeline, and God willing, Jeb will light somewhere and take hold one of these days, too. I want you to have the house, Kade, and that's the end of it."

Still astounded, Kade looked down at Mandy. She smiled at his expression. "Guess we'll have to go ahead and make something of ourselves," she said.

Kade turned back to his father, put out his hand. "Thanks, Pa," he said, still dazed. "Thanks."

Angus was flushed. "Get on that stage and get out of here," he said gruffly. "Sooner you get your business done down Phoenix way, the better. That ranch needs running, and you boys have hardly turned a hand to the place for a long time. At this rate, I'll have to wait for the baby to grow up and take over."

Mandy stood on tiptoe to kiss Angus's cheek in farewell.

Kade stopped in his tracks. "Baby? What baby?"

"Concepcion's and mine," Angus said.

Kade was speechless.

"If there's a God in heaven," Angus went on, apparently not realizing that he'd just set off a charge of dynamite, "it'll be a girl, and she'll have no need of a hundred square miles of scrub grass and bawling cows."

Kade recovered a little, grinned at the image his father painted, and wondered, as he put his hat back on, if the old man had any inkling that he'd just challenged fate and thereby guaranteed himself a hellcat of a daughter who'd fight her brothers tooth and nail for elbow room. Mandy linked her arm with Kade's, and he handed her aboard the stage.

"Are you thinking what I'm thinking?" he asked when they were both settled in the coach.

She laughed. "That you're going to have a sister and she's going to be a pistol?"

He nodded, delighted by the prospect of Angus and Concepcion as new parents.

Mandy smiled. "Yes—it crossed my mind."

"I'll be damned," Kade said, still grinning, feeling the whole rig shift as the driver climbed into the box to release the brake lever and take the reins. "A sister!"

69

THE RANCH OUTSIDE Phoenix was owned by Clark Kaplan, according to the information Kade had gathered before they left Indian Rock, and he and his wife, Eloise, were waiting outside when Kade and Mandy drove up in a hired buggy. The place was well kept, if not fancy, with a low-slung log house and a long porch shaded by a good roof.

"I don't see Mama," Mandy fretted, shading her eyes with one hand and peering into the blazing sunlight.

"Most likely, she's in the house," Kade reasoned calmly. "You said she was sickly."

Mandy hugged herself; even though it was only ten in the morning, the heat was already oppressive. In the high country, spring was still raw and new, with a tinge of winter to it, but down in the desert, with its lonely spaces and scattered cacti, summer was in full swing. "What if she's already passed?" she whispered. "I don't think I could bear that, her dying without my having a chance to say good-bye, I mean."

"Don't borrow trouble," Kade advised, reining in the mare, a sturdy gray rented right along with the buggy. "See the smile on that woman's face? She wouldn't be so cheerful if she had bad tidings."

Mrs. Kaplan approached them confidently, and sure enough, she was smiling. She was a small woman, but looked strong, and the light in her pale blue eyes was kindly. "Dixie's been waiting for you, ever since we got your wire," she said. "Come on in and I'll get you both something cold to drink." She turned and beckoned to her husband. "Don't just stand there, Mr. Kaplan. See to this horse and buggy."

Kaplan, a weathered and leathery man, half again as tall as his wife and wiry, took off his hat and strode over to greet them. "Howdy," he said with a nod, taking hold of the fittings and sparing a whole second word for the horse.

Kade got down from the rig and lifted Mandy after him. She felt a rush of emotion at his touch, perhaps because they'd spent the better part of the night making love in their hotel room. They had their differences, and always would, but their bodies agreed on everything.

Introductions were made, though they were unnecessary, as a matter of form. Then Mandy was walking toward the log house, toward her mother, her heart jammed into her throat.

Dixie waited in the front room, seated in a chair, a blanket spread over her knees. She was thin, and flushed, but her dark hair had been carefully arranged, and her eyes, greenish blue like Mandy's own, were bright with fretful anticipation.

"Amanda Rose," she whispered, and stretched out her hands.

Mandy rushed to her, embraced her. She felt as fragile as a fledgling in Mandy's arms, but she was still Dixie. Mandy wept as she held her mother, and so did Dixie.

"It was in the newspaper, about Cree and Gig," Dixie said

softly. "Leastways, they're both at peace now. I won't have you sorrowing over what happened, Amanda Rose. It wasn't your fault."

Mandy hadn't realized how badly she'd needed to hear those words from this particular person, until they fell upon her ears. "Thank you, Mama." She knelt beside Dixie's chair and nodded toward Kade, who was standing with his hat in his hands. "This is my husband, Kade McKettrick."

"Pleased to meet you, ma'am," Kade said, then colored up a little. Mandy hadn't guessed, before that moment, that he was nervous about meeting Dixie, and she was touched to see that her mother's opinion mattered to him.

"Aren't you a sight for these sore old eyes," Dixie said, and Mandy laughed through her tears, because some things never changed. Dixie was a woman who liked men, sons and brothers, husbands and lovers and strangers. "I'm depending on you to look after my little girl, you know."

Kade smiled. "I'll do that, ma'am, insofar as she'll allow it."

Dixie was clearly pleased, even a mite fluttery. "She'll allow it," she told him, her fragile arm tight around Mandy's shoulders, "or I'll know the reason why."

"Maybe I'll go and help Mr. Kaplan with that rig," Kade decided, and promptly retreated. Mrs. Kaplan had already vanished into the kitchen to mix up a pitcher of lemonade.

Dixie caught Mandy's face between her cool, papery hands. "Are you happy, Amanda Rose?" she demanded softly. "That's all I need to know. *Are you happy?*"

Mandy nodded. "Kade's a good man, Mama. Troublesome as a bee-stung mule, but good."

Dixie seemed merrily impatient, waving aside Kade's besetting sin. To her, it was probably a virtue. "Is there a babe started? I'd like to think I might be a grandmother sometime, even if I'm not here to see the day."

"We're working at it," Mandy assured her. "And of course you'll be here!" They both engaged in another spate of tears, though this time, they were mixed with laughter.

The visit had to be brief, since Dixie was frail, and they all took their lemonade on the front porch, Mr. Kaplan and Kade having carried Dixie's chair out there, in the hope of catching a stray breeze. There was plenty of good talk, but at a signal from Mrs. Kaplan, her husband allowed as how he'd better be about getting the rig ready to travel, and Kade went to help, but not before a meaningful glance passed between him and Mandy.

"I'll get your bed ready," Mrs. Kaplan told Dixie, who sighed and nodded her acquiescence.

"Kade and I have talked about this, Mama," Mandy said when she and Dixie were alone. "We want you to come back to the Triple M with us, so we can look after you ourselves."

Dixie laid a gentle hand to Mandy's cheek, and a sad smile was shining in her eyes as she regarded her daughter. "Guess you were about the only thing I ever got right in the whole of my life," she said wistfully. "But that's enough, I reckon." She paused, recovering her breath, then shook her head. "I can't go anyplace, Mandy. I'm all used up, and seeing you, well, that was all I was waiting for."

"Nonsense," Mandy whispered, near tears again. "You'll be better in no time—"

"No," Dixie broke in gently. "I want to rest, Mandy, and I'm asking you to do me the kindness of letting me go. You just love that man of yours. Have yourself a houseful of babies and make a fine life for yourself. You do those things, and I'll be dancing someplace for the joy of knowing you're happy."

"Mama—"

Dixie shook her head once more, her expression gentle, her eyes shining with tears. "Do as I say, Mandy. Cree and Gig and me, we're all part of the past, figures in a story that's already been told. You and Kade are what's real now. You go on, and don't make this parting any harder than it has to be."

Mandy hesitated, then nodded.

Dixie strained to kiss Mandy's cheek, and the touch of her lips felt cool and somehow faded, as though a part of her had already gone on ahead. "Go home, Amanda Rose. And don't you be coming back here to cry over a mound of dirt, neither. I'll be long gone."

Again, Mandy nodded.

Dixie squeezed her hand with surprising strength. "Go home," she repeated. "That's what I mean to do, and I daresay I might even find a welcome there."

Kade brought the buggy around, got down, and after a moment of utter stillness, walked toward them.

Mandy stood, then leaned down to kiss the top of Dixie's head. "Good-bye, Mama," she said, and went to meet Kade.

When she looked back, Mr. Kaplan was carrying her mother into the house. The chair remained on the porch, rocking a little in the breeze, as if a ghost were seated there.

Kade put an arm around Mandy's waist. "Ready?" he asked.

She looked up at him and saw her future in his eyes. She saw their children, and the home they would make together. The joys and sorrows they would share. "Yes," she said softly.

He took her hand, raised it to his lips, and kissed the knuckles. "I love you," he said, and she responded in kind from the deepest regions of her heart, the places that had been closed up and locked until she'd fallen in love with Kade.

They drove back to Phoenix, talking quietly along the way, checked out of their hotel, and boarded a northbound train.

When they reached Indian Rock, many long hours later, having ridden the stagecoach from Flagstaff, Angus was there to meet them, his face solemn, a telegram crumpled in one hand. Mandy didn't need to read it to know that Dixie had gone home, just as she'd said she would.

By now, she was dancing for sure.

Epilogue

KADE WATCHED, BAFFLED, as his younger brother rode toward the barn, hell-bent for yesterday, looking as though the devil himself were on his tail. He even glanced in the direction Jeb had come from, just to make sure old Slewfoot wasn't riding behind him.

Jeb was off his horse while it was still moving, the critter heading, reins dangling, for the open doors and the shelter of its stall.

"What the hell?" Kade muttered. Rafe, just riding in from his place across the creek, watched in puzzlement.

Jeb threw his arms wide. "You've got to hide me!" he yelled, and he looked and sounded dead serious, for all the comical picture he made.

Kade and Rafe looked at each other, then back at Jeb, both of them confounded. Rafe swung down from Chief's back and ambled over, pulling off his gloves as he came.

"Hide you?" Kade asked, bewildered. "From who?"

"Her!" Jeb yelled, and he'd gone white in the past two seconds.

"Who?" Rafe insisted, but a grin was taking shape in his eyes.

Jeb started to pace, throwing the occasional anxious glance in the general direction of town. "The she-cat who's after me, that's who!" No sign of the patented Jeb McKettrick arrogance now, no easy rhetoric, no smart-ass grin. Just one rattled cowboy.

Rafe chuckled and shook his head. "Maybe it's just me," he drawled, making a show of taking in the landscape, "but I don't see any she-cat. You running a temperature, little brother?"

Just then, a horse and buggy came charging over the grassy knoll on the other side of the creek. Kade squinted, saw a woman in a fancy bonnet and a blue-and-white-striped dress at the reins.

"That her?" he asked, curious, cocking his thumb.

Jeb all but jumped out of his skin. "Tell her I'm gone. Tell her I'm dead. Tell her anything." With that, he fled, rounding the bunkhouse at full gallop, just as he used to do when he was a kid and had earned himself a proper thrashing from one of his brothers.

Rafe let out a long, low whistle of exclamation, purely delighted.

Kade laughed.

Bold as Ben-Hur in his chariot, the lady in the striped dress drove that horse and buggy across the creek as if it were dry ground, making good use of the reins and raising a six-foot spray of sun-glinting water on either side.

"This," Kade said, "is gonna be good."

Rafe's grin was as wide as the mouth of Horse Thief Canyon. "Let's go and say hello to the lady. It's the gentlemanly thing to do."

She pulled up when she saw them, horse and rig dripping water, and Kade was taken aback when he got a good look at the woman's face. For some reason, he'd been expecting a clock-stopper, but she was breathtakingly beautiful, her dark blue eyes shooting flames, her wild and coppery hair doing its best to escape the bonnet. As if in capitulation, she wrenched the thing off her head and threw it to the floor of the buggy.

"Where is that lying, scum-sucking, yellow-bellied devil spawn?" she demanded.

Rafe and Kade exchanged glances.

"Which lying, scum-sucking, yellow-bellied devil spawn would that be?" Kade inquired cordially, tugging belatedly at his hat brim.

"Jeb McKettrick, that's who." She was flushed, but it only made her more fetching. "Where is he?"

Rafe grinned. "Hiding behind the bunkhouse," he said with an utter lack of conscience.

She was about to slap down the reins again when Kade caught hold of the harness. "Just one thing, ma'am. If you're going to kill our little brother, and it looks like you mean to directly, we'd appreciate knowing your name first."

"Chloe Wakefield," she said grudgingly, "and if you don't let go of that harness, right now, I might just run you over."

John Lewis's daughter. Kade stepped back, delighted, hands spread wide in a gesture of peaceful concession. He pointed helpfully. "That's the bunkhouse over there."

She was off, traveling at all the speed the poor horse could manage. Kade hoped she hadn't driven the hapless beast that hard all the way out from Indian Rock.

"Think we ought to go back there and save Jeb?" Rafe asked idly, straightening his hat.

Kade gave the matter due and leisurely consideration, rubbing his chin with one hand. "Nah," he said after a moment.

Rafe slapped him on the back. "You think she's the wife he's been bragging about?"

Kade shrugged, and the two of them started toward the main house. They had ranch business to discuss, there was fresh coffee brewed, unless Kade missed his guess, and Mandy and Concepcion had been baking pies all afternoon.

"I reckon so," he said.